THE RUNNING OF BEASTS

Bill Pronzini, born in 1943, a resident of Northern California, is one of the most prolific and talented writers of crime fiction in our time. Creator of the "Nameless" detective novels, Pronzini is the author of hundreds of published short stories, novels and anthologies, including the popular *Gun In Cheek* and *Son of Gun in Cheek* collections.

Barry Malzberg, born in 1939, a resident of New Jersey, represented the great Cornell Woolrich as a literary agent during Woolrich's last years. Malzberg's work has been described as a kind of "science-fiction *noir*," and in it he has absorbed the best in terms of Woolrich's influence. Malzberg, like Pronzini, has written and edited hundreds of stories, novels and anthologies.

THE RUNNING OF BEASTS

BILL PRONZINI and BARRY MALZBERG

Black Lizard Books
Berkeley • 1988

Copyright ©1976 by Bill Pronzini and Barry Malzberg.
Black Lizard Books edition published 1988. All rights reserved.
For information contact: Black Lizard Books, 833 Bancroft Way,
Berkeley, CA 94710. Black Lizard Books are distributed by Creative
Arts Books Company.

ISBN 0-88739-076-5
Library of Congress Catalog Card No. 86-72530

Manufactured in the United States of America

FOR BRUNI
and
FOR JOYCE, STEPHANIE JILL,
AND ERIKA CORNELL,
and
IN MEMORY OF JOSEPH W. FERMAN

> ... I will do such things—
> What they are yet I know not—but they shall be
> The terrors of the earth.
> —WILLIAM SHAKESPEARE,
> *King Lear*

EARLY OCTOBER

Note: after setting return to Cross

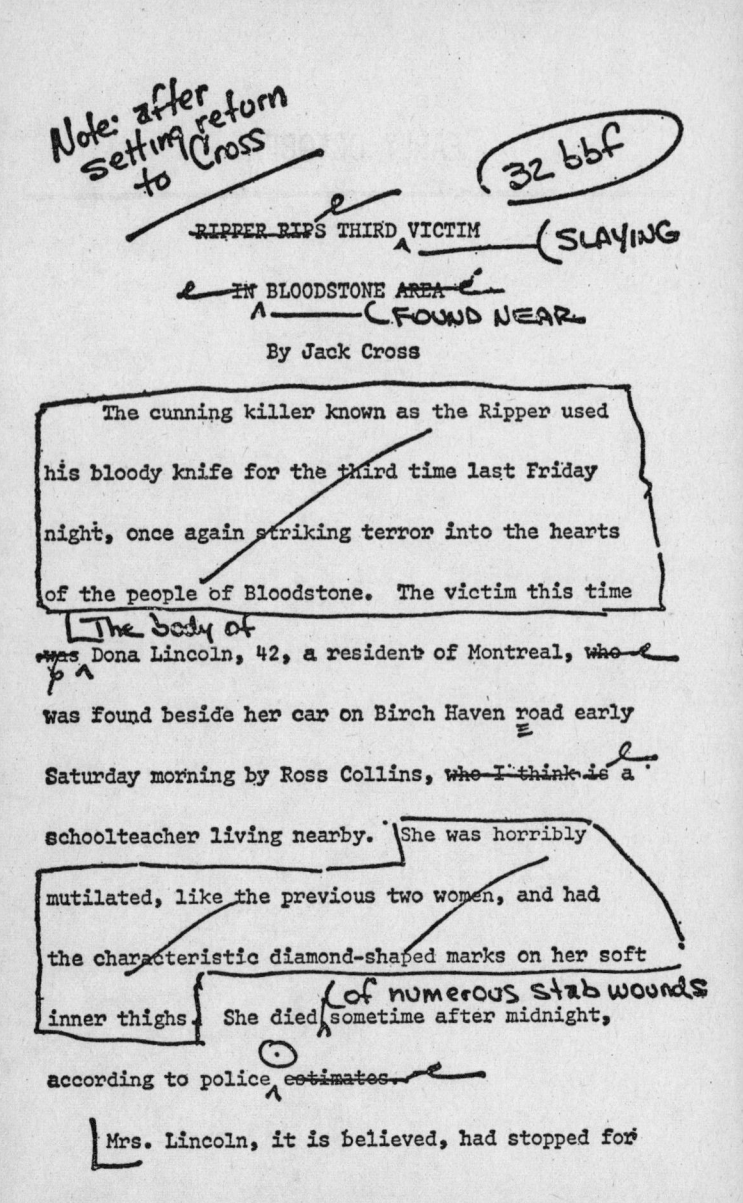

32 bbf

THIRD VICTIM SLAYING
FOUND NEAR BLOODSTONE

By Jack Cross

The cunning killer known as the Ripper used his bloody knife for the third time last Friday night, once again striking terror into the hearts of the people of Bloodstone. The victim this time The body of Dona Lincoln, 42, a resident of Montreal, was found beside her car on Birch Haven road early Saturday morning by Ross Collins, a schoolteacher living nearby. She was horribly mutilated, like the previous two women, and had the characteristic diamond-shaped marks on her soft inner thighs of numerous stab wounds. She died sometime after midnight, according to police.

Mrs. Lincoln, it is believed, had stopped for

the night in Bloodstone on her way from Montreal to New York City, where she was to visit her daughter. She is the first victim who did not live in the Bloodstone area. Does this mean something? We don't know as yet; neither does.

¶ Lieutenant Daniel Smith of the State Police, the officer in charge of the investigation, stated that similarities between the death of Mrs. Lincoln and two previous slayings this fall indicate a common assailant.

¶ The first victim, Julia Larch, 50, a resident of Maple Road, Bloodstone, was discovered by a skeleton maintenance crew at Colonial Village Amusement Park on August 4. The second victim, Arlene Wilson, 25, who lived with her parents at the Wilson Cabin Colony, was found three weeks ago, on September 16, near Pine Point. The Ripper is clearly stepping up his pace.

It is feared Bloodstone will become the object of national attention as a result of these murders. They have already been reported by the wire services, and were the subject of a poorly written article in this week's New York Sunday News in which Constable Keller was interviewed. I couldn't interview him; only the Sunday News can get to him. He is above the local press. Until 1969 Keller was with the Chicago Police Department, where he rose to the rank of sergeant before resigning under curious circumstances and subsequently coming to Bloodstone.

Dona Lincoln's daughter in New York City, and the remainder of her family in Montreal, have been unavailable for comment. So has Constable Keller. Lieutenant Smith ~~is the only one who will~~

~~I talk to me.~~ He said that the State Police were working on several possible leads, and is hopeful of an early arrest. They always say that, it doesn't mean anything, of course.

The obvious question remains.

When will the Ripper rip again?

Jack —
I've warned you before about this kind of irresponsible reporting. Don't let it happen again!

Plummer

Investigator's Report

Case No.: 417-H-6, 417-H-9, 417-H-11
Date of Report: 9 October
To: Captain Rolfe Jacobsen, State CID, Albany
From: Lieutenant Daniel Smith, OIC, Lake George
Identification: Summary of Investigation of Homicide (Multiple)

Reports from the County Coroner's Office indicate each of the three victims died of multiple stab wounds in the stomach and lower abdomen, perhaps inflicted by a butcher knife, hunting knife, or similar weapon. In each case there was also considerable mutilation of the abdominal area. No other area of the bodies was touched except for facial and occipital bruises and a series of small, diamond-shaped marks on the inner thighs of each. These marks in all three cases measured approximately one inch in diameter, penetrating the surface skin only, and were apparently made with some type of rough-surfaced metal object other than the murder weapon.

There was no evidence of sexual molestation; it has, in fact, been specifically denied in each of the coroner's reports.

Each of the victims was found in a semi-isolated area in or around the township of Bloodstone, Essex County. The only variants are that the third victim, Mrs. Dona Lincoln, was discovered beside her automobile, while no automobile was found in the vicinity of the first two victims, and that Mrs. Lincoln was a transient, residing in Montreal, Quebec, Canada. The first two victims were residents of Essex County. We have been able to uncover no relevance to these variants. In fact, they reaffirm our supposition that the person responsible is a psychopath, criminally insane.

Yet another distinct similarity between the homicides was the presence of several bloodstained tissues in the immediate vicinity of each victim. Forensic tests revealed the blood in each instance to be of the same type as the victim's, leading us to the supposition that the assailant used the tissues to wipe the murder weapon and possibly his own person. Investigation into the source of the tissues has yielded negative results. In each case they were of the same national brand, easily obtainable.

An empty pint bottle of Gordon's gin, found near the body of the second victim, Arlene Wilson—and which likely was discarded by someone other than the assailant in a manner utterly unconnected with the time or motive of the crime—yielded no fingerprints. A check of sales of that particular brand of gin in Bloodstone and surrounding communities also produced negative results, since it is a popular brand.

Remarkably enough, no other evidence of any kind has been found at any of the scenes or elsewhere in the area.

Interviews with the residents in closest proximity to the site of each murder, with other inhabitants of Bloodstone township, and with friends and relatives of the victims were conducted and have thus far given us no positive information. Attempts to retrace the movements of each victim on the night she was slain have been similarly futile.

Julia Larch, the first victim, was last seen at 10:40 P.M., when she set out on foot from the home of a family for whom she had been baby-sitting. Arlene Wilson was last seen at 11:05 P.M. at the Bloodstone Café, having left the café in her car at that time. The automobile was later found abandoned on Pine Point, approximately a quarter of a mile from her home and an equal distance from the location of the body. Dona Lincoln was last seen at the Witherbee Motel at 8:30 P.M., after having secured a room for the night from the manager, Mr. Arnold Witherbee. The manager did not see her or her car subsequently leave the motel grounds.

All three victims, according to the Medical Examiner's estimates as to time of death, were killed within three hours of the time last seen alive.

The possibility exists that the assailant was known to the first two victims, assuming that the assailant lives in or near Bloodstone township. This would explain, at least superficially, how the murderer was able to abduct the victims without creating a disturbance. In the case of Dona Lincoln, however, the chances are that the assailant was totally unknown to her.

Mrs. Lincoln's family claims that she knew no one in the Essex County area. It is conceivable that Mrs. Lincoln was accosted at the motel, there having been no other guests the night of the murder and Arnold Witherbee being hard of hearing. It is also possible that Mrs. Lincoln left the motel for some reason that night and was accosted elsewhere.

But in the absence of witnesses to any of the homicides, all of this must be seen as mere conjecture.

As previously stated, and as the media has openly suggested despite our efforts to reduce scare reportage, the brutal and apparently motiveless nature of these crimes would point toward a homicidal psychopath. But without motive or leads, there is little we can do except to retrace prior paths of investigation and increase patrols in the Bloodstone vicinity. And to advise residents, particularly female residents, since the crimes appear to be sexual in original impulse, to stay indoors after dark.

■

498 Bleecker Street
New York, New York 10008
12 October

Mr. John A. Reese
Managing Editor
Insight Magazine
894 West 37th Street
New York, New York 10036

DEAR JOHN:

Further to our conversation today, I'll try to wrap up my proposal for an article on the "Bloodstone Murders" in query letter form, on the basis of which I hope the Editorial Board will give me the go-ahead.

Background first:

Bloodstone, New York, is a community in the Adirondack Mountains, in what the lumberjacks used to call an "uphisted" or far-north county. It was founded, apparently, by one Peter Bloodstone, who was a minor official in Stuyvesant's Nieu Amsterdam until he went upstate hurriedly in the late 1600s for obscure reasons (which may have had to do with the fact that a lot of money, current exchange, was alleged to have accompanied him). Legend has it he committed suicide a few years later by jumping from a cliff and drowning himself in Woodbine Lake; the body was never found. You won't turn *that* up in the Chamber of Commerce brochures.

During this century, Bloodstone's piece of forest became a resort town. Current population is 453, by the *New York Red Book* before me. The Season—which offers boating, fishing, swimming, etc.—swells that population to several thousand. In the past decade, however, there has been a steady decline in tourism, owing to such reasons (among others) as the opening of the Northway, which bypasses traffic and therefore somewhat isolates the area, and rampant inflation on the one hand and more attractive tourist locales on the other.

Bloodstone is really two towns: what it is during what's left of the Season and what it is the rest of the time, which latter can best be expressed by what it *isn't*. It isn't "friendly," it isn't really part of the so-called mainstream, it isn't filled with sophisticated, engaging city types or even those witty, shrewd, taciturn folk of urban myth; it is not, in sum, a place where given any real alternatives, you'd particularly care to be caught dead. Isolation, parochialism, bigotry. Provincialism. Hatred of outsiders. Hatred of disadvantaged or ethnic or life-style minorities.

This, then, is the community in which there have now been three hideous mutilation murders since Labor Day. Internal evidence makes almost irrefutable a common assailant. Victims always female, bodies horribly slashed, a peculiar pattern of diamond-shaped marks on the thighs . . . you already know most of the details. Last week's *Sunday News* had a wrap-up with photos and grotesques, a short interview with the local constable, etc.

So why does *Insight* need anything from Ms. Valerie Broome? What can she offer, what perspective can she bring to these awful crimes that will make them more than sensationalistic *News* material?

In the first place: Bloodstone, as I said to you similarly at the beginning of our conversation, John, is my hometown; I spent the first seventeen years of my life there. I know the place as I will never know anything else, and I believe I can write about it—put on paper the soul of it—in a manner and at a depth that no outsider can hope to achieve.

In the second place: the interaction of Bloodstone with these murders is absolutely a microcosm, I think, of what is going on in America today. We've been through the charnel houses of all time in these past twelve years —assassinations, mass murders, public freakouts, private collapses, television spectaculars, grand funerals, small griefs, dead politicians, living politicians who are dead—and now, symbolically at least, it has all come home to Bloodstone, the American village. A pressure point where modern technology and alienated man are forced at last to meet each other.

That's the sociological part of it. But there's another part which is potently *psychological*. In the third place, then: recently I met a man named James Ferrara, a psychiatrist who makes out testifying for prosecution or defense, depending on who gets there first, on insanity pleas in criminal cases. He's done a few APA monographs for the *Journal* and dabbles in a little private practice, but he's really just on the fringes and bitter about it. More significantly, he has followed these murders closely and is intrigued by them, since he's also an amateur crime buff—the more violent the crime, the better, the bloodier, the more interesting; and he thinks that the killings in Bloodstone, the compulsive marking of the bodies, are characteristic of a particular kind of amnesiac fugue, a really complex schizophrenia in which the murders are being committed in a dreamlike state and the murderer does not know that he is the murderer.

I'll repeat that, it's the core of Ferrara's theory: *the murderer does not know that he is the murderer*. He goes about his business or to sleep, he wakes up and hears about the latest slaying, but he's just one of the townspeople or interested spectators, as repelled and horrified as anyone. A compartmentalization of the mind and spirit so complete that, in Ferrara's words, "the implications are shut away and the guilt is put away and the culpability is sealed off and nothing is left but the horror." Like certain theories of political assassination.

Ferrara also feels that the case is going to break fairly soon. Each murder, he points out, is building up greater and greater pressure in the walled-off section of the psyche which has been created by the murderer; the individual in his waking, functioning state feels a great but diffuse tension which he cannot adequately explain because he doesn't know where it's coming from, and in order to relieve that tension, he must kill again. But each murder is performed under greater stress, and so the partitions will finally crumble, possibly after a crime into a babbling confession to anyone at all, possibly during a crime so that the murderer will come awake to find himself doing it.

Ferrara is convinced of all this. I'm not necessarily convinced myself, but the prospect is both fascinating and chilling and makes a solid foundation for my proposed article. And if it turns out that Ferrara *is* right, *Insight* would have an exclusive of no little circulation value.

In some detail, John, that's it. I hope you'll find this suitable to pass on to the board, and that you'll share with me, at least in part, my excitement at the possibilities here. All I can add in closing is that while I've been successful with my past work, that success from the beginning has been with articles that were somehow peripheral to me. Not central. This one is.

As ever,

VALERIE R. BROOME

P.S. If you give me the go-ahead, I think Ferrara should accompany me to Bloodstone. His presence would add considerable depth, insight, and psychoanalytic authenticity to the piece. He says he'll offer his services for expenses and whatever "honorarium" you'd be willing to authorize.

NULL-TIME

One was fun with moans and groans but the truth of youth made two, that's three, three for me but I want more so it's got to be four, lance her for the answer and I'll marry five or six in the sticks for the cling of the clang of the rung of the gong at the old cold bold rule: off-center.

OCTOBER 18 TO OCTOBER 24

Saturday, October 18

BLOODSTONE

Bloodstone in mid-October was like the birch and maple and elms that grew in and around it: mostly bare and bleak, with only intermittent signs of life and color.

The village lay along the western shore of Woodbine Lake, a long, fairly narrow body dotted with little spruce-laden islands. The uniform, wooded slopes of the Adirondacks stretched on all sides, dull green in the foreground and blue-black in the distance, like a series of shadow images on the surface of the sky. U.S. Highway 9, which followed the curve of Woodbine and which became Main Street within the city limits of Bloodstone, sustained little traffic; most of it used the Adirondack Northway half a mile farther to the west, flat and free, straight up to Montreal. All but a scattering of the motels and cabin colonies were closed for the winter, as were Colonial Village and Fort Seneca to the north.

Bloodstone's small municipal beach, the long, sloping lawns of its park behind, and the public parking facility on Dock Street were empty. The information booth on the town green was closed, and so were the local office of the Northern Adirondack Historical Society, the antique stores and used furniture stores, the three realty offices, the false-fronted Republic Theater, Hammond's Bait and Tackle, the Adirondack Memory Gift Shoppe, and all the restaurants except for Bloodstone Café.

The Chamber of Commerce Bulletin Board carried a single listing on its wide face: JUNIOR CREATIVE WRITING WORKSHOP AND POETRY READING FIRST MONDAY OF EACH MONTH 2:30 AT THE LIBRARY. Underneath this, someone had scrawled the word "*fags.*"

The three hundred-odd adult residents of Bloodstone could purchase groceries and magazines and drug sundries at Safeway or Carter's General Store; they could cash a check or try for a loan at the Essex County Bank; they could buy a drink in Bloodstone Tavern, with its imitation chalet façade of brick and black-painted wood; they could fill their gas tanks at the Gulf station opposite the green; they could catch a bus for Lake George or Albany or Buffalo or New York City at the Trailways Depot next to the Gulf station; they could pray in one of the two plain white churches—Catholic and Baptist— on upper Main Street; they could, if they had need of the town clerk or the town constable or the fire department, go to the Bloodstone Municipal Center—a stone-faced, red-trimmed building on Whitehall Road, two blocks nearer the lake. But while they did all these things, they did them sparingly, so that at any given time of day there were no more than a few people on the streets and the old buildings had a huddled, wasted appearance. At night the village was empty and the scattered lights— sodium vapor arcs in the Gulf station, neon on the front of Bloodstone Tavern and Bloodstone Café, pale streetlamps, occasional headlights of a fast-moving car—increased the aura of desolation.

By late October the topics of conversation among the inhabitants had settled for the winter on money, politics in Lake George, football, the severity of the coming snows. Tourists were no longer mentioned. This year, however, there was another topic: the three murders committed by the apparently crazed, unknown assailant who had come to be known as the Ripper.

Most of Bloodstone believed that the Ripper would have to be an outsider; the crimes could be done by no friend, neighbor, or old enemy, and there was no one else in the town. This outsider, they said, murdered in Bloodstone either because he did not want to draw attention to his real home (New York City, most likely, they knew all about what was going on there) or because he had a warped, personal hatred for their community. They kept a watchful eye on the few strangers who came through at that time of year and were quick to report to Constable Alex Keller or to the state police any activity they considered suspicious.

Women, for the most part, heeded police warnings to

stay inside after dark, unless in going out they were accompanied by trusted male friends or relatives. Window shades were drawn, doors and windows locked tightly. The Ripper could not strike again, most of them reasoned, if he were unable to find another victim.

And so the town waited for the Ripper to be apprehended, or for the Ripper to go away; for the advent of winter, for Christmas, the new year, spring, and finally the beginning of the Season, such as it was, which would keep the town alive. The Season would come again, and so—unless reports of the murders had frightened them too badly—would the few thousand tourists. Patience. Patience and caution. It would all be over soon enough.

HOOK

Late Saturday morning Steven Hook turned his eleven-year-old Dodge past the sign, partially obscured by tall grass and sumac bushes, that stood in the V formed by U.S. 9 and the access road leading into the abandoned cabin complex. The sign said in eroded black lettering: HIDEAWAY H'SKEEPING CABINS • SLEEPS 2 TO 6 • OPEN ALL YEAR. Tacked to the upper right-hand corner was a shingle with the single word VACANCY printed on it.

He followed the weed-choked road to where the row of eight cabins crouched brokenly at the edge of a thick tangle of spruce and birch. The cabins were small, all of them once white clapboard except for one on the far left, Number Eight; that one, for some reason known only to the former and now dead owner, Forest Wicker, had been constructed from notched logs. Roofs sagged under a heavy weight of dead foliage; screen doors hung off-center from broken hinges; rusting iceboxes and pieces of decaying wooden furniture cluttered the partly enclosed front porches. Vegetation pressed the cabins on all sides but did not manage to conceal their ugliness.

Hook parked the car behind the cabin nearest Number Eight, where he always parked, and got out and walked around to the front. He was a lean, dark man with bright, expressive eyes and shaggy hair streaked with gray, a sardonic mouth that looked as if it would seldom smile. His movements were fluid and graceful, those of the accomplished actor he once had been. A girl in New York City had told him a long time ago that he walked like a cat and screwed like one too, all clawed fingers and teeth and throaty, growling sounds. That last bothered him, and every time he was in bed with a woman he remembered it and tried to be gentle—and did not always succeed.

He went onto the porch of Number Eight, opened the screen door, and stepped inside. Rotting spruce and pine needles littered the floor in the front room, kept company by a broken rocking chair and a mildewed mattress in one corner. Hook went into the tiny kitchen: a wooden half table, a chair, a disconnected gas stove, shelves holding bottles, jars, chipped coffee mugs, dust, more dead foliage, the unopened bottle of Seagram's hidden beneath a pile of filthy rags.

He stood looking at the rags. No, he thought, I'm not going to touch any of it, I'm not going to open it. He listened to the wind whistling coldly through the empty windows, blew on his hands, then sat heavily on the chair. He took the copy of *Tomorrow's Trots* from his coat pocket and folded it open on the table.

First race. Post time eight P.M., make that eight-oh-three. Claiming allowance for three-year-old colts and geldings. Seven horse looked fair, Bullet Hanover, three wins in the last four, morning line 5–2. Some chance. Three horse, Adios something-or-other, the probable favorite; though listed at 2–1, eight in the money in the last ten races at Yonkers, so you never could tell. Racing in B-1 and B-2 at Monticello and Yonkers, a soft spot in a claiming allowance, might go off at 6–5 here. So Bullet Hanover, here's to you, Bullet, might post at 2–1 anyway. Then again, the crowds were down to a couple of thousand at this time of year, and no good thing would get away at better than 7–5.

Too much, Hook thought. For that matter, now, why would they send a horse out of New York at this late date? They were obviously looking for a soft spot. Bullet Hanover down the pipe.

The small print blurred. Hook pinched his eyes, blinked several times, and then lit a cigarette. Try another. One horse, then. The one horse. 8–1 morning line; probably go to 12–1 with the other factors. A long shot. Coming off a strong fifth last time, from the eight post double-parked for the middle half a mile. A possibility. Better than risking even money on a goddamned downstate horse that might turn out to be crippled.

He could try it. But then again, the one horse in the ninth race last night had looked pretty good too; looked better at a zooming 15–1 at post time when Hook was already down sixty dollars. Only the one had broken at the first turn and had galloped off into the paddock with another thirty dollars of his money. Ninety dollars last night. Two hundred and twenty down for the week. Almost six hundred down for the month. So how did it *really* look for tonight? For next week? For next month?

Jesus, Hook thought, and stood. Abruptly he left the kitchen and went out to the front porch, stood there smoking and looking across the highway, beyond the closed Brickham Motel to the dimly perceived ruffles on the surface of the lake. Nothing moved within the range of his vision except those ruffles, and the only sound was that of dead paper-birch bark flapping in the wind. The aura of abandonment was omnipresent.

The Hideaway Cabins had been empty for a long time, since Forest Wicker had died intestate in 1968; Hook had found that out around town. They might have fallen into other hands except that there were no heirs, and if there had been, who would want a cabin complex in the late 1960s in Bloodstone? The old man had eked out a living for thirty years, the last ten of them probably draining what small assets he had accumulated as tourism in the immediate area collapsed.

No one visited them now except for occasional scavengers, adventurous boys, older kids looking for a place to drink beer or smoke pot. And Hook. Last spring he had pulled into the complex on impulse one afternoon, prowled through the cabins. There had been no special appeal that first time, but the following week he had gone there again, then again the next week, and finally two and three times a week right up until now. Maybe it was the melancholy solitude of the place that kept bringing him back. He had solitude aplenty at his cottage on Stone Bridge Road, on the lake just north of the village, but the Hideaway Cabins were different, at a new level of feeling. Maybe, Hook thought bitterly, maybe he was trying to make himself a tourist—symbolically trying to leave Bloodstone.

Well, he couldn't keep coming here after the first snows of winter began. Not until spring again, because the cabins, in their ramshackle state, offered no protection at all from the elements. It was bad enough this time of year, with the icy wind and the damp mists that came off the lake. He would stop coming here when the snows fell, all right.

The wind started his nose running, and he took one of the wad of tissues he always kept in his pocket and blew into it violently. Goddamned sinus on top of everything else. He snuffed out the cigarette against the outer wall and threw the butt toward the clutter of junk and detritus spread between this cabin and Number Seven, watched it bounce near the gluey mass of newspapers and racing forms and old programs, accumulated over past months and welded together by the elements in an amalgam of failure and hope.

He went back into the kitchen. And paused again in front of the pile of rags where the bottle was.

His mouth was dry. Reflexively he bent over, picked up the fifth, stared at it in the thin light. But he was not going to break that seal, he was not going to give in after six years of abstinence. He had bought the bottle in a bad moment two months ago, but that was all it had been, a bad moment, and he had beaten down the need. Still, it was self-torture to keep it around. So why not take it outside right now and smash it into a tree? No more temptation; out of sight, out of mind, out of life, out of pain. See how they run.

But he did not take the bottle outside. He didn't take it anywhere. He put it down again, used the rags to cover it, sat at the table, and hunched once more over *Tomorrow's Trots*.

KELLER

Constable Alex Keller was in the middle of a late Saturday lunch in his office at the Bloodstone Municipal Center when the two strangers, man and woman, walked in.

He put down his sandwich immediately, watching the two of them come forward to the low rail divider that separated the visitor's area from the more functional part of the office: his desk, a police radio unit, a glass-fronted cabinet containing a row of latch keys and a pump-action riot gun, a partially open door that led to the two small holding cells. Keller judged from their faces and postures that it was nothing urgent; then, irritated, he dropped his gaze to the desk top.

There were bread crumbs littering the neat surface, because the sandwich was on a hard roll and there was no way you could eat a hard roll sandwich without leaving crumbs. He didn't like people coming into his office when he was eating and there happened to be crumbs all over his desk. Eating, as far as he was concerned, was something of a private thing, which was why he always ate alone.

Keller folded the sandwich into its waxed wrapping, put it away in one of the desk drawers, brushed the crumbs carefully into the palm of his hand, dusted the hand into the wastebasket, and then wiped both hands on a paper napkin. He did all that without looking at the man and the woman; he did not look at them again until he had dropped the napkin into the wastebasket.

The man was short, glossy-looking, and had a fierce black mustache over a thin fag's scowl. He wore a fairly new suit that managed nonetheless to look shabby. Keller gave his attention to the woman, who was much more interesting. Sleek, slim, poised, self-assured. City girl. Dark, steady eyes with a little too much lavender shadow. Fine black hair parted in the middle and swept down her shoulders. Good legs, medium-sized tits showing through the open alpaca coat. New York, all right. Put ten women from ten different parts of the country in a police lineup, and he could spot New York City every time.

"Constable Keller?" she said.

"That's right." Keller got to his feet, adjusting the holstered revolver on his right hip so that it rode more comfortably, and crossed to where they stood. "What can I do for you?"

The woman smiled impersonally. "My name is Valerie Broome. I'm a writer on assignment for *Insight Magazine*."

"Oh?"

"This is my associate, Dr. Ferrara. We're here to do an article on the mutilation killings."

Keller felt a faint stirring of excitement that briefly chased the irritation. *Insight Magazine* was big business, nationwide, while the *Sunday News* maybe reached a couple of million who hadn't paid a penny for the supplement, who threw it aside before breakfast was over anyway. But he held the excitement in check. You had to be careful with people like this. Very careful. They could build you up in the public eye, give you a taste of fame, but just as easily they could rip you apart, destroy you. He had learned that and a few other things in Chicago.

"Dr. Ferrara?" he said.

"I'm a psychiatrist," the glossy little man said, and smiled as if handing him a business card. "An investigative psychiatrist specializing in the socially dysfunctional."

Keller decided to ignore him. He asked Valerie, "Isn't it a little unusual for a woman to be writing about violent sex crimes?"

"I've written about sex and violence before," she said. "Besides, I have something of a personal interest in what's happening here. I was born in Bloodstone, I lived here until 1965."

"I see."

Ferrara said, "Why do you call the murders sex crimes? There was no evidence of sexual assault, as I understand it."

"When a man goes around cutting up women like the Ripper does," Keller said, "there's always a sexual element."

"Really?" Ferrara had small, penetrating black eyes that seemed void of irises, like a bird's. "Entering their bodies with a knife instead of his erect penis, perhaps as a result of impotence? The knife as a penis substitute, blood for semen?"

Keller frowned. The irritation was back, sharper now. He did not like that sort of talk in front of women, and he did not like talk about impotence in any company. He also did not like the faintly superior, pedantic tone of Ferrara's voice. An investigative psychiatrist. What the hell was an investigative psychiatrist? "I couldn't tell you," he said flatly. "Sexual element or not, it has nothing to do with putting a stop to the Ripper. And I'm doing all I can toward that end."

Valerie said, "I understood the state police were in full charge of the investigation."

"Who told you that? Smith?"

"We haven't seen Lieutenant Smith yet. We just got in from New York a little while ago."

"Well, he'll tell you I don't have any official capacity when you do talk to him," Keller said, "but it won't be the truth. This is my town, and the murders happened within the city limits, and that makes them mine as much as the state police's. I've put as much work into the investigation as they have, maybe more."

"If you say so, Constable."

"You bet I say so."

Ferrara said, "He'll do it again, you know."

"What?"

"He's going to do it again—the man you call the Ripper. The whole point of the crimes is to attract attention, to convince himself of his own reality. Since he hasn't been caught yet, he'll keep on doing it until he is, until he's discovered, and in the process discovers himself, finds out who he is."

That didn't make any sense to Keller. He said after a pause, "He won't do it again. We'll get him before he does. *I'll* get him."

"Will you? How?"

"I'm not at liberty to discuss that. If you read the

piece in the *Sunday News,* you know I told that reporter the same thing."

"But surely you'd *like* to talk, Constable," Ferrara said. "The pressures of an investigation such as this, the obligations and responsibilities, must bear upon you very heavily. You begin to take it personally after a while, don't you?"

"I don't understand that."

"Well—a small rural town, in eventless stasis, and you its constable; the town possessing no enforcement problem of any significance; the constable in easy interrelation to the town; and then this terrible eruption. . . ."

"Did you say I'm incapable of handling the situation?"

"Do you feel incapable? There's no harm in ventilating your feelings, if so."

Keller stared at him. The irritation, now, had given way to rising anger. "Why are you here?" he said finally. "I can understand Miss Broome, she's a journalist, a writer for a big magazine, but why *you?*"

"Dr. Ferrara has some ideas about the murders," Valerie said. Her eye shadow seemed darker, as if her eyes were picking up splinters of light. "My editor and I felt he would make a useful psychoanalytic contribution."

"I've listened to his ideas," Keller said. "I don't care for them at all, what I've heard."

Ferrara said, "If you were to understand the psychological outlines of this case. . . ." He went on to give another theory, some crap about the Ripper not knowing he was the Ripper, the crimes committed in a stupor of some sort, but the girl cut him off before he was finished. She seemed to sense Keller's anger and to realize that further conversation at this point would only lead to greater antagonism. She said something about having other people to see and perhaps talking to him again later on and then prodded the glossy little bastard to the door.

When they were gone, Keller went back to his desk and sat in the chair. He took the half-eaten sandwich out of the drawer, looked at it for a moment, and threw it into the wastebasket. He had no more appetite, he had only the anger they had brought to him. Too much feeling, that had always been his trouble. Too much feeling and too much pain: the business in Chicago and now the Ripper. Maybe it was that, the overload of pain, he thought, which would—if you really, really looked for it —explain everything that had happened and would happen to him.

CROSS

James Jack Cross had always hated the house which his mother, Florence, owned and in which he had been raised.

The house sat alone on a low promontory overlooking the northernmost reaches of Woodbine Lake, the distant shapes of Fort Seneca and Colonial Village Amusement Park. Three-quarters of a century old, it was an odd combination of architectural styles dominated by Eastern Colonial: pillared, trimmed in elaborate wooden scrollwork, painted a solid white, with an exposed staircase along one side, a massive stone-and-mortar chimney, black 1890s gaslit lamps, and verandas circling it at ground and second-story levels. Cross had always thought of it, without humor but in a phrase he admired, as a tall, unevenly constructed club sandwich out of which some toothless mouth had gummed a few tentative bites.

When he brought his old Chevrolet six into the wooded front yard at four that afternoon, his mother came out on the front porch immediately and stood waiting for him. She had tinted her hair again since last Saturday, a lighter shade of red this time, and from a distance she looked an attractive thirty-five instead of an attractive forty-five. She was wearing one of his old pullover sweaters and dark slacks.

Cross went up onto the veranda. "Hello, Mother."

Florence kissed him on the cheek, stood back and looked at him gravely. "How are you, Jimmy?"

"I've asked you before not to call me *Jimmy*."

"That's your name, isn't it?"

"My middle name is Jack and that's the only one I use, you know that better than anyone." He brushed a hand through his unruly brown hair and pushed his glasses up on the thin slope of his nose; he felt gangly and awkward, as he always seemed to around his mother.

"You haven't answered my question," she said.

"I'm fine, wonderful," and he let her take his arm and lead him inside, into the front parlor.

It was a big, dark room with a stone fireplace covering one entire wall. Paintings in old oval frames, glassed-in bookshelves, and a large pillar-and-scroll clock filled the other walls. The furniture, heavy and ponderous, featured an antique Governor Winthrop secretary and Peterborough cabinets jammed with pewter and silver. Cross began instantly to feel depressed. The room, the house never failed to have that effect on him.

Florence said, "Would you like some coffee?"

"No, nothing."

Cross began to wander the room. It was very quite in there, except for the steady pendulum movement of the clock and sporadic crackles and creaks that came from the old house's stiffening joints. He stopped finally in front of the fireplace and turned to look across at Florence. The absence of strong light made her almost beautiful, he thought. Soft mouth, smooth skin, a little thick maybe in the waist and hips now, but not so much that it spoiled the contours of her body. Yes. Almost beautiful.

"Listen, Mother," he said, "I wish you wouldn't stay out here alone now. I don't like you being alone with the Ripper running around loose."

"We've been through all that before. I'm not in any danger as long as I keep all the windows and doors locked. And I have your father's old handgun upstairs, just in case."

"I'd still feel better if you weren't here alone at night."

"You could always move back, if you're that concerned."

"No," Cross said, "you know how I feel about this place. I couldn't work here. I couldn't live here."

"You lived in this house the first eighteen years of your life."

"The *worst* eighteen."

"Really, Jack? Do you really feel that way? I'm sorry for both of us, then." She sighed. "Even so, if I wanted to move elsewhere for the time being, where would I go? I certainly couldn't come live with you in that tiny cottage, even assuming you could push your Superman comic book collection far enough into a corner to make me a little room."

"You could move in with Plummer," he said.

Her mouth opened just a little. "I don't think I care for that suggestion at all."

"Everyone who cares knows that you and Plummer have been a lot more than just good friends for years."

"My relationship with Plummer is none of your business, or anyone else's. No matter what it is or might have been, I have no intention whatsoever of living with him. You want me to call you *Jack,* I'll do so; you do me the favor of dropping that subject."

"Have it your own way. You always do anyway."

Florence sat carefully on the Shaker rocking chair. "After all," she said, because she had to have the last word, "do I ask you about your personal relationship with Paula?"

Well, she wasn't going to have the last word this time. "Not directly," he said, "but you hint around enough. You'd like to know if Paula and I are sleeping together and you'd like to know if we're going to get married someday. The answers are yes and who knows? You see, Mother? *I'm* not afraid to be honest."

She seemed to flush faintly, although in the dim light he couldn't be sure. "You're being deliberately offensive, and I don't like it. What's come over you lately?"

"I'm not in the mood for a lecture."

"You've been acting rather strangely, Jack."

"That's a lot of crap."

"Nice language to use to your mother."

God. "I don't know why I come here," he said. "Every Saturday it's the same thing, just going around this way. And we get nowhere."

"Jack, *you're* not getting anywhere." She gave him one of her stern looks. "I had dinner with Plummer last night. He told me about that article you wrote for the last issue of the paper."

Cross' hands clenched. "What article?"

"You know perfectly well what article. Plummer was very disturbed."

"There was nothing wrong with that piece," he said. "It was a little emotional maybe, that's all. I wrote it the morning after the third murder, you know."

"Plummer thinks you have some sort of fixation about these killings. He says your work has gone downhill since they started."

"The whole town has a fixation about the murders," Cross said. He was angry now, and when he got angry his motor responses became almost paroxysmic; he knew that, but he couldn't do anything about it. "They're the most terrifying, fascinating events that have happened in this town since I was born. I'm a newspaperman, the news is my job, how can I *not* be caught up in what's happening?"

"You won't be a newspaperman much longer if you don't learn how to control yourself and your work. Do you realize how close you came to losing your job?"

"Stop patronizing me, for God's sake. You treat me like a damned kid. . . ."

"You've been acting that way, haven't you? Jack, either you do your job properly or you'll have to suffer the consequences. I won't intervene on your behalf."

Cross waved an arm jerkily; the hand and elbow seemed to move in independent ways, against each other. "Nobody's asking you to, nobody wants you to," he said. "Besides, I won't need Plummer's lousy job much longer. When I finish my book I'll be able to get a position on any paper in the state. I won't even *have* to work. I'll be a writer; I'll be out on my own."

"Your book," Florence said. "*The Ripper of Bloodstone,* wasn't that the title?"

"Working title."

"How much have you written so far?"

"A hundred and thirty pages. And it's the best work I've ever done."

"I'd like to read those hundred and thirty pages."

"Well you can't," Cross said. "I'm not going to let anybody read it until it's finished."

Florence sighed again, heavily. "Do you really expect to finish it? You've never finished a major project in your life."

"I'll finish this one, all right, and it'll be published."

"Suppose the Ripper is never caught? Have you thought of that?"

Cross stared at her. "Why do you keep doing this to me?" he asked suddenly. "Why do you find negatives in everything of mine? Sometimes I think you like the idea of me being a failure; that way, you think you've got control the rest of your life."

"Jack. . . ."

"It's not going to work out that way," he said. "You hear me? I won't let it work out that way. The Ripper's going to get me out of Bloodstone and he's going to put me on top and nobody is going to stand in the way."

Florence looked a little frightened in the dimness. "That's crazy talk. . . ."

"Is it? We'll see. We'll see about that."

She said something else, but Cross was on his way out, and he didn't hear it. Saturday afternoon, or at least the Florence part of it, was over. He opened the front door, walked rapidly to his car, and got inside. Florence came out on the veranda, gesturing, shouting to him, and then ran down toward the car. But he got it started and in gear and drove away before she reached him.

When the house and his mother disappeared beyond a curve in the lane, Cross began to feel better—much better. He allowed himself the smile he had been suppressing from the moment he walked out of the parlor. He had handled her just fine for a change. He had gotten the best of the Queen of Amateur Theatrics with a little melodramatic role playing of his own.

Clark Kent, by God, couldn't have done it any better.

SMITH

State Police Lieutenant Daniel Smith bent more intently over the board in the living room of Plummer's Bloodstone house and studied the situation.

Grave. Down by two in the bottom of the ninth, bases loaded, but two out and all his bench strength used up. Eddie Lopat was laboring for Plummer on the mound, but still had that incredible control, and *he* had no hitting. Nine to seven, three runs already in, but the rally looked dead.

"I'll try Gus Zernial," he said, looking up briefly.

Plummer nodded, riffled through the cards alphabetized on his side of the table, solemnly handed him one. Lefthanded batter with some power, some consistency, but now near the end of his career, little more than a .230 hitter who swung too quickly to wait out the base on balls. Years ago Zernial would have been the man you wanted to see up there, but not now. Far gone, thirty-seven years old. Still, he had no one else.

"I'll hit away," Smith said.

Plummer nodded, again solemnly, holding his pipe in his mouth. Smith leaned forward, put his finger gently to the spinner and then fitted the card tightly over the loop. He felt a little stab of pain in his stomach, but this time it could only be the pressure of the situation. "Okay," he said, and hit the spinner. It twirled and dropped after what seemed a long, hanging instant into *fly out.*

Damn! If it had not been a left-handed hitter against Lopat, if it had not been the low ERA Lopat card. . . . Well, that was all speculation. What could have happened and what came out of a situation were entirely different things.

"1953 Yankees nine, 1952 Athletics seven," Plummer said. He was a distinguished-looking man, with mild blue eyes and thick silvering hair, but his face in flush of accomplishment looked something like a teenager's. "You ran out of hitters, Dan."

"Yeah," Smith said, and pushed back his chair and stood. Standing took the cramping out of his stomach, and he felt a little less uncomfortable.

"Another game?" Plummer asked.

"Not just yet. Let's take a break."

Plummer nodded. "Think I'll have a cup of coffee. You want one too?"

"No." Smith felt another small twinge under his breastbone, put a hand there instinctively. "Maybe a glass of milk," he said.

Plummer got to his feet, looking at him gravely. "Stomach bothering you again?"

"No, it's all right."

"You really ought to see a doctor about those pains."

"Not serious enough for that," Smith said.

"It could be an ulcer. I had an ulcer twenty years ago. If you get them early and treat them right, they won't bother you; but if you ignore them, the damned things can open up on you and then you're in real trouble."

"I don't want to talk about it, Plummer."

Plummer started to say something else, then shrugged when Smith turned away; he went out of the room, into the kitchen. Smith sat in one of the overstuffed armchairs —a medium-sized man in his early forties with large, intelligent eyes, features that were undistinguished without being bland, and neatly trimmed brown hair. He forced his mind blank; the pain didn't bother him much unless he allowed himself to think about it.

Plummer came back with coffee and a glass of milk. When he handed the glass to Smith, he said abruptly, "The 1927 World Series, Dan."

"Pirates," Smith said in immediate response, "and the Yankees. Four games, Yankee sweep."

"All right. Last out?"

"Paul Waner, fly ball to right. The only World Series he ever played in." Smith paused. "1966 American League batting champion."

"Frank Robinson," Plummer said. "Triple crown. Three-oh-six average." He leaned forward. "Ned Garver."

"St. Louis Browns. Twenty-game winner in 1952. George Sternweiss."

"New York Yankees," Plummer said. "Batting champion 1945, lowest winning average in history until Yastrzemski's three-oh-one. Died in a railroad accident. Train went right off a collapsed bridge, and he drowned." He sipped at his coffee. "Wayne Terwilliger," he said.

"Terwilliger?"

Plummer smiled. "Right—Wayne Terwilliger."

"Infield," Smith said, "utility infield."

"No good. Team, years, position."

"Christ. Cincinnati Reds?"

"Nope. Give up?"

"No." But then, after a while, "Yes, goddamn it."

"Chicago Cubs," Plummer said, and winked at him. "Utility infield, mostly second base. Dodgers for a little while, too. Early fifties."

Smith felt another twinge of pain. He averted his eyes and drained the glass of milk.

The telephone rang. Plummer said, "Wayne Terwilliger, by God," and then went to answer it. He came back a moment later with a sober expression. "There's a girl named Valerie Broome on the line, wants to talk to you. She called your home and Marjorie told her you were here."

"Talk about what?"

"The murders. Her name's familiar, I think she used to live in Bloodstone when she was a kid. She says she's writing an assignment article for *Insight Magazine*. That's a pretty good publication." He said the last as if he found it hard to believe anyone from Bloodstone could be working for such an important periodical.

"When it comes to scare crimes like this one," Smith said, "none of them are any damned good."

"You'll get that maniac, Dan. We've all got confidence in you, you know that."

"Yeah. I'll have to see her, I guess."

"You can have her come over here," Plummer said with interest. "She's here in Bloodstone."

Smith said, "All right, why not?" and went away to the phone.

THE RIPPER

Blood on the veil, peeping through the veil, seeing her scuttle, leaping and lowering, now moving quick and quiet, dense and slow in the forest of the trees of the purpose of the need as I come down toward her but hiding deep within, within and forever, veiled.

Don't do it, she said.

Must do it, the oath.
No, no, no, no.
Yes. Here.
Where?
There, everywhere, I said and put it over and in, put it over and in deep and damp and stroke and lash and pouring through me then, hidden forever or at least for a while.
Break them, and the sweets come a-tumble.

HOOK

For a period of fourteen months during 1968 and 1969, Steven Hook had been an alcoholic.

He had not been much of a drinker, let alone a heavy one, when he had come to New York City from Dayton, Ohio, in 1958; but once there, he had discovered that it was something of a necessity for everyone struggling in the so-called public arts . . . and nothing was more public than acting. The parties and night life had more to do with getting ahead than talent, then putting in his hours in the Actors Studio. Still, he had handled liquor in moderation through the lean years, the succession of handyman and messenger and other part-time jobs that he had been forced to take to pay his way through the Studio, the minor roles at three dollars a performance Off-Broadway, his marriage to fashion designer Virginia Warren whom he had met at a party on the Lower East Side when they were both very obscure. Now only one of them was obscure.

But then. Ah, then. He had read for a Gene Ackers production of *King Lear*, hoping for Lear but ending with Edmund, which was still something of a plum. The production had been well mounted, and Hook had known that he was good, and although it all ran only fifty performances, he had discovered to his astonishment one morning in 1967 that he seemed to have won a *Village Voice* Obie Award for best male supporting actor.

That didn't mean a great deal to him, but it meant something to a few producers; he had been offered supporting roles in two Broadway plays and had taken what he felt was the best one. But that play folded after only three performances—and when he learned that the second offer was still open, and got the part, it also collapsed during the first week. His notices, which had been slight for the first part, were small and vicious for the second. The *Times* said that his overacting was symbolic of textual failure, although it was the director who had blocked him through every stride, every gesture. One of the magazine reviewers wrote that his motions resembled those of advanced paresis.

Bitterness set in, and that was when his drinking had become heavier and less regulated. He had once scheduled his drinking or at least scheduled the day around it; now there were no barriers between impulse and act. Ginny, mostly warm and encouraging in the early years, turned militantly feminist long before there was a movement to give a name to her rage. She took to laughing at his failure as her own career moved ahead. And after a while she also took a succession of lovers. When she openly admitted her adultery to him, he walked out and filed for divorce the next day.

So liquor became his wife. It insulated him against memory and had a way of splicing failure and success, so that after only a few drinks he could see his life as it should have been, would have been, except for circumstances beyond his control. It was a thin sea on which he could sail away the hours of each day and night. He could even work drunk.

The period of alcoholism had lasted fourteen months. Fourteen months of people and events seen through a haze as surrealistic as a *cinéma vérité* montage. Fourteen months of waking beside women whose names he could not remember and whose bodies only reminded him of Ginny's. Fourteen months of blackouts and hangovers, of old friends who stopped coming around and new friends who came only to drink, of phones that did not ring and money that vanished and jobs that fell away. . . .

And then, as the result of a single event, that part had ended too.

He had gone to a party in the Village, not by invitation but by design, having heard of it third hand, waiting until the party was in full swing because that was when the hosts let someone else answer the bell and almost anyone could get in and invade the liquor supply unnoticed. Off in a corner by himself, he had been working on half a tumbler of Wild Turkey, no ice, when a voice said, "Christ, love, will you look at what we've got here? Your sodden ex holding up another wall."

The man's name was Opsinger, a fringe producer whom Hook had known slightly and liked not at all. With him was Ginny.

When he first saw her it struck Hook as excruciatingly funny that out of all the parties in New York that night, he and Ginny should wind up together at this one. He began laughing, and once started, he could not stop. He stood there in the corner and laughed until his insides quivered; rolled his head back, howling. Conversation stopped; people stared. Ginny said contemptuously to Opsinger, "He's drunk, crazy drunk," and Hook said, "You bet I am, I am fucking drunk as a lord," and Opsinger said, "Suppose you watch that mouth, drunk or not, Hook," and still laughing Hook said, "Fuck you and fuck her too, if you're not already doing it, prick," and Opsinger shoved him against the wall very hard, the tumbler coming up and spilling Wild Turkey over Hook's jacket.

The laughter had gone out of him, and he was suddenly and terribly angry. The room began to spin, a woman shrieked and there were voices and pressure, and when his head cleared he realized that he had Opsinger down on the floor, choking him with one hand, smashing the other fist over and again into his forehead.

Defensively, then, he had passed out.

He woke the next morning in jail, with a blinding hangover and wanting a drink so badly that he couldn't stop the jerking of his hands. But he did not get the drink because he did not get out of jail. Opsinger pressed charges for aggravated assault, and Hook had no money for bail and no one to whom he could use his phone call to ask for it. A Legal Aid lawyer, who looked about nineteen and confused, shrugged and suggested that he plead guilty, and when he did that at the arraignment, a righteous old judge gave him a temperance lecture and ninety days, plus two years' probation. Ginny had not shown up in court, and he had never seen her again.

The ninety days dried him out and offered him time to think. The first thing he had decided was that he had to get out of New York City, and the second was that he would never act again in the theater because it was what had ruined him, and the third was that he would never take another drink under any circumstances. It frightened him, what he had done to Opsinger and what he might have gone on to do. All the more frightening was the fact that he had no memory of what had happened between the time Opsinger pushed him and when he found himself over the man on the floor. The blackout syndrome was where alcoholism really got serious.

Having made these decisions in the first few days, Hook stopped thinking altogether and waited patiently for his release.

The morning they let him go, he packed two suitcases full of his stored belongings and boarded a bus for as far upstate as his money would take him. The ticket got him to Cohoes, just west of Albany and a little south of Saratoga, and he found a job the same day as a janitor in a sort of combined bar-and-supermarket complex, an upstate phenomenon. There were times, while he was alone in the place, that the bottles of liquor shone like beckoning eyes —but he refused the invitation each time.

One evening a few weeks after his arrival in Cohoes, with nothing to do, he left his furnished room and took a bus to Saratoga Raceway. He had had a fondness once, in the short period when things were going well, for harness racing at Yonkers and a small knack, if not for picking winners, then for eliminating obvious losers and making intelligent stabs. This time he noticed that a trotter in the fourth race was called Broadway Farewell, and not without irony he bet it two and two, win and place. It started fast, finished well, came in at eighteen dollars and sixty cents, and was the beginning of the first winning streak of his then thirty-three years.

He went back to the track regularly after that. If this was going to be a new career—this had occurred to him instantly—then he had to be systematic. He had followed the forms, had come to know the horses' individual traits. After a while he developed a system of place parlaying on certain favorites which he felt would, and which did, make him a livable wage. He left his job finally and devoted all his time to Saratoga, going six days a week. And he continued to win: a winner at last.

Hook made five thousand dollars during the last six racing months of 1969, and bought the Dodge, and had no trouble staying on the wagon. Early in 1970 he began looking for a more permanent place because he was tired of hotel rooms and because the cost of living in the Saratoga area was higher than it needed to be. Eventually, he found the four-room cottage in Bloodstone. It was a little farther away from the raceway than was ideal, almost sixty miles, but it was cheap and quiet, and he enjoyed driving.

In the years following he had gone through a few pleasant, if passing, contacts with women and had lived comfortably; if he was not exactly happy, he had at least been content. He made thirteen thousand in 1971, his best year, and through this year he had averaged right around ten. But then, after a normal spring, things had begun, subtly at first but then not so subtly, to fall apart.

Women, accessible enough in the past, seemed to be at a premium and stricken with moods; he had not had sex for five months. The hundred-and-twenty-mile round trips to Saratoga were no longer relaxing, merely tedious. Bloodstone, once a sanctuary, seemed to be nothing more than an empty, lonely place suddenly filled by the gruesomeness of the Ripper killings. And, much worse, the system—particularly in the last two months—had gone completely off the rails.

For some reason that he could not pin down, he could no longer separate the false favorites from the real ones. Without that separation, the place parlay was no longer a system but only a matter of stabbing and luck and holding on. With almost ten months of this year gone, he had made slightly less than thirty-three hundred. And in these last months he was down—not even, not holding on. So much so, in fact, that he had gone off the parlays and was back now to where he had started from Cohoes: looking for long shots, reaching, begging, not in control.

In an obscure way the sudden collapse of this, his second life, seemed somehow related to the Ripper murders—the intersection of public and private disasters which had marked his life. A week after JFK's assassination he had lost out on a part that he had been verbally promised in an off-Broadway play, one that would surely have been a careermaker, since the play ran for sixteen months and was moved uptown. A few days after the shooting of Martin Luther King, Hook had learned that his second Broadway play was closing—the end, as it turned out, of his acting career. The afternoon of the day Robert Kennedy was killed he had found out about Ginny's lovers and officially ended their marriage and begun the serious drinking. Three nights after watching on television the horrors of the Chicago Democratic Convention, he had himself been mugged and beaten on East Fifty-third Street two doors from his building. And now, coupled with the brutal, senseless Ripper murders there was the collapse of the system and of his new life.

He was changing again, as he had changed in the Tombs in New York. But this time he did not know where that change was taking him, or what exactly was happening to him.

Steven Hook was terrified.

VALERIE

Valerie Broome and Ferrara spent an hour with Daniel Smith, the state police officer in charge of the homicide investigation, and Plummer, the owner of Bloodstone's weekly newspaper, the *Sentinel*.

The interview, if it could be called that, was far more amicable than the meeting with Keller had been. In the car after leaving the constable's office, Valerie had asked Ferrara for God's sake not to antagonize people by trying to psychoanalyze them; as a result, he had conducted himself with perfect grace, laying out his theories elegantly to Smith and Plummer, persuasive and polite. Everything went smoothly and easily—but with no more results than the Keller session.

Smith seemed competent and controlled and receptive to Ferrara's theories, but Smith also appeared to have no personal commitment in his investigation: a methodical man working in a methodical way. If you accepted the hypothesis that the Ripper would soon be compelled to reveal himself, and the case was therefore close to its own resolution, neither Smith's lack of personal involvement nor Keller's obsessive attitude mattered. But she still could not quite believe that the Ripper would bring about his own downfall, despite Ferrara's convictions. It was too pat, too simple, to fictionally ironic. And Ferrara, at least careerwise, was little more than a second-rate psychiatrist.

When they left Plummer's house, Valerie drove them— in the rental car which *Insight* had provided—back to the Homelite Motel, off the Northway two miles south of the village, where they had taken rooms. She left Ferrara there, telling him she wanted to spend some time driving alone, reacquainting herself with the town.

She drove the length of Main Street, and three miles south and three miles north on U.S. 9; she went past Johnstone's Wharf, the boat rental place where she had hired boats in the summers of her youth; she had a look at the house on East Lane where she had been reared and which was now in a state of disrepair; and she stopped for a time at the public school, Essex Union, a block west of upper Main. The school was a large two-wing old-fashioned brick building that looked like a correctional facility. She had spent half her waking life in there for twelve years, and seeing it again made her immediately and utterly depressed.

The whole area depressed her, far more than she had imagined it would. She really did hate Bloodstone, she realized. She had thought that after ten years of absence she had achieved a kind of objectivity and perspective, but that wasn't true at all. Now that she was here Bloodstone had instilled, insidiously enough, a sense of loathing and apathy, and she was not at all sure she could write about it without personal prejudice.

Valerie drove from the school to the small public park overlooking the municipal beach and the lake, left her car on the side of the deserted roadway, and walked down the brown sloping lawn. It was after five now, starting to get dark; the wind cut sharply, and the temperature had already dropped into the thirties. The mountains on all sides seemed bleak and remote, and the surface of the lake was gray and wind-rippled. It must have been a day like this, she thought, when Peter Bloodstone pitched off that cliff three centuries ago: the dark glass of the lake rushing up, slicing at his body when he crashed into it and shattered it and then disappeared forever inside it.

She sat on one of the wooden picnic benches, shivering slightly in the cold, and stared out over the lake. *Anybody in this damned place might be the Ripper,* that much she was sure of. Probably one of the common and upstanding citizens of Bloodstone, perhaps even the head of the town council. She had a fantasy vision, sitting there, of the councilman, whoever he might be, calling a press conference after unmasking or being unmasked as the Ripper and saying to the assembled news media, "Why did I do it? Well, you see, we don't like outsiders and we want to preserve our way of life. So we thought—the town council and I, that is—that a good colorful set of murders would help perpetuate rural America. So we drew lots, because it was fair that everyone have an equal chance to be the murderer, and I just happened to win. Isn't that something? Of course, there was nothing personal in any of this." Then he would raise a strong hand, and the rush of reporters to exits would instantly cease. "I do want you to understand one thing, though," he would say. "I took no pleasure in the crimes. This business of diamond-shaped marks on the thighs was just an extra added fillip. Why, I wouldn't take any pleasure from this sort of thing. I mean, if I did"— smiling winsomely—"if I did, I'd be a *monster,* wouldn't I?"

Valerie smiled grimly. Modern Dostoevskian shared guilt, and all that—there was a certain validity in the concept, ridiculous as the fantasy itself was. Anyone could be the murderer; everyone could be the murderer. So who was? And when would he strike again? *Soon,* Ferrara had assured her again on the way back to the Homelite. *Very soon. He is accumulating tensions rather than releasing them, as most obsessives, to their amazement and our pity, almost always do.*

Little spots of pale light began to wink on here and there in and beyond the park: streetlamps. Valerie realized that it was almost full dark now and then became acutely aware that she was alone in the park, alone in the darkness. Fear touched her. The Ripper went after women alone, women alone at night, and here she was, a woman alone at night. But he wouldn't strike this early, and in the middle of Bloodstone—or would he?

Time to get out of here, lady, she thought, and stood and started up the slope with the wind pushing at her back. She was thirty yards from the roadway when the headlights of a car appeared around a turn farther down, lakeward.

A fluttering began deep in her stomach. Now take it easy, she told herself, it's just a car, it's just someone on the road. But she began to walk faster, watching the headlights. The car was moving slowly, a hazy black shape behind the probing beams. And then, when it neared her car, it came to a drifting stop, lights gleaming dully off the polished metal.

Valerie stopped too. The fluttering intensified, and cold beads of moisture appeared on her forehead and beneath her arms. She came up on the balls of her feet, poised for flight.

The door of the other car opened and a man stepped out, moved forward to the perimeter of the headlamp glare. A big man with iron-gray hair and a tight, hard face, wearing a khaki uniform and a gun holstered on his right hip.

Keller. The constable, Alex Keller.

Valerie breathed out in a long, shaky sigh and forced her legs to carry her the rest of the way up the slope. When she got to her car Keller came up to her; he seemed to be smiling. "Everything all right, Miss Broome?" he asked.

"Yes," she said. Her voice sounded hoarse. "Why shouldn't it be?"

"You seem upset about something."

"No. Not at all."

"It's not a time for a woman to be out alone at dark—that was what you were thinking, right?"

"Yes," she said. *The Ripper could be anyone.* She reached for the door handle on her car. "Good night, Constable."

"Good night, Miss Broome," Keller said, and kept on standing there, looking at her.

Valerie got into the rental and fumbled the key into the

ignition and pulled away jerkily, lifting her eyes to the rear-vision mirror. Keller continued to stand there for a time, then returned to his cruiser. The headlights swung out to follow her. The three blocks to Main Street seemed to pass slowly, but she resisted the impulse to drive at greater speed. When she came to the intersection, Keller was a half block behind her. She turned south, past the Gulf station and the town green, and a few seconds later Keller came out in a slow turn, going the other way.

Immediately she veered to the curb and sat there feeling relieved and a little foolish. Tough New York girl. You bet. She had been more frightened just now than she had ever been in the jungles of the city, and with less provocation. Bloodstone had done that to her, as much as the threat of the Ripper.

The place was really getting to her.

She lit a cigarette and stared out at the empty street. This episode ought to send her straight back to the motel. And yet she did not want to go there: she did not feel like working, had nothing yet to *say*, no focus for the article, and she certainly didn't feel like listening to any more of Ferrara's pontifications.

The dull red neon sign on the front of Bloodstone Tavern, in the next block, caught her eye. A drink, that was what she needed now. A good stiff drink.

She drove down there, parked directly in front, and went in to get it.

KELLER

Ever since the discovery of poor Julia Larch, Alex Keller had lengthened his nightly patrols of Bloodstone township. He had had a cop's sense that Larch was going to be the first of many victims, couldn't pin it down any further than that. So he left his office at dusk every night and stayed out until well after midnight—driving each of the streets slowly, vigilant for any hint of trouble. He had been on patrol both times, when Arlene Wilson and that Canadian woman had gotten theirs, but not in the right place at the right time. This frustrated and enraged him, but it wasn't his fault. You couldn't blame him.

He had just begun his first circuit this night when he'd

confronted Valerie Broome. She had been pretty shaken by his appearance, all right, as though she were afraid that *he* was the Ripper. Well it might do her some good, throw a scare into her, wandering around in the dark that way.

He wondered again if that little bastard Ferrara was legitimate. Couldn't a man claim he was a psychiatrist and get away with it for a long time without having to show his degrees? He had heard of cases like that where quacks went into private practice, even had relations with women patients, before they were finally discovered.

And what did Ferrara, even if he was legitimate, know about what was going on here? What did he know about the Ripper or what Keller had to put up with or what this was doing to the town? He thought this was nothing more than a goddamned *case;* he didn't see any of the pain involved.

But the thing Keller had to keep in mind was that this Valerie Broome was doing an article for *Insight,* and since there was no way to call the two of them off because of the First Amendment and all that, he had to be represented in that article in as favorable a light as possible—particularly since he was the man who was going to catch the Ripper eventually. In fact, the smart thing to do would be to cultivate the girl's friendship and confidence. Give her a little background stuff that hadn't been released to the media.

Keller had a few theories about the Ripper himself. The fact that he didn't have psychological training or heavy language didn't mean he lacked insight. One thing he knew for sure: Ferrara's idea, what he'd heard of it, that the Ripper didn't know he was the Ripper was a crock of shit. The Ripper knew who and what he was, all right—crazy but cunning. There might even be a method to his madness. Maybe the killings weren't random at all. Maybe they were part of some overall, even long-range plan.

Those diamond-shaped marks on the thighs, there was another thing. Smith and the state police thought they represented some kind of puzzling clue that would, if you solved their significance, lead you straight to the guilty man. The press kept trying to say that they had symbolic meaning. But Keller thought they were meaningless altogether, no more important than the fact that the Ripper cut up his victims' lower torsos but left their breasts alone: all part of a homicidal maniac's blood rite. The Ripper wouldn't be caught because of those diamond-shaped marks; he would be caught through vigilance, dedication, and instinct.

Driving, watching and waiting, Keller paid close attention to each of the relatively isolated areas of Bloodstone. These were the sectors the Ripper seemed to prefer. It was still early in the evening, but then again, he might take to striking early simply because people expected him to strike late.

Which was precisely why he, Constable Alex Keller, realizing potentialities such as these, was the one who was going to get him in the end.

CROSS

THE RIPPER OF BLOODSTONE   Cross   add 142

into the bones. It would have to be Bloodstone. The Ripper
would have to have chosen it because the town was empty and
quiet, it was bleak and mostly deserted for the winter, and he
could carry on his cunning and terrible acts for months and
months, so the Ripper might have thought, before anyone could
~~get on~~ sniff out his trail.

But the important thing to realize is that from his point
of view, the victims deserved exactly what they were getting.
To him, what he was doing wasn't awful at all! Thus the vengeance he extracted was to him just and to us even more
horrible.

Take, for example, the diamond-shaped marks which he
inflicted on the ~~soft inner~~ thighs of his victims. To us these
were merely symbols of his demented thirst for vengeance.
But to him, I believe, they were of great meaning. Though as
I write this I cannot know the truth, I'm convinced it will be
borne out when the Ripper is finally caught that the marks
were symbols of power. Power translated into diamonds, for
the man who can give diamonds to a woman is the most powerful
of all men. I thought at first that there was some sexual
meaning to the marks as well, but I have decided that there
isn't except in terms of this great power he feels as he does
what he is compelled to do.

It was these insights I considered as I drove away from
my mother's house this afternoon in my old Chevrolet, which
I bought from Forest Wicker, the owner of the Hideaway
Cabins, before he died, and which is now starting to fall
apart. Thinking deeply, I found myself driving on the
Northway a few minutes later, due north on the Northway
toward the hidden and beckoning jewellike city of Montreal.

THE RIPPER OF BLOODSTONE   Cross   add 143
~~to the north,~~ I was not due to see Paula for hours and I did
not want to see her now anyway. There is never an end to her
demands on me, but she understands little, particularly about
the Ripper. The same is true of my mother. Neither of them is
capable of envisioning, as I am, the cruel lines of his ~~face~~
countenance, the wild light of power and vengeance in his
eyes, as he strikes again and again at his victims.

    All the corners of my mind sought still greater insight
into the Ripper as I drove through the grey afternoon.
Were these murders in Bloodstone his first or merely the
latest in a long string of such fiendish attacks? There are
thousands of unsolved killings in this country every year.
Could it be that he has murdered scores of women over the
past ten or twenty or more years? I couldn't remember any
other murders where the diamond-shaped marks were put on the
victims' thighs, but these symbols of his power may be
something new for him.

    Such a staggering possibility as this made me feel
uneasy, but I knew I had to set it and all my day's reflections
down on paper as soon as possible. Turning around at the
nearest exit, I started back here to my cottage. I began
thinking as I did of the victims themselves. How they must
have pleaded and begged for their lives! Particularly
Arlene Wilson, ~~who was a snotty bitch~~ who worked at the
diner on Route 9 and Clover Circle, and who, even though
she tried to keep it quiet, was going around and

HOOK

In October, Saratoga Raceway was not at all what it had been during the summer months. The mile flat track was long closed; only the harness raceway remained open. The society types who came to the track and then went to the terraces of the Hotel Gideon Putnam, the Skidmore girls and Rensselaer Polytech boys, sought indoor amusement for the winter; the tourists from Lake George and environs were gone. No one came to Saratoga in October except Steven Hook and fifteen hundred or so of his brothers and sisters in the gambling fraternity.

He got there at seven, one hour before the scheduled first post, and stood in the lower grandstand directly back of the finish line; he had never been able to sit at the track. While at the Hideaway Cabins that afternoon he had finally been able to work out his plays for the night, but he went over the selections yet again, drinking bitter coffee and chain-smoking and snuffling into tissues. The sky seemed gray and threatening; it would probably rain before the night was gone.

His system was reasonable enough: you split false and real favorites by post position, and you stayed off favorites running outside of the third slot from the rail. Simple as that. Favorite and an inside post, twenty to place; then all the winnings parlayed back—but never more than three bets in a row. Take the money then and go on home. It could mean a minimum of six thousand dollars a season, and it was a long season: from March through November up here. Only downstate did they run longer.

The system was reasonable, yes, but recently favorites had begun running out of the money in a proportion unencompassed by anything in his experience or charts. Night after night he was losing instead of winning two for three bets, and the hot streaks that he had often been able to carry through seven or eight races were gone.

Well, he thought, well tonight will be different. There is no yesterday and damned little tomorrow, but there is tonight, an excess of tonight, and we'll put on these bets and the horses will perform and there'll be no inexplicable conspiracy and they'll win. Place, that is. Place.

Hook did not believe it.

Eight o'clock came, and the night began. And at eight-oh-six he lost twenty dollars on the one horse, a 6-5 shot who held the lead until just short of the finish line, broke, and finished fourth. In the second race the play was marginal: there were two 5-2 shots, and the one of them running inside was a few dollars short of being the favorite. But he had pushed these often enough with no change in the overall statistics, and he thought that he could push this. Twenty dollars again, then, on the two horse—but the two's driver was too clever for his own good and got boxed in and finished third. Misses and miles, swallows and summers. Hook found he was out of cigarettes and had not brought an extra package, which was stupid because cigarettes cost ninety cents at the track; but he got a pack anyway, his third of the day.

He should definitely have skipped the third race. The even-money choice, a good horse, was running from post seven. Nothing else was close in the betting. But he did not skip the race; he bet fifty dollars this time, twenty-five to win and twenty-five to place on the seven, knowing he was breaking the system but doing it anyway. The seven showed nothing and was beaten by ten lengths.

Lear's Fool, all right . . . so in the fourth race the Fool went to the outside horse, Raider's Star, 45-1 from the six post with a late driver change. Long shots did win, after all. Fifty dollars again, spread twenty-five apiece win and show because that was the way to bet long shots; you doubled your money even on a third-spot finish. Except that Raider's Star finished fourth, which was the end of that, even though fourth was pretty good for a long shot. It just went to prove that he had picked a live horse, one that might even have come in with a little racing luck. . . .

He should have left then; the night was already a disaster. He was down a hundred and forty dollars, and by the system you never took half that loss in a given evening. You balanced off those occasional losses through the winning streaks. But how could he leave? He went back to the windows prior to the fifth race, standing surrounded by denim-clad men who were talking about a tip: the seven horse shipped up from Yonkers. A downstater was always a bet at a minor track like this, wasn't it? A downstate horse wouldn't be at a track like this unless it wanted to pull a fast one. Everyone knew that. So even though the horse was even money and even though it was running outside, he put a hundred win, a hundred place on it.

Hook stood cold and alone next to a grandstand pillar, clutching it for support. The marshal called the trotters, and the rain finally started, and the seven failed to get up to the gate on post. That should have meant a recall, only no downstate horse was going to get a recall at Saratoga. The seven pushed hard on the break to make up the ground, went full-gaited, and was twelve lengths behind the leader on the backstretch; it made up eight of those lengths, showing that it, too, was a good horse after all, and finished third.

When OFFICIAL went up on the tote board, Hook turned away trembling and shaken. Three hundred and forty dollars down; he might just as well have flushed it away in a toilet. Get out of here, he thought, get out now! The urge to bet the sixth race was thick within him—but thicker was the conviction that if he plunged on the sixth and seventh and eighth races, he would lose everything. Everything.

So he forced himself to walk out of there, out to the parking lot, past three grim-looking men, past a drunken woman who looked astonishingly like Ginny and who asked him if he wanted some fun, all the fun in the world for twenty dollars, *fast*. Rage and fear muddled within him. Things were falling apart, yes: crumbling into ruin just as were the Hideaway Cabins in Bloodstone.

Hook drove onto the Northway, handling the Dodge mechanically, headlights and taillights of the other cars flowing in the mist that the rain had become. Exit signs flashed by, exit roads leading to village leading to streets leading to taverns leading to bottles leading to— His throat felt spastic now, dry, and his palms sweated on the hard plastic of the wheel. He needed a drink tonight more than he could ever remember having needed one, and he knew that tonight he was going to take it, the only crutch he'd ever had.

He drove faster, going home to Bloodstone, going home to that first drink in six years: going nowhere.

SMITH

His wife said, "Danny? Is something the matter?"

Lieutenant Daniel Smith turned his eyes from the dull red glow of the logs in the fireplace and looked at her. She was sitting forward in her chair, smiling tentatively, one thick finger marking her place in the paperback she was reading. The chair was positioned directly beneath one of the Charles Cromwell Ingham regional prints she liked, and for a moment the soft, placid features of her face seemed as blurred as the blue Adirondack ranges in the painting; for a moment (and it was not the first time he had felt this), this woman, to whom he had been married for twenty-one years and who had given birth to his two daughters and who had shared exactly half of his life, seemed like a stranger.

"It's nothing, Marjorie," he said.

"Well, you look so sad sitting there."

Sad, Smith thought. Brooding, maybe; bothered certainly. But not sad. She almost always misread his moods; she never seemed to know how he felt, as if he were a stranger to her too. And yet, paradoxically, theirs was a comfortable marriage built on a passive affection that seemed as durable as it had been in the beginning.

"No," he said, "I'm not sad. I've just got some things on my mind."

"You did have a nice time with Plummer today, didn't you?"

"Yes."

"You said you tried out a new game and you liked that."

"I suppose so."

"Then what is it that's on your mind?"

"Work, mostly," he said. "The Bloodstone murders."

Marjorie shuddered and moved in a way that made the soft flesh of her body jiggle and dance. The jiggling and dancing had a mildly erotic effect on Smith; it always had. She was forty pounds heavier than she had been when they were married, upwards of one seventy now, but she still appealed to him physically. One thing you could say in her favor, he thought: she had never been placid in bed.

"I hope you catch him soon, the one doing it," she said. "Suppose the Ripper were to start killing women here in Lake George?"

Smith hated the "Ripper" appellation; anybody who used a knife on a woman automatically became the Ripper. But he said only, "He's confined to Bloodstone so far, and there's no reason to assume he'll go anywhere else. Don't worry, Marjorie. We'll get him."

She nodded, accepting that as she accepted almost everything he told her, and sat back in her chair and opened her book again. *Night Duty*. Another nurse novel. Marjorie read them in incredible quantities—if there was a nurse novel published in the last fifteen years that she had not seen, it was because it had not yet come to the Lake George area—and that was all she read. Smith had never seen her pick up any other type of book in all the years he had known her.

He watched her become reabsorbed in *Night Duty;* she read slowly, forming the words with her mouth. Then he sighed faintly and sat back himself, staring again into the fireplace.

He would have liked to talk over what was really bothering him, but he had never been able to discuss with her what was really on his mind. He had not even told her that he was almost sure he had an ulcer, because she simply would not have understood how this made him feel. How could you talk about anything as intense as that with a forty-one-year-old woman who thought you were sad when you were actually bothered and in pain, who still called you Danny, who read nothing but nurse novels?

He couldn't talk to anyone, he thought. Not his daughters, certainly. Carmen had gotten herself pregnant the year before and had married the boy, which he supposed was fair enough, and made Smith a grandfather at forty-two, dismaying him a little; she and the boy lived in Lake George, but they were concerned with their own needs and seldom came around except when they wanted to drop the baby off for an evening. Betsy, his younger girl, was fifteen and spent all her time talking on the telephone and listening to rock albums in her room, which was where she was and what she was doing now; he could hear the dreary beat of the music flowing like water through the ceiling.

He had a few acquaintances, state police people and civilians—Plummer was probably his best friend, primarily because of their mutual passion for baseball—but there was no real closeness with any of them. He might be able to discuss some personal matters, but none that really counted. If he had tried, it only would have made Plummer and the others uncomfortable.

One of the two things on Smith's mind tonight was that fluctuating pain in his stomach. The ulcer. Now, if he thought about it, he felt pain all the time. It had taken away his appetite when he'd returned from Bloodstone two hours before—he had less and less of an appetite these days—and he could not rid himself of the nagging fear of perforation. Plummer was right: he should see his doctor. But if he did, and it *was* something serious, there was no way to keep it from his superiors on the state police. Suppose they were forced to put him off on half-pay disability? Where would that leave him? He was terrified of surgery, too: sharp scalpel cutting into your flesh, then the probing inside. No, he was not going to go to his doctor unless the pain got appreciably worse, unless there was no other way to deal with it. In the meantime he would have to keep on drinking milk and eating soft foods; he had done some reading on ulcers, and that was what they advised. And he would keep on taking mild tranquilizers to relieve the tensions of the job, which was probably responsible for the ulcer in the first place. Certainly he had been in much more pain since this damned Bloodstone case had begun.

And that was the second thing, in some ways the major thing, bothering Smith. The homicidal maniac who went around cutting up women—and the visit to Plummer's house that afternoon by the woman writer, Valerie Broome, and the psychiatrist *Insight Magazine* had sent up with her.

The girl had seemed pleasant enough, if a little too emotionally intense: New York women, transplanted or in habitat, always seemed to be emotionally intense, as though the dark enclosure of the city had some sort of chronic hyperthymian effect on them. Still, she was all right; pleasing to look at, too. It was that psychiatrist, Ferrara—or rather, Ferrara's theories on the homicides— which kept preying on Smith's mind.

According to Ferrara, there was no order to the slaying. Chaos, senselessness, was at the core of the case. Anyone could be the assailant; everyone was potentially the assailant; worst of all, the assailant did not even *know* he was the assailant. The killer could even be a woman, someone like Marjorie, for God's sake, which was ridiculous. When you reached certain levels, Ferrara's postulations broke down completely.

And yet, there was still a chance, however remote, that Ferrara was basically right. And if he was, it made a whole new and disquieting ball game of Smith's investigations, of his approach to police work in general, and, by logical extension, even of his approach to life itself.

He had always believed totally in the concept that rational means led to rational ends, not only in law enforcement but in everything. The universe was an ordered place; things happened in a regulated manner, even though at first they might not seem to be regulated. As a result, methodology—going about things in a disciplined manner—was the key to his existence, to all existence.

But if there wasn't order to the Bloodstone murders, you could never solve the case through methodology—and this opened up the possibility that reason and discipline did not always have an effect on the scheme of things because there was *not* a scheme of things. Which in turn meant that he, Daniel Smith, in his commitment to methodology—and this was what was really bothering him, spoiling his quiet Saturday night at home—was right now little more than a court jester: a big-footed clown going through a bumbling series of maneuvers that meant nothing and would lead nowhere.

"Jesus Christ," he said, but quietly, and his wife, deep in her book, did not hear him. Nor would she have heard him then, he thought, if he had screamed.

FLORENCE

Florence Cross had always believed that bad thoughts could be put out of your mind by will, but now and then something would get into your consciousness and just stick there like a piece of food that you couldn't pry loose from between two teeth. What was stuck in her consciousness was the look in Jimmy's eyes when he'd talked about his book, *The Ripper of Bloodstone*, that afternoon. He had always been a moody boy who got excited by strange things that she couldn't understand, like those comic books he had been collecting since he was eight years old, but that expression today had been different.

She was brooding about it, still seeing him in her mind, when Plummer called her. He asked if she wanted him to come over, and she said no, and then he asked good-naturedly if she wanted to come over to his place, and she said no again. Plummer didn't argue with her. That was one of the better things about their relationship, not to say Plummer himself; he was more or less easy-going.

"I'll just lay out some solitaire here, then," he said. "Baseball again?"

"Got a new one. American League All-Stars from 1930."

"I don't understand why it means so much to you," Florence said. Then, tentatively: "Have you seen Jimmy today?"

"No. Didn't he come by your house?"

"Yes, but he was acting rather . . . oddly."

"Oh? In what way?"

"He didn't seem to be himself," Florence said vaguely. She really didn't want to go into details with Plummer. "That article you told me about—he hasn't written anything more like that, has he?"

"No. I would have told you if he had."

"Have you read any of this book he claims to be writing?"

"*The Ripper of Bloodstone?* No, I haven't."

"Has he talked to you about it?"

"He's been pretty secretive on the project," Plummer said. "Is something the matter, Florence? Something you're not telling me about Jack?"

"Of course not. It's just that I worry about Jimmy . . . Jack. He's an unusual boy, Plummer, you know that."

"We've talked about him enough," Plummer said, and his voice sounded weary. "Florence, I honestly think—"

"I don't care what you honestly think," she said, because she felt that he was going to start in again on the subject of Jimmy perhaps benefiting by some sort of psychiatric treatment. That was ridiculous, and she had told Plummer so when he'd first brought it up. There was nothing mentally wrong with Jimmy; he was just unusual. Yes, that was the right word: unusual. "I'll call you tomorrow, Plummer. Maybe we'll have dinner."

"I'd like that. If you want to, Florence."

"Well then I'm sure I will."

"Fine," he said. "Listen, keep the doors and windows locked tight. I worry about you, with this maniac running around loose."

"Yes," she said, "yes," and put the receiver down.

She went back to the parlor, where she thought she might read a magazine. But when she sat down with the latest issue of *Insight,* all that she could see was the way Jimmy had looked at her. His eyes were still in the room, dark and floating—and for a very long time then, Florence found that she could do nothing at all, that she was only very attendant to the sound of the clock working in contrarhythm to the querulous and strained feel of her heart as the eyes and the face moved together through her mind, separate, circling, then bound.

HOOK

The rain had moved north with him as he drove home from Saratoga, and when Hook parked the Dodge down the block from Bloodstone Tavern it was drizzling as it had been at Saratoga. Coming into town, he had passed the Hideaway Cabins and had almost turned in there for the cached bottle of rye; but he did not want to take that first drink alone, he wanted it with people around. He did not know why there had to be people around, and it didn't matter why; he didn't want to pursue it, he was reacting, not thinking.

Despite the fact that it was Saturday night, there were only three customers in the tavern: two old men over in one corner playing pinochle and a black-haired girl on the other side, alone at the bar and making ring pictures with her glass. The room itself was long and narrow, the bar at the upper end, four tables along the left-hand side, a pinball machine OUT OF ORDER and a jukebox on the right; the middle was as empty and beckoning as a coffin. Over the backbar and on the walls were a series of wooden plaques with cartoon drawings and puke-cute saying like OLD GOLFERS NEVER DIE, THEY JUST LOSE THEIR BALLS and SHE WEARS MINK ALL DAY AND FOX AT NIGHT; the biggest one read I'VE BEEN LISTENING TO YOUR TROUBLES AND I'D REALLY LIKE TO HELP YOU OUT. WHICH WAY DID YOU COME IN? It was little different from any one of a hundred neighborhood bars in which Hook had spent long portions of the New York years.

He took one of the middle stools at the bar, closer to

the black-haired girl than to the pinochle players, and laid a dollar bill in front of him. The backbar mirror gave him the image of himself: eyes glassy, sweat graying his forehead, cheeks flushed. His hands, folded across each other, were shaking.

The bartender came down the plank, a short, round man with a bushy fringe of white hair around his ears; he looked, oddly, like a mathematician. Hook did not know his name. Even though he had lived in Bloodstone for close to five years, he realized dimly that he did not know the names of ninety-five percent of the residents.

"What'll it be?" the bartender asked.

"Rye. Shot of rye. Beer chaser."

Nodding, the bartender turned to the array of bottles. Hook stared at his shaking hands, then stilled them by grabbing onto the bar edge. He became aware that the black-haired girl was watching him; he could see her head turned in profile in the mirror. But he kept his own head to the front.

The bartender poured a full shot glass, drew a beer from the taps, and set both down in front of Hook. Little winking highlights glistened from the dark surface of the whiskey. He thought he could almost hear the beer making popping sounds.

"You're that fellow who lives on Stone Bridge Road, ain't you?" the bartender asked.

"I'm that fellow, all right."

"Steven Hook. You play the horses."

Hook said nothing.

"Sure. I try to know everyone in town even if they don't come in here. Guess you prefer your own company, right, Mr. Hook?"

Hook still said nothing.

"Must be an interesting occupation, horseplaying," the bartender said. "Some people don't think so, some people think it ain't an honest profession. But me, when I heard around you followed them, I thought hell, everybody's got to be something and it don't matter what as long as it's legal. I like to put a couple dollars on the trotters myself now and then. Even buy *Tomorrow's Trots* down at the souvenir shop, the way you do, once in a while; they never handled it until you come to town and put in a special order, so I guess I got you to thank, don't I?"

"I guess so," Hook said. He took his left hand from the bar edge. The hand shook so badly that he pulled it back at once, tightened his fingers once more around the belled wood. Easy. Slow and easy.

The black-haired girl said, "Make me another Chivas and soda, Tony."

"I think maybe you had enough," the bartender, Tony, said. So now he knew something, Hook thought: half a man's name.

"Unh-unh," she said. "Not quite. Almost but not quite."

"Why don't you go write your article or whatever it is?"

"Scotch and journalism don't mix. Scotch and Bloodstone mix, though."

"What does that mean?"

"It means I probably made a very large mistake writing this very eloquent query letter which got me back to this fine little community, that's what it means."

"Well I guess maybe you did at that," Tony said. His voice was disapproving. "You're sure not the same girl I remember from a long time ago, Valerie."

"Ten years," she said.

"Ten years has sure changed you."

"Ten years changes everybody and everything, except maybe Bloodstone."

Hook watched the rye winking at him.

"What do you want to write up the Ripper for anyway?" Tony said. "That's nothing for a young girl to be writing about."

"What should a young girl writer be writing about? Marriage and childbirth and home canning?"

"That's right," Tony said seriously. "Maybe if you wrote about them things you wouldn't be sitting in here drinking half the night and making a lot of funny comments about the town you grew up in."

"Sexist bullshit," Valerie said.

Tony's mouth got very hard, and he turned from the girl. She shrugged again and got up, glanced briefly at Hook, and then went off in the direction of the rest rooms. When she was gone Tony shook his head, lit a damp cigar and leaned companionably toward Hook.

"What do you think about these Ripper killings, Mr. Hook?" he asked. "Pretty damned awful, ain't they?"

Hook winked back at the rye. "Awful," he said.

"Yeah. I mean, it ain't so bad for us men, but the women are scared spitless. My old lady's afraid to go outside by herself in the daytime now, and I can't blame her, you know? I mean, what the hell is the world coming to when people can't even walk the streets of their own town at night without some maniac ready to cut them up?"

"I don't know," Hook said.

"You read about them fag murders in Texas?" Tony asked, and blew smoke toward the pinochle players. "And that other bastard who killed all the farm workers in California? Mass murders, that's all you read about, and all the time going for bigger and bigger victim lists. I mean, what's the goddamn world coming to?"

"I don't know," Hook said. "I just don't know."

"I grew up with Julia Larch, the first one the Ripper killed, and I used to kid around with Arlene Wilson at the diner. I *knew* these women. If the state police and Constable Keller don't find the Ripper pretty soon, there's some of us going to do the job ourselves."

Valerie, the black-haired girl, had come back to the bar. She moved over to where Hook was sitting and took the stool next to him. "Vigilante committee, is that what you're saying?" she said to Tony. "A bunch of idiots with guns, beating the brush and turning over rocks, ready to shoot anything that moves."

Tony looked at her narrowly. "You don't live here no more, Valerie," he said. "You don't know what it's been like the past couple of months."

"Don't I?" she said. "Oh don't I?"

"It's making the town sick," Tony said, "and nobody can keep on living in a sick town."

Valerie began to laugh softly, shoulders shaking, eyes almost shut.

"What the hell's so funny about that?" Tony said.

"Tony, Tony, this town's been sick for years. Don't you realize that?"

"I don't realize nothing of the kind." He looked angry now. "Valerie, I don't want to hear any more from you. I mean it, you keep that kind of stuff to yourself or I'll put you right out of here."

"Give me another Chivas and soda, Tony."

"No. You had enough, I'm not going to serve you any more."

Hook had been listening without really hearing anything they had said. He kept staring at the glass of rye, just trying to get himself under control, and now he thought that he could do it, now he thought that he would be able to take this first one. He let go of the bar edge again and moved his hand across the surface, sliding it, closed his fingers around the shot glass, putting the beer out of his mind because it was a distraction, he shouldn't have ordered it in the first place. He pulled the shot glass toward him.

One of the pinochle players called to Tony for a refill, and Tony went away. The girl, however, turned on her stool and looked frankly at Hook.

He picked up the glass, held it, lowered his head over it, and got his mouth almost to the rim. He could smell the rye, the sharp, raw fumes of it, and all at once his stomach turned over and the hand began to shake more violently than before and the glass slipped from his grasp and spilled the glistening liquid over the bar. Oh Jesus, he thought, I can't do it, I can't do it, maybe I don't even *want* to do it. He got one of the tissues from his pocket and wiped at the sweat on his face.

"What's the matter?" Valerie said. "Are you sick?"

He blinked at her.

"You look pretty bad," she said sympathetically.

"I'm not sick," Hook said and thought: Yes, I am, I'm sick all right.

"The town's getting to you too, isn't it? Not just the murders—the *town*, the people, the life-style."

"I don't know what you're talking about."

"Maybe you won't own up to it, but you do, Mr. Hook.

71

By hook or by crook, you do." She laughed humorlessly, then cut it off. "Haven't I seen your face somewhere before?"

In every bar in Manhattan, in every grandstand in upstate New York, he thought. "No," he said. "Maybe."

"I've heard your name, too. You wouldn't be a celebrity, would you?"

"Only to myself," Hook said.

Tony came back and looked at the spill in front of Hook; he got a rag and began to mop it up. "Get you another one?" he asked.

Yes, Hook thought. But he could still smell the raw odor of the one he had been unable to take; his stomach lurched again, and he felt a sudden and overpowering urge to get out of there, to escape that poisonous reek. "No," he said, "no," and pushed himself up and away toward the door.

When he was outside he stood with his face uplifted to the cold, gray drizzle, breathing openmouthed. His stomach stopped lurching and emptiness came in—and he realized that he had not eaten anything in twenty-four hours.

He was *hungry*.

It was funny enough in a grim way, and his shoulders jerked with silent laughter. He wiped rain from his face with his coat sleeve. It hadn't been the drink that had brought him home. What he had come home for was food at the Bloodstone Café.

Headlights swept toward him on the slick street, and the car drifted over to the curb directly in front of where he stood. Hook saw that it was the town constable's cruiser. The constable, Keller, rolled down the window glass and looked out at him and said, "What's going on?"

"Nothing," Hook said. "Nothing at all."

"Why are you standing there in the rain?"

"I was just on my way up to the café."

"Yeah? You live here in Bloodstone, don't you? Seems like I've seen you around before."

"I live here," Hook said.

"What's your name?"

"Hook. Steven Hook."

"Address?"

"Fifty Stone Bridge Road."

"All right," Keller said. "Go on about your business, then. And don't stand around in the rain anymore."

"Whatever you say," Hook said. Fuck you, Constable, he thought. He put his hands in his coat pockets and trudged up the empty sidewalk toward the café.

CROSS

In bed with Lois Lane, on top of Lois Lane, inside Lois Lane, Clark Kent rocked in hard, steady, confident rhythm, clutching at her thin, soft breasts and listening with relish to her moans of joy. She had climaxed six times already; he had been moving into her for an hour; he could move into her all night. His staying ability was limitless because still unknown to Lois (although she must surely suspect by now; they had been seeing each other for such a long time), he was the Man of Steel—and the Man of Steel was endowed with great powers which flowed from all parts of him and most notably from his mighty steel shaft.

But it was time to end it now. She could not take much more of this unrelieved pleasure. Too much pleasure could become pain, and the Man of Steel inflicted pain only upon those who would do evil, never upon his beloved Lois. Clark Kent began to move faster, faster than a speeding bullet, more powerful than a locomotive, and then he whispered, "Now, Lois, now!" and allowed himself to begin emptying waves of molten steel into the soft and gripping core of her.

She stiffened underneath him—but not in ecstasy—and cut off the moans of joy; closed hard around his massive metal penis. The muscles within her held him too tightly, hurting him, dissolving the rigid steel to mere flesh, taking away the keen edge of his own pleasure. The she shoved up against him, forcing him out of her, struggling, rolling away.

"Damn you, Jack!" she said. "Damn you!"

Cross twisted into a seated position, panting, and blinked at her. At Paula, Paula Eaton. "What is it? What's the matter?"

"You know what the matter is." She pulled the sheet over her body, sliding to the far side of the bed.

"No, I don't."

73

"You called me Lois again, Jack."

Cross felt himself flush. "Lois? No, I said *your* name, I said Paula. . . ."

"I'm not going to stand for that kind of thing much longer," she said angrily. In the darkness her narrow face looked hard, seemed to glow as if with a small inner fire. "And don't think I don't know who you mean when you say Lois, because I do."

"Paula. . . ."

"I know you a lot better than you think I do."

"Now, Paula, listen—"

"It better not happen again," she said. "If you have to fantasize in order to make love to me, that's your business; I don't want to know about it, I don't even want to imagine you're doing it. Our lovemaking isn't very good for me as it is. How much fun can I have when you finish in less than a minute every time?"

"Less than a minute?"

"Every time, Jack. You haven't given *me* a chance to finish in so long I don't remember what it's like. You won't even *try* anymore. It's not so important that I always finish, I'm not obsessed by it, but I don't enjoy feeling used either."

Cross felt embarrassment and irritation. He shouldn't have to put up with this, not after having had to put up with Florence earlier. "It's not my fault," he said. "I can't help it if you can't hear right, if I don't excite you the way you excite me."

"Oh Jack," she said, "when will you ever grow up?"

The irritation clawed at him. "Grow up?" he said. "I'm grown up. You think that you can pull rank on me because you're older, Paula? I'm not one of your junior high school students, you know. I'm your lover, you know."

She sighed.

"I'm entitled to be treated with respect," he said.

She sighed again, looked away from him. Just like Florence, he thought. The same kind of weary, patronizing sigh, the long-suffering tilt of the head. She really *was* like his mother in a lot of ways, and this bothered him. He didn't want the woman he was sleeping with to be like his mother; that sort of resemblance had undercurrents which made him feel uneasy, even though it shouldn't because as long as you were conscious of something, it couldn't harm you, could it?

Cross reached over and turned on the lamp on his side of the bed. Paula's bed in Paula's house on the northern edge of the village. They always made love there. Making love in his own cottage (he couldn't quite explain this) would have been impossible, but in her place it was natural. He looked down at her, watched her turn her head slightly, like an animal, to avoid the sudden light. She didn't *look* like his mother at least, and that reassured him. What she looked like was a schoolteacher in her mid-thirties: short dull-brown hair and a mouth that was too narrow and eyes that squinted often. He caught hold of the sheet and drew it to her waist, held it there against her. She made a token effort to recover herself, gave it up, but kept her face averted.

Cross stared at her breasts. Small, tiny-nippled; thin. He had never thought a woman could have thin breasts, but there they were. Indisputably thin, that was the only word for them. He continued to stare for a time, and then he lowered his head to the one on the left and began to suckle.

"Stop that, Jack," she said, but she didn't push him away. After a moment she lifted one hand and held his head. "Jack," she said.

Clark Kent suckling the breast of Lois Lane with his powerful mouth muscles, giving her pleasure. . . .

No, Cross thought, and pulled back and stretched out supine, no longer touching her. He really should try to control that fantasy of his. It was harmless, everybody had some sort of sexual illusion no matter how they tried to conceal it, but it *could* get out of hand, he had to admit that. He wasn't Clark Kent, for God's sake; he was Jack Cross. Still, every time he got into bed with Paula, the fantasy recurred and excited him far more than she alone ever could. Which was not to say that he found Paula exactly unexciting, but still, everything helped. Well, he would definitely have to keep from calling her Lois again. If he couldn't resist the fantasy itself, he could at least keep it inside himself.

After a time Paula said, "Jack, I think we ought to talk."

"About what?"

"About us."

"What about us?"

"We've been sleeping together for two years now, and we've been engaged, if you can call it that without a ring, for almost as long as that. I think it's about time we made some definite plans."

Apprehension flowed within Cross. He came up to one elbow. "Marriage," he said.

"You say 'marriage' as though it's a dirty word."

"Don't be silly. There's nothing wrong with marriage, I think it's fine."

"But not for you and me."

"Not yet, Paula. I'm not ready for it yet."

"When *will* you be ready for it?"

"I don't know," Cross said. "Why do you keep harping on marriage? We've got the same kind of relationship now that we'd have if we were married."

"No, we don't. You come over here two or three nights a week, we talk a little and then we make love and then you leave again at two or three in the morning. Is that a relationship, Jack?"

"I think it's fine."

"For you, maybe. But I want us to be together every day of the week; I want an end to this skulking around. I'm tired of being Miss Paula Eaton, I want to be Mrs. Jack Cross."

Cross had heard all this before; he was silent.

"And I don't want to live alone any longer," she said. "I don't like living alone in the first place, and those murders make me terribly afraid."

"Don't worry about the Ripper," Cross said. "You don't have anything to fear from the Ripper."

"That's easy for you to say. You're not a woman."

"He won't come after you."

"You talk as if you knew him, for Lord's sake."

"In a way," Cross said. "In a way I do."

"What does that mean?"

"You'll find out when you read my book."

"I don't want to hear any more about your book."

"It's all going to be there, all the insights."

"I want to talk about marriage," Paula said. "Not about the Ripper and not about your book."

"You brought it up, Paula. I didn't start this."

"Don't you care about me? What I want or how I feel? Or is this book of yours and the Ripper and your collection of comic books all you really care about?"

I do not have to answer that, Cross thought. But he said, "I care about you, Paula, you know I do." He got off the bed abruptly and began to put on his clothing.

"What are you doing?"

"I'm hungry," he said, which was only a little part of the truth. The major part was that he did not want to listen to any more about marriage. When the Ripper was caught and when he had written his final chapters and gotten the book sold and his career on the way, maybe then. Maybe then. "What have you got to eat?"

"Nothing. I didn't feel like going shopping today."

"Well I guess I'll have to go out for a sandwich, then."

"Jack," she said.

"What?"

"Jack, there's something. . . ."

"Christ, what now?"

She closed her mouth, held her lower lip between her teeth, and looked at him uncertainly. Then she said, "No, let it wait."

"What is it?"

"Let it wait for a little while. I'll tell you."

Cross shrugged perfunctorily and reached for his shirt. He had thought for a moment that she was going to try the old Oh-God-dear-I'm-pregnant business. He wouldn't put it past her; she would do anything to get him to marry her.

Paula said, "Are you really going out now?"

"Didn't I say I was?"

"Do you mind if I go with you?"

She said that with resignation, and when Cross looked at her again he could tell that there wouldn't be any more talk about marriage tonight. "Of course not," he said. "Why should I mind?"

77

He watched her swing her legs out from under the blankets and stand and walk toward him. She was an ungainly creature who needed darkness or clothing to find the grace that she did not have. Still, she didn't look half bad naked, thin breasts and all; she really didn't look half bad.

Ah, Lois, good old Lois, he thought, and smiled at her almost tenderly.

KELLER

Shortly before midnight, with five full circuits of Bloodstone completed, Keller turned his cruiser west onto Shaker Creek Lane, a county road winding through heavy woodland two miles north of town. So far it had been a quiet and uneventful night; he had encountered few cars and fewer pedestrians, plus two asshole state troopers shirking it in their parked patrol car over near Fort Seneca. But just when you thought nothing was going to happen, something generally happened. The Ripper would never catch *him* flatfooted.

Keller drove slowly, peering through the damp windshield, wipers clattering; the rain was coming heavier all the time, moving, as it almost always did, from downstate. Occasional houses were interspersed among the trees, and farther out there were two fairly large rock quarries. But for the most part, the area was dark and lonely.

When he neared the entrance to the first quarry, he decided to take the dirt road which ran through it and onto the hill above. It was a dead-end road used only by the big gravel trucks—but then, you never knew. He drove onto the road slowly, the cruiser jouncing on the uneven surface, the wavering headlights turning birch boles into luminescent bars through the rain and mist. The car was three years old, and the shocks were gone. He should have new equipment every year just as they did in every town with any self-respect. But who cared here in Bloodstone about professionalism, except Alex Keller?

The two ramshackle quarry buildings were huddled black shapes; a bulldozer sat near them, jaws lowered and closed like a grotesque animal in repose. Keller shifted into low and started the laboring climb toward the rim.

At the top there was a small, cleared area—and the moment he came around the last curve he saw the car parked there, back where the line of trees began again.

It was an old car, battered and dusty, one he didn't recognize. A sudden grim elation took hold of him. The Ripper! He jammed down on the accelerator, lips flattening in against his teeth, right hand dropping to unsnap the flap on his holster. Then he swung the wheel hard and stood on the brakes, sliding the cruiser across the rear of the other car to block escape. Even before it had stopped moving, Keller had the service revolver free and the door open. He came out running, caught the other car's door, and jerked it open, dropping back a step immediately and into a crouch, the gun extended at arm's length.

There were two of them inside, all right—but it was a boy in his late teens and a girl a year or two younger. The girl was naked to the waist, arms folded across small, hard breasts; she made a half-keening, half-screaming sound. The boy had one hand in front of her, as though in protection, and the other hand fluttered toward Keller: his body wiggled on the seat like a fish on a line. "For God's sake," he said in terror, "for God's sake!"

Keller straightened, relaxing pressure on the trigger. The elation was all gone now, and he was coldly and savagely angry in a new way. "What the hell do you think you're doing here?"

They had seen his uniform now and their fear changed to a kind less intense: fear of authority and discovery rather than for their lives. Turning away, making little whimpering noises, the girl fumbled for her sweater and bra. The boy kept staring at Keller's gun; he could not seem to stop blinking or swallowing.

"What the hell are you doing here?" Keller said again, louder, and put the gun away. He stood then with his hands balled into fists, drawn and menacing.

"We . . . we were just parking for a while," the boy said shakily.

"I don't know you. Where do you come from?"

"Pottersville," the boy said. "Pottersville."

"Thought you'd drop it in in Bloodstone, right? Sneak over here and do it in the dark. What's your name?"

"David Warren."

"Driver's license," Keller said.

The boy produced a wallet, took the license out with trembling fingers. Keller looked at it, read the address, and threw it back at him. "Her name?"

"Sandy," the girl said. She was crying now. "Sandy Morgan."

"I ought to run the both of you in and call your parents."

"No!" the girl said. "Oh my God, please . . . "

"Listen," Keller said, "don't you know there's a killer running around loose in this area? He's murdered three women, do you understand that?"

"We didn't think . . . " the boy started.

"That's right, you didn't think. Suppose I was the Ripper, boy? I'd kill you right now and then do to your girl there what he did to those other three—cut her up, take a goddamned knife to her."

The girl began crying more brokenly. The boy looked at Keller in a helpless way, dropped a hand to the girl's head, and then seemed to think better of it; he brought the hand up in almost a parody of a salute.

"That's right," Keller said harshly, "That's exactly what I'd do if I was the Ripper."

"God. . . ."

"No God," Keller said. "Stop calling on God. There's just me. Now the two of you get out of here and don't come back again. Don't park *anywhere* after dark around here. You want to screw around, you do it in Pottersville. You hear me?"

"Yes, sir, yes."

Keller turned abruptly and went to the cruiser and backed it to one side. The other car's engine stuttered to life; the lights came on and the car rolled into jerky motion. The taillights winked like frightened red eyes in the misty rain, descending, and then vanished around the curve.

Keller sat in the cruiser, taking long, deep breaths to get

himself calmed down. Stupid fucking kids! Like rabbits, just wanting to crawl all over each other, not thinking. Well, he could have been the Ripper, all right. The Ripper out prowling and coming on them here in this isolated spot and killing the boy—that would have been a break in the method, but it could have happened that way—and then cutting up the girl with her hard little tits and putting the diamond-shaped marks on her thighs. . . .

He might have saved both their lives, catching them as he had. But he might have killed them too, and that was really what had shaken him up. Not because he could have been the Ripper, not that. Because in that first moment he had pulled open the door of their car, he had in his excitement come perilously close to squeezing the trigger and shooting them both.

VALERIE

Minutes after Hook left the tavern, Valerie stood impulsively and went out into the rain. She looked along the street and saw him in the next block, just turning into the Bloodstone Café. She hesitated a moment and then began walking rapidly up the sidewalk in that direction, well aware that following him this way might be a foolish act: *the Ripper could be anyone.* But he intrigued her, and she had had just enough alcohol to make her give in to her impulses. Besides, she was certain she knew him from somewhere; she had that same strange feeling of intimacy you sometimes had for people who didn't know you but whose pictures or persona were part of the apparatus of your life. She had never met Jacqueline Kennedy/Onassis or Margaret Mitchell or Richard Nixon, but were they truly unknown to her? And if she didn't find out who he was, it would bother her for a long time.

She entered the café—a brightly lighted room with chalked menus on blackboards behind the lunch counter on the right. Hook was sitting in the middle of five yellow leatherette booths along the left wall. She walked toward him, saw his gaze come up and steady on her. "Hello," she said. "Do you mind if I sit down?"

He shrugged. "Help yourself."

She sat opposite and studied him frankly. Pleasant-looking man, with an odd depth to his eyes. Damn, she *did* know him; but she still couldn't quite place him. "Do you come from New York City, Mr. Hook?" she asked.

"Not so recently that I'd want to admit to it," he said.

"How long ago?"

"Six years, give or take."

He seemed to have accepted her following him matter-of-factly, which might mean only that he was too apathetic to care. But then again, Valerie thought, there was a kind of vanity in it too. A long time ago, if not recently, this was the kind of man who simply took it for granted that a woman—even an attractive woman, no false modesty in Ms. Valerie Broome—might follow him.

She adjusted her coat, then decided to take it off: did that and laid it over the back of the booth. "Do you feel any better now?" she asked him.

"I don't feel any worse."

"Why were you so upset in the tavern?"

"Does it matter?"

"I just asked. You don't have to answer."

"I don't think I will," Hook said, and a waitress in a checked dress came with a chicken salad sandwich and set the plate down in front of him. She asked Valerie what she would like, and Valerie said a cup of coffee, and the waitress went away again.

Hook glanced at his sandwich, shook his head, and lifted a napkin from the container and shook it out carefully on his lap. Valerie watched him silently. What she ought to do, she was thinking, was to drink her coffee and then go back to the motel and to bed. This second meeting with Steven Hook wasn't leading anywhere—where had she thought it would lead, anyway?—and besides, the heat of the café was bringing her near sobriety with just a whisk of sickness in it.

But Hook looked up at her then, and said abruptly, "All right, I'm being impolite. Christ, it's been so long since I've talked to anyone I've forgotten how to go about it. Yes, I feel a little better than I did in the tavern. Not much, but then again I've had a very bad night. Very bad."

There was pain in his voice, and Valerie had always been sensitive to pain in others. She immediately forgot about the motel and about the hint of sickness. "Personal problems?" she asked.

"The running of beasts, mainly."

"Pardon?"

"Horses," he said, "the trotters. I'm a horseplayer."

"Yes, I heard Tony Manders say that in the tavern."

"A professional horseplayer," Hook said. "I make—made—my living from it. Only tonight I lost three hundred and forty dollars. I've lost almost a thousand for the month. The system I've been using doesn't work anymore, it's all collapsing, and I don't know what to do about it."

"Maybe it's just a run of bad luck."

"Luck doesn't have anything to do with it, not now. I should get out, I want to get out, but I don't know what else I'd do. I don't know where I'm going."

"You haven't been a horseplayer all your life, have you?"

"Just the past six years."

"What did you do before? Can't you go back to whatever that was?"

"Not anymore," Hook said.

The waitress brought Valerie's coffee, went away silently.

Valerie watched steam spiral up between her and Hook—and something clicked in her memory. She saw his face and his name suddenly in black and white, in newsprint. "The *Village Voice,*" she said. She felt excited, the way you do when you've just had a satisfying revelation. "You were an actor, you won an Obie Award a few years ago for a role in an Ackers production of *King Lear*. I knew I'd seen your name and your face somewhere, the *Voice* ran an article with photos."

"That was a long time ago," he said. "A lifetime ago."

"What happened to your career? Why did you give up acting?"

"Acting gave me up. It just collapsed—my career, that is. So I got out and came up here and took up horseplaying. Now that's collapsing too." He picked up his sandwich, took a small bite, put it down again. "Look, I'd really rather not talk about me anymore. Let's talk about you. Didn't I hear the bartender say you were a writer?"

"Yes. On assignment for *Insight Magazine*."

"I'm impressed. And you used to live in Bloodstone?"

"Long ago. As you said, a lifetime ago. Mr. Hook—"

She had been about to maneuver the conversation back to him; he struck her as being a tragic and enigmatic man —an actor turned horseplayer, two intriguing professions about which she knew little enough—and he fascinated her. But the front door opened in that moment, and she saw Jack Cross come in with a thin, pale girl. She knew him at once, saw him look at her and seem to jerk and stare in recognition.

"Crap," she said under her breath.

Hook said, "What?"

Valerie shook her head and watched Cross and the girl come down to the booth, the girl holding tightly to his arm. Hook turned to look up at them, frowned as if he too were displeased by the intrusion.

Cross said, "You're Valerie Broome, right? Class of '65?"

"Uh-huh. And you're Jack Cross, Class of '66."

"I knew it was you," he said, and seemed to want to dive into the booth against her; his eyes were bright and moist. He looked, Valerie thought, little different in ten years: still lean and ungainly, with the same horn-rimmed glasses and short brown hair coming to a point near his forehead. Just an older version of the boy she had know in the school journalism club.

"This is Paula Eaton," Cross said, and the thin girl smiled mechanically and seemed to tug at him. He ignored her, looking at Hook. "I think I know you too, don't I?"

"That's possible," Hook said. He picked up his sandwich.

"Sure, you're the horseplayer. Well"—to Valerie again —"how about if we join you?"

She didn't say anything.

"Jack and I can take another booth," Paula said.

Cross said, "Oh no, Paula, this is wonderful. I haven't seen Valerie in ten years." He dropped into the booth next to Valerie, pressing against her delicately. For just an instant a look of hatred came across the face of Paula Eaton;

she took the seat opposite, next to Hook, who did not look at her.

The waitress appeared, and Paula said she wanted nothing, oh maybe just coffee, but Cross ordered a full meal enthusiastically. Then he said to Valerie, "It's great seeing you, it really is. You know, I had a terrible crush on you back in school. I guess you wouldn't remember, but I did."

She remembered. As a matter of fact, she remembered those years very well, bits and pieces of her history still clambering back into memory. But that didn't matter at the moment; what mattered was the thought that she was losing this man Hook, who had started to come open to her a little but who was now grimly eating in the corner of the booth, his eyes dull and somewhere else. She didn't want to lose him, damn it; in ordinary circumstances she could deal with Jack Cross—he was surely as harmless and helpless as he had ever been—but the thought of losing Hook was infuriating. It might have been emotional, but just as likely it was simply a journalist's pride: a story which had finally come in in part after frustrating delay, but which was now being held by the source, who wanted further assurances.

"What brings you back to Bloodstone, Valerie?" Cross asked her. "You're not coming back to live, are you? I know your folks've been dead a long time, so it can't be a homecoming visit."

He had always had grace, she thought wryly. "No, I'm up here to do an article on the murders."

"Oh," he said, and paused. "Ah, going to spec it?"

"I'm on assignment for *Insight Magazine*."

"Oh," he said again. There was a much longer pause, during which Paula said to Hook, tentatively and defensively, that she was a schoolteacher at Essex Union. Hook said nothing.

"Well, that's a good magazine," Cross said. "They gave you an assignment, huh?"

"I've done three articles for them," Valerie said.

"Three. That's pretty good. Do they pay well?"

"Not badly."

"All on the front end, right? I mean, you don't have any subsidiary participation, any royalties—"

"There are no royalties on magazine articles," Valerie said. "Books. On books there are royalties."

"But for foreign editions, if they do it overseas—"

"Flat fee. Just a flat fee."

"Oh," Cross said. "Well I knew that, of course, I just thought with a big magazine like *Insight,* you know. . . ." He trailed off, only to start again. "You're a successful writer, then."

"I manage."

"You sound like you've done really good for yourself."

"Fair. Just fair."

Cross cleared his throat. "I'm writing a book on the murders," he said.

"That's very interesting."

"It's a nonfiction novel under the working title of *The Ripper of Bloodstone*. I'm telling it from the point of view of myself, the framing consciousness as the murders erupt."

"Uh-huh."

"I'm working on the newspaper here, too, but that's just until I get the book done."

"When will you have it done?"

"Well, he said, "I don't know. It all depends on when the Ripper is caught, doesn't it?"

"Please don't talk about the Ripper," Paula Eaton said.

"Paula's afraid of the Ripper," Cross said to Valerie. "She—"

Hook seemed to come to life. "I'm afraid of the Ripper too," he said. "What's wrong with being afraid of the Ripper?"

Paula looked at him gratefully. Cross blinked and said, "Well, nothing. I don't blame her, of course." He blinked again; then, to Valerie: "I don't have a contract for my book yet. I mean, I haven't tried to sell it on an outline or anything. I feel the best thing to do is to just get it finished and then put it up for open bids as a polished, completed work. You get more money that way."

"That's a point."

"Don't you?" Cross said. "I mean, you're in New York; you know publishing, right? Is it better to go for a contract on just a piece of it or write the whole thing first?"

"I've never written a book," she said.

"Just articles, right?"

"Right."

"Well, I just don't think you can sum up the Ripper in an article, no matter how good it is. It's a major subject, a major treatment is necessary." Flushed slightly, he leaned closer and asked her what she knew about agents, should you get one before you sold your first book or after?

Valerie said it all depended, and watched Hook hunch again over his sandwich; he seemed to have retreated within himself once more.

The waitress came over and put Cross' meal in front of him. Meat loaf, mashed potatoes, and string beans. Hard rolls and butter. A chocolate milk shake.

"Now me, personally, I don't see the use of an agent," Cross said, and picked up a roll. "I think that if you want to do something, you have to go right out and do it all by yourself."

THE RIPPER

Need and greed, slake and plunge in the hills of the valleys of the dust of the mountains, down and down the chilly blue, on and on the crazylights . . .

Sunday, October 19

SMITH

Usually Daniel Smith divorced himself completely from police work on his days off, but Ferrara's theories were still heavy on his mind when he awoke Sunday morning. He knew it would be impossible to relax at home, and so he went to his office and spent an hour studying his files on the slayings. If the assailant did not know he was the assailant, if the case *was* a grotesque, there was nothing to support the idea in either the forensic reports or his own reports, but neither was there anything to negate it.

All right, what he had to do was to go back over familiar ground, try to establish the pattern that had to be hidden beneath the surface. Methodology. Conclusive proof that Ferrara was wrong.

Bloodstone was at the center of the case, that was obvious; the crimes had happened in or near the township, and logical extrapolation made it likely that the assailant lived there, or had lived there. But could you investigate an entire town? Perhaps, he thought, if you went at it patiently. From that point of view, then, you could start with the constable—the one man who ought to know the town as well or better than anybody.

Alex Keller had no official capacity in the investigation of the murders, of course, but he seemed to have put in as much work on the case as Smith had. He was the town constable, but maybe there were other reasons, too, which Smith could only guess at. He knew little about Keller, had had little contact with the man even after the homicides started. Plummer had told him that Keller had been a uniformed officer in Chicago at the time of the convention riots and had been forced to resign as the result of a violent incident that had received national attention. In any case, Smith simply hadn't considered Keller as being particularly competent; relatively intelligent, yes, but lacking in discipline and insight.

But maybe he had been wrong. Maybe Keller's investigation had as much validity as his own. And maybe Keller had insights, after all, which might be of use to Smith, to which Smith could apply his own methods; he was willing to try anything now that would bring about a rapid solution to the killings.

He drove up the Northway and then into Bloodstone to the Municipal Center. But when he walked up to the entrance to the constable's office, he found the door locked; a hand-lettered sign in one corner of the glass said Keller could be reached at his residence, 47 Whitehall Road, in the event of emergency.

That address was a half block away, lakeward, and Smith decided to walk it. He went down the sidewalk, through a thin carpet of dead elm and maple leaves. Gray-veined clouds hung thickly over the lake, and the light filtering through was monochromatic; just below them, an arrow formation of Canadian geese, flying southward for the winter, made loud honking sounds that combined with the ringing of churchbells in a curiously plaintive medley.

Number 47 was a tiny, shabby green cottage set behind a screen of untrimmed tamarack bushes. Somehow Smith had expected Keller to live in better quarters, and he found himself frowning as he went up onto the porch and pressed the bell.

Keller opened the door almost immediately, wearing a pair of neatly pressed uniform trousers and a white shirt. He looked tired, Smith saw, faintly haggard, as though he had not been sleeping well of late; a series of red lines ran through the whites of his eyes. He also seemed wary, the way a man will when he doesn't quite trust the presence or intentions of another.

"Well, Lieutenant," he said. "Now what brings you here?"

"I'd like to talk to you, if you don't mind."

"About what? The Ripper?"

"May I come inside?"

"As a matter of fact, no," Keller said. "Nothing personal, but I don't discuss business inside my house or even on the front porch of my house."

Smith had not expected anything like that, and it put him on the defensive—as if Keller's were the position of authority, not his, and he were being rebuked for having bothered a superior officer. Irritation formed inside him. "I see," he said, because he could not think of anything else to say.

"If you want to wait up at the office, I'll be along in a few minutes."

"I'll wait," Smith said, "but you'd better not make it long."

He turned and went down off the porch and back up the sidewalk. He sat in his car, and the irritation continued to build; his stomach had begun hurting him again. But then he thought of the house Keller lived in, of the way the front room had looked through the open door: Spartan furnishings, no visible personal touches. Like a cell, all just like a cell. He did not know why, but that made him feel a little better.

Keller drove his cruiser into the lot eight minutes later and got out with several sheets of newspaper in his hand and unlocked the office. When Smith followed him inside, Keller was at his desk spreading out one of the sheets of paper. Without looking at him, Keller said, "Take a chair, Lieutenant."

Smith remained standing just inside the divider.

"Suit yourself," Keller said, and shrugged. He went to the wall cabinet and removed the riot gun and a handful of square-headed latch keys from inside, carried them back to the desk, and set them down carefully on the paper. Then he sat and took a cloth and a can of metal polish from one of the drawers. "Now what is it you want?"

"I'm not sure I want anything now," Smith said. "I don't much care for your attitude, Keller."

"That's too bad," Keller said equably.

"I had an idea we might exchange ideas on the murders, but there doesn't seem to be any point in it."

"Probably not. Why the sudden urge for cooperation, Lieutenant? It couldn't be because you've run out of possibilities on your own, could it?"

"Hardly."

Keller daubed polish on the cloth and began rubbing briskly at one of the keys. "Well it doesn't matter," he said. "I'm going to get the Ripper, you know. I'm going to bring him in. You'll take him over eventually, but I'll have the satisfaction of locking him up right here in one of my holding cells. With this," and he held up the key.

"Just how do you propose to get him?"

"Diligent police work. I'm working on a few angles."

"What sort of angles?"

"Oh, just angles. I don't think I want to talk about them."

Smith made fists of his hands, then put them inside the pockets of his coat. "Listen, Keller," he said, "if you come up with anything concrete, you'd damned well better report it to me. I'm the officer in charge and I advise you not to forget it."

"I won't. Is there anything else, Lieutenant?"

"Nothing else," Smith said tightly.

Outside in his car, he thought that damn it, he should have realized it would be useless trying to talk to a man like Keller. Keller didn't have any insights or any angles either. He knew even less than Smith did. He was all bluff and arrogance, a bull in both the literal and slang senses of the word.

Well all right. He didn't need Keller, the hell with Keller. Methodology would lead him to the truth.

Unless Ferrara was right. . . .

HOOK

At the Hideaway Cabins, inside the kitchen of Number Eight, Steven Hook spread out the new issue of *Tomorrow's Trots* and stared at the listing for the first race. Then, viciously, he tore it in half and pitched the pieces across the room.

He glanced at the shelf where the rags hid the bottle of rye. Then he shook his head and lit a cigarette and let himself think again of the girl, the black-haired girl, Valerie.

She was attractive, and he had not had sex in five months; she had seemed genuinely interested in him, and no one had been interested in him in a long time. But it was more than that. It was the way she had looked at him in the café, before the other two came in, and the way she had looked at him when Cross' droning voice had grown overwhelming and he had had no choice except to excuse himself and hurry out. Her eyes had been lustrous and warm, empathic and pained and alive. They were mirrors in which he had had a glimpse of himself as he had been at her age. They were pools in which a man could immerse himself and forget some of his own pain and fear.

I should go find her, he thought. I should apologize for leaving so abruptly last night. I should talk to her, get to know her. I should find out if she has anything for me, anything at all.

But he only sat there in the cold, ruined clutter of the cabin, smoking and thinking of her and of her eyes.

CROSS

THE RIPPER OF BLOODSTONE   Cross   add 147'

CHAPTER TWELVE

I was born in circumstances of pain and deceit, so it
was understandable that I should grow in full maturity to
the awesome power and reliability of uncertainty. Uncertainty has followed me all my life, has characterized
my life, and I can see why people can think of me as being in
pain even now.

But one must start at the beginning, at the quintes-
sential core. ~~of all strangeness from which we are multiply~~
~~wrenched,~~ I was born on September 23, 1949, the son of James
Cross Senior, a vigorous man in early middle age, and his
wife Florence, only a teenager then of stunning attractive-
ness who was even at that time performing acts of adultery
with ~~one sometimes by~~ Plummer. It must have been some
sudden understanding of these acts which caused the
unfortunate Senior to drop dead one morning of a stroke
while cultivating flowers in the rear garden, his only
hobby. Senior must have had a wrathful vision, all right,
for he fell nose first into a bag of fertilizer; his last
earthly glimpse, then, was of s---, which figures. For-
tunately for his devoted widow and helpless child, Senior
had collected life insurance policies the way other people
collect bottles. At least fifteen of them were found in his
travelling case, and although the companies were disgruntled
they could hardly prove suicide. Was it suicide? Had
Senior prepared the way for his fall by picking up a physical
here, a mortality chart there? We will never know.

THE RIPPER OF BLOODSTONE   Cross   add 148
It is questions like this which paralyze me into the awesome power and reliability of uncertainty.

The young widowed Florence was grief-stricken for approximately twelve hours. Then she continued her relationship with Plummer as before. Early on I knew something funny was going on between them. I have always been very observant. Sometimes they would disappear into her bedroom at night and I would listen at the door but they were quiet about it. They would never admit their affair to me, though. They didn't care about me. Or maybe Florence cared too much. I have never been sure about that.

When I was eighteen years old, I attended the State University of New York at Harpur College, but after two years, when my journalistic and literary talents felt confined and limited in expression, I obtained through Florence a position with Plummer on his then-weekly newspaper, the Bloodstone Sentinel. His previous editor had been arrested for hit-and-run driving while drunk and is now confined to the state facilities near Buffalo.

The most important thing I did after taking the position with Plummer was to get this cottage where I now live, which is located on Clear Creek Road one mile south of the village and three miles to the west, and is very secluded, the perfect place for a writer to work. If I had continued to live with Florence, my life would have been a disaster. As it was, being on my own, my writing style developed rapidly until it became what it is today. Also I met Paula and started sleeping going with her.

The front room of this cottage contains this desk at

THE RIPPER OF BLOODSTONE   Cross   add 149
which I now sit and two beenbag chairs and a leather sofa.
It also contains my collection of superhero comic books.
On the wall over my desk are my prize possessions, a pair
of 2x3 foot, full-color sketches of Clark Kent and Lois Lane,
which an artist I knew in college did for me for twenty-five
dollars each.

I wish Paula looked like Lois, or even Valerie Broome,
who is an old school acquaintance I met again last night and
~~who I always wanted to go to bed with~~ who says she is writing
an article for Insight Magazine. But Paula doesn't look
like anybody but Paula and reminds me only of Florence. And
she just won't stop harping about marriage. I ought to
break off with her, but I like her well enough. ~~and I like
sleeping with her.~~ So I have to keep putting up with her, at
least until the Ripper is caught and this book is finished
and sold. Then I can decide whether or not to marry her or
whether I should go to New York City. There are sure to be
girls in New York, girls always flock around successful
writers, they like nothing better than to go to bed with
them and maybe go down on them, Paula would never do that for
me even though I asked her several times.

This isn't going very well at all. I'm going to have to
redo these pages, they are too personal, they don't have
any place in a book like The Ripper of Bloodstone. Why did
I want to write this chapter anyway? I am merely the
focusing eye/controlling consciousness/detached
observer/partial participant here and really have little
to do with the great denouement which is to follow.

VALERIE

When Valerie drove them into the deserted parking area that served both Fort Seneca and the amusement park called Colonial Village, Ferrara said, "This is a charming spot. Fine place for a murder, wouldn't you say?"

"That's not very funny."

He gave her a fatherly smile. "Your trouble is you tend to become emotional about things. Clinical detachment, dear; you'd be better off if you adopted it."

Valerie said nothing. She parked the car, and they got out into a cold, sharp wind. The fort sat on high ground to their left, removed from the lake by a hundred yards of sloping, patchy lawn; it was a large red stone-and-mortar structure with five triangular wings that would give it, seen from above, the approximate shape of a star, built initially in 1764 and completely restored and turned into a state landmark and minor military museum in 1937. Heavy iron four-pounders were spaced at intervals around the ramparts.

Colonial Village, stretched out on the western end of the cove, was enclosed by a high wooden fence; all that was visible as they walked toward it was the tops of a few of the buildings inside and the shuttered concession stands flanking the locked entrance gates. When they reached the gates, Valerie read a sign wired to one of the halves: WARNING—PRIVATE PROPERTY. TRESPASSERS WILL BE PROSECUTED. She smiled wryly, remembering from her required local-history course in high school that the colonials had often "warned out" uninvited strangers, so as to keep their villages "pure." Things hadn't changed much in three hundred years in this part of the country, she thought.

She peered through the gate's cyclone fencing, down the long main street of the village. She had been here a couple of times in her mid-teens, just after it was constructed, and her opinion of it now was the same negative one it had been then. The buildings lining both sides of the street—merchant and artisan shops, peasant houses, incongruous souvenir and refreshment stands—still had a cheerless, phony aspect, made grimmer by its current desertion. At the far end the complex's tallest building, the meetinghouse, stood in a small grassy square; it faced north, whereas the original meeting-houses in real colonial villages had always faced south so as to be "square with the sun at noon." As an amusement park and as a historical replica, Colonial Village left quite a bit to be desired.

Ferrara said, "Is this the north gate? Or is there another one?"

"To our right and a couple of hundred yards along," she told him. The north gate was where the Ripper's first victim, Julia Larch, had been found two months ago; the lock had been broken off, and the body had been lying crumpled some distance inside the grounds, in a clump of ferns.

They followed the high wooden wall, into and beyond a small copse of spruce. The wind was getting colder, it seemed to Valerie, and she could feel goose bumps forming on her arms. This was a pretty bleak place, all right, and she had to admit that Ferrara's opening comment had been accurate: it damned well *was* a fine place for a murder.

When they came on the north gate, Valerie put her face up to the fencing. Boarded-up booths and partially dismantled rides. Beyond them was a small man-made lake, fed by a canal from Woodbine Lake outside the enclosure, that appeared to have a greenish, polluted tinge to it; on its near bank, the outsized facsimile of a ducking stool—a long wooden beam with an iron-banded armchair affixed to the upper end, resembling an elevated seesaw—pointed toward Bloodstone like an accusing finger.

Opposite the gate was the clump of wood ferns which had cradled like a palm the body of Julia Larch.

Valerie shivered slightly and stepped back, and Ferrara took her place. She glanced around at the swaying branches of the trees, at the leaden sky, and listened to the wind moan funereally. She felt jumpy now, and was getting jumpier by the minute. It might be conversion hysteria —one of Ferrara's terms—but she could imagine how it must have been for Julia Larch, how she must have felt when she died; Valerie shivered again and wondered if she would have the same edgy reaction to the scenes of the other two murders. It was natural enough if she did, she supposed, and the intensity of her reactions was one of the reasons for her success in the parajournalistic business.

"I think I've seen enough," she said to Ferrara. "Let's go back to the car."

He turned to look at her. "This place is really bothering you, isn't it?"

"No."

"Of course it is." He continued to look at her.

He really has got funny little eyes, she thought. Bird's eyes. Cold eyes. She felt a faint stirring of apprehension, the way she had in the park in Bloodstone last night when the constable had driven up—and then told herself she was being foolish again. Ferrara was the last person in the world to be afraid of.

"I'm going back to the car," she said. "Are you coming?"

"I'll be along in a minute. I find this place fascinating."

Valerie went back along the wall, walking slowly until she was into the trees and then hurrying. When she got to the car she slid in beneath the wheel and locked the doors, then started the engine and put the heater on high.

Outside, the wind skipped leaves and debris across the asphalt lot. In the distance, across the lake, she could see the buildings of Bloodstone crouched like animals above the water. Somewhere over there, the Ripper walked: hiding, waiting, watching—

Stop it, she told herself. Think about something else.

And found herself thinking of Steven Hook, of how much she had wanted to talk to him and how angry she had been when Jack Cross and his girlfriend intruded; of the greater anger and the curious sense of loss she had felt when he hurried out and away from her. . . .

KELLER

In Chicago in 1968 Alex Keller had gone out to do a job, only to do a job, and he should have been able to handle the demonstrators, he should have been able to hold onto himself. He was forty-five years old and twenty years on street duty; if he could not handle his share of a bunch of fags, punks, junkies, and whores, then he deserved no sympathy. The word had been made clear enough through Daley that they were not to take any shit, that they were mostly on their own to keep it under control the best way they could, which meant that they could do almost anything they had to do, the department and Daley were behind them all the way. At least, that was how he had understood it.

So Keller should have been able to handle it—and he had been, there in the heat and light of those streets; he was not even near to losing control of himself, working crowd control near the park that second day and hanging back, directing the attack rather than participating in it. Pretty good shape, pretty good control. Only then it had all gone completely out of hand, and it was not his fault, none of it was his fault.

It was the girl's fault, really: she had been the catalyst. She had come right up to him, love beads dangling around her neck, and she had said, "Why don't you make love instead of war? Why do you have to stand there holding a club in your hands instead of a woman?" She was a little kid, nineteen years old maybe, long, thin hair, long, thin body, suspicion of breasts under her sweater. And she had said, "You know why you guys are doing this?" with a sweetness in her voice, the breathy voice of a whore, almost as if there were a message she was trying to get across. "Because you're afraid of yourself, afraid of your bodies, afraid of the power of love."

Keller had been astonished; he could not believe what he was hearing. But still he had controlled himself, had only backed her up tight against a building, saying Get out, get out of here right now. You never went out of control with a woman, you never hit a woman. But she said, "Wouldn't you really rather be in bed now making love to me?" and had touched her breasts, what there were of them, with a little suggestion, and then the boy had come from somewhere and taken her arm, another long-haired kid with glasses and a flowered shirt. "Marie," he said to the girl, "come on, come on," and she said, "I'm just trying to speak to the cop here about love," and he said, "Marie, leave it alone, it's time to split," and she said, "I don't think he can fuck, that's his real problem. I really don't think he's able to fuck," and something had gone out of Keller then, or maybe it had simply gone into him, he was never quite sure: he had turned on the long-haired kid, turned on him, and moved in on him; he could not hit the woman, but the freak who had brought her into Chicago, who had set her up for this, was different game.

Keller lifted the club and brought it down on the kid's head, and the glasses jumped, and blood started to move downward onto the shirt flowers. The kid spun, screaming, and Keller got him a second time behind the neck, and there was a choking noise like a dog coughing, and the kid slid down. "No!" the girl was screaming. "No, no, what have you done?" and Keller said I've killed him, the bastard, and bent in the clutter to find the kid under his feet; lifted the club again, centered it just the way you might center a woman's vagina—he was really halfway over the edge.

Then hands were on him from the outside, a net of hands, and he was being dragged away. He started to go for his gun, but something slapped that hand down, and then he realized that he was being held by three of his fellow officers that he didn't recognize. "Man," one of them said, "man, didn't you see what was happening, that was on camera, on *camera*," and Keller, scuttling back in their grasp, looked to see the heavy boom coming out of the near window of the building, another circling from the parapet, small glowing lights, and realized that what he had just done had been picked up on the remote relays that the networks were sending out into the street.

His first thought was that he was only sorry he had not gone the whole way, killed the fag bastard on coast-to-coast TV just the way Ruby had killed that other bastard; but by the time they had pulled him to the periphery of the action, he had already gotten control of himself again, and he could see that it was pretty bad. He was not an uncontrolled or uncontrollable man; it had been a single lapse. Keller could clearly understand that what he had done would have serious consequences because that sort of thing couldn't be rationalized away, no matter how much sanction you had. It was not only a matter of its having been picked up on television, but that you simply didn't *do* something like that.

The other cops asked him if he was all right, and Keller said yes he was okay, and they had looked at him in a tentative way and then left him and he had spent the rest of the patrol on the fringes, very damned frightened for himself. He even thought about going to one of the emergency hospital areas they had set up down the block, to try to locate the kid and say how sorry he was, but that was obviously ridiculous, and besides, he wasn't sorry, not that way; the kid had deserved everything he'd gotten, it was just unfortunate that Keller had been the one who had had to do it.

The convention went on, and what he had done to the kid was shown on CBS in black and white remote to millions of television viewers. A week later he was called into the commissioner's office and told by the assistant commissioner that they were in a fairly tough position and perhaps he had better resign. The AC said that Keller had every sympathy in the world, and that as far as he and the commissioner were concerned, Keller had done the natural and normal thing; but there was a hell of a lot of heat coming down, not the least of it from the Democratic national organization itself, which insisted that something be done, so they had no choice except to take some kind of steps. "You mean that I've got to be sacrificed," Keller said, and the assistant commissioner said it was something like that, not exactly but close, and offered him three-quarters pension, which for twenty-five years in wasn't too bad. But then again, he had never done any of it for the money. From the army through patrolman, he had done what he had because he believed it was for the best and because he was dedicated. He even thought that he could justify what had happened on moral grounds and that most of those watching on TV were on his side. But there seemed to be no point in going into that with the assistant commissioner. The AC looked abstracted and disturbed, and seemed to have a great deal more than Keller on his mind.

So he had gotten out quickly and quietly, and a friend with contacts back east had told him about the Bloodstone constable's job, which was just opening up. Keller had nothing else, no other prospects—police work was all he knew—and he had driven out for the interview, two days one way, and decided that he liked it. It seemed to be just what he needed; he needed isolation and some cold forest in which to work out what had happened to him and where he would go from there. They appeared to be fairly pleased with him in Bloodstone, too. He had been honest about Chicago, and they had told him that they felt strongly about strict enforcement of the law. Their salary offer had been sixty-eight hundred to start, with escalating raises—low, they realized, but the best they could manage. With his three-quarters pension, more than ten thousand annually, money was the least of his problems; he had grabbed at it.

He went back to Chicago and got his belongings together and flew out then via Albany; and in December, 1968, there he was, all set up. At first he had thought that it would just be a two-year job while he decided what to do next or until the heat blew over in Chicago and he reapplied quietly for his old job. But he found to his surprise that he liked the area. Two years stretched to six and beyond, while he was still wondering if he should stay. Then the Ripper business had begun, and he had put aside all thoughts of leaving Bloodstone. The town had accepted him at a very tough period in his life, and he was not about to abandon it now. Without him it would be helpless, because the state police didn't care about Bloodstone, Daniel Smith didn't give a damn if the Ripper was caught as long as his own responsibilities to the case were covered.

After he had settled in Bloodstone, Keller had taken to driving to Albany to look for a whore in the bars around the captiol area whenever he got the need, whenever he felt that he could perform all right (he had been having trouble that way ever since what had happened in Chicago, he couldn't understand why). Since the Ripper had gone to work, though, he had not gone to Albany at all; he wasn't about to fuck away downstate while the Ripper was on the prowl, even though the need within him was strong and sure, and he knew he could perform and perform the way he had in the old days.

Just one more reason why he had to break the case and break it soon: The Ripper was getting his, but until Keller got the Ripper, he couldn't get *his*.

THE RIPPER

Off-center in the tangle he saw her moving, and filled with purpose he clung to his need, moving, moving with the thing. It scuttled, he pounced. "No," she said, "no," but "Oh yes," he said, "ah yes," he said, then that last rising leap as she, the thing saw what was about to happen and later, later—

—he put the knife, here comes—

—the knife up and out, in and to her, dancing, the chains of blood singing and the thing shrivels around the hard point, there in the sand she lies. He brings the knife in again, and again, ring the thing, and she does not move, she is his now, bride of darkness, bride of death, all seeking of need she lies there, the queen of pain and run, I wanted to run, but one more thing to do in the sand of the shore of the whore, the bells of our union clinging and clanging and ringing and ranging into the place of the diamonds, the diamonds, the diamonds.

HOOK

The cry of a loon, somewhere on or near the lake, pulled Hook from thin, shadowy sleep. He sat up in the old wicker chair, rubbed at mucus-grained eyes and then looked at his watch. After ten. God, he had been asleep for almost three hours. He had gotten back to his cottage on Stone Bridge Road at seven, from an aimless Sunday drive through the northern country, and had come at once onto the enclosed rear porch and stretched out in the chair. He thought he remembered dozing off almost immediately, with Valerie Broome somewhere in his dreams. Three hours. Had it really been that long? It felt like minutes; it felt as if he had been moving in and out of time.

The sleep hadn't done him much good; he was still tired, tight-nerved. And yet, underneath this, there was a curious alertness, as if he were responding to subsonic pitch, not heard but yet perceived. He ought to go to bed, but he knew that he would have trouble getting back to sleep, and the thoughts, the fears, which had worked at him through the day, dulled enough by weariness to let him doze, were back in heavy focus.

Outside, the loon cried again, mournfully. Hook lighted a cigarette and stared out through the wire screening. The overcast had thinned enough so that a pale moon was visible in the night sky, laying a dim wedge of light across the surface of the lake. The wind was down, soughing faintly through the tops of the trees.

He decided to take a short walk along the lake and through the woods. Walking, he had found, sometimes helped him relax, and he liked the quiet, the solitude of the land after dark. He liked the Adirondacks; it was only Bloodstone itself that had soured for him.

Hook stood from the chair, stubbed out his cigarette, lit another, and left the porch. He went along a mossy path to the narrow strip of beach at the foot of his property. From there he could just see the low promontory to the north on which the house belonging to Florence Cross sat outlined against the gray-black sky. To the south the trees stretched in an unbroken line a fifth of a mile, ending then at the first of three contiguous motels, all shuttered for the winter. The village proper began just beyond there.

Hands buried in the pockets of his jacket, he walked along the beach to the south and entered the trees. The air was chill, biting, and tasted of frost and winter; the night now was without sound except for the crackle of his steps on frost-matted leaves. The pale moon shone hazily through bare-branched paper birch, turning the smooth white bark almost luminescent, lighting the way for him.

But the walk did not relax him tonight. Apprehension began to tug at the perimeter of his thoughts and then grew, insinuating. He did not know what was causing it; it wasn't strong enough to turn him back to the cottage, but it wouldn't let him alone either.

When he came out of the trees at the first of the closed motels, the feeling sharpened abruptly. A tight chill moved along his back. He stared at the dark buildings, at the slender boat dock extending into the lake, at the fingernail slice of beach. The wind rustled branches behind him, singing in a soft, empty voice.

He entered the grounds of the motel, the Terra Alta, and angled toward the beach. The same loon—it could be that same one, trailing him, watching him—cried again, very close. He fumbled yet another cigarette into his mouth, struck a match that flickered and died in a gust of wind. He stopped, almost to the waterline now, raising the matches and cupping his hands.

And saw the huddled shape of something shining white and black in the thin moonlight at the beach's upper edge.

The chill worked along his back again, and he dropped his hands, the cigarette fell from his mouth; he forced his legs to carry him toward the shape. He began to know what it was before he was halfway there. His stomach spasmed, but he kept on walking until he could see the shape clearly and recognize the whiteness as naked flesh, the blackness as blood and a long, tangled fan of hair as he tracked the line of the body upward. The dead face seemed to glint at him, expressionless, like an electric bulb in a ruined socket.

He stared at the face for several pulsebeats, then turned in a rush and ran away from there, between the motel buildings toward U.S. 9 beyond, with the image of what was undeniably the fourth victim of the Ripper burned forever onto the surface of his mind.

KELLER

When Keller looked up into the cruiser's rear-vision mirror, he saw a man come running onto the highway fifty yards behind, waving his arms like a confused signalman.

Keller's groin shriveled into a painful knot. The premonition that had come over him half an hour before had been right; he'd known that it would be, he always trusted his instincts and they were almost always failproof. The Ripper was going to rip again tonight, and he was going to do it somewhere north of the village. That was all, but that was enough. There was no explaining it, you couldn't explain instinct. So he had begun patrolling U.S. 9 back and forth to the north, the cruiser leveled down to thirty, watching carefully and not seeing anything, not seeing the man—*the Ripper? was it the Ripper?*—when he drove past the entrance to the Terra Alta but seeing him now, back there waving his arms.

Keller braked the cruiser, veered to the right and then swung into a tight turn across the highway. He dragged the revolver from its holster, driving with his left hand on the wheel. The dark figure came up rapidly in the headlights, not moving out of the cruiser's path; a stunned rabbit. Keller recognized the excited white face, put a name to it. Hook, Steven Hook. The horseplayer from downstate who had arrived in Bloodstone just about the time Keller had. The man who had been standing alone, strangely, in the rain last night.

Was *Hook* the Ripper?

He tapped the brake again, and a thought brushed against his consciousness, a thought as soft and electric on the exterior of the brain as the caress of a woman's hand on the thigh. *He could run Hook down, run right over him.* If Hook was the Ripper, that action would end the case and the reign of terror once and for all; he would be a hero, nobody would blame him for running down the Ripper. . . .

The vision was so palpable, so large on the screen of consciousness, that Keller gasped aloud. But the sound broke the vision like glass, and reflexively he put the brake pedal all the way to the floor, twisted the wheel so the the cruiser slid past Hook, close but not dangerously close; Hook disappeared from sight. Keller brought the cruiser to a yawing halt thirty feet farther away, pulled on the emergency brake, and stumbled out.

Hook was coming toward him with uncertain movements, half running. When they were a few feet apart he stopped and said thickly, "Jesus, man, you almost ran me down. . . ."

Keller leveled the gun. "What are you doing out here? What's going on?"

"Another one," Hook said. He looked at the gun, looked at Keller's face, looked at the gun again. "Another Ripper victim, down on the Terra Alta beach. I found her just now, oh God I saw what he did to her. . . ."

"What the hell were you doing on the Terra Alta beach?"

"I was out for a walk. I—"

"This time of night? On a night like this?"

"I like to walk at night," Hook said. He made a snuffling sound, rubbed at his nose with the back of one hand, and then produced a tissue from his pocket and blew into it heavily.

Keller's eyes narrowed. "Get over to the cruiser."

"What for?"

"Get over to the goddamned cruiser!"

Hook shook his head uncomprehendingly, but did as he was told. Keller shoved him against the rear fender, kicked his legs back, spread him out, and went over him with his free hand. But he found nothing on Hook: no knife, no weapon of any kind. He prodded Hook to the front of the car, into the headlight glare and the pulsing stink from the engine, and examined his clothing carefully, his hands. The clothing was clean, the hands were clean. No blood. No bloody blood.

But that still didn't let Hook off the hook, Keller thought. Then he thought: Hook off the hook, bloody blood. He forced down a nervous laugh. Hook-hook, bloody-blood. He was so keyed up he felt light-headed, like a balloon about to burst. Take it easy, he warned himself. Just take it slow and easy, don't lose control.

Hook said, "What's the idea of shoving me around?" There was anger and agitation, fright and bewilderment in his voice, but that could come from just having killed number four too, Keller thought, it would fit the pattern of guilt as well as that of innocence. And he had a pocket full of tissues, that was very interesting too.

"I'm not taking any chances," Keller said, "not with anybody." He backed away two steps and lowered the muzzle of the revolver so that it pointed at the asphalt between them. "All right—who is she this time?"

"I don't know. I saw her face, but it was . . . it—"

"You didn't recognize her?"

"No. No."

"Did you see anybody else down there?"

"Nobody else, no."

"Any sign of anybody else?"

"No."

"You were just walking along and you found her there?"

"That's right, I told you that."

"Show me where she is."

"Hadn't you better call for help first?"

"Don't tell me how to do my job," Keller said, "I know what I'm doing."

Not taking his eyes off Hook, he went to the driver's door opened it, and leaned in and lifted the handset off the radio unit. He put in a terse call to the Bloodstone state police substation. Then he took the flashlight from the clip under the dash. "Now show me where she is," he said.

Hesitantly, Hook led him down toward the lake. Keller put the flash on and swept it left and right as they went. The arcing beam picked up nothing animate. The only sounds were those of their steps and of the wind.

When they neared the beach, Hook stopped and pointed and said, "Over there. I'm not going near her again, I can't stand to see her a second time."

"Stand right here, then," Keller told him. "Don't move."

Hook nodded, and Keller went down to where the body lay, shone the flash on it. His stomach kicked faintly, but otherwise he had no reaction; he had seen two of the Ripper's victims up close like this already, he knew what to expect. And this was another of his victims, all right, there was no doubt about that. Torso slashed open, diamond-shaped marks visible on one thigh; to one side, scattered over two or three yards of sand, were several bloodstained tissues. White tissues this time. The first time they had been blue, and the other two times pink, and now they were white.

The same color as the ones in Hook's pocket.

The woman's face looked up at him, and when he bent closer he knew her. Her name was Linda Simmons. She was in her thirties and lived in Bloodstone and worked at a concession stand at Colonial Village during the Season. So the son of a bitch was back to local women again. It was Keller's job to protect the local women, he was charged with that and he would do it, but Christ, he couldn't be everywhere at once. His intuition wasn't that good. It wasn't his fault that she had died tonight; he would have saved her if he'd had the chance. Part of it was *her* fault, for that matter. She shouldn't have let him get at her; she shouldn't have been out where he could get at her.

Keller moved away, playing the flash, looking for further evidence. But there was nothing in the immediate vicinity except those bloodstained tissues, and he wouldn't have time to search the entire area before the state police arrived. He hadn't wanted to call them, but Hook had made him realize that he had to do just that. There hadn't been any way around calling them and doing it immediately, not with a witness present; they'd have his ass if he failed to follow procedure. Smith particularly. Smith would like nothing better than to find an excuse to come down on him because Smith knew that Keller was going to solve this case; he knew that Keller hadn't just been blowing wind this morning. Smith wasn't fooling anybody with his clumsy little trick of pretending to want cooperation; he was running scared.

He looked up at Hook again and saw him sitting slumped now on a post, the glowing end of a cigarette off-center between his lips. Keller rubbed at his mouth with the back of his gun hand, and focused on the upraised gun as he did so, and felt his palm begin to sweat around the butt. That might be the Ripper sitting up there, he thought. I might already have him, by God; I might have beaten Smith and the rest of them to the Ripper right here tonight.

He kept on looking at Hook, looking at him past the barrel of the revolver. *Are* you the Ripper, Hook? No blood, no knife, not now, but you act pretty funny, you've got damned funny habits. You could still be the one, and if you are, Hook, if you are. . . .

From up on the highway and not far away, he heard the approaching scream of sirens.

Slowly Keller lowered the gun and holstered it. He no longer felt light-headed; he felt calm, very calm. If you are, Hook, he thought again, and turned back to the body of Linda Simmons.

THE RIPPER
Next!

Monday, October 20

BLOODSTONE

On the morning after the death of Linda Simmons, Bloodstone was a paradox of brooding fear and seriocomic carnival.

Three brutal slayings of women warranted a certain amount of media attention, but the fourth seemed somehow to lift the whole business onto an even grislier and therefore more newsworthy plane. The Ripper was becoming prime-time, front-page fodder, at least on the East Coast, and because he was, a dozen wire service and news syndicate reporters, along with press people and camera crews from New York City and a variety of other places, descended on the village. They took over the Homelite Motel and spent their time visiting the scene of the latest murder and the scenes of previous murders, trying to interview principal figures, and speculating companionably among themselves. Some were openly resentful of the fact that the seating capacity of the Homelite bar was only a couple of dozen and of the further fact that Bloodstone Tavern was the only other open bar in the vicinity.

Tony Manders said bitterly to his wife that the influx of reporters was like watching roaches stream into a Manhattan apartment, looking for garbage. But he raised all the drink prices at the tavern by twenty-five cents each, ordered his wife to make sandwiches that he sold at a dollar apiece, and offered to play liar's dice with anyone who was interested. He was very good at the game and took in an extra seventeen dollars by noon.

In the Homelite bar, meanwhile, several of the press encountered James Ferrara, who said he was a New York psychiatrist. Without telling them why he was there, he volunteered to hold a press conference at which he would explain his theories on the crimes. But just as the reporters became interested, an attractive black-haired girl who seemed to be involved with him appeared on the scene and told Ferrara to shut up, something about an exclusive hold. Then she took him away mumbling to himself.

Six additional state police units were assigned to cover Bloodstone, and the small substation, under the command of Lieutenant Joseph Rocca, was ordered staffed by a minimum of four troopers twenty-four hours a day. Daniel Smith, as the officer in charge of the investigation, requested that he be able to move his working assignment to Bloodstone and remain there until the case was finished. Captain Rolfe Jacobsen of the State CID in Albany approved the request immediately.

A young reporter from Buffalo, walking along the lake not far from the Terra Alta Motel, gathering atmosphere, managed somehow to pitch himself off a hummock of ground into the icy waters. He couldn't swim and nearly drowned before his cries attracted troopers, who rescued him.

John A. Reese, editor-in-chief of *Insight Magazine,* telephoned Valerie Broome at the Homelite to ask her how the article was progressing and when he could expect pages so as to determine the exact slant and format. Valerie put him off with such perfect vagueness that it took Reese half a day to realize, drinking his third lunch martini, that she had told him absolutely nothing.

The residents of Bloodstone gathered on street corners or in stores and private houses. They were all grim and angry and desperate; it was their lives, or the lives of their friends and families, which were threatened. And they were leery of all the media people, of any outsiders who couldn't be labeled as tourists, and bitter and unnerved by the unfavorable public eye which was beginning to focus on them. A few of the more militant residents, such as Tony Manders, urged vigilante action in the form of armed citizen patrols. But others argued that that was futile. In the first place, they said, the state police wouldn't allow it and there wasn't any way they, the citizens, could go on armed patrol without official sanction; in the second place, they said, they had no idea who the Ripper was—an invisible enemy—and unless they could catch him in the act of killing another woman, which was unlikely and not to be wished for anyway, they would have no way of differentiating between the killer and any honest man who might happen to be out alone at night. Still others suggested that the town council be impelled to pass a temporary ordinance to the effect that no women be allowed on the streets after dark without an escort, with fines to be levied against foolhardy violators. Nothing concrete came out of any of these debates and discussions.

An overzealous Schenectady reporter's second dispatch ended: "One can say then that on the day after the fourth murder, Bloodstone is a disturbed little island in a lake of blood, haunted by the malignant specter of the man they call the Ripper." His editor cut the line, pointing out that first of all it was purplish, and second of all Schenectady was not that far from Bloodstone and their obligation was to entertain informatively, not repel, their readers, to say nothing of their advertisers. "Maybe a deal could be worked out with the Ripper on that," the reporter said, but not to the editor and only much later.

SMITH

Early Monday morning, in the small office he had appropriated at the Bloodstone substation during the night, Daniel Smith stirred sugar into his fourth cup of warm milk and read tiredly over the homicide report he had just finished typing.

He had not been to bed since Sunday night, and the lack of sleep was beginning to tell on him; his body ached with lassitude, his stomach was bothering him continually, and his eyes were thick-lidded, gritty. Except for the sugared milk, he had not eaten anything in fourteen hours, and that made him even more nervous and irritable.

When Keller's call on the fourth murder had come in last night, Smith had been at the substation—having come there after supper to talk to Rocca, the resident commander; he had spent the day reinterviewing the families and friends of the first two victims, going over familiar ground: an exercise in futility. He and Rocca had arrived at the Terra Alta Motel within ten minutes of the call, and at first Smith had been oddly annoyed that it was Keller who was the first law officer on the scene. But

Keller had been calm and businesslike in explaining his role in finding the body of Linda Simmons, and Smith's annoyance had vanished eventually.

The beach, the motel grounds, and the surrounding woods had been thoroughly searched, without yielding any evidence except the ritualistic presence of bloodstained tissues. A lengthy interrogation of Steven Hook had produced no leads either. The man had been badly shaken by his experience, that had been obvious, and Smith could find no contradictions in his story. But was it still possible that Hook was the assailant? Was it possible that he could have killed the woman in some sort of blackout state and then come awake to find the body . . . ? Ferrara's damned theories intruding again. He had forced them out of his mind angrily, had taken Hook home.

Then he had set about tracing the victim's movements.

Linda Simmons had been thirty-six, a divorcée with a ten-year-old daughter in a semiprivate school in Rochester. She'd lived alone in a house on Cadwallader Road, southwest of Bloodstone. Smith and Rocca searched the house with negative results, then questioned her neighbors, none of whom had seen her at any time Sunday. She was a moody and private woman, they told him, and seemed to have few friends and no male interests that they had known about; she hadn't been particularly attractive. Her one passion, or the only passion the neighbors were aware of, was photography. She had had several pictures published in *Adirondack Life* and a few other regional periodicals, which explained the tear sheets—mostly night studies of woods and lakes and mountains—tacked on her bedroom and study walls. There had been no camera in the house, and with the moon out, Smith had thought, it was exactly the kind of evening which would attract a nature photographer who specialized in night studies.

When they finished with the neighbors, there had been a call from one of the trooper patrol units. Linda Simmons' car had been found hidden in the brush near a small body of water called Warm Pond, two miles northwest of her house and a half mile due west of the Terra Alta. Smith found the camera inside the car when he got there, along with her purse and most of her clothing. The lens was smashed, and there were traces of blood on it. There was no other sign of blood in or around the car, which meant the assailant had apparently used the camera to knock the woman unconscious; then, following the probable pattern of the three other slayings, but for no evident reason, he had transported her to the motel grounds, where he had killed her.

Smith canvassed the houses near the pond and learned nothing. Back at the substation, he spoke with the Essex County Coroner, with the forensic people who had come up from Lake George, with other officers: nothing. The camera surfaces carried no latent prints; Smith had felt sure from the beginning that the assailant wore gloves, and this tended to confirm it.

At dawn he and close to a dozen other troopers had begun canvassing Bloodstone, asking questions, searching for anyone who might have seen Linda Simmons prior to her death. They found no one.

All that was in the report he had just finished typing. What was also in the report, if not directly stated, was the incredible fact that the assailant had now killed four women and had not made a single mistake doing it. He was obviously a beast psycho, he obviously commited the crimes in a state of intense passion, and yet no one had seen or heard him except for the victims, and he had left no clues. That was, in Smith's world, impossible; but it had happened. Ferrara's theories, in his world, were also impossible. . . .

"Damn it!" he said aloud, and put the report down and slapped a palm on it. The assailant had to make a mistake sooner or later, or he had already made some subtle one and Smith just hadn't found it yet. There was no getting around the fact that the case had become personal for the first time in his career, and so it was time to admit that and to work around the clock if necessary until he had the assailant in custody, could talk to him, extract piece by piece the information which would prove that from the start there had been a methodology to it and a set of motives which he would be able to comprehend.

Smith took the bottle of Visine from his shirt pocket and tilted his head back and put a half dozen drops in each eye. That gave him temporary relief from the grittiness, the soreness. Then he finished his milk, stood, put on his rumpled suit coat, and went out and down the short hallway to Rocca's office.

He told the resident—a tall, bony man a few years older than himself—that he was going into the village again. Rocca said, "Dan, you ought to get some sleep. There's not much more you can do right now."

"I'll sleep later," Smith said. "I want to have another talk with the Simmons woman's neighbors."

He went out of the building through the rear entrance, to avoid the reporters congregated in front. They had been trying to see him for hours now, and he had nothing to say to them. Ordinarily he had no objections to these people, they were only doing their jobs, as he was; but this time, with no more information on the fourth murder than on the previous three, he didn't want to face them.

His car was parked beside the small garage in back, and he went to it and put his hand on the door latch. Just as he did that, a man in an old corduroy jacket with leather elbow patches came out from behind the garage and hurried toward him. Smith knew him well enough: Plummer's kid reporter, Jack Cross.

Cross looked disheveled. His hair was wind-flattened over his forehead, and his clothes were more wrinkled than Smith's. Cheeks flushed too, but not from the wind. He waved a small spiral notebook and said excitedly, "I knew you'd come out eventually, Lieutenant. You can spare me a couple of minutes, can't you?"

"I'm afraid not," Smith said. He opened the car door. "I'm not giving out statements to the press, not yet."

"The press? Hey, I'm Jack Cross, you know me. Those others are out-of-towners, I've been on this case from the start."

"You're still the press, Jack."

"Yes, but I'm writing a book about the Ripper. I told you that before. *The Ripper of Bloodstone.*"

Smith winced and felt his stomach burn. "No statements," he said. "I'm sorry."

"Listen," Cross said, a little plaintively, "I've got to know some of the details. For my book, not for the paper.

I don't know much at all; nobody bothered to call me last night, not even the Plummer. I had to find out about it when I came into the office this morning."

"No statements," Smith said again.

"You've *got* to talk to me. Keller won't talk to me; nobody will talk to me. But you always talked to me before. Plummer's your best friend, after all, and I'm—"

"When I'm ready to issue a statement you'll be notified."

Cross plucked at his sleeve. Annoyed, Smith brushed the hand away. Cross blinked at him and then stepped back and waved the notebook again in jerky motions that seemed almost paroxysmic. "Linda Simmons was the victim, that much everyone knows," he said. The tone of his voice had changed to one of near desperation. "And the horseplayer, Steven Hook, found the body and Keller was on the scene first and you came just afterward. But what did you find? Are there any clues? Were there diamond-shaped marks on the—"

"No comment," Smith said, and got into the car.

"The bloodstained tissues, how many were there this time?"

"No comment."

"What about the—"

Smith slammed the door and started the car.

Outside Cross shouted, "Why won't you talk to me? Damn it, why won't anybody talk to me? I'm Jack Cross, I'm writing a book that's going to make all of you famous, don't you understand that?"

God, Smith thought. He backed the car around, turned it quickly toward the driveway. The last glimpse he had of Cross, the kid was standing spraddle-legged, face stained dark red, shaking an upraised fist violently.

Except on television, it was the first time in his life Smith had ever seen a man shaking a fist at anyone.

VALERIE

She had found out from the press people, who were now all over the Homelite Motel, that Steven Hook had been the one to discover the body of the Ripper's fourth victim, and she decided that she would go over and interview him. From the perspective of the in-depth, penetrating article which she was going to do, the reaction of a witness to the product of the atrocities was critical. (The man who had found the corpse of Dona Lincoln had refused to talk to her, and the maintenance crewmen and the state trooper who had discovered the first two victims had so far been "unavailable for comment.") She had every professional reason, then, to talk to Hook, get an impressionistic report which would tie strongly into the background.

Bullshit, lady, she told herself. You want to go over and talk to him because you understand what a ghastly experience it must have been for a man as sensitive as he seems to be, and because you want to see him again and this is the first decent excuse you've had.

She went out and started for the rental car, and Ferrara was coming across the lot from the direction of the motel coffee shop. They reached the car at the same time. Valerie said, "You haven't been talking to those reporters again, have you?"

"No," he said shortly. He still seemed a little miffed that she hadn't allowed him to set up a press conference. "I've been having a late breakfast."

"All right." She reached for the door handle.

"Where are you going?"

"Out to interview the man who found the body last night."

He seemed to perk up a little. "Really? I'd like to go along then."

"Why?"

"For the same reason as you, of course," Ferrara said, and his eyes glowed faintly. "A firsthand account of the discovery of a victim. I expect it should be quite interesting." He went around to the other side of the car and got inside.

Valerie felt oddly aggrieved. She didn't want Ferrara along, because she wanted to talk to Hook alone; she had the idea that she might be able to draw him out again, as she had begun to do before the Jack Cross interruption on Saturday night. Still, under the circumstances, it was probably unlikely that Hook would be drawn out about anything but last night's experience. All she could hope to do on a personal level—and Steven Hook had become something of a personal matter, like it or not—was to reestablish contact. She could order Ferrara to stay here at the motel, and he would no doubt comply; but he wouldn't like it, and knowing him as she did, she realized he might just get it into his head to talk to reporters after all. Seeing Hook alone wasn't that important, not just now anyway.

She took the wheel and drove them out of the Homelite. Ferrara said, "This man's name is Hook, isn't it? Steven Hook?"

"Yes. I met him at the café the other night."

"Oh?"

"He's a sensitive man, Jim, and I'd appreciate it if you would let me handle things. Don't start any of your psychological probings, the way you did with Keller on Saturday."

Ferrara laced his fingers together across his chest. "You know, Valerie," he said, "you really ought to be more careful."

"What's that supposed to mean?"

"You've been going out alone quite a bit, at night as well as during the day? You were going out alone to see this Hook person? As I've said often enough, anyone in this town can be the assailant. Anyone at all, Valerie."

"Hook found the body," she said. "*Found* it."

"Which means nothing in terms of guilt or innocence. The state of amnesiac fugue—"

"I know, I know. But Hook simply doesn't strike me as Ripper material—okay? I told you, I've already met him."

"The Ripper doesn't strike *himself* as Ripper material," Ferrara said. "I advise you to bear that in mind at all times."

They went north through the village, heading for the address Valerie had found easily enough in the telephone directory, and finally turned onto Stone Bridge Road. The cottage appeared down at the end of the road, on the lake —a weathered wooden structure, painted brown, with screened porches front and rear. A long time ago, she recalled vaguely, it had been occupied by a family named Douglas, Carter and Mary Douglas.

When they reached the entrance drive, Valerie saw Hook halfway between the porch and an old Dodge parked to one side. He stopped, seemed about to bolt back toward the cottage, and then appeared to recognize her through the windshield. He stood waiting as she braked the car near him, as she and Ferrara stepped out.

She had felt herself very much on top of this second meeting with Steven Hook, certain of the approach she would take and the questions she would ask, but when she saw him up close, she was no longer sure of herself. He looked terrible: eyes wide and showing too much of the whites, little gray lines crosshatching his unshaven cheeks. She felt compassion, pity, pain—too much feeling, perhaps, for a man she hardly knew.

"Hello, Mr. Hook," she said softly.

"It's good to see you again," he said, and he seemed to mean that. He looked at Ferrara, who stood with hands behind his back in a posture of attentiveness.

"This is James Ferrara," she told Hook. "He's a psychiatrist from New York; he's assisting me on the article for *Insight*. We—" And she stopped, because she had almost gone on to say that they were just acquaintances, that there was nothing intimate between them. Now why should she feel the need to say something to him like that?

Hook nodded. "I suppose you came to talk about what happened last night."

"Well—yes."

"I don't want to discuss it," he said. "I've been fighting off reporters all morning so I wouldn't have to discuss it."

"I can understand that. I just thought . . . well. . . ."

"Don't apologize. You're only doing your job, I half expected you might be around." There was a thin sheen of sweat on his forehead. God, Valerie thought, he really does look terrible. It was not only the remains of shock, but something much deeper, something approaching grief.

She said reluctantly, "Maybe we'd better go then."

"I might be able to talk about it later," he said. "Later."

Ferrara, studying Hook with his penetrating bird's eyes, said to him, "You still see her, don't you, Mr. Hook? In the eye of your mind, fixed there."

Hook seemed stunned. "How did you know that?"

"It's quite natural psychological reaction," Ferrara said. "The images of horror tend to—"

"Jim," Valerie said warningly.

But Hook was standing stiff-backed now, staring at a point beyond both of them. The contours of his face rippled with emotion. "I thought it was all outside of me," he said after a long moment, more to himself than to them. "From the beginning I thought that I could keep the killings outside of me just like everything else for the past six or seven years. It wasn't that I had anything against these people, against the town. They haven't bothered me; I owe them something just for leaving me alone. But when I saw her there on the beach, saw her face, I realized it was *people* this madman has been killing, people, like the women I see in the stores every day. . . ." He broke off, shook his head; then: "I keep seeing her, that's all. And I feel confused. All the questions, Keller and Smith and Rocca and the reporters. Especially Keller. He treated me like I was guilty of something last night. I just found her, only that. I just found her."

Valerie's throat felt tight. She had an impulse to reach out and touch him but did not give in to it.

Ferrara said, "The constable is an extremely projective man, Mr. Hook. He sees his own guilt, I fear, everywhere around him, in all others."

Blinking, Hook's eyes refocused on him. "His own guilt?"

"I don't mean by that that I think he's the assailant, of course. But then he is not to be excluded, either. No one may be excluded. You see—"

Valerie said Ferrara's name again, more sharply, but Hook seemed almost sickly fascinated by the little man. "What are you getting at?" he asked. "Why can't anyone be excluded?"

Ferrara looked at Valerie with a perverse little smile that said he had been specifically asked to explain this time and he was therefore going to explain. Then, with the same elegance that he had used with Smith and Plummer on Saturday, he laid out to Hook his theory of the crimes.

Hook appeared to Valerie to back away, to recoil, although his position remained immobile. "That's horrible," he said. "My God, that's horrible!"

"Yes," Ferrara agreed solemnly. "However, it is the only explanation which fits the ritualism, the blind selection of victims."

"He has no idea that he's the murderer? No consciousness of his acts?"

"None."

"Then what does he think he's been doing when he's killing these women?"

"He slips into timeless time," Ferrara said, "and immerses himself. Then he emerges into normal time with a weak but to him credible explanation of the lapse. Sleep, perhaps, would be the most likely one. In any case, his rationalization is acceptable to him."

"Horrible," Hook said again.

His face looked even grayer, and Valerie wanted once more to reach out to him. She knew that he would not have resisted, might even have let her come in against him; but she could not do it, could not move her hand. She only stood there, looking at him, the sound of his voice echoing inside her head, saying *Horrible, horrible*.

KELLER

With the state police everywhere, goddamn reporters everywhere, dominating available witnesses and overrunning the scenes of Linda Simmons' abduction and murder, Alex Keller decided to work on a more indirect line of investigation. When you were dealing with something like this you had to try everything, work on every angle, no matter how slim it might seem. So, late that morning, he went to see the woman who was Steven Hook's closest neighbor—Florence Cross, the red-haired bitch who everybody in Bloodstone knew was balling with Plummer —to find out if she had anything to tell him about Hook.

Hook had been on his mind ever since last night, insinuatingly. The man's story had sounded reasonable to Smith, that was obvious, but Keller thought that business about walking alone in the woods at night was pretty strange and suspect behavior. And so was standing alone in the rain, face uplifted, laughing to yourself, as he had been Saturday night. Not only that, but Hook was a horseplayer, a race track sharpie—the kind of rim-of-the-law son of a bitch who was capable of just about anything; Keller knew that from Chicago, he knew all about horseplayers. Hook might be innocent, all right, but then again he might not be. At the least, he was worth further examination.

Keller rang Florence Cross' doorbell, and she opened the door right away. She seemed tired and frightened and more willing to talk to him. Which meant the Ripper was working on her mind, too. Well, the Ripper got to all of them sooner or later. Sooner or later.

She led him inside, into the dark parlor. Keller watched her walk, the way her hips moved underneath her skirt; he ran his tongue over his lips. She was too damned sensual for her age, he thought. He knew her hair was dyed and that she used plenty of makeup to cover the age lines in her face, but still, no woman with an adult son should radiate the aura of sexuality that she did. Unless that little piss-brain Jack Cross wasn't really her son, unless he was adopted or something.—

He sat uncomfortably on an elegant straight chair and asked her about Hook, making his questions sound routine so that she wouldn't intuit what he was really after. But she had nothing to tell him which added to what he already knew. She couldn't see Hook's cottage from the promontory, because of screening trees, and she hardly knew him; in fact, she couldn't recall ever having spoken to him. Plummer, who made it his business to know everybody in Bloodstone, had told her that Hook had come from New York and had been an actor once. If he had ever done anything to offend anyone or leave behind a recollection of odd behavior, she wasn't aware of it.

And that was that. Maybe Plummer could tell him something, Keller decided; he would have to see Plummer next. He stood up and said, "I guess that's about all. Thanks for your time, Mrs. Cross."

She plucked at one of the buttons on her blouse. She had nice tits, big and firm. The whores in Albany had big tits too, but all of them were soft—soft and mushy and hanging. Maybe that was part of the reason why he sometimes wasn't able to get it up; he had never liked soft, hanging tits. . . .

And she said, "Are you making any progress at all, Constable?"

"Yes," he said. "We're making plenty of progress."

"Well, but do you have any leads or clues or whatever?"

"I can't talk about that. But I'll . . . we'll get the man before long, don't worry."

"Are you sure it's a man?"

"Oh, it's a man, all right."

"What would he look like?"

"What? What's that?"

"What would he look like, Constable? Would he be a big man or a small man? Would he be old or young?"

"I don't know," Keller said, and frowned. "Why do you ask that?"

"I just want to know if you have any idea what type of man he is. Morbid fascination, I suppose you could call it."

"We have a general psychological profile," Keller said. "The appearance doesn't matter."

"What sort of psychological profile?"

"He enjoys killing women."

"Well yes, of course," Florence said. "But why? Why does he enjoy it? Is it because he hasn't been able to get along with them, because women in his life have failed him somehow?"

Keller felt his nerves tightening, felt himself becoming upset—and didn't know why. "I don't know," he said. "I can't answer that."

"Could it be something in his past? Some sort of emotional shock?"

"I don't know," Keller said again. He backed away a step.

"Would he be married or not married? Would he be doing this because in an unconscious way he needs help terribly and he's trying to attract attention—"

"Unconscious? What do you mean, unconscious?"

"Doing what he does and not knowing why he does it."

"No," Keller said. "No, that's not possible." He had an overwhelming need to get out of there. "I don't have any more time to talk, Mrs. Cross."

"But can't you—"

He shook his head and then turned and hurried quickly away from her, into the hall and outside. She had really upset him; there was sweat under his arms. But it was ridiculous that he should be upset; there was nothing to be upset *about*. And he thought of Ferrara on Saturday, the little bastard's theory about the Ripper not knowing he was the Ripper. But he kicked that thought back into his subconscious. Control, control, you couldn't let little things bother you. When little things started bothering you, you were in bad shape; Chicago had taught him that. Forget about Florence and her big tits and her damned questions. Concentrate on the Ripper, the Ripper—

What type of person *was* the Ripper?

CROSS

The offices and printing plant of the Bloodstone *Sentinel* were located in a white frame building with a rusticated stone façade, a block off Main on Dock Street. Jack Cross returned there a few minutes past noon that Monday, parked the Chevy in the narrow asphalt lot at the rear, and came around and inside through the front entrance.

There were four old wooden desks in the newsroom, a teletype machine from which all news items outside a radius of twenty miles were derived, a hot plate on a long table, and several framed past-issue front pages—all dealing with major national events. The front pages dated from the time before 1964, when the newspaper had been a twelve-page daily rather than a twenty-four-page weekly, and always gave Cross the vague feeling that life must have been more exciting then: he had missed the good years.

Except for the only other full-time employee, Marjean Goodie—who was an amalgam of advertising manager, writer of church and social news, and receptionist—the room was empty.

Marjean Goodie. That was some name for a fat girl with stringy hair and a poor complexion and muddy-looking eyes; if there was anything she wasn't, Cross thought, it was a goodie. He didn't much care for her anyway. She had taken a freshman year in journalism at the Newhouse School at Syracuse before dropping out to "enter the world," as she put it, and spent half her office time criticizing his work and the other half giving him little wistful looks when she thought he wasn't watching. Another one like his mother. All the women he knew seemed to be like his mother. But at least Paula was *thin*.

Marjean said, "Anything breaking, Jack?"

Anything breaking, Jack. She was always saying things like that—pseudo-reporterese, Newhouse Center stuff no doubt. "No," he said shortly, and went to his desk.

"Did you talk to Lieutenant Smith?"

"He's not giving out any statements yet."

"Well, did you interview Steven Hook?"

"No. He wouldn't open the damned door when I told him who I was. But I'll see him later. He'll have to talk to me eventually; they all will."

She sighed (a Florence sigh, a Paula sigh—Christ!). "It gives me the shudders just to think about that maniac running around loose. They'd better catch him pretty soon. I mean, this whole thing is enough to give anybody a nervous breakdown."

Cross took off his coat.

"Plummer is in his office," Marjean said. "He told me he wanted to see you as soon as you came in."

His underlip trembled and protruded. He didn't want to see Plummer. He hadn't, in fact, wanted to come back to the office at all. Now that there had been another murder, now that things were moving forward again, what he wanted to do was to fill in the details he didn't have and then go home and start putting it all down in *The Ripper of Bloodstone*. But Plummer wouldn't allow that, of course, and he couldn't afford to tell Plummer to go to hell, not yet; and nobody would cooperate with him about the death of Linda Simmons, about anything. If you wanted to look at it one way, only the damned *Ripper* was cooperating with him.

"You'd better go on in, Jack," Marjean said.

"All right, all right." He walked over to the closed office door at the rear of the newsroom and went in without knocking, because he knew Plummer didn't approve of sudden entrances.

Plummer scowled at him from behind his desk, the way

Perry White always scowled at Clark Kent and particularly at Jimmy Olsen. But he didn't have Perry White's flair, he never said anything really individual like "Great Caesar's Ghost!" All he cared about was screwing Florence and not making any waves, and all he talked about was baseball.

When Cross closed the door, Plummer said, "Where have you been, Jack?"

"Out on the fourth killing."

"Find out anything new?"

"Not yet."

"Ugly business," Plummer said, and shook his head. "But when you do your story, play it down: just the facts, no embellishments. And don't use the word 'Ripper.' The town is frightened enough without our contributing to it with yellow journalism."

"All those other press people are going to play it to the hilt," Cross said. "You want us to be the only ones not coming to grips with the truth."

"What they do isn't my concern," Plummer said. "I'm only concerned with what the *Sentinel* prints. We have to live here, Jack."

Not much longer, maybe, Cross thought. Not me, anyway.

"So I don't want sensationalism and I damned well don't want another article from you like the one on the last murder. Is that understood?"

"All right," Cross said. Old bastard. "All right."

Plummer began to fill one of his pipes from a glass desk jar. "There's an antique auction in Heavenly Lake this afternoon, starts at two o'clock. I want you to drive over and cover it."

Cross stared at him. "Auction?"

"That's right."

"The Ripper got number four last night," Cross said, "I don't have all the facts yet, the town's in a turmoil, and you want me to cover an auction in Heavenly *Lake?*"

"The murder is hardly the only piece of news that's going into this week's issue," Plummer said. "You've been neglecting your other work again, chasing around on the murders, and I won't stand for it. I'm paying you good money to do a job and I expect you to do it."

Good money: a hundred and fifty dollars a week. But Plummer's voice was hard and sharp, a tone Cross knew all too well, and it meant that there wasn't any use arguing with him or trying to make him understand. Clark Kent could argue with Perry White, but Plummer wasn't Perry White and this wasn't the *Daily Planet* and Jack Cross wasn't Kent. Let the old bastard have his way, then. All that mattered was *The Ripper of Bloodstone*. Nobody could take that away from him, and nobody could keep him from writing the truth.

"All right," he said again, and turned and put his hand on the doorknob.

"Jack," Plummer said.

Different tone of voice, but Cross knew that one just as well as the other. He turned back, and sure enough, there was a paternal glint in Plummer's eyes. Employer to kindly father figure. Old bastard. "Jack, your mother's been pretty worried about you. I think you should stop in and see her tonight."

Cross didn't want to listen to any lectures which was what this would lead to if he argued. "Okay," he said. "Whatever you say."

"Good boy." Plummer lit his pipe, got it drawing. "How's your book coming?"

"Fine," Cross said. Now what?

"Maybe you could bring in what you've written one of these days. I'd like to read it."

I'll bet you would, Cross thought. So you could take it right to Florence. "I'm not ready to show it yet," he said. "I've got to polish it up, it's just a rough draft."

"I could give you some objective comments before you put it into final."

"I'll let you see it as soon as it's finished," Cross lied.

"I'm looking forward to it." Plummer's pipe had gone out, and he paused to relight it. "Did you know about the psychiatrist who's up from New York City?"

Cross looked at him warily. "Psychiatrist?"

"He came with Valerie Broome. You remember her, of course."

"I saw her Saturday night. But she didn't say anything about a psychiatrist."

"Well his name is James Ferrara and he's a consultant on the article she's writing for *Insight Magazine*. She's an assignment writer for them now."

"I know," Cross said.

"This Ferrara has some interesting theories on the murders," Plummer said. "Not for publication in the *Sentinel*, but you might be able to work them into your book. He's staying over at the Homelite."

Plummer didn't particularly give a damn about *The Ripper of Bloodstone;* he was suggesting Cross see this psychiatrist because he thought an interview might lead to a professional connection. As if once he got talking with a psychiatrist on any subject, the urge to put himself into treatment would be overpowering. Florence had told him once, indignantly, that Plummer had been hinting around about him benefiting from a shrink; it was because Plummer didn't understand how sensitive he was, she said. Probably mistook uniqueness for some sort of instability. She refused to hear any more about it from Plummer, which meant that she was on Cross' side in this respect, at least. She knew there was nothing wrong with *his* head.

Still, even though Cross was aware of Plummer's intentions, the old bastard may just have put him onto something worthwhile after all, something worth a follow-up. If Ferrara *did* have some interesting theories on the Ripper, they could work neatly into the book. Opinions from a qualified psychiatrist would give it an important air of authority, which would in turn give even more solidity to his own insights.

"I'll look him up," Cross said. "I'll do just that."

Plummer nodded, satisfied. "Just make sure it's on your own time, Jack. Right now we've got an auction to cover in Heavenly Lake, right?"

"Right," Cross said, and left the office and left the building and went immediately to talk to James Ferrara.

HOOK

Hook could see her face, moving up and up through the refractory levels of memory; but sometimes it was the face of the dead Linda Simmons and sometimes it was the face of Valerie Broome, and he did not know which seized him more. He could see *Tomorrow's Trots,* charts and figures on a horse without a name. He could see the drink before him in Bloodstone Tavern, the rye winking at him and then spread in a glistening stain across the bar. He could see the bottle buried deep under the rags in Number Eight of the Hideaway Cabins, ten short minutes away. He could see the shapes of Valerie and Ferrara turning away from him earlier, toward the car, her stride hesitant (or was that only his imagination?), and feel the unspoken cry choking in his throat: *Stay, don't go away.* And he could see Ferrara's glossy features, hear Ferrara's voice saying *The Ripper does not know that he is the Ripper; he enters timeless time,* and his own voice saying *Horrible*—and that was almost the worst of all, that above everything else which he could not bear.

Faces, *Trots,* drink, bottle, shapes, cry, features, voice, Ripper, horrible. . . .

And he realized, sitting there in the front room of his cottage, that after years of not thinking at all he suddenly had too much to think about, more than his rusted equipment could handle. Poor Edmund. Poor, poor Edmund!

SMITH

On his way back to the substation again—frustrated, possessed of the same lack of substantive information as before—Smith felt a stab of pain in his stomach so sudden and severe that it took away his breath and almost caused him to lose control of the car.

Gasping, he fought the wheel and braked to a stop on the shoulder of the road. The pain came again and again, spasming, and he had a stark mental image of the ulcer perforating, swirling blood that would fill the reservoir of him, of bleeding to death inside. Holy Mary, Mother of God! He clasped both hands under his breastbone and held them there, tears leaking from his eyes as he battled panic.

His stomach spasmed a fourth time . . . but then the pain ebbed, modulated once more into the familiar dull ache. When he could breathe normally again he took his hands away and pulled a tissue out of the box on the dashboard and wiped sweat from his face.

Perforation. He had never taken seriously the possibility of perforation; Plummer's warnings were too abstract. The ulcer was just something he would have to learn to live with, he'd thought, like his marriage. He had always believed that nothing truly terrible would ever happen to him. In his methodical universe, all could be accounted for except his own death, but that was somewhere in the future; he would not have to deal with it as the man he was now.

But he had never had a sudden, crippling pain like this before. He ought to see his doctor for sure now, and yet, suppose the doctor wanted to put him in the hospital? He couldn't let himself be taken out of the investigation, not at this point, not with all the things on his mind and the absolute need to see the case through to the end. The ulcer just *couldn't* be that bad; the tension, the lack of sleep were primarily responsible for the attack he'd just had. All he had to do was to take it a little easier, get some sleep right away, start eating regularly again, force the tension down mentally as well as physically. He'd be all right. He *had* to be all right.

Slowly, very slowly, Smith took the car back onto the road. His hands, slick on the wheel, were trembling.

KELLER

When Keller got out of the cruiser in front of the office of the Homelite Motel, the door to the adjacent bar and coffee shop opened and Jack Cross came out. Keller watched him veer over and thought: Little piss-brain—but he didn't move from where he stood beside the cruiser. He felt strangely upset by Florence Cross' questions, and his thoughts and reactions were dull instead of sharp, overlain with the kind of thin haze you felt when you'd been drinking. Too much pressure and too much feeling, and the price of both was pain.

Cross said, "I want to talk to you, Constable, get a statement from you. About Linda Simmons."

"No. I don't have anything to say."

"You were the first police officer on the scene," Cross said. "You can tell me—"

"I'm not going to tell you a goddamn thing."

"You can't avoid me indefinitely, I represent the people and the people have a right—"

"Get away from me." Keller started for the office.

"There's nobody in there," Cross said. "They're all in the coffee shop, listening to James Ferrara."

Keller stopped. "What do you mean, listening to him?"

"*He* doesn't mind talking, I just talked to him myself. He's a New York psychiatrist, but you already know that. He says he met you on Saturday."

"He's been talking about me?" Keller said tightly.

Cross moved over in front of him again. His lips twitched, as though he wanted to smile. "He mentioned your name a couple of times."

"What did he say?"

"Why don't you ask him? And why don't you ask him about the Ripper, too? He knows what he's talking about."

"He doesn't know anything," Keller said. "He's a quack."

"Oh no, he isn't. He's got everything nailed down just right about the Ripper. He says the Ripper doesn't even know he's the Ripper, doesn't even remember killing all those women; that he's a kind of schizophrenic—"

"Bullshit!" A wad of anger and sickness moved inside Keller's stomach. "That's a load of bullshit."

"I think it's the best theory yet," Cross said. "It puts a whole new light on the case; it backs up my own ideas about the Ripper. I've been on the right track all along, but you wouldn't even take the time to listen to me, none of you would."

"I've heard enough out of you right now, Cross."

"Well you'd better listen to *Ferrara,* then."

"I don't need to listen to bullshit."

"Then why are you here? There's nobody else here except a lot of press people and you didn't come to talk to them, did you?"

Keller put a hand on Cross' chest and shoved him violently; he could not help himself, it was reflexive. Cross staggered backward, almost fell. His eyes were enormous, glistening, behind his glasses. "What's the matter with you?" he said in a squealing voice. "You didn't have any right to do that!"

"Get out of here," Keller said. "Stay the hell out of my way from now on, you understand?"

"You'll be sorry you treated me like this," Cross said. He was trembling, and his arms jerked in spasms, like a puppet's. "You'll be sorry when you read my book, it's all going to be in there about you."

Keller started toward him.

Cross backed away across the lot and then ran to where his car was parked. He threw himself inside clumsily, all arms and legs. The Chevrolet accelerated out of the lot, clutch grinding, motor missing badly.

Keller stood motionless. The feeling of disconnection had deepened now; his attention swung loosely, shifting within him like a pinball. Then, after a long time, or what seemed like a long time, he focused on the entrance to the bar and coffee shop. What the hell *am* I doing here? he thought. I don't want to see Ferrara, I don't want anything to do with that little quack bastard. He doesn't know anything about the Ripper; nobody really knows anything about the Ripper; nobody knows why he does it or what type of man he is.

Shambling, all arms and legs himself, Keller got back into the cruiser and drove away from there.

THE RIPPER
Waiting . . .

Wednesday, October 22

VALERIE

Valerie Broome had had her career breakthrough in 1969, when the girl next door in the West Side apartment building in which she lived was raped.

The girl had tapped frantically on her door at two A.M., and Valerie had gone to help her and eventually to call relatives and the police. Later on, with the girl's full cooperation, she had taped an in-depth interview. Her ten-thousand-word article, which appeared two months later in the *Village Voice,* brought her very little money but a small reputation. The piece—an interweaving of documentary recollections juxtaposed against autobiographical snippets from Valerie's point of view and more objective statements by psychiatrists and social workers—had been a deep cry of outrage which had signaled, in the words of the *Voice*'s copywriters, the beginning of an emerging women's consciousness.

Shortly thereafter, the managing editor of *Insight* had contacted Valerie to request an impressionistic article on the fear of rape, sort of a semifictional account of the stream of consciousness of an attractive, lonely girl in New York and how she faced the possibility of rape every moment of the day. She had gotten five hundred dollars for the three-thousand word article and another assignment on rape among lower-class women, but at that point she had been tired of writing about rape and afraid of becoming stereotyped into a limited subject which would surely, if sadly, pass from the magazines. Instead, she had on her own done a long article on the interconnections between the judiciary and the Democratic clubhouses in Brooklyn, which *Insight* had published—and at about the same time an anthology called *Rape: The Crime in the Name of the Law,* with her *Voice* article as the title piece, had been published and had become a best-seller. So with almost no sense of transition she was a successful writer, in fact, a rather notorious one, although she did not feel she had done anything of significance. That feeling had not much altered since.

In the meantime she had been able to leave her job as an editorial associate for one of the blander women's magazines and find a larger apartment in the West Village at three times her former rent; she had also been able, because she was a celebrity of sorts, to appear at Seminars, on panels, even on the lecture circuit. She had subsequently written two more pieces, very long ones: one for *Insight* on sex therapy and sex clinics, and the other an intense three-part profile for the *New Yorker* of a retired Senator who had once been the majority whip and the powerful chairman of two key committees, now living widowed and alone in a Washington hotel. This last article had won an award from the National Society of Magazine Writers, and several publishers had been willing to offer major contracts if she would commit herself to a slight updating and expansion of the thirty-five-thousand-word piece. She did not, for reasons that she could only partially explain, accept the contracts, and she did not attend the awards dinner. Once again she seemed to have achieved a small success not through her own sensibility but through the appropriation of someone else's.

Until the murders in Bloodstone had triggered her discussion with John Reese, and her subsequent assignment, she had done little for six months except a few reviews for general-circulation magazines and thirty pages of disorganized notes for a novel. But she would probably never be a novelist because nothing in her own experience or background seemed to have the richness or complexity which she could find in article subjects, and her subjects were then refracted through her style in such a way that editors had referred, not disapprovingly, to her "stenographic" approach, to her ability to make virtually no interposition of writer between subject and reader. The girl who had been raped was interesting, the old Senator more so, but what was Valerie Broome? She was a twenty-seven-year-old girl, reasonably attractive, passably talented, who had struggled out of a small upstate community which had contributed nothing to her sensibility but absolute stultification, and her father had operated a tobacco shop/newsstand—a painfully dull and shy old man who could not understand why she seemed unhappy with Bloodstone and who, in Valerie's sophomore year at Cornell, had been run over and killed in a freak accident on upper Main Street. His estate amounted to just about enough to bury him, and when she returned to campus, only slightly grief-stricken, Valerie saw no reason ever to return to the town again. All her possessions were at Cornell, and she had had a full scholarship plus a part-time job in the school bookstore.

But none of this—nor her graduation with honors and her turndown of a PhD instructorship in favor of going to New York to enter publishing and pursue the ambition to be a writer—was material for the fiction she hoped to do. It was possible, in fact, that if the girl next door had not been raped, Valerie's career might not have existed and she would have remained an editorial associate on the women's magazine.

She had met a few men in New York and had gone to bed with a couple of them, but they seemed a little put off by her. Which was understandable: she put herself off. Men seemed more comfortable talking with her in formalized situations. She made them happy in bed, but the series of transitions necessary to get from here to there were labored rather than easy and natural; she could not open up to them, the relationships never seemed to progress beyond the superficially personal and therefore always ended amicably but coolly. And now, at the age of twenty-seven and back in Bloodstone after ten years, she had met Steven Hook. He was good-looking, but not all that good-looking, and forty years old or thereabouts and tired and beset with internal problems. Still, there was something irresistibly fascinating about him, above and beyond his acting career and the horseplaying and the past few years buried—why?—in Bloodstone. For the first time, there was something more than superficially personal in her feelings, something about him that touched her deeply.

She could not shake the thought that in an entirely alternate frame of reference, this was the kind of man she could have loved. . . .

Sitting now in her room at the Homelite, Valerie pulled the sheet of paper out of her portable typewriter and crumpled it and threw it at the wastebasket, where it bounced against all the others. Three hours of work last night and several hours this afternoon had produced exactly three workable pages of what Reese had indicated to her would likely be a serial piece of at least three installments.

She looked at her watch, and it was a quarter after six. Wednesday was almost gone. She pushed away from the desk and went to the window and looked out into the motel courtyard. Early in the afternoon, thick clouds had finally overcome the pale sun which had shone on Bloodstone since Monday, and now, with the coming of darkness, they had a restless, bloated look. It was going to rain again.

She wondered dimly, without caring much, where Ferrara was. She had kept him with her most of the time during the past two days—drawing him out further on his theories and his impressions of Bloodstone for the article, visiting the scenes of the second and third murders, interviewing those few individuals who were willing to be interviewed—but she knew that he had found time to talk to members of the press anyway, even after she had warned him not to. Some of the media people had been pulled out of Bloodstone when it became apparent that nothing else was going to break immediately; but most of them were still firmly entrenched at the Homelite, and a wire service reporter had tried to buttonhole her in the coffee shop last night, mentioning Ferrara's name and wanting to know his qualifications as a consulting expert. Well, what could she do about it? Ferrara was Ferrara.

And Bloodstone is Bloodstone, she thought, because that was one of the reasons why she was finding it so hard to write. For the first time she had material which was completely hers, and that was what she had thought she wanted; but on inspection, it turned out that much of her strength had come from being outside of her work, from giving little of herself to it. Bloodstone demanded an involvement whose level she had never touched. As she'd feared on Saturday, she had been overwhelmed by the place, she could not put it down on paper so that anyone who had never been there could understand it as it really was. In fact, maybe *she* didn't understand it as it really was, and never had.

Turning, Valerie went back to the desk and stared at the empty typewriter. Useless. She could sit there for the rest of the night without accomplishing anything more. She wasn't going to work then; all right, what *was* she going to do? Well. Well, there was one thing she could do. She had resisted it the past two days, because she was certain where it would lead, but resistance had never been her particular strength. Fools rush in, she thought. Fools and knaves. The town bred them, nurtured them: fools and knaves.

She got her coat from the closet and went out to see Steven Hook.

KELLER

Patrolling again: headlights tunneling, roadways retreating beneath humming tires, darkness all around, emptiness all around. Keller feels, not for the first time, that he has been existing in a state of perpetual darkness and mobility these past few weeks—no contact, no daylight, alone in eternal night, searching for the Ripper and (it occurs to him disturbingly) for something more, something inside him that he won't quite be able to understand until the end of it all.

He tries to think of the whores in Albany, the whores waiting for him at the end of it all, but the naked bodies on the screen of his mind are those of faceless women torn open, glistening with blood. He shakes his head, aching head and rubs at his burning eyes and wonders if tonight he will be able to sleep. He stares harder through the windshield.

Shadows crouch and flee and return as the cruiser moves through the night: animal prowling within a metal shell, seeking the prey that preys on helpless prey; hungry, weary, angry in the endless black.

Patrolling again. . . .

HOOK

He opened the door and Valerie Broome was standing there on the porch. Hook could not remember later whether he had heard her knock or whether he had simply gone over to the door in obedience to an impulse—which might say something profound about levels of communication.

She was wearing a short black coat, and he noticed that although it was only damp outside, not raining, her hair gleamed as if wet. "Well," he said, "come in."

She entered and looked at him seriously, slowly, her eyes questing; then she glanced around the cluttered, dusty room.

"It's a mess, isn't it?" he said. He closed the door. "I'm not much of a housekeeper."

"Don't apologize, Steven. May I call you Steven?"

"Yes, of course." His mouth felt curiously dry, metallic. "I'm glad you came again," he said.

"Are you?"

"I almost went to see you a couple of times."

"Why didn't you?"

"I don't know. I think I would have, eventually."

She took off her coat, one swift, graceful motion that seemed somehow intimate. He took it from her, draped it over the back of a chair.

"Are you feeling better?" she asked.

"A little. It doesn't bother me quite as much as it did, her face doesn't haunt me now." *But yours does,* he wanted to say, foolishly.

"What have you been doing?"

"Staying away from Saratoga."

"No more horseplaying?"

"No more horseplaying," he said.

"Have you decided what you're going to do?"

"Not really. I thought about going job hunting in Lake George, maybe finding an insurance agency or a bank that would take me on. But that seemed pretty silly. I'm thirty-nine years old, you know, and I've never worked in an insurance agency or a bank, and an ex-actor turned ex-horseplayer isn't likely to be considered a good trainee risk."

"There are other jobs."

"Sure. Dishwashing or portering or the like. I've been there before, and I'm not ready or willing to go back again."

"So you've just been sitting here—alone—the past two days."

"Mostly, yes."

"Did you ever think you spend too much time alone?"

"I don't have any friends here. Or anywhere, for that matter."

"That sounds a little pathetic," she said frankly.

"It is." He paused. "What have you been doing?"

She said, "I haven't been working."

"Oh?"

"I can't do the article. I'm supposed to be writing the first installment of what's now going to be a fifty-thousand-word piece. Only I can't seem to get started."

"Why not?"

She looked at him steadily. God, he thought, those eyes are compelling. "Reasons that will probably work out," she said. "Maybe."

He gestured toward the couch. "Would you like to sit down?"

"No, I don't think so."

"It's a little uncomfortable, standing here."

She moved closer to him, so close that he could smell the scent of her hair: soft, musky. "Let's not fence, Steven, all right?"

And he knew what she was thinking then, had maybe known it from the first moment he saw her on the porch. There was no surprise in the knowledge, but no vanity either. He felt a gentleness that he did not know was in him and reached out and put his hands on her shoulders, slowly worked them up over the bulky sweater she wore until the tips of his fingers touched her neck. The skin there was soft, seemed translucent. Her hands touched him too, then, drew him closer, and he said, "Valerie, I—" and her touch became more insistent, and she said, "No, don't talk. Later we'll talk about a lot of things, but not now."

He put his mouth against hers, and there was a slow moment of pressure, then yielding, then openness, and then a long, blank time at the end of which he realized that they had come into his bedroom, with the old scripts and manuals on racing and unlaundered clothing all around. He felt shame, wanted to say something apologetic, but she said against his mouth, "Don't talk, don't talk," and more time passed and their clothes were gone, her body shone like marble in the light, and then they were pressed together, caressing, in the rumpled gray arena of the bed. Still the gentleness within him, her hands fire, her mouth fire, and slowly, slowly she took words and cries from him which were not in his voice as he settled into her, hardness immersed in softness, breaking. . . .

SMITH

Smith set up the baseball game in his room at the Witherbee Motel. It was called Computer Baseball, and it was one of his favorites that he had brought along to help him relax, help him think, during the waiting hours.

You played it by choosing what pitch you wanted your "pitcher" to make and then inserting the appropriate card into a simple memory bank. The other player, if there was another player, then inserted either a "take" or "swing" card, and a small screen lit up and told you whether the pitch was a ball or a strike or a hit batsman (if "take") or whether it was a swinging strike or a groundout or fly out or base hit of one type or another (if "swing"). There were also "steal" cards, "sacrifice bunt" cards, "intentional walk" cards. Strategy was important, as in a real game, and if you played it alone, you bisected yourself so that one part literally tried to outsmart the other, concealing intention—

Ferrara: "The assailant bisects himself, turns one part

of himself against the other. He does not know he is the assailant."

Smith shook his head angrily. Damn it, there was no equation that could fit both baseball and mass murder. None. He put in a card for fastball, put in a take card, and the screen flashed STRIKE. He put in the card for curve, inserted the swing card, and the screen flashed FOUL BALL. He slid in the curve card again, then the swing card, and the screen flashed SWINGING STRIKE.

Strike three and you're out.

Smith lost all interest in the game. He stood and shut off the overhead light and lay on the bed, knees drawn up, staring at the ceiling and listening to the steady, sour burble of his stomach. He had never felt so depressed, so hamstrung. Nothing was going right, everything seemed to be working against him: the impotence of his investigation so far; constant hassling from reporters and townspeople; his wife turning uncharacteristically petulant over the fact that he had moved in here for the time being instead of commuting back and forth to Lake George; the fixed ache and worry of the ulcer (he hadn't suffered anything resembling a second severe attack, but he was plagued by the thought that it *might* happen again); even a goddamn toy baseball game. Three strikes and you're out. Damn Ferrara and damn this case!

The sounds in his stomach grew louder, like water boiling, and he farted. Immediately he felt the need for defecation, and got up and went into the bathroom. He sat on the toilet, farting steadily now, filling the cubicle with odor, unable to make his bowels release. He had been having trouble that way for days—something to do with the ulcer, something to do with the tension. . . .

The telephone rang.

Smith sat up straight, came onto his feet. *Ring.* He fumbled at his underpants and trousers, got them up around his knees. Starting out, he staggered sideways into the basin and cracked a forearm painfully. *Ring.* Son of a bitch! He came out and duck-ran toward the bed. *Ring.* Struggling, he pulled his pants all the way up and pitched himself onto the edge of the bed, face flushing, and dragged the receiver off the hook just as it started to ring again.

"Smith," he said.

Rocca's voice, tight and clipped, said, "You've been wanting action, Dan; we've got it."

His stomach burbled loudly. "What?"

And Rocca said, "Somebody just tried to kill Florence Cross."

THE RIPPER

Up the downside, down the upside, down and down, groaning and moaning and clinging and singing in the ice-capped mountains, cold and loose, hanging loose, loose as a goose among the diamonds. . . .

CROSS

In the *Sentinel* newsroom, where he and Plummer and Marjean Goodie were putting the weekly edition to bed, Jack Cross leafed through a stack of filler, looking for a two-inch item to close a hole on page three. Some newspaper, he was thinking, but without bitterness. Half of it was devoted to filler.

Actually, he was in better spirits than he had been in weeks. Since Monday, he had learned most of the details of the Linda Simmons murder, succeeded in interviewing both Smith and Steven Hook, stayed far away from Keller (he would take care of Keller in *The Ripper of Bloodstone;* he would devote a whole chapter to Keller), fabricated a story on the Heavenly Lake antique auction from a telephone conversation with the sponsor after it was over, gathered information on several other assignments without covering any of them directly, deftly avoided his mother, had sex with an oddly introspective Paula and managed not to call her Lois, and completed another five thousand solid words on the book. The way the book was progressing was the main reason for his good humor. The chapter he'd written on Ferrara and his theories was some of the best writing he'd done so far, if not *the* best. He'd really gotten it all together now, particularly in the closing paragraph:

And thus the man outside merges with the man inside, the two of them fused and reborn as the Ripper, who descends knifelike through the night toward his victims . . . the way Superman ascends knifelike through the night toward the victims of others. For the Ripper is the antithesis of the great American hero, of all that we hold to be Good and Right. He is Superman in the mirror: the Dark Prince, the Prince of Sleep.

Cross smiled, thinking that it was prose like that which could win him the Pulitzer Prize.

And then the telephone rang.

VALERIE

In the night, suddenly, there were sirens.

Valerie was in the kitchen when she heard them, making coffee and thinking of the way it had been in bed with Steven (good; better, in some ways, than it had ever been), trying to analyze the breadth and depth of her feelings for him and not quite succeeding. She turned immediately from the stove and hurried out into the front room, and he was already at the window. She went to him, saw that his face was tight and pale. She touched his arm. There were more sirens now, a half dozen or more, some close by and others echoing in the distance; all of them together created a shrill, piercing, unrelieved scream, like the cries of the damned.

He turned to her. "God," he said. "God, not again."

KELLER

When Keller got there, less than ten minutes after the call had come over his radio, the area near the Cross house was swarming with state police.

The Bloodstone dispatcher had given no details, just a standard "Ten-thirty-one-X, attempted homicide, all units Code Three" and then the Cross address. But Keller had known instantly that it involved the Ripper: the Ripper striking again where Keller wasn't (eight miles away to the west), outmaneuvering him yet again, out-cunning him. And the worst of it was that "10-31-X" meant offense in progress against a female, attempted homicide *in pro-*

gress, and that heightened the chances of both identification and apprehension by the state police before Keller could get there.

Two blue-and-yellow patrol units were pulled into a tight V on the access road that led up to the promontory, blocking admittance. Keller slid the cruiser to a stop in front of them. He had the window down, and he yelled out to one of the troopers, "Did you get him yet? Do you know who he is?"

"I don't know much of anything," the trooper said. "We just got here."

"I'm going up."

The trooper hesitated. He knew Keller, they all did, but he obviously wasn't sure what his status was in this situation. But Keller was not going to wait for sanction. He swung the cruiser onto the soft outlay, wedging it around the patrol units, and then came back onto the access road, tires shrieking.

The surface of the promontory was as brightly lighted as a football field: glaring yard lights, fixed headlights on four additional patrol cars, at least three flashlights flickering among the trees and bushes. Most of the windows in the house were illuminated, outlining the structure against the black, threatening sky. Keller recognized Smith's car parked near the porch—even that bastard had beaten him to the scene—and took the cruiser in behind it. He got out, revolver drawn, flashlight in his left hand, and ran to where a young trooper had appeared at the edge of the near woods.

"You haven't gotten him yet," he said, stating it now.

"Not yet," this trooper said. "Looks like he got away clear."

"Has he been identified?"

"No. Mrs. Cross says she didn't get a good look at him."

The Ripper was still his, then. He said, "She's all right?"

"Just shaken up. She's inside with Lieutenant Smith."

"What the hell happened here?"

The trooper said he wasn't sure of the full story, but as far as he could determine, Florence Cross had gone to the woodshed at the back for some kindling, and when she came out again a man in dark clothing jumped out at her with a knife. She'd run back to the house and locked the rear door and got her late husband's pistol, but the assailant had scraped around outside without trying to break into the house and then had vanished. "She's pretty damned lucky," the trooper said. "If he'd caught her, she'd be number five right now."

"Yeah," Keller said. He was glad she wasn't number five, that she hadn't been hurt. Of course he was glad. But if anybody else *did* have to get it, it was too bad that it couldn't have been a bitch like her. Only the bitches never got it; it was the decent ones like Linda Simmons and Julia Larch who wound up as the victims. Well, if *he* was the Ripper, he'd have—

Jesus. Jesus Christ! He had finally managed to get out of his head all that quack psychological bullshit that had upset him on Monday, he'd been functioning in tight control, and now it was trying to start working on him again. No, goddamn it, not this time. Not from now on. The name of the game was control, and he wouldn't let it slip anymore, not for even a few seconds.

Abruptly he turned away from the trooper and went into the dark woods. He put on his own flash: one more light flickering, moving off-center in the night.

SMITH

Florence Cross, face blanched, hands clasped between her knees, sat in the Shaker rocking chair in the parlor and shook her head slowly, continually, like a doll's on a broken spring. "I've told you and *told* you, Dan," she said, "I just. . . . I was too frightened and it was too dark for me to get a good look at him. All I remember is a shape, a silhouette."

Smith paced back and forth in front of her. In the minutes immediately after Rocca's call, on the way here, he had felt a strong emotional uplift, but now frustration and doubt were moving in again. The assailant had *failed* this time, and that should have been the break he had been waiting for. Yet even in failure, the assailant retained his incredible luck, his total anonymity. No apparent evidence, no apparent leads, no break, nothing at all except the sour, lingering kiss of insanity and chaos.

He said again, harshly now, "Christ, Florence, isn't there *anything* you can tell me about him?"

Her head continued its broken, negative wobbling. "No," she said. "I'm sorry . . . no."

"He just jumped out at you with a knife."

"Yes."

"What kind of knife?"

"Big. A big knife. With a long, thin blade."

"Thin? A few minutes ago you said it was thick."

Her eyes flicked, settled on the knot in his tie. "Thick, thin, I don't remember exactly, it all happened so fast. Dan, I was terrified."

"All right. You don't have any idea where he might have come from, where he might have gone?"

"No. He was just there, and then he was gone."

Rocca came back into the house then, into the parlor. Smith turned to look at him, but Rocca said, "Nothing yet, Dan," and Smith slapped impotently at his thigh. The pain in his stomach was sharp now, and getting sharper, but he ignored it, he refused to think of it.

Florence said, "Are you sure Jack has been notified? Are you sure he's coming?"

"I told one of the troopers to call him from the substation before I left," Rocca said. "He'll be here, don't worry."

"I need him," she said.

Smith couldn't take another minute in there with her; he needed movement, activity, no matter how futile. He said, "Stay with her," to Rocca, and went out for another look at the area around the woodshed.

HOOK

"They've got the road blocked," he said. "We won't be able to go up."

"Damn," Valerie said softly.

But Hook was relieved; he didn't want to be on the scene of another murder; he didn't want to know what had happened up at the Cross house. He hadn't wanted to come even this far, but Valerie had insisted on coming, and he had not wanted to let her come alone. He had just slept with her, he felt protective toward her—but it was more than that. She had filled an emptiness in him, opened up feeling in him as her own feeling came out, and she was someone solid and warm on which he had been able to lean at a time when nothing else had solidarity and warmth. A different kind of crutch from the one supplied by alcohol: support for the crippled spirit. He didn't want to lose her yet tonight, particularly tonight. He did not want to be alone.

He took the Dodge off onto the side of the road, and they got out. There were other cars there, other cars arriving: press people, local residents, more state troopers. Small groups milled about, sending out words in nervous, angry blocks of sound. Hook stood to one side, away from the others, and watched Valerie trying to talk to one of the troopers on the roadblock. The trooper wouldn't tell her anything, she said when she came back a moment later, except that there hadn't been another murder. Definitely there had not been another murder.

Thank Christ for that, Hook thought. At least for that.

He listened to the voices around him and felt the wind blowing cold through the night, carrying with it now the beginning drops of a cold, thin rain. He took Valerie's arm, held his body against hers.

The wind, the night, the roadway, the people—all of it, all of them—were wrapped in the odor of fear.

CROSS

The moment Cross came running into the house, Florence threw herself at him and clung to him with her fingers bunched in his coat. Immediately, holding her, he began to feel awkward. When he had gotten the telephone call from the state police telling him what had happened here, he had run out of the newspaper office blindly, the words *The shit, the filthy shit tried to kill my mother!* running through jumbled thoughts like a leitmotif. But now that he was here, now that he had visual confirmation that she was unharmed, the urgency had drained away, leaving only relief and confusion and the feeling of awkwardness.

He looked over Florence's head and saw Lieutenant Rocca watching them from in front of the fireplace, sympathetic and uncomfortable. Cross tried to move her away from him, but she held on desperately, making little sobbing sounds. He had an urge to pat her head, but that struck him as ridiculous; he kept his hands motionless on her back.

Half a dozen seconds passed, silently, and then the front door banged open again and there were hurrying steps. Cross knew it had to be Plummer even before the old man came into the parlor. Plummer had shouted after him as he ran out of the *Sentinel* building, but he hadn't answered or stopped, so the old man would have followed in his own car, there had been headlights behind Cross all the way out.

"Thank God you're all right, Florence," Plummer said in a shaky, breathless voice, and stepped around into Cross' view. His face seemed even whiter than Florence's. He reached toward her, touched her tentatively, and she raised her head and looked at him in a blank way and then pressed closer to Cross' chest; she wasn't reacting to Plummer at all, and though he didn't know why, that made Cross feel vaguely pleased.

He found his own voice. "It's all right, Mother. The police are here and I'm here. I came as fast as I could."

"It was terrible," she said against his chest. "It was awful, Jack. . . ."

Plummer said, "Don't talk about it, try to forget it. Maybe if you lay down—"

"I don't want to lie down," she said. "Let me be, Henry. There's nothing you can do."

Cross saw Plummer flush faintly, turn away, and he knew it was because she had called him *Henry*. Plummer hated that name, for some reason, and wanted everybody to call him only Plummer—and this must have been the first time Florence had ever used his given name. That pleased Cross, too, in the same vague way.

He managed finally to disentangle himself from Florence, stood her away from him. Her eyes were strangely glazed. Shock, he thought; he said, "Henry's right, Mother. You'd better lie down. You're pretty unsteady."

"Yes. Yes, if you say so, Jack. If you come sit with me. Will you do that?"

He hesitated; he didn't want to sit with her, and yet it was obvious that she needed him after what she had just gone through. *The filthy shit tried to kill her with a knife....*

Rocca said, "Go with her, son."

Cross nodded and said, "All right." Then, still feeling awkward, he took her past Plummer and out of the parlor and down the hall and over the threshold of her bedroom.

KELLER

There was nothing for him to find in the woods, and Keller went across the edge of the yard and around to the rear. The woodshed was there, flanked by a pair of bare-branched black cherry trees; not much else except for a couple of Scotch pine and a small grass plot with arched and roseless rose trellises at either end. He moved away from the house, playing the flash beam in a restless arc, picked up a dirt path and then frowned when he saw that it led to a low handrailed platform at the edge of the promontory.

He went there, and the platform became a landing for railed steps leading down the cliff wall. The wall—stratified limestone festooned with ferns and lichen—was steep enough so that the steps were switchbacked. At the bottom, in the black lake water, he could see the outer portion of a rickety wooden pier.

Had the Ripper come this way, instead of through the woods in front and to the south, or down the access road? By boat, maybe? It was possible; the Ripper was capable of any action, any maneuver.

Keller descended to the first switchback. From there he had a better viewing angle of what lay in both directions below. The lake came up against the cliff wall to the north, but to the south there was a rocky strip that stretched from the pier to low sloping terrain forty yards distant, where foliage grew flush with the waterline. So the Ripper didn't have to have come by boat at all. He could have walked here through those trees and then along the rocks to the steps.

Not seeing any sign of recent passage, Keller came the rest of the way down. The flash beam showed him nothing but blank, warped boarding, the length of the pier. He climbed down onto the rocks, where phosphorescent little waves shone in the light and there were drifting tendrils of mist. Body bent, head bent, he picked his way slowly among the stones.

Near where the foliage began, the probing flash revealed something crumpled and white lying partially hidden behind one of the chunks of limestone.

Keller pounced to it and caught it up between thumb and forefinger. It was a tissue, a white tissue like the ones at the site of the Linda Simmons murder: damp, but not disintegrating, as it would have been if it had been there for any length of time; something moist and mucilaginous at the center. He held the flash up close to it, couldn't verify but thought he knew anyway what that substance was. He felt a stab of revulsion submerged in a wave of excitement. The tissue had been dropped here by the Ripper, he was certain of it. It had the *feel* of the Ripper on it, just holding it made his fingers tremble.

Carefully he put the tissue into his coat pocket, against the jail key that he had taken to carrying with him, the key he would use to lock up the Ripper. Then he went over the rest of the rocky strip, a short way into the foliage, but there were no further signs and no further evidence.

When he returned to the steps and climbed up again to the promontory, it had just started to rain. Off to his right he saw another flashlight bobbing toward him at an angle through the drizzle. The man behind it, Keller saw as he neared the house, was Smith. Their paths intersected, and both of them stopped.

"Oh," Smith said, "Keller. When did you get here?"

"Few minutes ago. Why? Don't you want me around?"

"That's a stupid damned question," Smith said, and made an impatient gesture. "You find anything back here?"

Keller took the jail key out of his pocket, carefully, and bounced it in his hand. "Nothing," he said. "Nothing at all."

THE RIPPER
Stupid stupid, stupid stupid, the diamonds are mine!

Thursday, October 23

BLOODSTONE

The town council, responding to pressure from the panicked residents, called an open town meeting for Thursday noon at Essex Union. Daniel Smith and Alex Keller, among other officials, were summoned to give an accounting of the progress of the investigation to date and to set forth a concrete plan of action to protect the lives of Bloodstone's women until the Ripper was apprehended. Notices, hastily mimeographed, were put up on the Chamber of Commerce bulletin board and in store windows, but they were unnecessary. Every man and woman in the area knew about the meeting, by word of mouth, within an hour of the town council's decision.

Those press people who had been pulled out of Bloodstone earlier in the week returned, along with a dozen more of their fellows and additional mobile television units from Rochester, Syracuse, Montpelier, Ottawa, and Montreal. Most of the press were looking forward to the town meeting as something tangible on which a new dispatch could be written, because as things stood at the moment Florence Cross was in seclusion and Alex Keller and Daniel Smith and everyone else who knew anything of last night's attack were unavailable for or refused comment.

James Ferrara was also looking forward to the meeting. He was convinced that even if it meant losing his honorarium from *Insight Magazine,* he would be able to set up a recorded interview with one of the major television newscasters on the scene. He said to Valerie Broome, who had appeared again at the Homelite after mysterious absences last night and this morning, that in all likelihood the Ripper himself, in his normal persona, would be in attendance—which was exactly the angle he intended to use to promote the interview.

CROSS

When he came out of his cottage a few minutes past eight thirty, into cold gray light and a dripping mist, Paula's car was just swinging in from Clear Creek Road.

Oh Christ, he thought. He didn't want to see Paula this morning; he didn't want to put up with her. The attack on Florence had shattered his good spirits and put him in a low, depressed mood: the horror, the outrage, the sense of personal violation. And Florence hadn't helped matters any, wailing and crying and clinging to him and demanding that he stay the night. He loved her, he supposed, she *was* his mother and he was afraid for her, but what could he do? He couldn't spend all his time holding her hand, and he couldn't stay in that house, he really hated that house; besides, the state police had promised to post a guard. He wanted her safe and unharmed, but by God he wanted her to leave him alone.

So he had gotten out of there and come home and started to work on *The Ripper of Bloodstone* and had turned out one of the best sections yet, five pages of personal stuff that he had really been able to sink himself into. But after he had written it, he'd felt overtaken by the depression. It wasn't just a book now; the Ripper had come into his *life*.

Cross watched Paula park her compact behind the Chevy and get out and come over to him. She looked concerned, a little frightened, a little . . . what? Determined? "Hello, Jack," she said gravely.

"What is it?" he said. "Why aren't you at school?"

"The school's been closed for today and maybe indefinitely. Haven't you heard about the town meeting?"

"Oh," he said, "the town meeting." He *had* heard about it, from Plummer who had called him an hour ago; but he had still been half asleep and he could hear Florence's voice in the background. He wondered again if Plummer had spent the night with her. Probably not. Not with the state police guard. And not after the way she had treated him; she had made it clear enough to the old bastard who counted more in her life.

Paula was saying, ". . . just awful what happened to your mother last night. I'm so very sorry, Jack."

"She wasn't hurt," he said. "It could have been a lot worse than it was."

"It was terrible enough." She sighed her Florence sigh, embellished it with a little shudder. "When will this madness end? When will that fiend be caught?"

She really could be melodramatic at times, he thought. For a schoolteacher, she didn't know anything about nuances and subtleties. For a schoolteacher, as a matter of fact, she was pretty stupid altogether. He said, "They'll get him, don't you worry."

"Before he kills anyone else?"

"Maybe. You can't tell about that."

"I've been half frantic, alone at my place; I keep hearing noises and imagining all sorts of things."

"You'll be all right."

"I know now why you didn't come over last night," she said as if he hadn't spoken, "but I needed you, Jack. I really did."

"Tonight," he said. "I'll come to you tonight."

"*Late* tonight, I suppose." There was a sudden sharpness in her voice; her mood seemed to shift. "So you can sneak in the back way without anybody seeing you."

"We've got to be careful, Paula."

"Why? Why do we have to be careful? Everyone in Bloodstone knows we've been sleeping together; there are no secrets in a place like this. Isn't it about time we brought it out into the open, Jack? Isn't it about time we stopped playing games with each other?"

"Listen, Paula," he said, "I've got a lot of things on my mind, I've got to get to the office—"

"No. *You* listen. I know you're under strain, and I know how terrible this attack on your mother has been for you, but I can't go on the way we have been. I just can't, Jack, not anymore." She drew a long, heavy breath. "I want you to marry me. As soon as possible."

Anger flared inside him. "For God's sake, are you going to start that again? What's the matter with you? The Ripper's stepping up his pace, he tried to kill *Florence* last night, and you come out here and want to talk about marriage—"

And she said, "Jack, I'm pregnant."

The words stunned him. He blinked at her behind his glasses, mist on the lenses so that her face seemed aqueous, off-center, like a face seen underwater. "Say that again."

Paula looked at him steadily, mouth cut down at the corners. "I'm pregnant. I'm going to have your baby."

"I don't believe you," he said. His voice was hoarse and brittle, and his hand trembled as he took off his glasses, wiped them on his shirtfront and then put them on again. "You're lying to me."

"I'm not lying. I went to the doctor Monday and he gave me the results late yesterday. I was going to tell you last night; I *had* to tell you this morning. I can't live with it alone any longer."

And it was the truth. He could see it in her eyes. Not the old false pregnancy gambit, she really was going to have a baby. The kid isn't mine, he thought desperately, the bitch has been sleeping with someone else . . . but that *wasn't* the truth and he knew it. Nobody else would have her, and she didn't want anyone but him. She'd done it to trap him; he'd never expected her to go that far, but she had, she'd gotten pregnant to trap him. . . .

"For Lord's sake," she said, "don't look at me that way! It takes two you know, I didn't do it all by myself."

"Abortion," he said. "You've got to get an abortion."

"No."

"It's legal. Everything's legal in New York now."

"No. Abortion's a sin, it's murder. I won't murder a helpless infant."

"Embryo," Cross said. "Fetus."

"I won't do it," she said flatly. "I thought all that through last night and I won't do it under any circumstances. You're going to have to face the responsibility, that's all; you're going to have to be a man now, Jack."

He began to feel detached, as if he were watching all this from some high place. Like Superman, looking down from the heavens: removed, suspended above all activity.

"There's only one answer," Paula said, "and you know that as well as I do. We have to get married, Jack—the sooner the better. I'm almost three months along; it won't be long before I start to show."

Cross stared at her with his objective, detached eyes. Thin, pathetic, with that mousy hair and those bovine eyes. Lines in her face, crow's-feet beneath her eyes. God, he thought, she's *old*. Old, old. Seeing Valerie for the first time in ten years had been a more shocking experience than he had even thought at the beginning; *that* was the way a woman should look, that was the kind of woman he should have. But Paula . . . in five or six years Paula would be a crone, thin breasts hanging like sausages, soft, quiescent curve of her body turning hard and grainy, wrinkles forming, blue veins bulging like roots close to the surface. Why hadn't he seen that before, the way she really was and was going to be? In passion's grip you saw nothing, he had read that somewhere, but he could see it now, he could see what she would become, the future before him in the gray, wet morning: suffocating, perilous, dead.

"Paula—I need some time to think," he said.

"Think about what? Are you going to marry me or not?"

"I'm going to do the right thing, don't worry about that. I'm going to do the right thing." Control had seeped back into him, detached control; his body relaxed, and he managed a small reassuring smile. "I just need to work out plans, that's all. You can't expect me to make any on-the-spot decisions, not after you've hit me with something like this and on the morning after Florence was attacked. Not when our whole life together is at stake."

"You'd better make the right decisions, Jack. I won't stand for anything else."

"I will, Paula. Now why don't you go on home? I'll call you later today, I'll come by tonight. We'll talk then; I'll have everything worked out by then."

She yielded a little, but she was still determined and still wary. Steel to his steel under her fluttering. "Oh, Jack," she said, "I know we'll have a good life together, I just know it," and came forward and started into his arms.

"A good life," Cross said, and deftly held her off. He took her arm gently and guided her to her car. "A good life, Paula," he said, and handed her into the driver's seat, held the door, closed the door with a *thwok!* Behind the mist-streaked pane, she looked now like an insect: an old, thin, strange insect frozen in glass. He gave the pane an intimate pat and said, "Tonight, Paula," and smiled again and stepped back.

She looked out at him, still frozen there, for several seconds: confused, hopeful, old. Then she started the car and backed it and turned it and drove away into the mist.

Cross watched the car until it was out of sight. Then he went to the Chevy and got into it and sat there brooding. The feeling of detachment left him, the feeling of control vanished, and he was agitated and morose again. He didn't know how he was going to handle Paula; he didn't know what to do.

What would Clark Kent do if he knocked up Lois Lane?

HOOK

*Still, comrade, the running of beasts and the ruining heaven
Still captive the old wild king.*

The lines had been turning around in his head all morning, dredged up from a dim recess of the subconscious. James Agee had written them, he seemed to recall —part of a poem from somewhere which Ackers had read to the cast before the final rehearsal of *King Lear* as giving some kind of unique and final insight into the play. Maybe it did; but if so, Hook could no longer remember what the insight was.

He paced. The cottage, Valerie gone, had become an empty and oppressive call. He had managed to get her to stay with him last night, and with her there—to hold, to talk to—he had felt better, calmer; but now that he was alone, all of the jigsaw-piece uncertainties began to cut at him again with sharp little edges. *Still captive the old wild king. Still jagged those old wild uncertainties.*

He was going to have to get out of there pretty soon. Maybe drive down to Lake George and go through with the job hunting, get to an agency or something. He was low on money, and if he didn't find a job within the next couple of weeks, he would run the risk of eviction. Which wasn't all that negative a risk, he thought, considering the way things were in this town. Only he still did not know where else he could go. And maybe, at the core, Bloodstone was Everyplace: no matter where he might drift to, what he might find, it would be the same for him there as it was here. Thomas Wolfe: *You are your world*. And up yours, Mr. Wolfe. Blow it out your ass, Mr. Agee.

He wished Valerie would come back. He wished he would never see her again. He wished that he could make love to her for the rest of his life. He wished that she had never come to Bloodstone. He wanted what she had done to him, and he could not bear what it was doing, because *still* he could feel her against him in the night, *captive* as he touched the softness of her breasts, *the* sudden gentleness in him as he made the *old wild* motions mounted atop her like a *king*. . . .

"Bullshit," he said aloud. "It's all bullshit."

SMITH

There were some things bothering Smith about the attack on Florence Cross: little inconsistencies, deviations in the modus operandi of the first four slayings.

They had started to bother him in the substation last night, after he had come back from the Cross house and started to type up his initial report, and they continued to bother him until he finally got off to sleep much later, near dawn. The major thing was the fact that the assailant had *failed* this time, and there were two corollaries to that: the fact that he had run away almost immediately, and the fact that a bloodlusting maniac with a knife ought to have been able to deal with Florence Cross, a small middle-aged woman taken by what she claimed was complete surprise, in the forty yards between the woodshed and the rear door of the house.

If the assailant was that slow, that inept, that brutally direct, that quick to flee, why hadn't any of the other victims escaped, or at least escaped long enough to sound an alert? And why, after four attacks on women out alone at night, would he have decided to go after one at her home? Then, too, Florence's account of what happened was full of contradictions, such as the one about the size of the knife. Shock, maybe, but he had the feeling something else was involved, that she was lying, holding back information.

Smith could see two possible explanations. One was that the inconsistencies and contradictions meant nothing, proved nothing, except that the case *was* entropic—one gigantic inconsistency from the beginning. But he refused to accept that interpretation; he would not give in to that.

The other explanation was that the man who had attacked Florence Cross was not the same man who had butchered the previous four women. A *second* potential murderer. Lunatic violence had a way, Smith knew, of awakening repressed psychosis in other individuals, giving them just enough impetus to push them over the edge into savage acts of their own.

The prospect of that was just as appalling to him because it complicated matters, presented a possible, wholly new case—one which would take time away from his investigation into the mass killings. But he had no choice except to follow up on the possibility, confirm it or deny it.

The question, of course, was who? Who might want Florence Cross dead? Her son, Jack? He was a little strange, that was true, but through his own relationship with Plummer, Smith had known Florence and Jack for a number of years, had seen the boy on an occasional basis since puberty, and it was his judgment that Cross was harmless. Still, the two of them had never seemed to get along that well, and there might be hatreds hidden beneath the surface which could have exploded into violence. But Cross had been at the newspaper office at the time of the attack, had in fact been the only person Florence wanted to have with her afterward.

Plummer? Well, Plummer was his closest friend—although he didn't really *know* the man, what went on inside him. Only Plummer, too, had been at the *Sentinel* at the time of the attack. . . .

Smith went to the Cross house again early Thursday morning and spent another hour interrogating Florence. The deeper he probed with her, the more personal and intense his questions, the more nervous and upset she became. She was concealing some knowledge, all right, he was certain of it now. Could it be that she had, after all, recognized her assailant? Or if not that, that she had a suspicion as to who it might be and was keeping it to herself for some foolish reason of her own? Whatever it was, he could not drag it out of her.

So the people he wanted to see next were Plummer and Jack Cross. Maybe neither of them was a suspect, but they might know something which would help to clear up matters.

Smith drove to Plummer's house, and found it deserted. He went from there to the *Sentinel* building.

The newsroom, he saw as he entered, was empty except for Marjean Goodie, who sat typing at her desk. When Smith approached, she took her fingers off the keys at once and looked at him. In spite of who he was, her expression appeared to be guarded, diffident. Everyone in Bloodstone was guarded and diffident, now, to the point of paranoia. They didn't trust *any* outsiders, and they didn't trust themselves; they avoided all contact, passed one another on the street without word or glance (he had noticed that the past couple of days), locked their doors and drew their blinds and shut themselves away physically and mentally. Fear did that to you, Smith thought. It robbed you of personality, turned you into a colorless segment of a singular mass. Specious defense mechanism: if you made yourself faceless, nothing could happen to you because you couldn't be seen by the thing or things you feared.

Tell that to Ferrara, he thought. Ferrara would love that.

"May I help you, Lieutenant Smith?" Marjean asked.
"Is Plummer in?"
"No, he hasn't been here at all today."
"Do you know where Jack Cross is?"
"No. He hasn't been in either. I guess he must feel awful about what happened last night. Wasn't that an awful thing? I don't know what I'm doing working here alone this morning; if I'd known nobody would be in, I

wouldn't have come. But I'm going to the town meeting and then I'm going straight home and stay there. Don't you think that's the wisest thing to do, Lieutenant?"

"Yes," he said. He could feel his stomach burbling, and a chattering around the edges; but he was not breaking wind anymore, and he knew that the sounds of his distress were quiet. "Do you have any idea where Plummer might be?"

"Maybe home. Have you tried his house?"

"He's not there."

"Well, I guess he could be with Mrs. Cross."

"I've been to her place, too," Smith said. "He'd left a while before I arrived."

"I just don't know, then. But . . . well, I might have an idea where Jack is, after all. Paula Eaton called just after I came in at eight, asking for him. He could be with her someplace."

"Paula Eaton," Smith said. "She's his girlfriend?"

"Actually I think they're sort of unofficially engaged. I mean, there hasn't been any announcement or anything, and Jack won't talk about it. I guess they're also. . . ."

She stopped. The way things were in Bloodstone now, she was reluctant to share confidences with anyone, but Smith knew from past contact that she was a gossip—one of those drab little people who feed vampirically on the actions and emotions of others, because there is nothing in their own lives to sustain them.

He said, "Yes, Marjean?"

Need won out over reluctance, as it almost always would. "I guess they're also *lovers*," she said. "There are people who claim to have seen him leaving her house early in the morning, like he's spent the night, you know?" She flushed slightly. "I never thought of Paula as being that kind of girl, but then Jack is sort of good-looking in a boyish way and we've all got biological needs, haven't we?"

Smith nodded. Then, making his voice casual: "Do you suppose Mrs. Cross has any other male friends besides Plummer?"

"Mrs. Cross? Oh no. You know yourself how close she and Plummer are. I mean, you're good friends. . . ."

"Is there anyone you know of who might have a grudge against her? Might have reason to strongly dislike her?"

"No. No one." Marjean frowned. "Why are you asking all these questions, Lieutenant? Does it have something to do with the attack last night?"

"My job is to ask questions," he said, and smiled at her. She had told him all she knew, he decided, and if he pressed it anymore, she was liable to figure out what he was leading into, and then it would be all over town. "May I use one of your phones?"

"Oh sure, of course."

Smith got Cross' number from her and dialed it, and there was no answer. Then he looked up Paula Eaton's number and dialed that: no answer. He made a mental note of Paula's address—he would see her at her house or at the town meeting if she was there—and then thanked Marjean for her help. He went out quickly to where he had parked his car in front.

The wind coming off the lake was cold, tinged with the breath of winter, and he tugged the collar of his coat tight around his neck. There had been rain on and off during the night and early morning, and while it had been hours since the last precipitation, the skies were heavily threatening. Dock Street was nearly empty, as was Main a block to the west, and the buildings had a forlorn, aged look, like rows of old men sitting alone with dull and distorted memories.

The pain started when Smith reached the driver's door of his car.

It bloomed in the unmerry chatter of his stomach, small and warm at first, then gathering intensity, then stabilizing for a moment. He straightened up and pressed his left hand hard against the spot, just below his breastbone. No, he thought—and it began to spread again, growing hotter, and just as he had three days ago, on Monday, he imagined an implosion, the ulcer perforating, blood swirling to fill the spaces around organs. The image brought terror, and he put out a hand to the cold metal hood of the car, leaning against it, holding himself while the pain magnified, stabbed and burned, stabbing, burning—

He went to his knees, doubled over, unable to breathe.

Tears squeezed out of his eyes. Knives, guns, maniacs: you expected those risks when you were a police officer, you could live with them, and if it had to be, you could die by them. But not an ulcer, not internal destruction; that was absurdity, farce. *Here lies Daniel Smith: died of a perforated ulcer while engaged in the performance of his duty. Requiescat in pace.* Oh my God. . . .

Help me! he shouted mutely. Help me!

And the pain began to ebb.

He felt it sliding back, gentling, burning becoming warmth becoming burbling coolness—all as rapidly as it had come on. He could breathe again. The wind blew chill against his face, and he shivered and opened his eyes and realized he was kneeling on the street, struggled up to brace his body on the car. Sweat soaked him, drying like paste in the cold.

Across the street a man and a woman stood watching him with dull, empty eyes. Down toward Main, in front of a boarded-up antique shop, a teenager slouched against a parking meter. What's the matter with you? Smith thought. Why didn't you come to help me? What kind of people *are* you?

KELLER

The substance on the tissue Keller had found the night before was nasal mucus.

"Snot?" he said. "Are you telling me it's *snot?*"

The chemist in Lake George, to whom he had taken the tissue early that Thursday morning, was affronted. "The term is nasal mucus," he said primly. "And yes, that's what I'm telling you. If you doubt me, have it analyzed somewhere else. Frankly, I don't know why you brought it here in the first place; there are state forensic people, after all."

"This is a private matter," Keller said. Then: "I was sure it was something else."

"Is that so? What did you think it was?"

"Semen."

"I could have told you it wasn't that the minute you brought the tissue in," the chemist said. "Hell, man, it had a greenish tinge. Have you ever heard of greenish semen?"

He made a chuckling noise. "Of course, now, maybe one of those little green men from outer space we're always hearing about. . . ."

Stupid bastard, Keller thought. "Listen," he said impatiently, "what about that greenish tinge? What does it mean?"

The chemist didn't like the fact that his joke had gone unappreciated; his mouth turned prim again. "It means that the individual who used the tissue has a sinus problem, probably a chronic low-grade infection. Heavy congestion of discolored mucus in the sinus passages always indicates infection."

"That's all?"

"One more thing: the individual is a smoker."

"How do you know that?"

"Traces of tobacco tars. It's all in the report. Who should I send the bill to?"

Keller caught up the manila envelope containing the tissue and the report. "I'll pay you out of pocket," he said.

The chemist shrugged. "Twenty dollars."

"How much?"

"You requested laboratory tests and evaluation. Twenty dollars is the standard—"

"All right," Keller said, "all right." He gave the chemist two tens from his wallet and went out without saying anything else. Stupid bastard.

But on the drive back to Bloodstone, he concluded that the information might have been worth twenty dollars after all. Okay, the substance on the tissue was snot, which told him that the Ripper had blown his goddamn nose and dropped the tissue in those rocks either before or after the attack on Florence Cross. The Ripper's snot, the Ripper's tissue. And if the chemist knew what he was talking about, the Ripper had a chronic sinus condition and smoked cigarettes or some other form of tobacco.

Steven Hook had been snuffling and blowing his nose Sunday night at the Terra Alta Motel.

Hook again.

Keller had asked Plummer and a few others about Hook since Monday, but they hadn't been able to tell him any more than Florence Cross had. No one seemed to know much about him. Well, he *could* be the Ripper, all right, and if he was, Keller had the inside track because Smith and the rest of the state police didn't suspect him at all. He would have to have a talk with Hook today, and he would maybe have to search Hook's cottage, and he would have to find out more about his background, and he would definitely have to keep an eye on him. One way or the other, he would find it out before much longer.

The bloodhound is on the scent, he thought, and his lips pulled in a thin, little smile. Alex Keller, the Bloodhound of Bloodstone, is on the scent of the bloody bloodspiller and may even have to spill *his* blood when he finds him. . . .

VALERIE

It was a quarter of twelve when Valerie and Ferrara arrived at Essex Union. The parking lot was already filled, and grim-faced people filed up the steps to the gymnasium wing in groups of two and three.

The gym was small and cramped, with roll-back bleacher seats; for the town meeting, however, they were using folding chairs set in even rows across the hardwood floor. At the upper end was a high stage—the gym doubled as an auditorium for a variety of school and community functions, Valerie remembered—and on the stage were two long tables and more folding chairs, a small podium with a microphone, and two men struggling to remove a heavy piece of prop scenery. Basketball standards hung from the ceiling, one of which was suspended directly in front of the stage, cranked up out of the way; the hoop, the net, reminded her of a gallows.

The building was jammed with townspeople, press people, television equipment. Valerie wondered vaguely why the meeting had been opened to the press, allowed to become a kind of public spectacular, when the town so obviously and so vehemently hated the attention of the outside world. Well, that was Bloodstone for you, she thought. No consistency of action or reaction, and at the core, ultimately self-destructive.

She scanned the crowd for Steven Hook, but there was no sign of him. She had called him an hour earlier, to tell him about the meeting, and he'd said he might as well attend. Still, she would not be surprised if he stayed away. She had felt like staying away herself; only that would have been an admission of weakness, and a shirking of professional obligation besides. And while being a part of the school again, becoming one with the Bloodstone masses again, was as depressing as she had expected it to be, she was finding that she could deal with it simply by having approached it in stages.

As she allowed Ferrara to lead the way to two empty chairs on the far right, she saw Plummer and Alex Keller and Daniel Smith mount the steps to the stage. She also saw Jack Cross standing alone against the bleachers near the front, busily writing in a notebook. An unlit cigarette clung to one corner of his mouth, and he was wearing a hat pulled over his forehead; there was nothing in the band, but she imagined that if he had had a press card, it would be prominently displayed there. There but for the grace of God, she thought wryly, goes Valerie R. Broome, product of the same environment.

Ferrara had been in a gregarious mood all morning, expounding at great length, saying things like: "The Ripper is entering an entirely new phase now, a sea change of personality, as it were, with a felt role reversal; the next thing he might do is to turn himself in." But when they were seated, he became quiet and thoughtful; his eyes moved restlessly about the gym. Finally, he said to her that he had better use the rest room before the meeting began and excused himself and hurried away.

She might have expected a psychiatrist to come up with a better excuse than that, but then, he was really an unimaginative little man. Where he was going, of course, was to talk to reporters, probably one of the television people. And the hell with him. She no longer cared what he did or didn't do; it had been a mistake to bring him to Bloodstone with her in the first place.

She tried to concentrate on the meeting. No good. She thought of Hook, and that was much more pleasant—or it was until the level of thinking reached questions like *what did he mean to her?* and *what effect did last night have on her?* and *where if anywhere would their relationship go now?* Then her mind rebelled and closed. She seemed to have reached a state where she was walled off not only from the meeting but from her own psyche.

At length a heavyset man made his way to the podium —the head of the town council, she supposed—and began to pound for order. Valerie sat up straighter in her chair. Through the ragged amplification of the microphone, the blows on wood sounded instead as though they were striking human flesh.

HOOK

The meeting had already begun when Hook came in. He hadn't wanted to come at all, but it was better than sitting alone in his cottage, better too than driving down to Lake George to look for a meaningless job; and Valerie would be there. He stood against the wall to one side of the entrance doors, looking for her, and finally located her sitting on the far right: purple scarf tied around her hair, face small and white and smooth in quarter profile. He thought about going over there, but all the chairs around her were occupied; he stayed where he was.

From the podium a man Hook had seen around Bloodstone, but whose name he didn't know, was saying that everyone should remain calm, that matters were in competent hands, that the presence of the state police representatives at this meeting showed the responsiveness and dedication of their public officials. "We had hoped that Governor Carey, or at least our state assemblyman, could be here as well," he said, "but owing to prior commitments in Albany they were simply unable to attend. However, both have sent their assurances that they will see to it everything humanly possible is done to—"

"We want results, not a lot of windblown assurances!" a man shouted from the floor, and there were mutterings of agreement and a smattering of applause.

The podium speaker appeared to flush slightly. He exhorted everyone again to remain calm and then called on

Lieutenant Smith "to tell us exactly how the investigation is progressing."

Hook stared at the shifting bodies in the chairs, at the backs of heads—faceless heads. Dimly, he remembered on Monday telling Valerie and the psychiatrist, Ferrara, that while everybody and everything in Bloodstone had once been outside him, no real personal awareness, he had finally realized after finding the body of Linda Simmons that there were *people* involved, very personal issues. Only now that he was here among a concentration of those people, he felt it all slide outside him again. Defense mechanism, maybe, but none of it seemed to have any reality, any immediacy. In fact, with all the television equipment and media people around, it was like watching a TV show—watching it while it was being filmed, so that you were there and yet not taking part in any real sense.

He leaned heavily against the wall. Length and width, no depth, he thought. Two dimensions: gray on gray.

KELLER

Sitting at a corner of the stage, Keller realized bitterly that his presence was only going to be a token one. They probably wouldn't even ask him how *his* investigation was progressing; they just didn't have enough faith in their own constable to expect that he could do anything about the Ripper that the state police weren't already doing. Maybe they didn't think he cared, when the truth was, he cared too much. He had an impulse to stand up and shout it to them: *I care too much! And that's why Alex Keller, no one else, is going to put an end to all this.*

But doing that would be a relinquishing of control, and he could not allow that to happen again. He would have to keep it all inside him, then, as he always had, and if no one ever really understood the truth, as least *he* would know it. The price of feeling is pain. . . .

At the podium Smith was giving a technical summation of his investigation thus far, speaking calmly and clearly into the microphone, but Keller did not listen. He noticed, now, that Steven Hook had come in and was standing at the back of the gym. He let his attention focus on Hook. The manila envelope containing the Ripper's tissue and the Ripper's snot felt warm in one pocket of his uniform jacket. In the other pocket, the jail key felt warmer still.

SMITH

Even under the echo of his amplified voice and the stirrings and murmurs of the assembled people, Smith could hear the steady rumbling in his stomach. He felt himself wanting, needing, to fart, and desperately held it back; he was certain that if he allowed it to come out, it would be enormously loud and impossibly vile, and there would be a moment of stunned silence and then wild, mindless laughter. He could not stand that; now above everything else, he could not stand being laughed at.

"And so we *are* making progress," he was saying, "please believe that. But until we make an arrest, we need your full cooperation if there are to be no more homicides. We have ten units on full-time patrol in this area, but you must realize that they cannot begin to cover every inch of ground; they can't be everywhere at once. Each and every one of you must remain indoors after dark. Do not go out unless it is absolutely necessary, and then only in the company of others. Secure your houses and don't open your doors to anyone until you're sure of who it is. If you see or hear anything of a suspicious nature, notify us immediately—"

"We've heard all this before," a voice said from one of the front rows. "And we're cooperating the best we can. But how long can we live this way? That's what we want to know: how long are we supposed to live in fear before you get the Ripper?"

There were angry shouts, a sudden growing undercurrent of hostility.

"Listen," Smith said, "please listen—"

"Do you or don't you have a suspect?" somebody asked.

"We do not have a suspect at this time. However—"

"Just what leads *do* you have?"

"We have an established modus operandi—"

"That doesn't mean a thing!" a man yelled. "All that

talk about forensic examinations and laboratory analysis . . . none of it means anything! You don't have any leads at all, do you? You're no closer to catching the Ripper now than you were at the beginning!"

People began to come up onto their feet, some of them shouting. And Smith knew that he had lost control of the situation, that the meeting was about to erupt into chaos. The media people knew it, too. He could see them pressing forward eagerly, taking notes, moving hand-held cameras over the crowd. He tried to think of something to say to restore order, but there was nothing, nothing, and he only stood there impotently, holding back the thunderous fart that had formed in his rectum, thinking that the man who had just yelled was right because he wasn't, he just *wasn't*, any closer to finding the assailant than he had been at the beginning.

CROSS

Cross wrote rapidly in his notebook, in the private shorthand he had developed in college. Everyone was standing now, creating a babble of noise that bounced and rolled off the high walls of the gym; Cross could feel the floor shake. This was turning into a real event, he thought; maybe he would devote an entire chapter to it. The people rising up against the lies and false promises of authority . . . no, that sounded like Commie stuff, he would have to find another way of putting it. But they had plenty of right to be angry, he was angry himself; after what had almost happened to Florence last night, he knew exactly what they were feeling.

Who is going to get the Ripper, if not the state police? he wrote. *Is anyone going to get him? Or will he, like that other Ripper of long ago, like the Prince of Darkness he is, go on and on unpunished?*

A woman shouted, "What we ought to have here is martial law!"

Frank Wilson, the father of the Ripper's second victim, said, "That's right! Mobilize the National Guard, seal off the town, and search every piece of property and every car going in or out. That's the only way that beast is ever going to be caught!"

A desperate cry for martial law. Might be the answer . . . but is the Ripper too cunning even for the National Guard?

Up onstage Smith was saying that that was impossible. You couldn't declare martial law for something like this, no matter how terrifying it was to the people of Bloodstone; there were too many risks of repression and loss of individual liberties. And even if that weren't the case, the chances were at best remote that the National Guard would be able to accomplish anything more than trained investigators.

What does the Ripper care of repression and loss of individual liberties?

Smith gripped the edges of the podium. "You're not thinking rationally, any of you," he said into the microphone. "I tell you, we can handle things, we are handling them. All we need is a little more time—"

"You've had three months and four women!" somebody shouted. "How much time and how many more women do you need!"

"We're not miracle workers," Smith said. His face, Cross noticed, looked from this distance to be the color and shape of an apple. A Red Delicious. He wrote that down. "We can only do so much with the evidence at hand, it's a slow and methodical process. But we're getting closer to finding out who the assailant is—"

"You'd better get him damned soon!" Tony Manders bellowed. "Because if you don't, and if you don't call in the National Guard, we'll have to do something about it ourselves!"

Potential vigilante action. Draw parallel with Old West?

"Let me warn you." Smith said, "if any of you takes the law into his own hands, he's liable for arrest and prosecution like any common criminal—"

"So now you're calling *us* common criminals!"

"I didn't say that. For God's sake, will you listen—"

"No! We want action, results, no more words!"

Cries of agreement; the building was becoming chaotic. Smith threw up his hands in a frustrated, angry gesture and turned away from the podium. A woman screamed at him that he was a fascist, and Cross thought that was ridiculous; he knew what a fascist was, or was pretty sure he knew what a fascist was. Better double-check it. Plummer and old Fred Jordan, the head of the town council, took over the podium and tried to get everyone calmed down. But nobody listened to them; nobody was listening to anyone but himself.

Which was another pretty good observation, Cross decided, and put it down in his notebook.

HOOK

Out of the shouting, milling people, Valerie emerged and pushed her way quickly toward the entrance doors. Hook motioned to her, and she saw him and came to him, touched his hand; she looked very glad to see him. "I can't stand any more of this," she said. "It's like watching a lynch mob get started."

"I know," Hook said. "Christ, I know."

They went out into the gym's small front lobby. But before they reached the outer doors, Hook heard footsteps hurrying after them—and a moment later Keller fell into step beside him and caught his arm, saying, "Just a minute. I want a few words with you, Hook."

The three of them stopped. Seen this close, Keller's eyes seemed to have a film over them, but Hook was not sure whether it concealed or showed feeling. The constable's mouth was set authoritatively, and his whole body appeared tense.

Frowning, Hook said, "What about?"

"Not here." Keller glanced at Valerie. "Where we've got some privacy."

Hook watched her eyes move between Keller and himself. She seemed about to say something to the constable, then shrugged. "I'll wait for you outside, Steven," she said to him. "In the parking lot."

"All right."

Valerie went to the doors, looked once more at him over her shoulder, and walked out.

Keller said, "The two of you are pretty friendly."

Hook didn't like the tone of his voice. He wanted to say *What business is it of yours?* but instead he said, "What is it you want?"

"Alone. Alone, Hook."

Keller nudged him with his body, the side away from his holstered gun, and turned him back the other way. They passed the gym entrance, and the people inside were still eddying together and shouting; the stage was now empty.

"All a lot of crap, don't you think?" Keller said. "We don't need the National Guard or any damn-fool vigilantes to get the Ripper, do we?"

"I don't know," Hook said.

"Well we don't. We don't even need the state police."

Hook shook his head and followed Keller through a door in the opposite wall, down a short corridor and into a deserted locker-room area. They halted near a glass-windowed cubicle that would belong to an athletic instructor.

"Well?" Hook said then.

Keller gave him a long, penetrating look, eyes motionless. The scrutiny made Hook feel uncomfortable; he shuffled his feet slightly, and because his sinuses were acting up again, began snuffling. "Well?" he said again.

Keller said in a sly way, "Better blow your nose."

"What?"

"Your nose is full of snot. Better blow it."

Hook looked at him blankly.

"I said blow your goddamned nose!"

"Christ," Hook said, but he took a tissue from his coat pocket and blew into it.

"White," Keller said. His eyes glittered. "All right, give it to me."

"What?"

"The tissue. Give it to me."

Hook felt an expanding sensation of unreality. Confused, he extended the tissue. Keller took it out of his hand, opened it carefully, and squinted at the blob of mucus. "Greenish tinge," he said. "I thought so, I knew it."

"What are you talking about?"

"Snot, Hook. I'm talking about snot."

"Snot? For God's sake—"

Keller took a small manila envelope from his jacket pocket, extracted from it a second white tissue. He held the two tissues up in front of Hook's face. "Both yours," he said. "Your tissues and your snot."

I don't believe this, he thought. I don't believe we're standing here talking about snot and tissues, what do snot and tissues have to do with *anything?*

"I found this one near the lake last night," Keller said. "At the foot of the promontory below the Cross house. You dropped it there, Hook."

And suddenly, Hook began to understand. He felt his mouth working, but only as an irritant on the panel of his face; no words came out.

"The Ripper uses tissues to clean off his knife," Keller said. "But when he doesn't use them for that, he might use them to blow his nose. Isn't that right, Hook?"

"Jesus." Hook made an involuntary step backward. "Jesus, you can't think . . . you can't suspect *me* of being the—" He could not say it. His mouth caught on the *R,* and the rest of it would not come out.

"The tissue hadn't been there long," Keller said. "Dropped sometime last night, the way I figure it."

"I was home all last night." He was sweating now, and a thin horror had begun clipping, clipping at his brain like sharp little shears. *He thinks I'm the Ripper.* "I didn't attack Florence Cross; I couldn't have done a thing like that. I was *home* last night."

"Can you prove that?"

"Yes! Valerie was with me, Valerie Broome. The girl I was just—"

"I know who Valerie Broome is." Keller's mouth had gotten tight. "What were the two of you doing?"

"Talking. Just talking."

"Screwing?"

"Talking, what difference does it make? I was home, I couldn't be the"—he got it out this time—"the Ripper. . . ."

Keller moved in on him, tapped the tissues against Hook's chest. "This is your tissue and your snot. You can't deny that."

He put a hand to his mouth, wiped away saliva. "All right, maybe it is, I do a lot of walking near my place, I could have dropped it anytime. . . ."

"I told you, it had to have been dropped sometime yesterday."

"Well maybe I was walking over that way yesterday afternoon, before Valerie came over."

"Maybe?"

"I was out yesterday afternoon, I think it was over by the promontory. I don't remember exactly."

"You don't remember what you did yesterday? Come on, Hook, that's pretty hard to believe."

"I can't help it, it's the truth. I've got a lot of things on my mind, a lot of problems. . . ."

"You bet your ass you have," Keller said.

Hook could smell the constable's breath: sour, fetid, as though he hadn't brushed his teeth in a month. Teeth, snot, tissue, Ripper. "Listen," he said, "listen, Keller, lots of people use tissues, just because I use them doesn't mean I'm guilty of anything. I found one of the victims, don't forget that. I found her and I hailed you."

"Just the kind of clever thing the Ripper might do," Keller said.

"I'm not the Ripper. Ask Valerie about last night. She's waiting out in the parking lot, she'll tell you."

Keller stared at him in that penetrating way. Hook held the eyes as long as he could, but the film had come over them again, and it was like matching stares with a dead man. He averted his face, fumbled a cigarette into his mouth, and struck a match with hands that quivered. Finally he looked back and said, desperately now, "I'm not the Ripper!"

Keller smiled.

SMITH

Smith left the gymnasium quickly and quietly, by the fire exit behind the stage. He could not deal with these people any longer or with the reporters who would have been waiting for him if he had tried to go out the front way. His stomach was still churning, but now in the familiar dull, sour way. Alone in the confines of his car, he

finally released the fart that he had been holding back—
and it came out small and painful and odorless. All that
discomfort for nothing. *All* of it for nothing.

Push ahead, he thought grimly. Get right back to work.
Cross and Plummer were still here at the school, but he
remembered that he had not seen Paula Eaton anywhere
in the crowd; he had met her a couple of times, briefly,
in the company of Jack Cross, and he knew her by sight.
He dredged up the mental note he had made of her
address and drove there.

She was home. She hadn't been able to bring herself to
attend the meeting, she said; she wasn't feeling very good.
Her body was stiff against the doorsill, and her face was
impassive, vaguely vacuous. She did not invite him in,
although neither did she give him the impression that she
would refuse him entrance if he requested it. She didn't
seem to care one way or the other.

After two minutes with her, Smith knew that she had
nothing enlightening to tell him. She answered his questions about Florence Cross with monosyllables, a general
air of preoccupation, and no apparent interest in why he
was asking them. The only times a spark of life showed
in her eyes was when he mentioned Jack Cross' name.
Unlike Marjean Goodie, Paula seemed interested in no
one else's private life except her own and its intersection
with Cross'. And if Florence had interfered in their relationship, it apparently hadn't been strongly enough to
foster any animosity in the Eaton woman; even the attack
on Florence hadn't affected Paula, except perhaps in terms
of the effect it had had on Cross.

Smith thanked her and said he was sorry to have bothered her, and she nodded in that abstracted way and
immediately retreated into the house. He went back to
his car. Now what? Locate Plummer and Cross, and if
they couldn't or wouldn't tell him anything either, then
another session with Florence. The only way to get the
truth out of her was to keep hammering at her; eventually
she—

The police radio under the dash crackled, and the voice
of the Bloodstone dispatcher requested acknowledgment
from Unit A.

Smith caught up the hand microphone and touched the Send button. "Unit A," he said. "What is it, dispatch?"

"We've just had a call from Captain Jacobsen in Albany," the dispatcher said. "He wants to see you immediately, sir."

"Where? In Albany?"

"Affirmative."

"What for?"

"Well, he apparently received word about the town meeting, I'm not sure just how. He seemed pretty upset."

"Shit," Smith said and then realized that he had automatically depressed the Send button and the word had gone out over the air. That made him even angrier. "All right, dispatch, put in a call that I'm on my way. Ten-four."

He slammed the microphone back onto its sprocket. Goddamn it! Everything and everybody continually seemed to be working against him: not a single clue in four psychopathic homicides, an attack on Florence Cross that probably hadn't been perpetrated by the mass assailant, a chaotic town meeting that made him out to be a bumbling clown, and now a pointless conference in Albany a hundred miles and two hours away. He could, would, overcome all of these obstacles with patience and absolute confidence in the ordered universe—but how long would it take? And how many more obstacles would there be before methodology finally took him to the truth?

VALERIE

Valerie waited in the school parking lot, standing alongside her rental car and wondering what Keller had wanted with Steven, why they were taking so long in there. Keller's eyes had been a little strange, filmy, and she hadn't liked the way he looked at Steven. Still, there was no point in worrying or trying to speculate about it. She would find out soon enough.

Townspeople had begun to flow out of the gym, still talking loudly and making angry gestures to each other. There was no sign of Ferrara in the outflux, and she supposed that he was still talking to reporters and television people. If he didn't put in an appearance by the time she was ready to leave, he could find his own way back to the Homelite. In fact, maybe she would let him find his own way back to the Homelite even if he did put in an appearance. . . .

Uh-oh, she thought then, because Jack Cross had appeared on the steps and was looking in her direction. And sure enough, here he came, walking toward her in that awkward stride of his. She had nowhere to go to evade him, except into the car and lock the doors, which was foolish, so she stood stolidly and waited and hoped that Steven would come out of the gym immediately.

But he didn't, and Cross stopped in front of her and pushed his hat back on his forehead, pushed his glasses up on his nose, and said, "Hi, Valerie. That was some meeting, wasn't it?"

"Some meeting," she said.

"I wasn't too surprised to find out the state police don't have any real leads. I guess none of us were. I mean, if they did have any real leads, they'd have arrested the Ripper by now, wouldn't they?"

"I imagine they would."

"What I think, and I hope I'm wrong but maybe I'm not—nobody is going to run the Ripper down. Not the state police or vigilante groups or anybody else. He's just going to go on and on."

That possibility had crossed Valerie's mind too, but she did not want to dwell on it with him—or with anybody else, for that matter. She said, "That's not a very pleasant prospect."

"No, it isn't," Cross said seriously. "I'm going to write a section on the idea in *The Ripper of Bloodstone,* my book. If it turns out he isn't caught, after about a year or so, then I'll use that section as the final chapter."

"I'm sure it will be very profound."

"I think it will. It's a good book."

"So you told me."

Cross hesitated, and his eyes flicked behind his glasses. He seemed to be gathering himself toward something. At length he drew himself up and said, "Say, Valerie, I, uh, I was wondering if you'd like to have a cup of coffee or something with me at tht café? We, uh, could talk some more about the case, maybe exchange some ideas? I've got a few that might help you with your article."

God, she thought, he's asking me for a date. "I'm sure you do," she said. "But I'm afraid I can't. I'm waiting for someone."

"Oh? Who?"

"A friend."

"Dr. Ferrara?"

"A friend," she said.

"Oh." He colored slightly, embarrassed and a little hurt. But Valerie remembered the way Paula Eaton had clung to him on Saturday night and how he had treated Paula, and she had no sympathy for him. He was really a pretty pathetic case. "Well, maybe some other time. I guess I'll go on home then and get to work on the book." He backed away. "It's a good book," he said again, and turned and hurried off through the lot.

Valerie shook her head and then promptly forgot about him. She began to pace back and forth restlessly. Where was Steven? Another five minutes passed, and finally she saw him emerge and come down the steps, Keller at his side. She frowned a little; then, as they approached, the frown deepened. She could see that there were little blotches of sweat on parts of Steven's face, something she had never seen on anyone else. You either sweated or you didn't, that was metabolism, but he seemed damp on his right cheek, dry on one temple, damp on the other temple—

Keller said without preamble, "Miss Broome, I want the answer to one question. Where were you last night around nine o'clock?"

She kept staring at Hook. He looked almost as badly upset as he had been on Monday, and his eyes were imploring.

She said, "Why?"

"Just answer the question, Miss Broome."

"All right, I was with Steven."

"All evening?"

"Yes, all evening."

"Doing what?"

"I don't think that's any of your business."

"Was he out of your sight for any period of time?"

"No."

"Not even for fifteen or twenty minutes?"

"Not even for five minutes," she said.

"Are you willing to swear to that under oath?"

"Why should I have to swear to it under oath?"

Hook said, "The constable thinks I could be the Ripper."

"What?"

He said it again; his voice sounded shaky.

"My God, that's ridiculous!"

"Is it?" Keller said.

She felt herself becoming very angry. She didn't like Keller or his manner or that filmy look to his eyes. "Do you have anything to back up a wild idea like that?"

"Bits and pieces," Keller said. "Bits and pieces."

"Which means you don't have anything at all, particularly after what I just told you. Now why don't you leave Steven alone? He couldn't be the Ripper and you know it."

Could he? something cool within her asked in an offhand conversational tone. Her journalistic voice. *Are you really that sure? Anyone could be the Ripper, anyone at all. And you know better than to shut off even the remotest possibility until it's completely disproven....*

She saw Steven's face, open and suffering, and hated herself for allowing doubt to enter her mind. "Just leave him alone," she said again, but the words seemed to come out thicker this time, less angry. "Leave us both alone."

"All right," Keller said. "For now." He directed it to her, but he was looking at Hook in a hard, fierce way, as though trying to penetrate the outer shell and examine what lay within.

Then he spun on his heel, in an almost military aboutface, and left them alone in the cold wind.

She tried to think of something to say to Steven, but her mind had gone blank on her. She could not even bring herself to touch him, though she wanted to. He could not be the Ripper, he simply could not. . . .

"I'm sorry, Valerie," he said. "I didn't want to get you

involved, but I had no choice. He really shook me up inside there; he's an obsessive if I ever saw one, and I've never been very good with that type of person."

"I'm glad you involved me," she said. "What got him started on you, anyway?"

"Snot," he said.

"What?"

"Snot." His mouth pulled up at the corners, as if he wanted to laugh, but he made no sound. "I don't want to talk about it right now, okay?"

"Okay. Are you all right?"

"I will be in a little while. Let's go somewhere for coffee and food."

She nodded. "The café?"

"Not in Bloodstone at all. Somewhere else."

"Yes," she said. Anyone could be the Ripper, but not Steven. "I think that might be best for both of us."

"How did I ever get here?" Hook said quietly, but he was asking the question of himself, not her.

THE RIPPER

Time for strife, time for a wife, time for a life. Soon. Soon. Soon. Soon. Soon. Soon.

KELLER

Keller went back to his office at the Municipal Center and put in a call to the Bureau of Criminal Identification in New York City. He gave his name and position to the man who answered and requested a check on Steven Hook. The BCI man said he would get to it when he could and call back.

Keller sat brooding for a while about Hook and Valerie Broome. She was either lying outright, or she had been with him last night and he had slipped away long enough to make the attempt on Florence's life. One or the other. He couldn't understand why she would want to protect Hook. She was laying him, of course, that might have something to do with it; she was from New York City, too, a New York woman no matter where she'd been born, and all of them were a little crazy. Whatever her reasons, he was sure that she was lying. And so was Hook.

To pass the waiting time, Keller swept out the office and the holding cells, took liquid cleaner to the walls and woodwork and furniture polish to the desk and chair. Finally, after two hours, the telephone rang, and it was the BCI man.

"We've got a yellow sheet on one Steven Hook," he said. "Not much: one arrest for drunken and aggravated assault in 1969. Ninety days in the Tombs, two years' probation."

Keller said, "Well now, that's very interesting."

"If you say so," the BCI man said.

"Was that assault against a woman?"

"Nope. Man."

"No other felony arrests involving women?"

"Like I said, just the one."

Keller put the phone down. Not much in itself, maybe, but it was one more bit, one more piece in the overall picture he was constructing of Hook. The more bits and pieces he found, the clearer that picture became. Pretty soon now, it might become clear enough to show conclusively that Hook and the Ripper were one.

HOOK

It wasn't working between them.

Hook and Valerie had gone from the Essex Union to Pottersville and had spent two hours over coffee and tasteless sandwiches. Then they had come back to Bloodstone to pick up his Dodge, and he'd suggested they go to his cottage, but Valerie had turned that around without actually saying no and they ended up instead in her room at the Homelite, sitting apart and talking over more coffee and too many cigarettes. And it just wasn't working between them.

She had tried too hard at first to recapture the mood of last night, and he in turn had been unable to shake the depression Keller had brought to him and had grown more and more reticent. Their conversation had degenerated until, now, it was desultory and a little strained. They had not talked about Keller or about the Ripper, and yet those subjects seemed to hang in the air between them, suddenly glistening and poisonous. He knew what it was, after a while, and she knew it too. He kept waiting for her to put voice to it, maybe get rid of it that way, but she didn't, and it seemed she wouldn't.

Hook got up from his chair under the humming central heating unit and went over to where she was sitting on one of the twin beds. He put a hand on her neck, as he had last night, and leaned down and drew her toward him. She came against him willingly enough, her lips open when they touched his, but his hand, still on her neck, felt a tightness, a holding back. He broke the kiss abruptly, straightened, and moved away.

In a dull, heavy voice he said, "Let's get it out into the open, Valerie. You think it's possible, even in the smallest way, that I might be the Ripper after all."

She looked at him with a shocked expression. But she said nothing.

"You know I'm not," he said, "but some part of you is afraid that I could be."

"No, Steven—"

"Yes." He moved back to the bed and stood looking down at her. She returned his gaze, her eyes full on his and yet somehow removed. "Yes, that's exactly what it is."

"No," she said again, but there was no force to it. She turned her head to one side. "Oh God," she said.

He picked his coat off the other bed, swung around in the same motion, and walked across to the door. She said his name, and he paused with door open, glanced back to see her standing now, arms straight down at her sides: perfect 1890s portrait, cameo of her face framed in light. Then he stepped outside and shut the door quietly behind him.

Thunderheads, barely perceptible in the new darkness, lay over the lake to the south like piles of filthy laundry. The air had a sharp, metallic odor, very still, not a breath of wind. Hook sat in the Dodge with his hands resting on top of the wheel, staring over at the closed door to her room. It did not open.

He could see the dial of his watch, and it was twenty minutes until six. All right, he thought. Home? Or somewhere else? *Where* else?

At length he started the engine, engaged the gears, and, with no sensation of conscious choice, began driving.

SMITH

Smith got back to Bloodstone at seven o'clock.

The meeting with Captain Jacobsen in Albany had turned out to be more bitterly significant than he'd anticipated. Jacobsen was getting heavy heat from state officials, and the events at the Bloodstone town meeting—which he had learned of through a telephone call from an unidentified county official who had been there—made it certain that he was going to get a lot more heat. The assailant had to be caught and caught fast, he said, and if Smith couldn't get the job done, then maybe he would have to be taken off the investigation and somebody else put on, nothing personal. There hadn't been anything Smith could say in his own behalf; Jacobsen knew there were no leads, knew Smith was doing all he could, but he wasn't about to put his own position in jeopardy by going to bat for him. Smith asked tightly how much time he had, and Jacobsen said a few days, it depended on whether or not there were any more incidents, and then he had gotten out of there with his stomach burning and a thin rage pulsing in his temples.

Shit or get off the pot. Strike three and you're out. Nothing personal—except that it was as personal as it could be now: the assailant or himself.

He drove through the village, and it had the look and feel of a ghost town. All the buildings along Main Street were closed and dark, including Bloodstone Café and Bloodstone Tavern and the Gulf station; streetlamps shone dully on empty sidewalks. Dying town, huddled in the night. Scene of carnage, scene of chaos, scene of frustration. . . .

He went to the substation. Rocca had nothing to tell him, except that all the patrol units were out and reporting at regular intervals. Smith felt tired and hungry, but he couldn't afford to take the time to rest and eat. *A few days, it depends on whether or not there are any more incidents.*

He got back into his car and headed it for Florence Cross' house on the promontory.

KELLER

For the third time Keller rapped on the outer screen door of Hook's darkened cottage, and for the third time there was no response. He reached out and tested the latch: locked. He came down off the steps and went around to the rear and tried the porch door there.

That one was unlocked.

Keller switched on his flashlight, opened the door, and entered the porch. The beam picked up a chaise longue, a round wooden table, a short Formica-topped counter along the lefthand wall. He examined each of these carefully, found nothing. Then he went into the front room, and the light showed him that Hook was a slob on top of everything else: dust and crap everywhere. He searched the furniture, books and what looked like playscripts on a tier of shelves, the fireplace; even shone the flash up the flue, looking in vain for loose bricks.

Into the bedroom then. He opened the closet and rummaged through it, pulled out dresser drawers, got down on his hands and knees and looked under the bed where Hook had probably had sex with Valerie Broome. Nothing. He straightened, stepped into the bathroom, lifted the lid on the toilet tank, and went through the medicine cabinet and linen shelves. Nothing. The kitchen next. Knives in one of the drainboard drawers, but everybody had knives in their kitchen. Nothing special about these, not even particularly sharp; furnished goods. He opened the refrigerator, the freezer compartment, looked under the sink, sifted through flour and sugar containers. Nothing.

No bloodstained clothing, no bloodstained knife, not even a pair of gloves in the entire cottage.

Keller was only mildly disappointed. The Ripper was cunning and clever, and if Hook was the man he was after, it wasn't surprising that he hadn't left anything incriminating here. It sure as hell didn't exonerate him, any more than Valerie Broome had exonerated him at the school earlier.

He wondered again where Hook had gone tonight. Back on the prowl, maybe? The Ripper had failed to get Florence Cross, and that might make him all the more desperate to succeed again and quickly. Would he try Florence a second time? Not likely, especially not with a state trooper on guard at her house. Time to get back on patrol, Keller thought, let instinct guide him. If Hook was somewhere in Bloodstone, he would find him and then he would watch him very closely.

He left the cottage through the rear porch, came around to the front, crossed Hook's yard and Stone Bridge Road to where he had parked the cruiser in heavy shadow. Thunder rumbled in the distance, and as he swung into a U-turn and started back toward U.S. 9, lightning split the sky in a jagged blaze. Thick drops of rain began to spatter against the windshield.

A sudden interesting thought came to him then: I wonder if he gets a hard-on when he kills them? He would have to ask the Ripper about that when he finally put the blocks to him. He would definitely have to ask him about that.

HOOK

He was thirty miles down the Northway from Bloodstone, moving rapidly through a thickening drizzle, before he realized that he wasn't just driving purposelessly. His subconscious mind had all along been taking him to Saratoga.

The insight made him transfer his right foot from accelerator to brake, and the sudden braking caused the Dodge to fishtail slightly on the wet pavement, to jump lanes. Jesus! He got the car under control and, because there was little traffic on the highway, did not come close to harming anyone but himself. Sweating, he reduced his speed to thirty, holding the wheel tightly in both hands.

He couldn't go to Saratoga anymore, he had already

made that decision; he would lose every last cent of his money if he did. So why had he been going there? Self-destruction, maybe that was it: some latent death wish hidden away in a corner of the psyche. . . .

Ahead, an exit loomed in the rain. He took it, then took the overpass there and came back onto the highway north-bound. He increased his speed, sent the car skimming along the wet empty road.

Where am I going? he thought.

CROSS

THE RIPPER OF BLOODSTONE   Cross   add 179
know where I'm going. I have made my final decision, and it
is irrevocable.

I'm going to leave Bloodstone as soon as the Ripper is
caught. Or if he isn't caught, I'm going to leave Bloodstone
in exactly one month to the day.

After I got back home this afternoon, I thought about
things very carefully, because I had put off thinking about
them with all the other things on my mind and the town
meeting, the chapter on which I'm going to write next. The
more I thought about them, the more I realized that this
decision is the right one. I can't marry Paula. She and the
~~little bastard~~ child she contrived to have by me will never
have the chance to stifle my life and my career. After all,
I thought, Clark Kent would never let Lois Lane stifle his
career in a similar situation.

It will take some doing, but with the strength of
my decision behind me I will find a way to put Paula off.
It's just a matter of keeping my poise, keeping her off-
balance with perfect control. Then, when the time is right,
I'll simply pack my clothes and slip out during the night.
Where I've decided to go is New York City. I have a few
dollars in the bank, and I'll find an apartment in
Greenwich Village and do the final draft of this book there,
if I haven't already done it here. No one will ever know
where I've gone. Not Paula or Florence or Plummer. No one.
It will be a clean break, a new start, everything I've
always wanted. ~~Including those girls I've heard about who
like to go down on writers~~

189

THE RIPPER OF BLOODSTONE   Cross   add 180.

There goes the telephone again, but I'm not going to answer it this time either. It's either Florence or Paula, and I'm not quite ready to talk to either of them. I'll have to see Paula later, of course, and maybe I'll even stop by and talk to Florence for a while. I think I can face her now, in light of my decision, and keeping her happy and off my back is important too until the right time comes for me to leave for New York City, south on the Northway.

When I meet a new girl I won't let her start interfering with my life and my career, that's for sure. I've had enough with Florence and Paula. And Valerie Broome, too, who had absolutely no right to treat me like I had leprosy or something when I asked her to have a cup of coffee with me today, which was something I wouldn't have done if I wasn't so attracted to her, she's really a very exciting woman. ~~I can't help wondering who she was waiting for today, who her friend is and if she's going to bed~~

I should put an end to this and get on with the section on the town meeting, after which I'll do the section on my new theory that nobody is going to get the Ripper at all. But I don't feel like doing those yet. I think what I'll do right now is to go out and have a few beers at the tavern. I haven't had anything to do with the out-of-town reporters, but now that I think about it it's probably a good idea to get to know them, especially the ones from New York because they can give me some hints about getting along in Manhattan. After that, I'll go to Paula and

VALERIE

She got into her nightgown and called the desk and told the night manager that she wanted no calls under any circumstances; then she checked to make sure the door was secured, shut off the lights, and got into one of the twin beds. She lay there for a long time, waiting for sleep and listening to the rain against the windows and the whine of the central heating unit.

After a while she stopped thinking of Steven, or at least Steven and sleep blended, and she passed into darkness.

If she had hurt him—this was her only consolation—she had hurt herself almost as much.

BLOODSTONE

Bloodstone Tavern owner Tony Manders sat at the table in his dining room, with the book on New York State law that he had gotten out of the school library open in front of him. He had just finished reading the section on martial law, which, as near as he could make out with all the fifty-cent legal words, seemed to back up what Smith had said at the town meeting about its being impossible to declare martial law in the area. He began looking for the statutes covering citizen arrests.

And then his wife screamed.

It was a shrill, wailing cry that brought him up out of his chair, sent him running into the kitchen. She was standing at the sink, hand to her mouth, eyes protuberant with terror and focused on the rain-streaked window. Manders went to her, grabbed her shoulders. "What is it, Gena? For Christ's sake what is it?"

"Outside, outside!" she said desperately. "I saw someone out there, someone moving around over by the barn. A man . . . Tony, maybe it's the Ripper!"

Manders' mouth twisted into a rictus of fury. "Did you get a clear look at him?"

"No, no, I just saw him moving, a shadow. . . ."

He released her and leaned close to the window. The yard lights were on—he always kept the yard lights on now—but he couldn't see anything. He spun away, ran into the living room, got one of his hunting rifles out of the gun case there, jacked a shell into firing position, and ran back into the kitchen.

His wife said, "No, Tony, don't go out there. . . ."

"You bet I'm going out there," Manders said grimly. "Relock the door after me and call the state police."

He went out. His wife relocked the door, returned to the window; her hands fluttered at her mouth like fat white insects. She saw him move across the yard, the rifle butted against his shoulder, swaying from side to side. Then he disappeared from sight, behind the barn, into the trees beyond.

A moment later, there was the flat crack of a shot.

Gena Manders made a soft, keening sound, held her breath. She waited one minute, two, three, but he didn't reappear.

"Oh God," she said, "oh God," and flung herself across the kitchen toward the telephone.

PAULA

Paula Eaton left her house at eight thirty, hurrying through the rain to her car. Jack had not called her, and he had not come to see her as he'd promised. She had telephoned him at home, without getting an answer, and then she'd tried the newspaper office and his mother's and hadn't gotten a response at those places either. She knew he sometimes didn't answer the phone when he was working, so chances were he was home after all.

She had to see him, they had to talk: she could not stand the waiting, the equivocation, a minute longer. The confrontation this morning had started out the way she'd expected—Jack wanting her to get an abortion, trying to back away from his responsibility—but then he had changed to a tack she still didn't understand. Had he just been trying to get rid of her, or had he been sincere in wanting a little time to himself to think and plan for their future? Did he really intend to marry her? In her confusion she had let him send her away, and that had been her mistake.

Paula drove slowly down U.S. 9, through the village. When she reached Clear Creek Road, the surrounding night seemed completely empty, filled with claps of thunder and penetrations of lightning. The wind seemed to penetrate the glass and metal around her, to gust within despite the fact that she had the heater on as high as it would go. She began to feel apprehensive; the night, the storm, unnerved her. She had always been afraid of the dark anyway, and the Ripper killings had from the first added fuel to that fear. She wondered if she wasn't a fool tempting fate by coming out alone this way. But Jack hadn't left her any choice; she *had* to know what he was going to do about her and about the baby.

Two miles from his cottage, headlights appeared in her rear-vision mirror.

She was aware of them instantly, and her heart began to stammer. There had been lights behind her on Main Street, she remembered that now, but she hadn't thought anything of it then. But was it the same car, following her? No, that was irrational; it was just somebody going home, somebody who lived out this way, maybe some scared woman like herself. . . .

The headlights grew larger in the mirror.

Coming faster, Paula thought. The fear in her deepened: became cold and palpable and urgent. It's nothing, you're overreacting—but suppose, suppose. . . . Drive faster, get away from those lights, get to Jack's cottage. Only she wasn't a good driver, and she was terrified of speed and wet pavement. Turn around then. Turn around and go back to Main Street; go home where it was safe!

The entrance to a narrow side road that wound away through thick forest to the south—Hobbler Way—appeared in her own lights, just ahead. In confusion and terror, she slowed the car and turned it into the road. She fumbled at the shift lever, gears grinding, got it into reverse and twisted the wheel, twisted on the seat, and began to back up.

The headlights were almost on her now, the dark shadow of the car came into view; then it slowed abruptly and cut over behind her, blocked her off.

Paula's foot jammed onto the brake pedal, and she shifted frantically into drive; the car bucked forward—and then the engine stalled. A scream rose and was stillborn in her throat. Lock the doors! She jabbed at the door buttons, had to do it twice before she succeeded in depressing both of them. Her fingers twisted the ignition key, but the motor only coughed and whirred emptily. She turned on the seat to stare out through the rear window, saw the door of the other car open and the familiar gray-black shape of a man step out. He came forward and bent into the frame of the door window. When Paula shifted position again, facing toward him, she saw that he was smiling.

Recognition made her body sag against the seat back, drained away some of the fear. She swallowed thickly, watched him make an easy lifting gesture toward the door button. His mouth formed the words "Open it, Paula. Open the door."

The way he was smiling, the familiar presence of him, said that it was all right, she had no reason to be frightened of *him*. Impulsively, Paula flipped up the button. And he reached out, still in that casual way, and took hold of the handle and opened the door.

The wind came into the car, cold, cold; drops of rain stung like ice crystals on her skin. She heard from somewhere the faint shriek of a siren. Then he said softly, "Hello, Paula," and the smile was fixed now, frozen: frieze. He held out his hand to her palm up, four fingers curled in against it and the index finger extended like the blade of a short, blunt knife.

Understanding moved through her in slow, horrifying tremors—too late. "Oh my God," she said, and her voice was a half scream lost in the rain and the darkness and the dancing, singing wind.

THE RIPPER

Closing in, putting it in, making it ring, making it sing, light and leap, binding, ringing, singing, kniving, and kniving be the song. . . .

KELLER

The cruiser's police radio burst into staticky life. "All units, all units," the metallic voice of the Bloodstone state police dispatcher said. "Ten-thirty-one, all units Code Three to Manders home, forty-seven nineteen Bebout Lane four miles northwest Bloodstone village. Repeat: ten-thirty-one, all units Code Three to forty-seven nineteen Bebout Lane four miles northwest Bloodstone village. All units acknowledge ten-twenty and ten-twenty-three."

Keller said, "Fucking shit son of a bitch!" and slapped the dashboard viciously with the palm of one hand. It was the Ripper again; Hook had gone on the prowl again, all right. But it was happening as it had happened last night, a taped replay of last night: state police called in first, on the scene first, he some distance away with instincts dormant, wrong place at the wrong time again, again, again. Well, they wouldn't run him to ground tonight either. They wouldn't get him.

He hit the button for the siren, flicked on the flasher light on the dash, swung the cruiser into a skidding U-turn, and went hurtling through the Ripper-filled darkness.

CROSS

Bloodstone Tavern was closed, the whole town was closed up tight, and so Cross turned the Chevy toward the Homelite Motel, the Homelite bar. But halfway there, he realized suddenly that although he was twenty-six years old, he had never once, not once, had a drink in the company of other men.

The knowledge was shocking, in its own insidious way as appalling as the pregnancy news from Paula: a simple fact of normal life that had somehow evaded him. It was the most natural thing in the world for a single man to have friends, to go drinking with them occasionally, but he had no friends, he had no one to go drinking with, and he had not even *known* these things were missing from his life.

Cross stopped the car on the side of the road, his face and neck flaming. He couldn't go to the Homelite now, he couldn't just walk in there with all of those out-of-town reporters around; the fact of his virginity (and that's what it was, he was a virgin in comradeship) would show on his face and in his voice. They would all know, and they would all laugh behind their upraised glasses.

He sat there for a time, and then he began driving again, aimlessly now, up and down streets and roads shining wetly in the rain. Only the factor of his control over the ancient steering, the chattering clutch, seemed to bind him to circumstance. Alone in the car, alone in the night. No friends. Clark Kent had friends, even Jimmy Olsen had friends, but not Jack Cross. Alone. . . .

After a long while—or it might have been a short while, he was utterly disconnected—he heard sirens around him, hanging in the storm. He blinked and saw that he was on Main, across from the Catholic church. Flashing lights appeared behind him, and he pulled automatically to one side to allow first one and then a second state police car to rush screaming past him.

The Ripper? Had the Ripper struck again so soon?

Abruptly he became engaged again. Maybe he didn't have any friends, but by God he had the Ripper. No virgin there, he was as experienced as anyone. He swept his hat off the seat, jammed it down on his head, and took out after the lights and sirens.

SMITH

When he got to Cross' cottage, a light burning within made amber rectangles of two facing windows but there was no sign of Cross' car. Smith parked near the front porch and went up and rapped on the door: no answer. He swore softly. The kid had always seemed to be hanging around, but now when Smith wanted to talk to him, he couldn't make a connection.

He hadn't been able to make *any* connection tonight. Florence Cross had been home, but the trooper on guard there said that she had taken a sedative and had gone to bed early. He'd rung the bell anyway and had gotten no response; the house had remained dark. Then he had gone over to Plummer's, and Plummer hadn't been home.

A few goddamn days. . . .

Smith took out his notebook and wrote a short note, similar to one he had written to Plummer, instructing Cross to call him immediately at the Witherbee Motel. He signed it, slid the paper under the door, and then hurried back through the icy rain to his car. When he drove back onto Clear Creek Road, the thumping of the windshield wipers made a monotonous counterpoint to the hollow drumrolls of thunder. Wind buffeting the car forced him to drive at forty.

He became aware that the radio was strangely silent, and glanced down at it—stared at it. The toggle switch on the set was flipped up to Off position. Christ, he must have shut it off coming out here; he couldn't remember shutting it off, but he must have. What the hell was the matter with him, doing a stupid thing like that?

He reached down to the toggle, and just as he did that, his headlights picked up, not far ahead, the dark form of a car sitting in the middle of the entrance to a narrow side road. He jerked erect, leaning over the wheel. Shadows crouched off-center among the trees on both sides of the car up there, retreating under his lights, but nothing else moved within his vision.

When he was twenty yards from the vehicle Smith pulled in behind it at an angle, so that his lights gleamed blackly off its metal surfaces. His stomach had begun to hurt him again, and he could feel his nerves contracting. He unbuttoned the flap of his holster, put his hand on the butt of his gun. Still nothing moving in or around the other car. He put the transmission lever into Park, left the engine running and got out and went around to the driver's side of the other car. The interior was empty, but on the front seat, tipped on its side, was a woman's brown leather handbag.

Up the side road, something winked redly.

Smith saw it at the periphery of his vision, pulled his head around, and stared in that direction. The rain seemed to be falling in long, isolated sheets now, like thin slices of plywood dropped from the sky: nearly impenetrable. But above the cry of the storm, he thought he could hear a low, vibrant humming.

Taillights, he thought. Automobile engine.

He hesitated, looking back into the abandoned car, looking at the purse on the front seat. Redness flickered again down the road, so briefly that it was almost subliminal; it pulled his eyes back. He seemd to hear the motor sound again, slightly louder now, as though accelerating.

That decided him. He ran back to his car, noting by a signpost that the side road was called Hobbler Way. He put the headlights on high beam, edged around the other vehicle, and went up Hobbler Way at increasing speed.

Blackness.

The sheets of rain.

Lightning cut suddenly across the tops of the trees, but its brief glare revealed only emptiness. He drove faster, nearing the spot where he had seen the first—

Wink.

Pinpoint of red this time, seen through the rain and the forest growth; red and black and the yellow glare of his lights. . . .

White.

Mound of white on the left, among the trees.

Smith slowed reflexively, and the hairs came up on the back of his neck. His stomach kicked, throbbed, but his bowels were quiet and empty. Lightning glittered again, turning the sky flashbulb bright for an instant—and the perceived white mass took on form, substance, became the focus of his attention. He braked the car, sliding it across the road and onto the berm, came out and ran toward the white object and stopped when he was close enough to identify it as the body of a woman.

Lances of pain from the ulcer. It was a woman he knew this time: Paula Eaton.

The rain hammered down on her, cleansing the gaping wounds in her torso, diluting the blood and staining the leaves beneath her. Newly dead: the assailant, the maniac, had done this to her only minutes ago. It was his car Smith had seen and heard; he was on this road, he was minutes away, he was *here*. The son of a bitch had run out of luck at last; he had killed one too many women.

Back inside the car, Smith slammed the transmission into gear and careened down the road. But he did not put on the red light or siren. Don't let him know he's being pursued, let him think he's getting away clean again. Smith fumbled below the dash with his right hand, got the microphone off the radio, started to speak and remembered that he still hadn't turned the set on. Savagely he hit the toggle switch.

"Unit A," he said into the microphone. His voice sounded thin, cracking, like brittle ice. "Unit A."

The dispatcher's voice said, "Ten-four, Unit A. Where are you? We've been trying to reach you."

"Listen: I've got a ten-thirty-three-X, homicide, Hobbler Way off Clear Creek Road. Pursuing suspect south on Hobbler. Code Two emergency, ten-seventy-eight. Do you read, dispatch?"

There was a slight hesitation; then, "Jesus, Lieutenant—the Ripper?"

Even the troopers were calling him that now, no discipline. "Affirmative!" he shouted. "What's the matter with you, dispatch?"

"We had a call fifteen minutes ago from a man north of town who claims the Ripper was on his property, after his wife. I put out a ten-thirty-five on it, Lieutenant. All units on the scene."

Smith, slowing into a turn, felt again the mocking suspicion of absurdity, of manipulation by lunatic forces beyond his control and beyond his comprehension. Enraged, he shouted, "False alarm, that was a false alarm! It's happening here on Hobbler Way, the victim is one Paula Eaton, and the assailant is here! Get me some assistance, dispatch. He's not going to get away this time, you understand!"

"Affirmative," the dispatcher said quickly. "Ten-four."

Smith dropped the microphone across his lap, came into another turn, came out of it. Darkness, rain: nothing. But the assailant was up there somewhere, up there ahead. For the first time he was dealing with cold reality instead of something obscure dancing out of reach.

In the distance he saw crimson flickers again, like drops of blood glistening on the wet black canvas of the night.

HOOK

Lights cut in and out of Hook's vision, illuminating the rain, as he drives. He still does not know where he is going, or maybe he does. Maybe he has been heading for one place and one thing ever since he left Valerie, and Saratoga was only the long way around.

I couldn't be the Ripper, he thinks. If I was, I'd know it at every level of my being. There is no such thing as a totally fractured personality, one part unaware of the other part. That is a myth. It's a myth and a lie.

I couldn't be the Ripper. . . .

KELLER

There was no roadblock at the entrance drive to 4719 Bebout Lane, as there had been at the Cross access road last night, but the yard was filled with state police cars.

Keller drove past three parked civilian cars, a small knot of eager, hurrying men with cameras—reporters, fucking vultures—and took the cruiser into the yard and brought it to a stop, siren dying, under a skeletal sugar maple. He knew the place; it belonged to Tony Manders, the owner of the tavern. Manders was a hothead and his wife a bitch, so at least the Ripper was picking the right victims now.

He slogged toward the house, a big white frame with a barn in back and a vegetable garden on one side. There were lights showing in all its windows. A trooper in a black slicker was stationed at the foot of the porch steps, and Keller went up to him and demanded to know what had happened. The trooper told him.

"But you didn't get him, he's still loose," Keller said.

"Yeah. Still loose. Manders says he chased him into the woods out back, fired a shot at him. Thinks he might have hit him, too; anyway, he heard some kind of cry."

"All right," Keller said.

The rain was torrential now, and he returned to the cruiser. More cars arriving out on the road—more reporters, some of the braver townspeople. He noticed Cross' old Chevrolet and the kid standing beside it, peering across the road. Then he reached inside for his slicker and flashlight.

The radio crackled, and the voice of the dispatcher said, "All units. Previous alert ten-twenty-two. Repeat: previous alert ten-twenty-two. Ten-thirty-three-X, homicide, emergency Code Two, Hobbler Way three miles southwest Bloodstone village. Repeat—"

Keller straightened reflexively, banged the back of his head on the door frame, and held back a cry of pain and fury. Goddamn false alarm, summoned all the way over *here* on a fraud when the Ripper was ripping number five ten miles away! Back and forth, always too late or too early or too far away. He felt cheated, badly used. And now this new alert—was *that* a fraud too? The homicide, female, was verified, but was there actually an officer in pursuit? Which officer, then? Smith? Smith's car wasn't here, that was who it had to be. Unless Smith was the Ripper, chasing himself, laughing at Keller, leading him merrily along . . . no, not Smith, that was ridiculous. Hook. Smith was a fool, but Hook, Hook was the Ripper.

"Units three-seven and four-one," the dispatcher was saying, "to vicinity of intersection Hobbler Way and Cadwallader Road. Units three-two and three-five standby intersection Cadwallader Road and U.S. Nine. Unit four zero to intersection Hobbler Way and Clear Creek Road. All units acknowledge, ten-sixty-two. . . ."

Keller stared through the rain at the state police cars strewn around the yard. None of them was occupied; the only trooper in sight was the one at the house that he had just talked to. Keystone Kops, chasing around through the woods, leaving their cars and their radios unattended. By Christ, *he* was the only one who had heard the dispatcher's message. So it might work out all right after all—*if* this wasn't another fraud, *if* Smith was really in pursuit of Hook, of the Ripper.

He slid into the cruiser, looped it around with the tires spraying thin streams of muddy water. He went out of the drive and turned left on Bebout Lane, containing his speed until he reached the first turn so as not to alert the reporters that anything new was coming down. The dispatcher's voice droned over the radio, repeating his message, but Keller didn't reach for the microphone to acknowledge. He would come into it silently this time; come in soft like a bloodhound, like the Ripper himself: without warning, relentless, implacable.

No more bullshit, he thought. This better be it and no— more—bullshit.

CROSS

He watched Keller's cruiser come out of the Manders driveway and move away toward Bloodstone. Now that was pretty curious. Cross stared over at the front yard, and none of the state police units showed signs of leaving. Then where was Keller headed to? Normal speed, and no red light or siren—but was he onto something anyway, some new development the troopers didn't know about yet?

That had to be it. Cross didn't know how or what—he didn't even know what was happening across the way— but instinct told him that the constable would never leave the scene unless it was very important and also involved the Ripper. Whatever else you could say about Alex Keller, he wanted the Ripper as badly as anyone did.

Immediately, Cross made up his mind to follow the constable. Now that he had made those other important decisions about his personal life, he had become a new man, capable of making *any* decision and knowing that ultimately it would prove to be the right one.

He ran to the Chevy—long, easy, steel-legged strides— and became one with it and launched himself after Keller.

THE RIPPER

Didn't have to be that way, could have been better, could have been higher, harder, faster, deeper but the thing wouldn't resist, just lay like stone in the rain falling, falling away, all of her stone, and I reached to bring the blood to her but the blood would not come, stayed roiling within her, no blood, no life to her, bare fingers digging at the stone, bare and seeking to bring the warmth but oh no, nothing at all, nothing within her, stone, stone is stone and in that stone no blood no knowledge no liver no spleen no organs no life then but death against her piling the wall clinging and ringing off-center to the dead thing that screamed like life in my hands. . . .

SMITH

Ahead of him now, as he emerged from a series of serpentining curves and started down a long incline, he could see the intersection of Hobbler Way and Cadwallader Road. Both of them were empty, empty, within the screen of his vision. He hadn't seen any more of the taillight flashes, although a moment ago he had thought he heard the roar of an engine, very close; now he realized that it could only have been the sound of *his* car, magnified and reverberated back to him by the encircling trees.

Which way? Which way, damn it? Left toward Bloodstone, or right deeper into the countryside? He braked sharply as he came on the intersection, slid partway out onto Cadwallader Road. Rain-soaked darkness in both directions. The pain in his stomach was intense, flatulation underneath it, hurting him from waist to neck—the sharp, tearing pain of perforation. But he wouldn't perforate; he refused to think of that. Instead, he had an image of the girl, Paula Eaton, lying back there on the side of the road; but then his mind closed again, overload and circuit blank, and he was once more staring at blackness, at emptiness, at—

—a tiny flare of blood-red color, far down to the left.

He flattened his lips against his teeth, cramped the wheel, and took the car, yawing, that way. He couldn't gain on those taillights, they remained the same maddening distance in front of him, but at least he hadn't lost the assailant, at least he was still in pursuit.

The redness vanished again.

Smith rejected the urgent impulse to increase his speed. The car felt loose around him, floating, sending out spumes of water in its wake, and he was afraid of losing control. The staticky voice of the Bloodstone dispatcher penetrated his consciousness; he caught up the microphone. When the radio was silent he said, "Dispatch, this is Unit A. Still pursuing suspect, east now on Cadwallader Road. Intercept situation, U.S. Nine and Cadwallader. Ten-five. Advise location of backup units en route."

"Ten-four," the dispatcher's voice said scratchily. "But . . . well, there *aren't* any units en route yet. I can't raise a single response from anyone at the previous ten-thirty-five."

"What? Jesus Christ, dispatch!"

"I'm sorry, sir. I don't know how it could happen, but they must all be in the field—all of them. No one seems to be monitoring."

Absurdity, chaos. Clown burlesque. Dumb show. Smith was sweating now, sweat in his eyes combining with the sheets of water outside to give the night the shimmery distortion of a dream. "Put me on the air!" he bellowed. "Tach two!"

"Affirmative."

Smith clenched the microphone, waiting for the dispatcher to switch the frequency. Rain thudded like bullets against the hood and roof of the car. A cut of lightning came, showed him nothing on the road ahead, but off to his right, on high ground, he saw a familiar landmark: the creeper-festooned ruins of an old stone mill. Less than a mile to the intersection of U.S. 9.

The radio was cleared to Tach 2. Smith said, "Unit A to all units," and repeated the 10-codes for emergency response without red light and siren, officer in need of assistance, past tense offense report: homicide. He gave his position, requested immediate acknowledgment.

There was no response.

"Acknowledge!" he screamed into the mike. "Acknowledge, you sons of bitches!"

Unrelieved static.

Smith screamed it again, heard himself screaming, and cut it off. He sleeved his eyes clear of sweat. Chaos everywhere, but not here, he wouldn't let it happen here.

A quarter of a mile from the intersection, he topped a rise and saw the taillights again, glimmering just beyond the Northway overpass.

"Suspect approaching U.S. Nine," he said automatically. "Pursuit less than one-fourth mile on Cadwallader Road. Code Two intercept."

Silence.

He took the car through a shallow dip in the road, then into a long S-curve, then climbing to another rise. When he reached the top of that one, the road ahead was as nearly straight as a piece of loosely stretched string. He could see the intersection, and the taillights were there, splashes of crimson just turning south. Then they winked out again beyond a hillock.

With no more curves between himself and the intersection, Smith chanced a ten-mile increase in his speed. The car, drifting, planed toward the overpass, across it. He said into the mike, voice rising again, "Suspect now proceeding south on U.S. Nine below Cadwallader Road. Pursuit one-fifth mile, approaching intersection. Code Two intercept. Acknowledge. All units acknowledge."

The radio said nothing at all.

When he came on the intersection he braked to twenty, swerved far to the left, saw that U.S. 9 was clear, and made the turn south. The rear end tried to break loose, but he battled the wheel until the tires found traction, held it; the car straightened again on a point. He could smell the sour odor of his sweat, could feel the clamminess of it under his arms and bathing his groin. From neck to waist he felt empty. His stomach had stopped hurting, but the absence of pain was somehow more frightening now than the pain itself had been.

The highway, slick and twisting beneath the rain, was as void of traffic as the county road. No headlights, no taillights. Wild urgency hammered at him. There were a half dozen roads that intersected along here, half a hundred places where the assailant could leave the highway and disappear. Did he know he was being pursued? Had he seen the headlights in his mirror? If he wasn't suspicious, he would keep driving until he reached a fixed destination, and Smith would have a chance of tracking him all the way. But if he *was* suspicious. . . .

Smith's hand was white around the microphone. I'll have all your asses if he gets away, he thought. You'll all be sad fucking clowns if he gets away.

The odometer clicked off seven-tenths of a mile, eight-tenths, nine-tenths. Thunder rumbled, lightning flashed out over the lake. The road was still empty of light and movement ahead and behind. Lost him, gone again, lost him lost him lost him—

Saw him.

Came through a dogleg in the highway and saw him: flickers of red, cones of diffused yellow, tracking away at a right angle to the west.

In that first moment of recaptured contact, Smith thought the other car had turned off onto an intersecting road; then he recognized the area, the sign on the edge of U.S. 9 up there, the staggered row of ramshackle cabins beyond the headlights of the other car. Abandoned complex: Hideaway Cabins. He had passed them dozens of times driving into Bloodstone from Lake George. Dead end, at least for a car. Smith reduced his speed to forty, thirty-five, thirty.

And doubt brushed his mind again. Why would the assailant be going there? *Was* that the assailant? He hadn't seen the car turn onto the complex's access road, it could have come from the opposite direction. . . .

Smith lifted the microphone to his mouth, thumbed the button on its side. He reported that the suspect was now on the grounds of the Hideaway Cabins complex, three miles south of Bloodstone village on U.S. 9. But he was still talking to the dispatcher and to himself.

The headlights of the other car swung around to the left, outlining one of the broken, sagging cabins; then the brake lights flared. Abruptly, both winked out. The car had stopped, shrouded in rain and darkness.

Have to go in there alone, he thought. Have to take him myself, my responsibility, mine from the beginning. Proof positive of an ordered universe. Maybe.

The pain started in his stomach again, sparks of it hot

and stinging, as he cut his own lights and brought the car forward and onto the access road.

HOOK

Hook got out of his car and made his way through the weeds to Hideaway Cabin Number Eight. When he was inside, in the middle of the kitchen, he stopped and blinked several times as lightning briefly illuminated the room. What was he doing here? And immediately he moved to the wooden shelves, to the pile of rags there, and took out the bottle of rye. He held it tightly in both hands.

Now he knew exactly what he was doing here.

No, he thought, I don't want a drink. Valerie, peace of mind, a new life—but not a drink. Then, in his mind, he saw the body of Linda Simmons, lying on the Terra Alta beach; heard the nightmare wailing of sirens; heard Keller's voice accusing him of being the Ripper; felt the stiffness in Valerie's body when he had touched her tonight. His hands shook, his mouth was arid. Thirty-nine years old. Thirty-nine years old and no future. He scratched at the cap seal on the bottle, tore it free.

I don't want to do this, he thought, and pulled out the cork. I don't want to do this, he thought, and tilted the bottle to his lips. "I don't want to do this," he said aloud, and drank.

Bitter heat in his throat, in his stomach. Six years! He gagged, drank again, gagged, drank. His knees felt wobbly, and he put out a hand to the wall to steady himself. Then he began to hiccup, body convulsing, sounds sharp and hollow in the cold, damp room. Then the hiccups stopped, as suddenly as they had started, and he moved away from the wall.

Warmth flowed through him.

The trembling stopped, his mind turned the consistency of cream.

He swallowed more of the rye.

Valerie had been a crutch, but this was a better one. Yes, a better crutch. Best crutch. Now really, why had he fought it so long? This was the answer, always had been:

the real crutch of the problem. Fuck off, old wild king, old Ripper. No pressure here, not anymore. Hah!

Christ on a crutch, here was a proper crutch!

KELLER

He was just coming out of the village when Smith's radio voice told him that the Ripper was at the Hideaway Cabins.

Keller bore down harder on the accelerator, a tight smile working at the corners of his mouth. No fraud this time; his instincts, active again, told him that. All right, Smith, he thought, all right, you Keystone Kop, just hold him there. Don't try to take him, don't do anything. I'm coming, I'll be there in less than five minutes.

Four minutes, three miles, and the Hideaway Cabins appeared, buildings huddled behind the curtain of rain. He saw the shape of something creeping on the access road, lightless—Smith's car; he couldn't see the Ripper's car at all. Give Smith that much: he was moving slowly, lights out, blocking vehicular escape. Just stay in the car now, stay in the car, I'm coming.

But not straight in, that wasn't the way to do it. Smith might panic; Smith might get in his way, Smith might blow the whole thing. Come in blind, on padded feet. Like a bloodhound. Don't alert Smith and don't alert the Ripper. Move in from the rear, sniff out the quarry, and then pounce before either of them knew what was happening.

Keller put the cruiser in darkness, slowed, turned onto an overgrown, mud-rutted road that cut off the highway just this side of the Hideaway Cabins. Once the road had led to a house set well back among the trees, above and to the left of the complex; the house had burned down two years ago and nobody used the road anymore except kids looking for a private place to hump their girlfriends. This little section of ground was a disaster area: first the Hideaway Cabins, then the house. But tonight it would be something else entirely.

SMITH

When he was a hundred feet from the nearest cabin, he coasted the car to a stop and switched off the engine.

Then he reached up and took the plastic globe off the interior light and unscrewed the bulb. He rolled down the window because the sluicing rain made the windshield impenetrable, and off to his left, fifty yards away, he could see the other car angled against a decaying log between two of the cabins. Nothing moved over there. Nothing moved anywhere except the storm.

Smith clenched his teeth against the pain in his stomach and drew his gun.

CROSS

The moment he saw Keller shut off his lights and turn onto the dead-end road, Cross knew that this was it. Keller was after the Ripper; the Ripper was somewhere nearby, the whole thing was going to come to a climax right here tonight. He felt exhilarated, adrenaline flowing.

He would have to play it cautious, though. He was an observer, a chronicler of the pain and horror that the Ripper had brought to Bloodstone. He couldn't become directly involved, because direct involvement meant the possibility of bodily harm—and of all the individuals in this case, he had to remain unscathed in order to record the complete story. On the scene, yes, but removed from it too.

He saw something moving on the grounds of the Hideaway Cabins.

The Ripper! he thought instantly. So that was where he was and where it would end. He was there, and Keller had turned up the dead-end road because he intended to move in from the rear flank. But was it just the two of them, Keller and the Ripper? Or was somebody else there too? Somebody had to have alerted Keller, which made it probable there was at least one more man on the scene. Smith, maybe. It *should* be Smith, that would tie it all up neatly. The Hideaway Cabins, Smith, Keller, the Ripper. And Jack Cross, who was writing a book called *The Ripper of Bloodstone*. Beautiful, dramatic. A devastating final chapter!

He turned his car as dark as the others and swung over to the side of the highway, near the entrance to the dead-end road.

HOOK

He carried the bottle into the cabin's front room, staggering slightly. He was drunk now, he knew he was drunk, and he no longer cared. It was good to be drunk; it was fine to be drunk; it was a fine crutch all right, no doubt about that. In fact, he felt almost cheerful. Things always seemed more pleasant, life a little more carefree, when you had a few drinks inside you; he should have remembered that long ago. The world was a better place when you had an edge on, yes sir, yes indeed.

"These eclipses do portend these divisions, *fa sol la mi*," Hook said to the bottle. Tom O'Bedlam's speech on the heath; good old Edmund, good old King Lear. "Excellent foppery of the world," he said.

Rain blew in through the broken windows, the broken front door. But the storm didn't bother him at all. Nothing bothered him right now. He tilted the bottle, lowered the bottle—and through the window, in a sudden bright flash of lightning, he saw the car parked down the way, the figure of a man silhouetted inside.

Evasion of whoremaster man! And the warmth went out of him; he became conscious of the cold in the cabin. He went to the window, squinted through the wet dark. The man was still sitting inside the car. Just sitting there. Hook's heart raced; he no longer felt almost cheerful, he felt, now, anxious, scared.

His fingers clutched the bottle, clutched the windowsill. An aura of menace grew within him, very real, very immediate, and caused the short hairs to rise on his neck; the man out there was a threat to him, *after* him.

Hook's thoughts whirred and clicked fuzzily. Whoever it was must have seen him drive in or seen the Dodge from the road. Not the state police. He hadn't seen the car very clearly in the cut of lightning, but the roof line was smooth, no flasher light; and a trooper wouldn't just sit out there that way. All that talk about vigilantes at the town meeting today . . . an armed private citizen? Or—

Keller.

Jesus, Keller?

SMITH

Smith got out of his car and approached the parked vehicle, hunched over and breathing thickly through his mouth. When he came up to it he saw that it was an old Dodge, empty, and he recognized it immediately. It belonged to Steven Hook, the man who had found the body of Linda Simmons; he had seen it in Hook's driveway that night, when he accompanied the man home.

So it was Hook. Hook was the assailant. Unless this *wasn't* the car he had pursued from the scene of Paula Eaton's murder. But then what was Hook doing here at an abandoned cabin complex in the middle of a stormy night? But then what would the assailant be doing here?

It must be Hook.

Maybe it wasn't Hook. . . .

Smith stood motionless for a moment, looking for a flicker of light or some other sign to tell him where Hook had gone. He saw nothing. Finally he pushed through a swath of high grass, skirted a patch of thistle, and flattened himself against the wall of the cabin nearest the Dodge. The wind-driven rain struck his hands and face like slivers of ice, but inside, down in his guts, the ulcer sent out more glowing, stinging sparks. He wanted to fart, to relieve the pressure, but he could not break anything loose from the cavity inside.

He edged up onto the porch, poked his flashlight through one of the glassless windows, and snapped it on. Emptiness. He put the light out again and came down off the porch and crossed to the adjacent cabin on his left.

The sparks kept on getting hotter, sharper.

KELLER

He came downslope through the trees at the rear of the cabins, on a straight line from where he had left the cruiser on the muddy dead-end road, and crossed a narrow, shallow stream that paralleled the row of buildings. The Ripper was there, all right, he could almost smell him—the smell of corruption. It wouldn't be long now, not long at all.

The Bloodhound of Bloodstone was zeroed in.

CROSS

On a hillock overlooking the cabins, Cross crouched at the bole of a spruce and watched and waited. He had a ringside seat here, and you couldn't ask for any more than that, no literary observer could. He couldn't remember when he had been so excited.

A tine of lightning showed him the figure of a man moving along the front of the cabins. Smith, he was sure it was Smith. Perfect! Now—where was the Ripper? He could see part of the woods to the rear of the complex, and a second lightning flash revealed what might have been movement among the trees back there. Keller? Or the Ripper? Boy oh boy oh boy.

A phrase popped into Cross' mind, spontaneously, the way the really good stuff always did. *In the black, the black figures maneuvered like pieces on a blood-spattered chessboard.* Better get that down on paper, he thought. By God, better get *everything* down on paper—the final chapter written as it happens! A first in the history of the nonfiction novel, better than Capote witnessing the execution of Perry and Dewey in Kansas; a literal tour de force, a Pulitzer Prize for sure. *As I write this, the Ripper is about to be unmasked and brought to justice. Like you, the reader, I await the final moment of truth. . . .*

Cross took out his notebook and pen, shielded them somewhat from the rain with his body and the folds of his coat, and began writing in blind and furious shorthand.

HOOK

From the window he saw the man out front, the menace, leave the car and move stealthily through the high weeds toward the Dodge. The black rain obscured the figure, made recognition impossible.

Hook backed into the middle of the room. Self-protection, find a weapon. The bottle? Not the bottle, he put the bottle down on the floor. Frantically he probed the darkness, felt out a broken piece of two-by-four the length of a yardstick on the rotting mattress near the kitchen. He caught it up, stood listening.

The hammering of the storm shut out all other sound.

Into the kitchen, to the rear door. He edged it open, put his head out. Shadows danced everywhere; the night was alive with shifting, dancing, running shadows.

He lifted the club and went out and ran along the rear of the cabins until he came to Number Five. Then he edged around the corner to the side wall and leaned back against it. He was trembling. He had no real cause to be afraid, but now that he was outside here in the rain and darkness, he was terrified. Menace crackled like lightning in the wet sky.

And the wind in the trees made a ripping sound. . . .

SMITH

Smith had checked three cabins, all of them deserted, and was just coming to the steps of Number Four when the agony burst through his stomach.

He had known it might happen, but he still wasn't prepared for it—the same way you knew you were going to die someday but were never really prepared for death. You just kept plodding along, trying to do your job, trying not to think about possibilities and inevitabilities. So Smith had kept moving, kept looking for Hook, and now, all of a sudden, this one possibility had become absolute.

The pain was incredible, much worse than either of the two previous attacks. It straightened him up and then kicked him backward; it took his breath away, so that the cry that rose in his throat had no voice. A part of his brain was filled with the agony, but another part remained strangely objective, poisonously circumspect. It's not supposed to happen like this, that part said. I'm chasing a probable killer, I'm a cop after a killer here. . . .

Absurdity.

Dumb show.

Clown.

Then there was nothing at all but the pain.

CROSS

Something has happened to Smith! Through the moaning thunder of the storm I see him stagger backward as if shot, then fall onto the steps of a cabin. But there was no muzzle flash from a gun, and neither Keller nor the Ripper has put in an appearance. Smith seems to writhe in agony . . . what has felled him?

The tension continues to mount inexorably.

KELLER

There was movement along the side wall of the fifth cabin.

Keller came to a standstill on the slope fifty yards away and craned his head forward, as though on a point; his nostrils flared. Shadows separated again, and he saw the man there, Hook, the Ripper. He made a low sound like a baying in his throat, swung the revolver and his flashlight up, and began to run.

HOOK

Above the cry of the storm Hook heard the slither and pound of footsteps behind him. He whirled away from the cabin wall in a crouch, lifting the length of two-by-four, cocking it behind his right ear. A cone of light lashed suddenly through the rain and darkness, found him, cut at him like the blade of a knife.

"Hook!" a voice bellowed. "I knew it, Hook, I knew it was you!"

In terror, he stumbled a retreat. The two-by-four dropped out of his hands. Tom O'Bedlam, old wild king—get off the heath! Run, run, run!

"Hook!"

Behind him, a gun crashed. . . .

CROSS

It's happening, it's happening! A flashlight beam swirls bizarre patterns, Keller has arrived . . . a figure that can only be the Ripper emerges running from behind one of the cabins but I can't see his face yet . . . now Keller appears . . . a gun flashes . . . the Ripper continues to run . . . Keller shouts something lost in the wild wind . . . the gun flashes again . . . the Ripper lurches to a halt but he's not hit, he's surrendering, his hands raise as though in benediction.

Keller approaches him and now I strain my eyes for my first glimpse of the Ripper's true identity, the revelation . . . I hold my breath . . . in the black sky lightning flashes . . . ah! ah yes! I know at last who attacked Florence, I know the name of the Dark Prince. . . .

SMITH

Smith lay on the porch steps with his arm wrapped across his stomach and stared over at the two men who had run into view. Someone had come to assist him after all, and that someone was Keller: Keller had chased Hook, shot at Hook, caught Hook, was confronting Hook. Neither of them knew or cared that he, Daniel Smith, was down, maybe dying, less than fifty yards away.

The pain had lessened somewhat, but he still had no voice. He would have to go to Keller then, he would crawl to Keller if necessary because he wasn't going to die like this, he was not going to die like this.

KELLER

Hook's face was slightly off-center in the light from Keller's flash: features wet and ravished, eyes staring glassily. Now that Keller had the situation under control, now that he knew beyond any doubt that Hook was the Ripper, he smiled at him almost fondly. "You led me a merry chase, Hook," he said. "But it had to end this way, we both knew that, didn't we?"

"Keller?" In a dazed way, Hook shook his head. "Why did you shoot at me? I haven't done anything."

"Cutting up women is something. That's really *something*."

"Oh Jesus Christ—"

Keller moved in on him, frisked him fast and hard. Nothing. Hook just stood there: no blood on his clothing or on his hands, either. But that was all right. He could have washed it away in the stream in back, or even in the rain.

"Where's the knife?" he said. "Where did you hide it?"

"No."

"Did you get a hard-on when you killed them?"

"God, leave me alone."

"Did you talk to them? Did you tell them things while you were doing it to them?"

"You're crazy," Hook said desperately. He looked sick.

"Only one of us is crazy and that's you. Now you'd better tell me about it. How you felt when you cut them up, whether or not you got a hard-on, what you said to them, why you put those little diamond-shaped marks on their thighs, what you did with the knife—"

"Stop it!" Hook shouted. "Stop it, I'm not the Ripper!"

Keller sighed. Hook just wasn't going to admit the truth, and that was too bad, too bad. Maybe he could get the full story when he got him back to the Municipal Center —but a lot of things could happen before then, you never knew what might happen when you had a dangerous maniac in custody. Hook might try to escape, and Keller might have to shoot him: no warning shots this time, shoot to kill. That was a definite possibility, all right. He might have to shoot Hook dead long before he could bring him in.

His finger caressed the revolver's trigger.

HOOK

I'm not the Ripper, I'm not the Ripper, *fa sol la mi,* I'm not the Ripper. . . .

CROSS

The time has come for me to step down upon the scene for what will doubtless be a chilling and illuminating interview with the Ripper. Why did he do it? that's the first thing I'm going to ask him. Smith's fate must also be determined before the climax is complete. History perhaps will little note nor long remember what has happened here tonight, but for those of us who have lived it it is a night and a story that we will never forget.

SMITH

Smith crawled off the porch steps into the mud, came up onto his knees, and got one foot planted. I won't die this way, he thought again, and he lunged upward onto his feet. He swayed, staggered, redness swirling in back of his eyes. The ulcer, the hole in his guts, spewed fire (and blood? and blood?), but he bit down hard against the pain and held his balance.

Lurching, he started toward Keller and Hook.

KELLER

The sudden low, ululating wail of sirens, approaching on U.S. 9 from the north, penetrated the combined voices of wind and rain. At the same moment Keller heard them, he saw out of the corner of his eye a man shambling toward them. He turned, backing away from Hook but keeping the flashlight on him.

Smith.

He had forgotten all about Smith, but there he was.

The sirens grew louder.

And he saw yet another man coming down from the trees inland, hurrying, waving an arm, calling something that he couldn't hear.

Cross, piss-brain Cross.

Smith staggered and extended a hand, as if begging for help.

The sirens were very close now.

"Bastards!" Keller shouted in fury. "Bastards! Why couldn't you *stay* away! He's mine, I can do what I want with him because goddamn you, goddamn you, the Ripper is mine!"

HOOK

I'm not the Ripper, Hook thought, and bent over at the waist and vomited at Keller's feet.

SMITH

Keller is shouting, just standing there and shouting. But it doesn't matter because Smith has heard the sirens now and he knows that finally the help he needs is on the way. He stumbles to one knee, holding himself, and peers through a haze of pain and rain at the highway.

And two yellow-and-blue state police units, one on the tail of the other, appear with their flasher lights revolving hellishly. They swing in, sirens fading, and skid to stops behind his car. Gray-uniformed troopers burst out, and there is more shouting, and flashlights come on; movement flows around him in a montage of misty red and wet black and glaring yellow-white.

Hands touch him, slip away, come back again. "Don't let me die," he says, "I'll have your asses if you let me die," and feels himself slide bonelessly through the clutching hands and fall and fall and fall—

CROSS

There are troopers all over the place now, and I can't help but wish they'd waited about ten minutes longer, for they're going to take the Ripper away and hold him incommunicado and I won't get my exclusive, on-the-spot interview. This is too bad, but the important thing of course is that the Ripper has been captured, even though it disproves my recent theory that nobody would catch him, he would go on and on. And maybe I can interview him later.

I am still stunned by the fact that Steven Hook is the Ripper. Why, I ate dinner with the man last Saturday night! I knew I didn't like him then, but not why. The mysteries of human behavior and motivation cannot always be fully perceived by even the most astute observer.

As I stand writing this on the porch of Cabin Six, I see Keller stomping around in the mud, scuffling his shoes as though trying to clean something off them. Poor Smith has staggered and fallen into the arms of two uniformed men. Red lights flash, flashlights dance, thunder and lightning and rain . . . it is a situation fraught with the essence of drama. Now Lieutenant Rocca, who has just arrived, comes to Keller and they talk. Troopers lift Smith and carry him to a patrol car, shouting for an ambulance to be called. Other troopers shackle Hook's hands and lead him to still another patrol car. He is crying something . . . wait, yes, he is crying that he is not the Ripper. Hook is crying this because he believes he is innocent; as Ferrara has said, he does not know that he is the Ripper. Can he plead innocent in court by saying that he is not really the Ripper because the Ripper is someone else who has taken over his body while he was asleep? Is that a possible defense? Now the patrol car containing Hook drives away quickly, passing groups of media people who have just arrived out on the highway, unlike me too late.

Two troopers have noticed me finally, and they start toward me with drawn guns. . . .

Cross closed the notebook and put it away inside his coat. The troopers stopped in front of him, shone flashlights on him; they both looked pretty angry, probably, he thought, because they knew they should have gotten here sooner than they did. One of them demanded to know who he was and what the hell he was doing here.

He said, "I'm Jack Cross, I work for the Bloodstone *Sentinel*. I followed Keller out on a hunch, you see, I've been here from the beginning. What's *your* names?"

The troopers stared at him. "Our names?" the one who did the talking said.

"I'm writing a book on the Ripper, I'm going to put you into it. Everybody here is going to be in it, you'll all be famous."

"Yeah?" The talker exchanged a look with his partner. "Well, you just come with us."

He went with them through the rain to the cluster of patrol cars, and then the talker went away to where Rocca was now bending inside the car in which Smith lay. Cross noticed that Keller was standing alone in the middle of a patch of weeds, rain dripping from him, hands clenched at his sides, looking like an angry stone giant. *Angry stone giant.* He got the notebook out of his pocket again and wrote that down on a fresh page, shielding the damp paper with his body. He didn't like Keller, but Keller had caught the Ripper, and that made him the man of the hour. You had to give credit where credit was due, after all, particularly when you were writing a nonfiction novel which would lay out the full facts and background of the case. He was going to be fair throughout *The Ripper of Bloodstone* when he did the final draft. Fairness and accuracy were the marks of a great journalist.

Rocca and the one trooper approached him, along with another trooper whom Cross knew slightly because he worked out of the Bloodstone substation. "You've been here all along, Cross?" Rocca asked. There was a curious inflection in his voice.

He nodded. "From the first."

"Why?"

"I followed Keller out from the Manders place. I figured he was on to something, and boy, that's just what it was."

"You want to give me your version of what happened here?"

"Sure," Cross said, and told it to him with relish. The retelling made him all the more excited, and he had difficulty controlling his jerky motor responses.

A little incredulously Rocca said, "And you were up in the trees, taking notes, the entire time?"

"The entire time, right."

"Shock," the trooper he knew said.

That didn't mean anything to Cross. "What happened to Smith?" he asked. "Heart attack, or something like that?"

"We don't know yet," Rocca said grimly.

"Well, what about Hook? I mean, did you suspect him at any time? I didn't suspect him, not at all. Listen, can I talk to him after you're done interrogating him? I'd really like to get an interview with him. For my book, you know?"

The trooper he knew shifted uncomfortably, and his expression was pained. "Maybe he doesn't *know*, Lieutenant," he said to Rocca.

"Know what?" Cross said.

"About—the latest victim."

"Oh, I figured he got another one, and that Smith got onto him somehow and chased him here; I was going to fill all that in a little later." He paused. "Who was she this time?"

Silence.

Cross looked at them expectantly. "Come on," he said, "who was she?"

"Sweet Jesus God," Rocca said.

THE RIPPER

Just bones, good desserts, sweet meats and pretty things blue and new—but not so good, bad aftertaste, scared, hiding in the cling of the clang of the rung of the gong, old and cold and lost my bold beyond the diamonds. . . .

Friday, October 24

HOOK

Twelve thirty A.M., Friday morning.

Hook sat in a straight-backed chair in a small room at the Bloodstone substation, wrapped in a blanket they had given him so that he looked like a giant white larva in a gray cocoon. He was sober now, long sober, but sickness still roiled through him in thin waves. Sickness, and terror.

They had been hammering questions at him for two solid hours, in shifts. They hadn't touched him physically and they hadn't put glaring lights in his eyes and they hadn't denied him water or cigarettes. They just kept moving around him, sometimes three of them, sometimes four and five, circling him, throwing questions from the front and from the rear and from both sides. The same questions, over and over again.

"Did you kill those women, Hook?"

"No. No."

"Why did you go to the Hideaway Cabins tonight?"

"I don't know exactly. I go there sometimes. . . ."

"Why? Why do you go there?"

"I like it, the atmosphere. I can be alone."

"You *live* alone, don't you?"

"Yes."

"Well can't you be alone where you live?"

"It's not the same thing. . . . I can't explain it."

"Where were you before you went to the cabins?"

"Driving. Just—driving."

"Driving where?"

"I . . . I was going to go down to Saratoga Raceway, but when I was halfway there I realized I couldn't go. So I drove back, that's all."

"Why couldn't you go to Saratoga?"

"Because it's over. All over for me with the horses."

"You're on a losing streak, is that it?"

"Yes. A long, long losing streak."

"So you were driving and drinking, right?"

"No. Just driving."

"You were drunk at the cabins."

"I had a bottle there."

"Why? That's a funny place to keep a bottle."

"I bought it a few weeks ago but never opened it. I don't drink anymore. I don't drink anymore. I was an alcoholic once. . . ."

"You don't drink anymore, but you bought a bottle a few weeks ago and hid it at the Hideaway Cabins and got drunk on it tonight. That doesn't make any sense, Hook."

"I'm trying to explain. My life's been screwed up lately, nothing going right, a lot of pressure—"

"Pressure from the losing streak?"

"That's part of it. I bought the bottle in a weak moment, but I fought off the need for it. Only I couldn't bring myself to throw it away, either. Then I found Linda Simmons last Sunday night, and I couldn't get the image of the way she looked, the way her face looked, out of my mind, and then Keller started hounding me today, I told you about that, and then there was a . . . misunderstanding between Valerie Broome and me, and . . . I just couldn't take it anymore. You can understand how that is, can't you? I couldn't take the pressure anymore and I went to the cabins and got that bottle and started drinking. I thought that was what I needed, but it wasn't, it isn't, it only made things worse—"

"Is that why you started killing those women? The pressure?"

"I didn't kill them, I couldn't do anything like that."

"You've got a police record, haven't you?"

"Yes, but it wasn't a serious offense—"

"Aggravated assault is a felony, Hook. That's serious."

"I was drunk. That's why I stopped drinking."

"Do you always get violent when you're drunk?"

"No. Just that once."

"Why then?"

"I don't know. The man I assaulted was with my ex-wife at this party and he made some comments about me and I'd had too much to drink and I . . . I just lost my head."

"Maybe you lost your head again a few times since."

"No. No, I told you, until tonight I hadn't had a drink in six years."

"You came to the Hideaway Cabins from the north, right?"

"From the south. I was halfway to Saratoga and I turned around and came back, so it had to be from the south."

"But you were driving on Clear Creek Road."

"No. That's a county road to the west. I was on the Northway for a while, then on U.S. 9."

"Did you know Paula Eaton?"

"I met her, just briefly. Last week, at the café."

"Then it wasn't any trouble getting to her, was it?"

"I haven't seen her since that night. I didn't kill her, I didn't know she was dead until you told me."

"What did you do with the knife?"

"I didn't kill her!"

"Where were you when Florence Cross was attacked?"

"With Valerie Broome, I told you that too. She verified it to Keller this afternoon; she'll verify it to you."

"Have you known her long?"

"Just a week. We met last Saturday night."

"You became intimate friends pretty quickly."

"There's nothing wrong with that. . . ."

"Why did Keller start harassing you?"

"I don't know, it didn't make any sense to me. He's an obsessive. If you talk to him about it, you'll see what I mean."

"Why did you put those diamond-shaped marks on the victims?"

"I'm not the Ripper. God, I found the Simmons woman, I reported it to Keller, I wouldn't have reported it if I had killed her, would I? Would I?"

Hook wiped his forehead, blew his nose, lit another cigarette, and looked around at their hard, tight faces. He could hear the rain tapping, tapping on the roof. He wanted to crawl into a corner and fold the blanket over his head and curl himself inside it. He wanted to vomit again. He wanted to go home. He wanted them to leave him alone.

"Please," he said. "Please. . . ."

"Why were you at the Hideaway Cabins, Hook?"

"Why were you driving around in the rain?"

"Why did you assault that man in New York City?"

"Why did you start drinking again tonight?"

"Why did you kill them?"

Why, why, why, why, why, why. . . .

SMITH

When he became conscious again he was in a room with pastel green walls and a thick antiseptic odor—a hospital room. A white-uniformed intern and a white-uniformed nurse were standing beside the bed in which he lay, looking down at him. He felt emotion come over him, and the emotion was shame. He turned his head away from them.

The intern leaned forward. "Easy, Lieutenant. You're going to be all right."

Smith found a word. "Ulcer," he said.

"Yes. Do you have much pain?"

It was muted, he realized, with intermittent pulses of sharpness: bearable. He told the intern that, and then he said, "I didn't perforate, did I?"

"No," the intern said. "It wasn't quite that serious, although it could have been. We X-rayed you a few minutes ago; we'll know more when the pictures come in."

"What hospital is this?"

"Lake George General."

Smith nodded, swallowed heavily; he still had his face averted.

The intern said, "We notified your family, and they're on the way over. So is Dr. Metcalf."

He said nothing.

"Neither your wife nor Metcalf knew about this ulcer of yours, Lieutenant," the intern said. "Have you been getting treatment from another doctor?"

"No."

"You mean you haven't seen *any* physician about it?"

"No."

"Or told anyone about it?"

"No."

"For God's sake, why?"

"I had my reasons," he said.

"How long have you had pain?"

"A couple of months. Three, maybe."

"Have you had any other severe attacks?"

"No," he lied.

The intern looked at him gravely for a moment; then he and the nurse moved to one side and began whispering together. Smith closed his eyes. His mouth tasted cottony, and his limbs ached with fatigue. But he thought only of finding the body of Paula Eaton, of the chase—in his mind he could still see those red taillight flicks shimmering through the rain—and of the events at the Hideaway Cabins.

The intern's voice said, "Lieutenant?"

He opened his eyes and looked at the man this time.

"Do you feel strong enough to talk to one of your troopers? Personally, I don't like the idea of it, but I'm told it's urgent."

"Send him in," Smith said.

The intern and the nurse went out, and a moment later a uniformed trooper entered. He stood awkwardly, holding his hat in his hands. "I'll try to make this as quick as possible, Lieutenant," he said. "It's just that Lieutenant Rocca needs your account of what happened tonight as soon as possible. I mean, it's all pretty confused. . . ."

"Absurdity," Smith said. "Entropy."

"Sir?"

"Entropy. But there's order at the core and I've got to find it. I will find it."

"I don't follow, Lieutenant—"

"Did you arrest Steven Hook?"

"Yes, sir. He's in custody."

"Well, I'm not sure he's the man I was pursuing," Smith said. He didn't want to admit that, but he had no choice. Methodology demanded truth; methodology *was* truth. "Do you understand, trooper? I wish to Christ I was sure, but I'm not, I'm just not sure the assailant is Steven Hook. . . ."

KELLER

Keller was furious. "Let him go! What the hell do you mean, let him go? He's the goddamn Ripper!"

Lieutenant Rocca leaned back in the chair behind his desk, shook his head tiredly. "That seems highly doubtful at this point," he said. "I wish it wasn't; he's the only suspect we've turned up so far and I *want* it to be him. But we haven't found any evidence, not a shred of it, to link him to the homicides."

"Smith followed him to the Hideaway Cabins, didn't he?" Keller said. "Followed him from the scene of Eaton's murder right to there, didn't he?"

"Smith isn't sure Hook was the man he was following."

"What?"

"The trooper who accompanied him to the hospital phoned in a couple of minutes ago," Rocca said. "He got the full story from Smith when he regained consciousness."

Keller said angrily, "Why the hell isn't he sure it was Hook?"

"He didn't get close enough on pursuit to see the car at any time. He was trailing taillights, that's all, and there were times when he lost the lights altogether. One of those times was just before he reached the Hideaway Cabins. He didn't see Hook's car turn onto the grounds; he just saw it moving in there. It could have come from the opposite direction, all right, just as Hook claims."

"Oh for Christ's sake," Keller said.

Rocca said, "Dan's going to be okay, thank God for that. It was an ulcer attack, a bad one. He'll have to be hospitalized for a while, maybe have an operation—"

"I don't care about Smith's ulcer, I care about Hook! Goddamn it, he's murdered five women!"

Rocca leaned forward in his chair, looking suddenly very irritated. "We searched Hook's person and his car and his cottage and the Hideaway Cabins without finding any sign of the knife or bloodstains or gloves or anything else incriminating."

"He could have got rid of them somewhere, hid them in a thousand places. . . ."

"We did find evidence that Hook has been going to the cabins on a regular basis, just as he told us: stacks of racing forms, a bottle of liquor he kept there, some other things. That gives him a plausible reason for being there tonight. He's also got an apparent alibi for the time of the attack on Florence Cross. One you already know about, Keller. It's corroborated by a trooper's report of a routine check on Florence Cross' neighbors on the night of the attack, and Hook says you checked it yesterday afternoon with this woman writer, Valerie Broome, and she confirms that she was with him during that time."

"That alibi stinks," Keller said. "The Broome bitch is lying to protect him."

"Why would she lie to protect a maniac who cuts up women just like herself? She's only known him a week besides. Come on, Keller, use your head."

"He's got a yellow sheet in New York City, did you know that?"

"We know it," Rocca said. "He served ninety days for aggravated assault, and that was six years ago. The assault was against a man involved with Hook's ex-wife. So what does that prove? He has no other record of any kind."

"He's a horseplayer, a race track sharpie—"

"Which also proves nothing. There's no law against playing the horses. Look, we've been at Hook for three hours and we can't even dent his story. It doesn't make complete sense in certain areas, granted, but he's got emotional problems and he was drunk. He doesn't deny either of those things, and he didn't try to hide his record in New York City."

"I tell you, he's guilty as sin. If you'd let *me* in there with him, I'd have gotten a confession out of him by now."

"How?" Rocca asked sharply. "With your fists?"

"That's one way." He shouldn't have puked on my shoes, Keller thought, and took a quick glance down there again. He had rubbed at the polished leather with water and a rag, but he felt he could still see the stain glowing just under the surface: the Ripper's vomit. "That's the best way," he said, "the hell with your goddamn bleeding-heart liberals."

"What is it with you, Keller? What makes you so positive Hook is the man we're after?"

"I know it, that's all."

"But you don't have anything to back it up, do you."

He thought of the tissue, the snot—and knew what Rocca would say if he told him about them: *So you found a tissue at the foot of the Cross promontory, not on the promontory itself, and Hook admits that it might be his, he might have dropped it when he was out walking. What kind of evidence of guilt is that? You say the tissue had the feel of the Ripper on it; that doesn't mean a thing, either, and you know it. . . .*

"No," he said tightly.

"Then you've got something personal against Hook, is that it?"

"I've got five killings against him," Keller said, "and an attempted sixth. That's what I've got against him. And now you want to let him go. Jesus Christ, you can hold him for seventy-two hours without charging him—"

"I could, but what *good* would that do? Word would leak out before long that we had someone in custody, and people would start relaxing no matter what we said—the last thing we want to happen. Then when we let Hook go finally, and it looks to me like that's just what we'd have to do, they'd be even more panicked and have even less confidence in us than they do now. The way feelings are, there might even be fools like Manders who'd get it into their minds to go after Hook themselves, and for no reason except that they've convinced themselves he's guilty because we held him seventy-two hours on suspicion. Arresting somebody without evidence can be twice as bad as not arresting anybody at all in a situation like this; if you thought it over rationally, you'd realize that. Besides, Hook's not going to go anywhere. If he tries to run, it's an admission of guilt."

"You let him go free, he'll damned well go on the prowl for number six!"

"I'll have men keeping an eye on him. *If* he's guilty, he won't have the chance to go after number six."

"The hell he won't," Keller said. "He'll find a way, he's a cunning, murdering son of a bitch, and if he spills any more blood, it'll be on *your* hands, baby."

"The hell with it," Rocca said, "there's no point in trying to talk sense to you and I'm just not going to waste any more time. I've had enough tonight. You've got no damned authority in this investigation, and besides that I don't much care for the way you've been interfering, going off half cocked. Not notifying us of Smith's radio alarm may have cost the capture of the real assailant. . . ."

Keller felt the beat of his pulse in his cheekbones; his face seemed to be swelling. "Bullshit, Rocca," he said, "you and your troopers hadn't left your radios unattended out at the Manders place, you'd have heard the call the same time I did. You blew it yourselves and now you want to blow it again—"

Rocca stood up, his face richly veined. "I'm through talking to you, Keller, and through listening to you and through putting up with you. Get out of here, go home, and from now on stay the hell out of our way. Do I make myself understood?"

They glared at each other. Keller's hand throbbed; he could almost feel the impact of his knuckles with Rocca's beard-stubbled jaw. Control. Control. He took a deep, almost painful breath. "All right, Rocca," he said, "all right," and spun around and stalked out.

When he stepped through the front door of the substation a moment later, the press converged on him like wolves, nipping with sharp, eager teeth. Young, middle-aged, man, woman, fag, dyke—every variety of vulture you could think of. "I've got nothing to say to you," he said, and shoved through them toward his cruiser.

One caught his arm, a small bearded man in a plastic raincoat. "Give us a break, Constable. Who have they got in there? Does it look like they've caught the Ripper?"

Keller wrenched away from the man, shoved him, and sent him sprawling onto the rain-puddled concrete. The others fell away. The one he had shoved said, "Hey, hey, what the hell's the idea?"

"Vultures," Keller said. "You cost me in Chicago, but you'll never cost me again. Never, you hear me?"

He went to the cruiser, took it out onto the highway. And as he did so, a thought suddenly popped open in his brain like a flower; expanded, its colors as lustrous and delicate as petals. It wasn't so bad, after all, that they were letting Hook go. No, by Christ, it wasn't bad at all because it meant that he, Keller, could nail Hook again and this time do it the right way. The Keystone Kops had little interest in Hook now; Rocca had as much as said so. Which left him in a position of full control: he could handle Hook any way he saw fit.

The Ripper was still his, *all* his now.

And he knew—he could see it at the bright center of the blossom—exactly how he was going to break him.

HOOK

Lieutenant Rocca, along with one other uniformed trooper, took Hook out through the rear entrance and put him into a patrol car. The rain had slackened into a steady drizzle; the clouds in the morning sky had begun to fragment slightly, indicating that the storm had blown itself out. Around to the front of the substation several more troopers were holding the crush of reporters at bay —a diversionary tactic, Hook supposed dully, so that none of them would know he was being taken away or could identify him.

He still could not quite believe they were releasing him. The endless questions had instilled in him a sense of fatalism: they all thought he was the Ripper, nothing he would say or do would convince them otherwise, and they would lock him up pretty soon and tell him that he had better get himself a lawyer, even though he had waived the right to presence of counsel before the interrogation began. But then Rocca had come back into the room after a lengthy absence and had told him they were going to let him go. Just like that. No explanations, except that for the moment he had checked out to their satisfaction.

He had sagged in the chair—release of tension, followed instantly by a kind of numbing fatigue. "Thank God," he had said.

"You're still under suspicion," Rocca had said flatly, "so you make sure you keep yourself available."

"I'm innocent. You've got to believe that or you wouldn't be letting me go at all."

"If you are, you don't have any more worries. All right—we'll take you home. I'll have a trooper bring your car around later."

Now, in the patrol car, Hook sat with his arms wrapped across his chest. He was cold, bone-marrow cold, and he wondered how long it would be before he'd be able to get warm again. His head ached with hangover, his throat was sore and scratchy. He must have been out of his mind to start drinking again. Alcohol wasn't a crutch, it was a spear: you leaned on it and it cut through and then cut you up inside.

I could be dead now, he thought. Keller could have shot me instead of firing over my head, and I'd be as dead as poor Paula Eaton. . . .

They rode in silence the short distance to Stone Bridge Road. When they pulled up in front of his cottage, Rocca said, "Remember what I told you, Hook. The way it looks now you're as innocent as you claim to be, but if you do anything at all that makes you look the least bit guilty, I'll have your ass in a cell so fast you won't know what hit you. Understood?"

"Yes," Hook said. "I'm not the Ripper," he said.

Rocca got out and opened the rear door for him, then slid back into the front seat. The two policemen sat there inside, looking out at him. Hook stood uncertainly for a moment, finally turned and went up the steps and unlocked the porch door; entered and closed it again and leaned back against it. After a moment he heard the patrol car drive away.

Free. Home again, alone again.

He went into the living room, into the bedroom, without turning on any lights. He took off his damp clothing and put on fresh underwear, and just that way he lay uncovered on the bed. What would Valerie think when she heard about what happened tonight? Would the doubt in her grow so large that it could never be gotten rid of? He wondered if he should call her later or if she would call him. He wondered if there was anything left of their relationship.

I still don't know where I'm going, he thought.

A little while later, exhausted, he passed into a thin, thrashing slumber.

And came out of it suddenly, jerking upright, when something went *ping!* against the window glass.

He pawed at his eyes, got them into gritty focus. It was still dark in the room; he might have been asleep five minutes or an hour. *Ping!* He came off the bed, stumbled to the window, drew the curtains aside and stared out.

A man stood in the shadows beneath the dripping branches of a pine thirty feet away, hand upraised and then flung forward. *Ping!* A pebble: he was throwing pebbles.

Hook could not see him clearly, and his first thought was that it was a trooper. He knew Rocca might probably have him watched, accepted that. But a trooper wouldn't be throwing pebbles at his window, alerting Hook to his presence. . . .

The shape moved forward two steps, then a third, and now Hook could see him well enough to recognize him. A chill like grains of ice moved through his body, tightened his groin, started him trembling again.

The man watching the cottage, throwing pebbles because he wanted Hook to *know* he was there, was Alex Keller.

BLOODSTONE

Paula Eaton's murder made national headlines and all the major television news broadcasts and brought still more press people into Bloodstone. There were rumors that the state police had arrested someone, but had subsequently released him because of insufficient evidence; Lieutenant Rocca would not verify this, nor would Captain Jacobsen in Albany, nor would any other police or government official. No one seemed to know exactly who it was who had been arrested. Speculation included the young reporter for the local weekly paper, Jack Cross, who was apparently the fiancé of the new victim and whose mother had been attacked on Wednesday night, and Steven Hook, who had found the body of the Ripper's fourth victim. However, Cross could not be located for comment, and Hook remained secluded inside his cottage.

Several of the press who had been at the Hideaway Cabins filed reports that Lieutenant Daniel Smith had been rushed from the scene to the hospital in Lake George. The state police did not deny this, but neither would they reveal the reason why. A hospital spokesman would say only that Smith had been admitted for observation and was allowed no visitors.

What had frightened Tony Manders' wife, it developed, had been a young doe. This same doe was what Manders had shot; it was found in the woods, bloodied and nearly dead, by troopers just before they had finally been summoned away to the abandoned cabin complex, and had later been killed by Manders' nearest neighbor and hidden away in the man's cellar for butchering.

Manders told his wife that the false alarm was all her fault: if she hadn't cried wolf—or doe, as it happened—the Ripper might be in jail right now. She told him the false alarm was all his fault: he had gone outside with that rifle of his, after all, and while she had only seen the doe through the kitchen window, from a distance, he had gotten near enough to shoot it, and even in a storm a doe didn't look anything like a man when you got that close. Manders told her that if she didn't shut her face, he was going to have to hit her for the first time in their marriage. His wife, who was as big as he was and had a violent temper, told him that if he laid a hand on her, she would cut off his balls with a hatchet. There was no further argument between them.

Two residents of Bloodstone, both of whom had read the New York papers carrying interviews with James Ferrara, in which Ferrara had elaborated his theory of the murders, independently telephoned the state police substation. Both agreed angrily that the theories were "a crock, scare stuff, psychiatric mumbo jumbo," and one of them said, all right, if the Ripper didn't know he was the Ripper and anyone could be guilty, maybe it was the goddamn kike psychiatrist himself who was cutting up their women. The trooper who took this call patiently explained that that was hardly likely, and besides, Ferrara was of *Italian* extraction.

Fourteen other residents of Bloodstone drove to Albany, entered the State Capitol, and demanded to see the governor himself about calling out the National Guard. Governor Carey, it turned out, was in Rochester to address a Democratic Committee luncheon. He did, however, later issue a statement from Rochester, appealing to the people of Essex County to remain calm and to allow law enforcement officials to handle the situation.

Eleven additional residents, including Tony Manders and one member of the town council, met at the councilman's house to plan vigilante strategy.

A representative of a fundamentalist religious sect based in the Adirondacks, who also claimed to be a psychic, was interviewed on the *Today Show* in New York City. He said he had visited Bloodstone the day before, in the hope that he would be able to assist in the search for the Ripper, but that the psychic emanations had been so strongly and violently evil that he had been literally driven out. He stated further that he felt Satan himself had emerged in Bloodstone and urged everyone to pray for the town's salvation.

A prominent television anchorman taped a report in which he said the Ripper case had become the most vicious and frightening crime story of the year, if not of the decade. His cameraman said to a bartender later, after the tape was aired nationally, that what the Ripper case had really become was the best freak show since Watergate.

CROSS

In the hours since the Hideaway Cabins, Cross had shifted emotions many times.

Rage and disbelief. Rocca had to be lying to him, Paula could not be dead. He had thrown himself at the lieutenant, beat at his arms, shouting it: "Paula can't be dead!" Two of the troopers had pulled him away gently, held him.

Revulsion and pain. The look on Rocca's face, on the faces of the other troopers, had finally convinced him that it was the truth. He had a vague memory of sobbing, of leaning against the cold metal of one of the patrol cars with his hands pressed to his face, while images of Paula unfolded in his mind—images of her as she looked alive, he could not imagine her in death. And still could not.

Desolation. They had let him leave the cabins, been glad to get rid of him, and he had slipped away through the weeds and the darkness to where he had left the Chevy. And he had started driving blindly again: up and down, back and forth, rain and emptiness.

Relief. This came to him insidiously, working at the edges of his consciousness. He was out from under with Paula for sure now; she was no longer a threat to him, to his career. He could stay in Bloodstone as long as he wanted; he could leave Bloodstone whenever he chose.

Guilt. But Paula was dead, and he didn't want her to be dead, he had never wanted anything like that. It wasn't his fault, he had warned her against the Ripper, he had told her not to go out at night alone—and yet, maybe if he had gone to see her tonight as he had promised, she would still be alive.

Grief. She was *dead,* and he had cared for her, he had enjoyed sleeping with her and being with her. Now he had no one.

Hopelessness. No one except Florence. And he found himself driving up the access road to his mother's house. Yes, and coming to her was the right thing to do because she was the only one who cared, the only one who could give him comfort.

Bewilderment. It had taken him a long while to rouse her, and when she finally came to open the door for him, and he told her about Paula, she had reacted first by backing away from him, looking at him with huge, moist, shocked eyes. Then, when he babbled out the rest of the story, told her about the Hideaway Cabins and Keller and Smith and Hook being the Ripper, she had gathered him against her and held him as she had on Wednesday night, weeping.

Numbness. Sitting on the couch with her, hours moving away, his mind blank. Drinking cup after cup of hot coffee. Smoking cigarette after cigarette. Florence talking to him, saying words that he only half heard, until the dawn spilled gray light through the windows.

And now, fear. This has to do—and he is not quite sure why—with the trooper who has come into the dark old parlor just as the clock chimes eight. The trooper stands before him, towers over him; his head, his body seem enormous to Cross as he says, "Son, Lieutenant Rocca has some more questions to ask you and he thinks the substation is the best place to ask them. That's why he had me come looking for you."

"Can't it wait until later?" Florence asks. "You can see how upset Jack is, can't you?"

"Suppose you let me handle this, ma'am," the trooper says gently. "You've been through a bad ordeal yourself." He looks at Cross. "You want to come along with me now, son?"

"I don't want to go to the substation," Cross says. His voice sounds shrill in his ears, and he realizes his hands are spasmodic.

"Why can't the lieutenant come here?" Florence says. "Doesn't he have any heart, any compassion?"

The trooper shifts on his feet, looks in an uncomfortable way between her and Cross. "He'll have to come down to the substation," he says, "I'm sorry."

Florence sighs. The old Florence sigh, but magnified now, Cross realizes, almost pathological. She is taking all this harder than he is.

"What questions does Lieutenant Rocca want to ask?" she says. "Jack said he told him everything he knows at the Hideaway Cabins."

The trooper hesitates, moistens his lips, shifts his feet again. "The coroner has performed an autopsy," he says. "That's standard procedure in a violent homicide, you understand."

"We don't want to hear about that."

"Look, you're making this very difficult for me." The trooper pauses, and then he says, "Miss Eaton was more than three months pregnant."

Florence puts a hand to her mouth, turns to stare at Cross. Hands on his knees, he sits there. Just sits there. It is very quiet in the room. After a long while he raises his eyes to his mother's, and when he does he feels the fear in him change to yet something else, something which he cannot name.

The corners of her mouth, quivering, seem to bend upward in what might be the faintest ghost of a smile.

She is proud of him, he thinks.

VALERIE

Finally, after eighteen rings, Valerie picked up the telephone. Her wristwatch said it was five past eight A.M. "I told you I didn't want any calls," she said, but it wasn't an employee of the Homelite. It was John A. Reese of *Insight Magazine*.

"Do you know what I *went* through?" he said. "That stupid operator wouldn't put through the call, and then you keep me waiting even longer before you decide to answer."

"I'm sorry, John," she said. "I asked specifically that all calls be held off."

"I trust that's because you were up most of the night, working."

"Well—no. I went to bed early."

There was a thick pause. She drew her knees up, leaned back against the headboard. She felt huge, moist with sleep. Ferrara had come knocking on the door more than an hour ago, calling out to her, but she hadn't let herself wake up then; she almost hadn't let herself wake up to answer the phone, either.

Reese said, "Valerie, are we in the same world? Don't you know what's going on?"

"What do you mean?"

"The fifth murder, what do you think I mean?"

Her mouth opened; her hand tightened around the receiver. She was fully awake now, and it was suddenly very cold in the room. "Oh God, John, the Ripper killed *another* one last night?"

Another pause. "You didn't even know about it, for Christ's sake?"

"No. I was exhausted and I'm having trouble coping with this town and I just . . . I went to bed early. John—"

Reese said angrily, "Don't tell me you can't cope with that damned town of yours after *you* sought the assignment. I authorized a substantial advance for you; you're supposed to be on top of things in that lunatic asylum up there. Your friend Ferrara apparently is, he's getting his name in the papers here—all the fancy psychological theories that *we* were supposed to be buying. This is one of the hottest stories of the year, and you're huddled in bed because you can't cope with the town."

She swung her feet off the bed, stood up. "I'm sorry, John, I don't know what else to say. Except that I'll get right on it. Who was the victim?"

"A woman named Paula Eaton."

"Oh my God."

"You know her?"

"I met her last Saturday. Do the police have anything?"

"It's rumored they arrested someone finally, but they seem to have let him go again. Lack of evidence."

"Who?"

"How would I know?" His voice rose again. "You're there and I'm here and you're asking *me* questions! Get out and dig up the facts!"

"As soon as I hang up."

"I want at least seventy-five hundred words for the next issue," Reese said. "I've already got the art department working up a cover. We close the issue Saturday night, so I'll need your pages by midmorning. Don't worry about a polish; that's what we've got editors for."

"I'll hand deliver it," she said. "Sunday morning."

Reese paused again. Then: "Just how much have you written so far, Valerie?"

"Fifteen pages," she lied. "Four thousand words. And the rest outlined. The way it's set up, I won't have to rewrite because of the fifth murder, just drop it into the lead and a couple of other places."

"All right then. Make sure you give me some sidebar stuff by Ferrara, let him earn his goddamn honorarium. Anything that's left after the *News* picked him over, that is."

"That's all included," she said, "don't worry."

"I'm very worried. The only thing that will make me stop worrying is seventy-five hundred solid publishable words."

Reese range off, and Valerie replaced the receiver. She stood there for a moment in the cold room. Whom had the police arrested last night? That was the one question turning over and over in her mind. Whom had they arrested, and why?

Steven Hook? her cool journalistic voice said. *Was that who it was?*

No, she said, that's not who it was.

But it could be.

Steven is not the Ripper.

Anyone could be the Ripper.

I was with him when Florence Cross was attacked!

Then why these doubts, these fears? Isn't it because we're afraid we might have slept with a man who could be the Ripper?

God!

Valerie took off her nightgown and dressed hurriedly. She was just putting on her makeup when the state police arrived to talk to her about Steven Hook. . . .

KELLER

He had his hand resting casually on the butt of his revolver when the Ripper opened the door. "Morning, Hook," he said. "Get a good night's sleep, did you?"

The Ripper looked pale and haggard, eyes underlined in violet-black; muscles jumped in his face and hands. Keller had seen plenty of guilty men on the verge of breaking down, and this one had all the symptoms. It wouldn't be long now. Put a little more pressure on him, keep the pressure on, and he would crack wide open like an eggshell: confess, go after the knife and try to rip another woman, do something that would tie him up once and for all. He could take Hook any time he wanted now, rough him up, force a confession out of him, but that wouldn't stand up with the Keystone Kops or the bleeding-heart courts. No, he had to give them hard evidence when he gave them Hook, dead or alive. And dead was the best way; they couldn't find a reason to let him go again if he was dead. But he still needed the hard evidence. They had hung his ass in Chicago just for doing his job, and he wasn't going to give them or anyone an opportunity to hang his ass again.

"Leave me alone," the Ripper said. "Why can't you leave me alone?"

Keller said, "You shouldn't have puked on my shoes last night, Hook." He pointed his thumb downward. "They're my best shoes and they're ruined now, I'll never get the stain out or the smell out. You shouldn't have done it."

The Ripper hadn't expected that—keep them off-balance, that was the thing—and he looked sickly bewildered. His eyes bobbed down to the shoes, bobbed up again. "Christ," he said.

"But you'll pay for them," Keller said, and smiled at him. "One way or another, you'll pay for everything."

"Why are you doing this to me?" The Ripper ran a shaky hand across his face. "The state police let me go, they know I'm innocent. Why do you have to keep persecuting me?"

"Guilty people always feel persecuted," Keller said. "Particularly the homicidal maniacs. It's something I learned a long time ago."

"I'm not the Ripper."

"Sure you are, Hook. We both know that."

"I'm not, damn you! Listen, I'm not going to take much more of this. If you don't stop watching me, hounding me, I'll report you to Rocca."

"Go ahead," Keller said agreeably. "It won't do you any good. There's just no way you can put a bloodhound off the scent once he's got it. No way at all."

"Keller, for the love of God—"

"Don't talk about God to me," Keller said, "the Ripper doesn't have any right to talk about God to anyone." Then he took the latch key from his pocket and moved it slowly back and forth in front of Hook's face, like a trainer working a stunned animal. "You see this?" he said. "You know what this is, Hook?"

The Ripper stared at him, at the key, breathing through his mouth.

"It's the key to your future," Keller told him. "It's the key to the first of three or four or maybe a dozen cells, plain barred ones and padded ones, that you're going to spend the rest of your life inside. I'm going to put you in that first cell myself pretty soon, and this is the key I'll turn behind you. Then it'll be all over. No more knives, no more ripping, no more blood hard-ons. The end of everything. . . ."

"I don't have to listen to any more of this," the Ripper said. He started to back inside the porch, to close the door.

Keller stepped forward and wedged his leg against it.

Reflexively the Ripper pressed his weight into the wooden frame, trying to shut him out. Keller liked that; it was just what he wanted. He lunged violently into the door, left hand coming forward to bunch in the Ripper's shirtfront and then pull him to one side. The edge of the door scraped against Hook's side, flew inward, and banged off the wall. The Ripper struggled in his grasp, hands lifting to claw at the bunched fingers. Abruptly, Keller released him and moved back a half-step and transferred the key to his left hand and drew the revolver. He shoved the muzzle against the Ripper's chest.

"Come on," he said. "Come on, Ripper."

Hook did not move, looked as if he had stopped breathing. His eyes flicked between the gun and Keller's face; his own features were ashen, and there was sweat on his forehead.

Keller let him feel the pressure of the gun for a full minute, let him feel the *pressure* for a full minute. Then he pulled it back, moved it through the air in the same way he had moved the key. Finally, he put it away, keeping his hand on the butt.

The Ripper's mouth worked, but nothing came out. He seemed to sag against the doorjamb.

"The key or the gun, Hook," Keller said. "It's up to you. Now or later. Make it easy on yourself."

Hook wobbled his head: a desperate negative.

"Okay then," he said, and shrugged. "I'll be on my

way now—but not too far away. I'll be watching you, Hook. Everything you do, everywhere you go from now on."

Deliberately he turned his back on the Ripper, hesitated for an instant, and then went down the steps and across the yard in a slow, even stride. Behind him he heard the door slam, and smiled again. He had handled things just right, he thought, put on just the right amount of additional pressure. His instincts told him he wouldn't have to wait much longer; Hook was teetering on the edge, no doubt about that.

Walking, Keller saw no sign of the state police units that had been making periodic checks on the Ripper's cottage throughout the night and morning—he had waited until the last of those checks before going up to confront Hook just now—and of course there was no one but himself posted to watch the Ripper around the clock. Rocca had put on nothing but a superficial surveillance, which was just what Keller had expected; that stupid Keystone Kop had it in his head that Hook wasn't the man, all right. For Keller's purposes, that was working out all to the good.

When he reached the trees to the north he took up a position that allowed him a clear view of both front and rear entrances to the cottage. He would stay hidden there for a while and then he would move around to the other side. That way, the Ripper would never quite know where he was. There wasn't any way he was going to get out of there without Keller knowing about it.

Keller took the package of NoDoz from his jacket, swallowed another of the capsules. He had gotten the package and a bag of fresh fruit and a box of cookies when he had gone home from the substation last night to change into dry clothes. (But not different shoes. He would wear these shoes until the finish, track the Ripper to the finish in shoes which bore the Ripper's own stains.) Fatigue lay heavily on him, and he had a malignant headache, and his feet were chilled to the point of numbness. His sense of time was screwed up, too. It seemed to rush by for a while and then to slow down to a crawl, so that there was no clear perspective on lapses—something like heavy drinking. But none of this was important unless his alertness was affected, and with the NoDoz there was no danger of that for a long while yet.

He watched and waited.

SMITH

Smith was up and pacing back and forth in front of the windows that Friday morning when his wife and Dr. Owen Metcalf came into the hospital room.

Marjorie's placid face, like unkneaded dough, bore little marks of worry, and her hands moving together at her breast made a dry rustling sound. Metcalf looked irritated and disapproving; he was a thin, disagreeable-looking man, and that was more or less his normal expression.

"Marjorie tells me you're being a damned fool," Metcalf said. "Which means you're continuing in a consistent pattern."

"Think what you like," Smith said. "I'm leaving here today and that's all there is to it."

"You've got a severely ulcerated stomach, owing as much to neglect of medical attention as anything else. That attack you suffered last night came perilously close to perforation; you could still perforate at any time. Any sort of stress or exertion—"

"You've been all through that, Owen."

"Yes, but you don't seem to grasp the full significance of it. That ulcer could kill you, Smith, and I'm not exaggerating. If you won't consent to an immediate gastrectomy, then it's imperative that you at least spend several days in here where we can run more intensive tests and possibly treat it internally. The X rays—"

"I can't spend several days in here," Smith said. "I've got a job to do."

"There are others just as qualified as you to handle those sex murders in Bloodstone."

"They aren't exactly sex murders."

"Whatever they are, then. It's a dreadful business, but your life is at stake here as much as any potential homicide victim's. More so, because you're taking no precautions whatsoever."

"It's my case and I've got to see it through," Smith said. "You wouldn't understand it if I tried to explain."

"Is that so?"

"Yes, that's so."

He saw that Marjorie had turned from them and was looking out one of the windows. Irrationally, he felt a stirring of anger; that had always been her way, to deal with the difficult by turning from it. Each time they had problems with the children, arguments over money, troubles of any kind, she had moved to windows, other rooms, different moods. He had explained it to himself for a long while as an excess of feeling on her part, a delicacy of response so deep that she had to remove herself or risk intense pain. But the simple truth was: Marjorie was completely dull and stupid. He had married a dull, stupid woman. . . .

Metcalf was speaking to him, and he returned his gaze to the man. "What?"

"I said, I suppose then there's nothing further I can say to convince you of the foolishness of your decision."

"No, there's nothing more you can say. Look, Owen, I don't have any pain this morning"—which was a lie, although the pain was of the old familiar variety—"and I feel rested. I intend to take it easy; I won't exert myself or let myself get overly excited or tired. And I'll take the medicine you gave me and keep in touch regularly."

Metcalf grunted, turned for the door.

"When the case is finished I'll have the operation," Smith said. "I'll do whatever you want me to do."

"If you're still alive," Metcalf said coldly, and went out.

Marjorie was still staring out the window. Looking at her again, Smith noticed now that the upper third of a paperback book, another nurse novel, was visible inside the shoulder purse she carried; he could read the title: *Crisis in Ward C*. Dull and stupid, he thought. He went to stand beside her.

"Danny," she said, and one eye seemed to look at him while the other remained fixed on the window, "Danny, for heaven's sake why won't you listen to the doctor? He said you might *die* if you leave the hospital now—"

"I'm not going to die," Smith said.

"I just don't know why you're acting this way. You almost lost your life last night, and now you want to go right back up there to Bloodstone and risk it again. You never took your work so seriously before. Why are you so . . . so desperate now?"

Desperate, he thought. She had missed it again, misunderstood his mood and temper. He had always found reasons for this, too—some failure, perhaps, which any person might have in understanding another, even someone close to him. He looked at her face, and it seemed to blur again, as it had in the past. I know you, Marjorie, he thought, but we really are strangers now anyway. Strangers.

"Go on home," he said, "and bring me some fresh clothes."

"Danny—"

"Do what I ask. It'll be all right."

She turned to face him fully, and he watched the little creases of concern meld to other creases, marks which signaled acceptance. A dough-face, on which patterns were imposed. "Yes, Danny," she said, and he took her by the elbow and guided her to the door.

When he was alone again he went to one of the windows and stood looking down into a barren courtyard. Rocca had called an hour earlier to fill him in on last night: the finish at the Hideaway Cabins, the interrogation and eventual release of Hook, Keller's groundless obsession with Hook, the coroner's report that Paula Eaton had been pregnant, the questioning of Valerie Broome and Jack Cross. Smith was forced to agree that Rocca had made the right move in releasing Hook; without even a single scrap of evidence against the man, except his perhaps coincidental presence at the Cabins, it would have been pointless to hold him. On the surface, then, it looked like they were nearly back to where they had started, without leads or strong suspects. Rocca had said that, and his voice had sounded wearily defeated.

But Smith felt otherwise. The case was close to breaking, he sensed it. If he made certain moves, methodical moves, he would split it wide open. It was all up to him, despite the fact Rocca had told him that Captain Jacobsen, after learning of Smith's apparent incapacitation, was sending up another CID man to take over control of the investigation. He had to finish it as much for himself, his own peace of mind, as for any other reason.

No one understood how he felt, he thought bitterly; no one *could* understand it. Except maybe one person. Christ, there was one person who might understand at least part of it. That person wasn't Marjorie, and it wasn't either of his daughters (who were strangers to him too, he had realized that when he saw them here at the hospital; they were carbon copies of Marjorie, as though her genes had outweighed his in their creation). And it wasn't Rocca or Captain Jacobsen or Plummer.

The one man who could probably have grasped part of his feelings was Alex Keller.

FERRARA

James Ferrara said, "The assailant, or the Ripper if you prefer, has gone over the thin edge of unreason. The acceleration of the attacks is the primary symptom, of course."

He took another swallow of the Manhattan in front of him. It was either his third or fourth, he was not quite sure—he did not usually drink this much early in the day—but he was certainly holding the liquor well. The case, in fact, was making even more sense now than it had previously.

The group of press people in and around the booth in the Homelite bar were all staring at him intently. They seemed willing to listen to him for the rest of the day. One of them signaled to the bartender for another round of drinks, and Ferrara said, "No, please, no more for me." His voice sounded a little shrill, but the words were unslurred; fundamentally, he was in perfect command of himself.

"It's on me," the reporter said. "One more won't hurt."

"Well no, I don't suppose it will," Ferrara said. The reporters all laughed, and he smiled companionably. "Just the one, though."

"Sure. Go on with what you were saying, Doctor."

He cleared his throat. "You must consider the pressures bearing down upon the Ripper," he said. "We have already established the fact that the crimes are being committed in a kind of amnesiac fugue, a complex state in which the outward personality has sealed itself off from the perpetuation, but the irony of this complete severance of the personality—one part the 'good,' the known identity; the other part that of the 'Ripper'—the irony of this, as I was saying, is that each successful commission only leads to frustration. You see, the Ripper is not only satisfying complicated needs with these crimes, he is trying to reconcile the two parts of him, to make conscious acceptance of the murderous personality."

"Just a second, Doctor," the only woman reporter present said. "Are you telling us that the part of him that is the Ripper wants the other part of him to know it?"

"Precisely. If the crimes are successful, you see, then the recognition element has obviously not occurred and the assailant remains masked. This is unbearable to him. The crimes must become less and less spaced, increasingly outrageous, so that the fusion is made—" Ferrara swept out his arm to emphasize the point and knocked the Manhattan glass over. It bounced without breaking, rolled across the table; but there was no spillage because it was empty—he seemed to have finished the last of the drink. One of the reporters fielded the glass neatly and placed it upright in front of him.

"Sorry," Ferrara said. "I seem to have gotten a bit carried away."

The reporters laughed again, and he laughed with them. They were all on his side. Except, that was, for the woman. She said, "I just can't accept that theory, Doctor. It sounds pretty farfetched."

"Not at all." He took a cigarette from the pack beside him, lit it as the bartender arrived with a fresh round of drinks and set them out. "The whole point is, the man wants to be caught. That's the only way he can find out who he is, in effect, which was his primary motive from the beginning. To achieve identity. Self-recognition."

"I just don't understand how you can be so sure of this," the woman said. "I realize you're an accredited psychiatrist, but after all, your opinion is only one of many possible opinions, isn't it? You could be completely wrong."

"I could be," Ferrara said patiently, "but I'm not. As I've told you, I have made an extensive study of this case. Is it not without precedent, you understand, although the particulars are quite unique."

"It's a viable theory as far as I'm concerned," one of the men said, and the others nodded. "And a fascinating one, Doctor."

"Yes, isn't it?"

The woman was still skeptical. "Do you think he gets pleasure out of killing his victims, cutting them up the way he does?"

"Not in the accepted definition of the term 'pleasure,'" Ferrara said. "Which is to say he is not stimulated by his actions, sexually or otherwise. However, he seeks from them the 'pleasure of identity,' as it were, which of course disastrously eludes him."

"Well then, why does he kill only women? I mean, he could achieve this quest for identity just as well by killing men or even children, couldn't he?"

"No," Ferrara said. "The fixation, perverse as it is, is essentially heterosexual—perhaps even matriarchal. The surfacing of the Ripper persona is directly related to feelings of inadequacy or hatred or resentment, some shattering personal experience in his past or even in his present. Simply stated, then, he feels that through women his identity has been taken, and in order to find it he must kill them. Only women, that is to say."

"Wild," one of the other reporters said. "Even for a guy who goes out and cuts up women, this baby's crazy on top of that."

"I know what you mean," Ferrara agreed generously.

The female reporter said, "Suppose you tell us why you think the Ripper confronts his victims in one place and then transports them elsewhere to kill them? And what you believe might be the significance of the diamond-shaped marks."

"Signature," Ferrara said.

"I beg your pardon?"

"The diamond marks are the Ripper's signature, his way of identifying to all that he is the one responsible for the acts. Which is part of his search for identity, for discovery. As is his apprehension of the victim at one locale, his destruction of her at another. A desperate pleading for assistance in the fusion of self."

" 'Stop me before I kill again'?" another reporter said. "He hopes he'll be caught while transporting the victim from one place to another, *before* he can destroy her?"

"Essentially, yes."

But the woman said, "It seems to me, Doctor, that you're contriving explanations to fit your original hypothesis. I've got another possible answer, you know, just as plausible."

Ferrara frowned. "Have you?"

"The diamond marks are symbols of marriage, and the Ripper carries his victims away because symbolically he's taking them over the wedding threshold."

Ferrara realized that she was mocking him and decided he would not comment on what she had said. He took a careful sip from his fresh Manhattan. "Murder can be as positive a search for identity as sexuality, were you all aware of that?" he said. "It can be a voyage of self-discovery. Of course, it tends to get blunted far more rapidly than sexuality does."

The woman looked hostile now that he had refused to let her goad him, but the men nodded, still with him and waiting for more. Ferrara had another sip of his drink and wondered if he might not let them buy him one more, just one more, after this one.

While he was wondering that, and framing what he was about to say next, he glanced over at the door and saw that someone else had come into the bar, someone he recognized: Jack Cross.

HOOK

In the bathroom Hook splashed his face and neck with cold tap water. Straightening, he saw himself reflected in the medicine cabinet mirror: eyes that seemed to crouch deep in their sockets, dull-filmed and haunted; the skin on his cheekbones and around his mouth deeply lined and fuzzy gray in color, like petrified wood.

He turned away, dripping water, and went back into the cluttered living room. Cluttered and dirty. Like his life. All the time he had thought he was reconstructing his life, he had merely sat in the center of it, while at the edges, dangling off-center, all the planks and ledges of meaning had been collapsing. And now—

The telephone rang.

He jerked, twitched, at the sudden sound. His nerves felt ready to snap. Keller had done that to him, Keller far more than the events of last night: hounding him like a personification of Hugo's Javert, talking to him the way he had a few minutes ago, pulling that gun on him for the second time in twelve hours and the third time in the past five days. Should I call Rocca? he thought. Yes. No. I don't know. Why can't they *all* leave me alone?

Hook picked up the phone, as much to shut off the noise as to find out who it was. He held it against his ear, not speaking. Valerie's voice came through thinly: "Steven? Steven?"

She sounded upset, but her voice calmed him nonetheless; she was the only real calming force in his life just now, even after what had come between them yesterday. He sank into the nearest chair and pressed the phone more tightly against his ear, as if to draw her closer. "Hello, Valerie," he said. "My God, I'm glad you called."

"What happened last night?" she said. "What *happened?*"

"The Ripper killed Paula Eaton, poor Paula Eaton."

"I know that, I mean with you. Were you arrested?"

"Yes, but it was all a mistake—a terrible, grotesque mistake." He released a heavy breath. "The state police have been to see you, haven't they."

"Lieutenant Rocca was just here, yes. But he wouldn't give me any details about last night."

"I don't know many details," Hook said. "Lieutenant Smith chased someone away from the scene of Paula Eaton's murder, and he thought it might be me because he saw me driving into the Hideaway Cabins; but he never got close enough to see the car he was chasing, he was following taillights, and it must have turned off somewhere. The state police took me to the substation and questioned me, but they let me go again; they knew I was innocent." He did not mention the fact that he had seen patrol units checking up on him on two separate occasions this morning, before Keller had come knocking on his door.

Valerie said, "Why were you at those abandoned cabins?"

"Because I was in a bad way, mixed up. I don't remember much of what took place after I got there, it's all a blur." In self-condemnation: "I was drunk."

"You told me you hadn't had a drink in six years."

"I hadn't, not until last night."

"Why did you start again?"

"I told you, I was in a bad way. Keller, and then you acting as though you believed I could be the Ripper. . . ."

Beat. Just a single beat, like a normal hesitation before making a turn over a piece of business. But it was more than that, much more. "Oh Steven," she said in a low, painful voice.

"And there's still doubt in your mind, isn't there?" he said. "More doubt than ever. There'll be doubt until the real Ripper is caught."

"I'm sorry, I can't help it. I want to believe in you, I do believe in you, but so many things have happened. And just being in Bloodstone makes it all that much worse."

"When will I see you again?"

Beat. "I don't know," she said. "My editor at *Insight* called this morning. . . . I've got to do seventy-five hundred words on my article by early Sunday morning and I've only written seven hundred and fifty. I'll lose the assignment if I don't deliver—"

"Don't call us, we'll call you, right?"

"Please. Please, Steven."

"I need you," Hook said. "I need somebody, I don't have anyone, and Keller is outside right now; he's been outside all night, hounding me, because he's convinced for no sane reason that I'm guilty. I'm not guilty, Valerie, but I'm drowning."

Beat.
Beat.
Beat.

"I'll come see you later today, or you can come here,"

she said. "Just as soon as I can get some work done. I'll call you, Steven—I will."

And the line made an empty clicking sound.

He stood in sudden rage, slammed the receiver into its cradle, but as quickly as it had come, the anger drained away. Could he blame her, really, for her actions, her attitude? She had known him less than a week, and how can you *know* someone in that length of time, even if you've slept with him? Jesus, he didn't even know himself anymore, if he ever had. . . .

Ping!

He jumped, spun around, stared at the window. Then he ran there and pulled aside the curtains. There was nothing to see but the trees, branches swaying gently in the wind. But Keller was there, very close—and maybe he would come knocking at the door again, come *in* this time. If the man had crossed the line of sanity, then it might occur to him, too, that he didn't need to draw the line at the doorsill. He could just come in and unholster that gun yet another time and—

Hook could not finish the thought; it wouldn't happen that way, it would not. He came back to the chair, sat down, and clenched his hands between his knees. Sat there like that, sweating in the cold room.

Ping!

THE RIPPER

Time, feel time was no time before but nowtime is now and now and nownownownownownownow. • • •

CROSS

Cross stood peering through the dimness of the Homelite bar. Ferrara was there in one of the booths, surrounded by press people, laughing with them, drinking with them.

I never had a drink with anyone, he thought again.

I never laughed with friends or acquaintances.

I never even had a woman until Paula.

And Paula's dead, Paula's dead, Paula's dead. . . .

He saw Ferrara glance in his direction and then walked toward the booth, although it felt more as though he floated; he had felt that way every time he had taken a step since leaving his mother's house earlier with the trooper. It was not a Superman kind of floating; it had nothing to do with Superman. Nothing had anything to do with Superman anymore, or with Lois Lane or Clark Kent or Jimmy Olsen or Perry White. They were imaginary beings, comic book creations, and he had moved away from them now, could never go back to them. They could have nothing more to do with his life. The Ripper was real and he was real and both of them were alive and Paula was dead.

When he stopped in front of the booth, conversation stopped with him. The press people looked at him, seemed to recognize him; their eyes brightened, and their faces revealed interest. But Ferrara's eyes were not bright, and his face revealed only what might have been annoyance.

"Can I talk to you?" he said. "I need to talk to you."

Ferrara frowned and tamped out his cigarette. "As you can see, I'm rather busy at the moment. Perhaps a bit later—"

"I can't wait until later. I have to talk to you now; there's no one else I can talk to. I don't know what to do."

"Do about what?"

"About Paula, about the Ripper."

"I see. Well what do you *think* you should do?"

"I don't know," he said. "I want to see her, but I can't even imagine her dead; I don't want to see her dead."

"Then you shouldn't see her," Ferrara said. "By all means you should not see her."

"You're right," Cross said. "I won't. But what about the Ripper? What should I do about him?"

"I don't expect there is anything you can do, is there?"

"I thought the state police had him in jail, I thought I knew who he was. It wasn't so bad then. But they let him go because they didn't have any evidence. They said they thought he *wasn't* the Ripper. Lieutenant Rocca said that."

All the press people, in a body, seemed to lean toward him. "Who did they let go?" one of them asked. "Who did they think might be the Ripper?"

Cross shook his head; he did not take his eyes off

Ferrara. "Then they started questioning me, as if *I* could be the Ripper. She was your fiancée, they said. She was pregnant, they said. Where were you when she was killed, they said. It was awful."

Ferrara appeared to retreat deeper into the booth. "Everyone is a suspect, you must realize that."

"But not me," Cross said. "Not me, not me."

Ferrara said nothing.

"I'm a *victim,* that's what I am. At first I was just the focusing eye, the detached observer writing *The Ripper of Bloodstone*—but then he started to come into my life. First Florence, then Paula. Why? Why should he do that to me?"

"He has done nothing to you," Ferrara said. "His selection of victims is quite random. He does not even know you or anyone else exists, except of course for those individuals directly linked to his own tragic presence. What you feel—"

"I don't care about that now," Cross said. "I've got to do something, don't you see? First Florence, then Paula, and Paula is dead. I can't just observe anymore; I can't just go home and write my book. I've got to *do* something!"

Ferrara picked up his drink, drained it. The press people were staring at Cross in a hungry way now; one of them had started writing in a notebook, as he had been writing in his notebook last night. He was no longer one of their fraternity, his role *had* changed to one of full participant. The Ripper had seen to that.

"The death of your fiancée has placed you in a highly emotional state," Ferrara said. "I suggest you place yourself in the care of a qualified physician until—"

"No," Cross said. He felt himself begin to jerk in place, like an epileptic entering a clonic seizure, but he could not stop it. "I told you, I have to do something about the Ripper!"

"Just what is it you'd like to do? Hunt him down yourself, exact retribution for the personal torment he has caused you?"

"I don't know. I just have to do something."

"Permit me another suggestion, then. Seek out the

places at which the visible and the buried personalities of the Ripper merged, when he reunited with event by its discovery. Perhaps there you'll find direction."

"I'm not sure I know what you mean."

Ferrara's eyes appeared to roll sideways in their sockets, and he belched delicately. "What I mean," he said, "you should visit the scenes of the crimes."

Cross stared at him; the jerking lessened. Now he understood, and while he was still confused, not quite in complete control of circumstances, he felt that Ferrara had given him a purposeful course of action. "The scenes of the crimes," he said, and began to back off from the booth; the sensation of floating, at least, seemed suddenly to have vanished.

Two of the reporters stood up, and a third, who had been leaning against the side of the booth, took a step toward him. One of them said, "Just a second now, Mr. Cross."

Another one said, "Who was this man they had in jail and then released?"

The third one said, "You said your fiancée was pregnant, and that the state police had questioned you—"

He turned and ran to the door and through it and away.

SMITH

Smith finished signing the release form at the main desk in the hospital lobby, the letters of his name looking curiously round and childish as he slid the paper across to the duty nurse. He turned to Marjorie, took her arm. "We'll get a taxi to the office and I'll check out a car and drop you at home."

She nodded dully, stupidly, and they started for the entrance doors. And there was Plummer, just coming up onto the outer landing.

When Plummer pushed through the doors, he almost ran into them. He stopped abruptly and his mouth fell open. "Good God, Dan," he said. "What are you doing down *here?*"

"Leaving—isn't that obvious?"

"But I heard you were seriously ill, that's why I came. . . ."

"I'm not seriously ill. At least not ill enough to stay in here when there's work to be done in Bloodstone."

"He won't listen to the doctor," Marjorie said dully, stupidly.

"I was told you were brought here in an ambulance," Plummer said. "That you were unconscious. You can't just get up and go back to work after something like that, man."

"Don't tell me what I can and can't do, Plummer," Smith said. "And where were *you* last night?"

The abrupt question seemed to startle Plummer. "Why —I went over to my sister's in Whitehall." He paused, and pain flicked in his eyes. "I wanted to stay with Florence, at least for a while, but she . . . wanted to be alone." He paused again. "Why do you ask that?"

"I wanted to talk to you," Smith said. "I still do."

"About what?"

"About Florence. She's been acting rather strangely since the attack on her, wouldn't you say?"

"I suppose . . . yes. Yes, she has. But it was a terrible experience for her . . ."

"I want another talk with her too. A long talk."

"Why? She's told you everything she can."

"Has she?"

"Of course she has."

"I don't think so, Plummer."

They stood in silence for a moment, and for the first time Smith noticed that the man looked old. Somewhere between now and the last time he had taken a good look at him, Plummer had become old. And he felt, then, insight turning, enlarging: the same was true of Marjorie, which could only mean the same was true of him. Old, all of them. Christ. You just never knew what was happening to people, to yourself, until something forced you up against it.

Plummer said finally, "What are you trying to say, Dan?

Are you intimating Florence has been withholding important information?"

"We'll get into that later," Smith said. "The three of us together, because I want you there when I see Florence. As a matter of fact, suppose we do things the easy way. Instead of my signing out a car at the office here, I'll go back to Bloodstone with you after we drop Marjorie off. That way we can go straight to see Florence, and I can pick up my own car afterward."

Plummer hesitated, looking bewildered as well as old. "Dan, I just don't think you ought to be up and around—"

"I don't care what you think, what anyone thinks. Now are you going to take me up to Bloodstone or not?"

"Danny," Marjorie said dully, stupidly, "won't you please. . . ."

"Shut up. Just shut up, Marjorie."

She blinked at him, and then immediately, as he had known she would, she turned and stared out through the doors.

He said, "Well, Plummer?"

"All right," Plummer said, and by Christ, Smith thought, *his* voice was as dull and stupid as Marjorie's. Another stranger, he was surrounded by strangers. "Whatever you want, Dan, I won't argue with you."

"Good. That's exactly the way I want it."

They went out and down the hospital steps, turned a corner and followed the street leading toward the parking lot. Plummer, a little ahead of Marjorie and him, walked slowly, staring straight ahead. The cords in his neck showed, and the skin was crosshatched with age lines. Marjorie's face was blank, and age lines were prominent there too. What did the three of them look like? Smith wondered. What would someone—a rookie cop, say— think if he saw them on this cold, gray October day? *Three old people,* the rookie might think. *I wonder which of them is just being taken out of the hospital.*

It happened to everyone, that was the thing you seldom thought about but could never escape. Mays, who could no longer chase down those long line drives that he had once caught with ease. Musial, relegated to pinch-hitting roles in the hot St. Louis sun. Ruth, fat and struggling in Boston, falling down as he ran the bases. Dizzy Dean, his arm ruined, stumbling toward the dugout in Chicago. Ted Williams, circling the bases with his head down after that last home run. Only Koufax had gotten out in time, and that was a matter of doing it or losing all his stuff and eventually becoming a cripple. . . .

VALERIE

4.

death has always been an improvisatory business. The country, in fact, has commanded it to be that way: death as careless accident, death as unscored exit. (We are, after all, a consumer society; in the c.s., the only true sin is not to be able to consume further, i.e. to be dead.) So it has been something for the corridors or the dim abcesses of public buildings, the hidden parts of the private buildings.

Even in the more colorful, the more political deaths, the same hasty, improvisatory quality has persisted, raised in its more elfin moments to what might be considered the artlessness of the commedia dell'arte. Oswald in his undershirt blinking at Ruby's pointed finger (he could not believe that there was actually something there); Kennedy falling in the car in an explosion of roses, a finger twitching at his neck as if the bullet were an itch; Starkweather in his ruined ears looking across the prairies for someone else to kill because it was something to do; even the state funerals curiously misarranged, as with the Kennedy funeral train killing three on the tracks who simply could not comprehend that an actual train with an actual corpse was coming their way. Haste and improvisation afflicting the mass murderer or assassin no less than the dignified aging tycoon trying to breathe his remorseless last in a little open space.

But here in Bloodstone, New York, the improvisation— which still applies in the case of the five hideous murders to date— has taken on a pastoral tinge, much as if the transplantation of horror from what we think of as the more closed conventional spaces of death has necessitated different background, if not different scoring. One can conceive of the five female bodies in rigid frieze, features distended, eyes humorless and touched with horror; and yet one can also visualize a hint of scatology in their perception of death, the shriek of toilet humor which must underlie any apprehension of mortality and it just keeps coming out of me word after gleaming paragraph after smartly conceived image one after the other and all of it right in the John A. Reese and Insight vein that's the horror of it because the truth is

They are dead
They are hideously dead
Five women are dead
A homicidal maniac has killed five women here
And I am so sick of Smart Set
oh my god steven
i
am
so
sick
of

CROSS

He came down through the trees and the wet leaf mold to the rear of the Hideaway Cabins. This was not one of the scenes of the crimes, but there had been troopers all over the area where Paula's body had been found, and they wouldn't let him get anywhere near it. And Cross didn't want to go back to Florence's house, not yet and maybe not for a long time; the way she had smiled this morning when the trooper told her Paula had been pregnant—he knew it had been just that: a smile—had sickened him toward her again. So he had come here instead.

The state police had searched the cabins and the grounds last night, and if they hadn't found anything, there was probably nothing to find. But Hook might be the Ripper after all, the state police might have been wrong in letting him go, and that meant there *could* be some clue hidden here. Maybe the knife, the gloves, whatever instrument he used to make those terrible diamond-shaped marks. . . . (Oh Paula? Had the Ripper put them on Paula? No, he wouldn't think about that.) Those things were somewhere, the Ripper was somewhere and somebody.

Ferrara had steered him onto the right course, given him something positive to do about the Ripper, and he had to follow it as far as he could, as best he could. He was a full participant now, and full participation entitled him, forced him to join the hunt. For Paula. Who was dead. Was dead. Was dead.

There was a trooper stationed out front, sitting in his car on the access road; he was there, Cross knew, to keep out the press and any curious citizens who might come along. Which was why Cross had parked his car out of sight of the complex along the side of U.S. 9, gone up the road Keller had taken last night and then down from the rear.

But now that he was here, where should he start looking? Inside the cabins? Out here? Inside, outside, all around the town. Ins and outs. Something, somewhere. Paula.

He started toward the nearest of the cabins.

KELLER

Still waiting, still watching the Ripper's cottage on Stone Bridge Road, Keller listened to the wind, and it seemed to be saying *Chicago . . . Chicago . . . Chica-go . . .*

Oh yes, Chicago, he could never forget Chicago. Not even when he was closing in on the Ripper. It kept intruding on his thoughts; it wouldn't let him alone. They had nearly destroyed him in Chicago, that was why: how could you forget the place where you had nearly been destroyed?

But it hadn't been his fault, none of it; he had no reason, had never had any reason, for guilt. It was the girl, the kids, the bleeding hearts, the liberal press, the country itself—and too much feeling and too much pain. No one had considered him, though. Not then and not since. It had all been the kids: interviews with the kids, television close-ups of the kids with smashed heads, sympathy for the kids, excuses for the kids. No one had even been aware of *his* pain, *his* sacrifice. No one cared about him, or cared to understand his side of it.

Well all that was going to change. When he gave them the Ripper it was all going to be different. They'd have to listen to his side then; Chicago would have to listen and the country would have to listen. Even the whores in Albany would have to listen; they'd never laugh at him again when he couldn't perform (and that was just one more thing that Chicago had done to him). He would not be ignored any longer. He was an American as any of them, more so, and America belonged to him as much as to anyone.

He felt suddenly like laughing, but laughter would not have been professional, not here, waiting for the Ripper. Later. Later he would laugh, after he had given them Hook. And then he would go down to Albany and pick up one of the whores, and right in his cruiser, maybe parked right in front of the capitol dome, he would fuck the ass off her in the sheer throbbing joy of release.

VALERIE

The telephone was ringing.

She knew it was Steven, that he hadn't been able to wait for her to call him again. She should not have hung up on him so abruptly before, but the conversation had been too painful, too equivocal. Only, the hour since had been just as painful, just as equivocal; she couldn't write worth a damn, that was obvious. She had to come to terms with her feelings about Steven, and the time was right now.

She answered the phone, and he said, "I can't wait until tonight, Valerie, I've got to see you now, as soon as possible. I've got to talk to you."

His voice sounded good, she thought—a little high, a little fast, but essentially well-modulated and in control. The voice of a sane man who has gone through a series of major crises and suffered each of them deeply because he feels deeply. Inside he was still strong, stronger than she would ever have been if their positions had been reversed.

She said, "Talk about what, Steven?"

"Everything. What's happened here in Bloodstone, what's happened between us, what I'm going to do about myself. I've got to make some decisions, and I can't do it without help. I can't fight things through alone anymore."

She looked over at the desk with her typewriter and the pages strewn around it like dead leaves. Five women were dead and Steven was suffering, needing, and here she was, trying to put together glib sociology and varnished prose for *Insight*. Counterfeit again. Always counterfeit, nothing inside, just doing a cut-and-paste job on pain and assembling it into printed words. *Is* there anything inside me? she thought. Will the real Valerie Broome please stand up?

"Valerie?" he said.

He could not be guilty; he simply could not. If he was, she would have had some intuition of it long before Keller's questions yesterday, Ferrara be damned. And she did care for him, or at least there was not an absence of feeling. And he *had* been with her when the Cross woman was attacked. And they had gone to bed together, he had entered her, she had been filled by him. . . . God, it was inconceivable that she could have made love to a man who had killed five women.

"Do I have to beg you?" he said.

"All right," she said. "All right, Steven. Do you want to come here or should I drive to your place?"

"Neither," he said. His voice, now, seemed almost liquid with relief. "Keller's still outside; he'll follow me if I come there, and if you come here he might not even let you inside. He's gone over the edge, I'm terrified of him. I don't want him anywhere around when we talk."

"How will you get away from him?"

"I'll think of something."

"You won't do anything . . . dangerous?"

"No. Now we've got to decide on a place to meet."

She did not know why Johnstone's should pop into her mind at that moment; memories of youth, maybe; a familiar landmark. She heard herself say, "There's a boat storage and rental place, Johnstone's Wharf, about three miles north of the village. Do you know it?"

"I know it. That sounds as good as any; I'll meet you there in forty-five minutes." He paused, and then he said, "You'll be there, won't you?"

"Yes. I'll be there."

She put down the receiver, stood staring at it. I could not have slept with the Ripper, she thought again. And unless she met Steven, helped him, continued their relationship at least for a while, it meant that at some level she would be admitting that she might have done just that.

HOOK

Talking to her, Hook had had no idea of how he was going to get out of his cottage and away from Keller long enough for them to meet. The important thing then had been convincing her to see him. But now that it was arranged, he still had no idea of an escape method.

He went to the window that faced north and peered again through the curtains. Keller wasn't visible anywhere in the trees out there. He entered the bedroom and looked out to the south, and Keller wasn't there either. From the enclosed rear porch he scanned the rear of his property:

no sign of the constable. Christ, where was he? Out there somewhere, but it had been twenty minutes since he had thrown a pebble at one of the windows, and there was no telling when or if he would throw another one. Unless Hook pinpointed his exact location, he was liable to run right into him the moment he tried to leave.

he prowled the cottage from porch to porch, window to window. Time ticked away, and Keller remained hidden. If he couldn't locate him pretty soon, he would have to take a chance. Go out slow, maybe, and get into the car and let Keller follow him and then try to lose him somehow on the road..

He returned again to the rear porch.

And saw movement, off to the right among the trees.

Hook pressed against the screen door, staring. Fluttering of a coat flap, a quick flash of Keller's iron-gray hair. He was moving laterally from south to north, now almost directly behind the cottage and forty yards away.

Hook's reaction was immediate. He ran into the living room, caught up his jacket, palmed his car keys, and went onto the front porch. He opened the outer screen door quietly, stepped out. The Dodge was parked close by, facing toward Stone Bridge Road. He sprinted toward it, not looking anywhere else, and wrenched the door open and threw himself inside. The key slid into the ignition lock on the first thrust, and he twisted it, held his breath. The engine caught instantly. He dropped the transmission lever into Drive and pulled away, tires fanning gravel.

Coming onto Stone Bridge Road, he glanced back to his right and thought he saw Keller there, running out along the side of the cottage. He swung his eyes frontally again, barreled the car down the road. The only other house on Stone Bridge Road, a faded Cape Cod that belonged to a couple from Albany who used it only two months a year, came up on the right—and he saw something metallic glinting dully around toward the back.

A car: Keller's cruiser.

Impulsively, Hook hit the brakes and lifted his eyes to the rear-vision mirror. The figure of Keller filled the narrow glass, mouth open as though bellowing as he ran across the front yard, gun drawn and arcing over his head like a semaphore; the separation was several hundred yards. Hook cut the wheel hard right and took the Dodge up the Cape Cod's crushed-shell drive, brought it to a stop next to the cruiser.

Time. He needed more time. *Still captive the old wild king,* he thought. But not for long. He jerked on the emergency brake, leaned over and dragged out the small portable tool kit he kept under the seat. From inside he took a screwdriver and a ball peen hammer, carried them out of the car.

He could hear Keller shouting unintelligibly in the distance, but he couldn't see him from here. He bent by the cruiser's right front tire, curiously calm, and held the blade of the screwdriver against the rubber where it met the metal rim; then he drove the hammer against the plastic handle. He had to do it twice before the blade penetrated. There was a loud report, like a gunshot, and then the thick hiss of escaping air.

Hook dropped the tools, lunged back into the Dodge. The drive made a full loop of the Cape Cod and rejoined itself in front, so that he did not have to waste any time backing and turning. When he came out around the far corner, Keller was less than a hundred yards away in the middle of Stone Bridge Road. The constable's face seemed to shine redly in the cold daylight; the hand holding the gun snapped out in front of him, as if on command, and the elbow locked.

He's going to start shooting, Hook thought. He had known all along that this might happen, but until this instant he had not allowed himself to consider it. Sweat drenched him. He hunched over the wheel, feeling enormous and vulnerable, and came down hard on the accelerator. The Dodge bounced and jounced sharply onto the road again.

Keller fired twice.

Hook heard the sounds, closely spaced, even above the screaming of the engine and the tires, but the bullets didn't hit him or the car. It was like lightning: if you heard it, then you hadn't been struck. Warning shots? Or hurried misses? He dropped the transmission into D$_2$—more power—and began pulling away, opening up ground between them.

When he was almost to the intersection, a pickup truck rushed into his vision from the south. He jammed on the brakes to keep from sliding out into its path. As soon as it had gone by, he made the turn north onto U.S. 9 behind it, then looked back. He had one last glimpse of Keller falling away behind the screen of trees.

Hook shifted back into Drive, wiped his face with a tissue. He felt like an escaped criminal; that was what Keller had done to him. But he had done it to himself, too—flatting and destroying the cruiser's tire that way, running like a guilty man. Guilty man. And he thought for the first time of the state police units that had been assigned to check up on him today. Christ, it was sheer luck one of them hadn't come into the vicinity when he was running from Keller, when Keller was shooting at him. He would have looked guilty to *them*, all right, and they would have given chase, maybe shot at him too and maybe not have missed. . . .

Reflexively, Hook slowed his speed. Would Keller go to the state police now? He didn't think so; Keller would come alone after him, it was the only way an obsessive like that would react. Well then, *he* should go to Rocca, tell the lieutenant about Keller and why he, Hook, had done what he had. The state police would protect him when they had all the facts. A few minutes alone with Keller, and they would know that he had gone over the edge.

But first he had to see Valerie, talk to her, find something in her that would keep him together and help him find some sense of himself. In his state of mind, wise or foolish, that was the most urgent thing right now. And he had bought the time he would need; Keller wouldn't find him because he wouldn't know where to look.

As he drove toward Johnstone's Wharf, another little tendril of thought slipped into Hook's mind, a thin undercurrent of perception that he could not quite define. He seemed to have forgotten something, that was a part of it.

He had forgotten something vital. But what? A fact? An object?

What could he possibly have forgotten?

KELLER

"You son of a bitch!" Keller screamed as the Ripper's car vanished on U.S. 9. He still had his feet spread in a shooter's stance, gun arm braced in his left palm. "You goddamn fucking Ripper son of a bitch!"

He stood that way for a half a dozen more seconds, then lowered the revolver and jammed it viciously into its hoster. He ran up the drive and around behind the Cape Cod to his cruiser, knowing what he would find and then finding it. The Ripper had killed one of the tires—murdered it, emptied it of life the way he had emptied the life from Julia Larch and Arlene Wilson and Dona Lincoln and Linda Simmons and Paula Eaton. And now he was on his way to rip number six, Keller was sure of it.

He fumbled keys from his coat and dragged up the trunk lid and swung the spare out, began to fling jack components onto the damp earth. He should have killed the Ripper when he had him under the gun, shot him dead at the Hideaway Cabins last night instead of firing over his head, shot him dead this morning at the cottage and claimed self-defense, even the bleeding hearts couldn't argue with self-defense. He should have killed that kid in Chicago, too, smashed his fucking fag head to a pulp because that was what he had been asking for, what all of them had been asking for.

All right. All that was behind him. From now on he was going to do exactly what he had to do, what the situation called for and the hell with what happened later. A man was a man, and in the streets of Chicago or here in Bloodstone stalking a homicidal maniac, a man should always do what he had to do.

CROSS

Between Hideaway Cabins Seven and Eight, toward the rear, Cross came upon a heap of discarded junk: the shattered remains of chairs, the coil from one of the old-fashioned iceboxes, a decomposing mattress, a cracked toilet bowl, a rusted wood stove lying on its back, a wet glutinous mass of old newspapers and what seemed to have once been magazines.

He stopped there and leaned against the wall of Cabin Eight, rubbing a coat sleeve across his eyes. He had gotten inside the first six cabins through broken-out rear windows, and had searched them as quietly as he could, so as not to alert the trooper out front. He had not found anything except filth and rubble. But he wasn't ready to give up yet. He would stay here all day if he had to, until he had searched everything and everywhere he could think of.

The rusted wood stove caught his eye. The door in its belly was secured and did not look as if it had been taken off since the stove had been abandoned there. Inside would make a good hiding place, he thought. The state police might have overlooked it.

He moved to the stove, squatted in front of it. He tugged at the handle on the door, felt it yield, and the door came off with a little clanging sound—not loud enough to carry out to where the trooper was. Cross dropped the door to one side and then slid his hand through the opening, swept it slowly over the rough wet walls, encountered a small corroded hole near the bottom—

Something brushed cold and slime-furred against the back of his hand; something made a frightened chittering sound.

Rat, there was a rat in there!

Cross was terrified of rats; he hated anything small that moved. He ripped back his hand, scraping skin off the knuckles on a sharp edge. The rat jumped through the door opening, big and gray and red-eyed, and he lunged away instinctively and lost his balance and sprawled sideways into the disintegrating mass of newspapers and magazines as the rat scurried away. The accumulation separated like lumps of paste, and his cheek came in contact with one of them; he pulled back, hands moving under him, palms flat.

And he stayed that way, motionless on hands and knees.

The heel of one palm was resting against a hard, flat object beneath what was left of the papers.

Vertigo struck him; the day, the surroundings, whirled into gray mist. Time seemed to freeze. Then, slowly, the mist evaporated, and he felt his pulse thudding in his ears like the ticking of a rewound clock. The hairs on the back of his neck erected. He shivered convulsively, made a moaning sound in his throat. Then he began tearing at the paper, the magazines that weren't magazines at all but racing forms, something called *Tomorrow's Trots*.

The earth directly underneath had been scraped away, leaving a shallow depression. Within it, filling it, was a pair of dark-stained gardening gloves and a dark-stained kitchen knife with a slender, square handle.

The Ripper's gloves, the Ripper's knife.

Paula's blood.

Racing forms: Hook was a horseplayer.

Hook was the Ripper, Hook, it had been Hook all along, Hook had killed Paula.

Cross picked up the knife, not touching the gloves, and staggered to his feet and fled headlong up into the trees.

SMITH

They drove north in heavy silence, like two strangers— exactly what they were, he thought. Plummer kept their speed under fifty on the mostly empty Northway, his hands at the nine o'clock and three o'clock positions on the wheel in the manner of an old maid out for an afternoon drive. His mouth was set, prim and disturbed. There was something fussy and small about Plummer; Smith wondered why he had not noticed that before, too.

He ran his fingers back and forth, back and forth across the area just under his breastbone. The movement was only half conscious; the pain from the ulcer was still muted and steady. The farting had started again, but only sporadically: small, silent, odorless bubbles.

Through the windshield he watched the highway flow beneath them, the mountains surrounding them blackly on all sides. Finally he said, "Plummer."

"Yes?" Plummer said without turning his head.

"Who holds the all-time record for bases on balls in a single major-league game?"

Plummer turned quarter profile toward him then, his face clamped. "What kind of question is that, Dan? This is hardly the time—"

"Do you know the answer or don't you?"

"Jimmy Foxx," Plummer said automatically, tiredly.

"Right. With Boston in 1938."

"Dan, I don't like the way you're acting. You seem changed...."

"Maybe I am," Smith said. "Consecutive games played, National League."

"No. Good God, how can you even think about baseball now?"

"Gus Suhr, Pittsburgh, eight hundred and twenty-two from 1931 to 1937. My point." Smith smiled, but it was nothing more than a twitching of his mouth. "There's order in baseball, did you know that? It's a beautiful game. Order, symmetry, methodology, purpose, everything framed in numerals. Haven't you ever thought of it that way?"

Plummer gave him another strange look, then blinked rapidly several times and gave his attention to the road again. The silence rebuilt, thicker, more strained. Smith kept running his fingers across his stomach, staring out through the windshield and trying to think, now, of the National League record holder for the most total bases in a single game.

They were off the Northway and moving toward U.S. 9 before he remembered, with a feeling of satisfaction, that it was Joe Adcock. Eighteen, for Milwaukee. In 1954.

VALERIE

Except for the inevitable warping of time, the patina of shoddiness and emptiness that overlaid everything in Bloodstone, Johnsone's Wharf looked just as it had in Valerie's youth: a cluster of three buildings—a combination bait-and-tackle shop and rental office, a boat storage shed, and a private house—set several hundred yards off U.S. 9 on the lakefront. A slender channel dredged out of the shoreland paralleled the access road and parking area; in its center were two nearly empty rows of boat slips that extended out into the lake itself. Except for a teenage boy wearing an Expos baseball camp and making halfhearted repairs to the side wall of the office, the place was deserted.

She sat in her car in the parking area, faced up toward the highway. She had been there for ten minutes now, not thinking about anything, just waiting. The boy had come up to ask if he could be of help when she first arrived, and she had been curt in turning him away, even though she remembered dimly the eight-year-old child he had been; at least he had not recognized her.

When she saw Steven's car turn at last onto the access road, she opened the door and stepped out immediately. But he didn't pull in next to her. Instead, he drove over behind the storage shed. A moment later he reappeared on foot, hurrying toward her, and as he approached, she saw that he looked ghastly. She felt compassion and the faintest touch of anxiety, kept her hands in her coat pockets as he grasped her arms briefly and then backed away a pace.

"Poor Steven," she said softly. "It's been awful for you, hasn't it?"

"Bad enough," he said. "Listen, Valerie, I don't think we'd better talk here. I managed to get away from Keller, but he'll be out looking for me pretty soon and I don't want to take any chances of him finding me."

She frowned. "How did you get away from him?"

"Subterfuge," he said vaguely. "It doesn't matter."

"Where do you want to go, then?"

"I don't know. Somewhere else. We can take your car, but we've got to hurry."

She saw nothing in his eyes except pleading. *He is not guilty of anything; I have not slept with a mass murderer.* And immediately behind that thought was another, perhaps one that had taken seed in the back of her mind at the same time she had remembered and then suggested Johnstone's Wharf earlier. *There's a place where we can be completely alone, free in emptiness; and if we go*

273

there, if I'm alone with him there, nothing will happen because he is innocent, he is innocent, there'll never be any more doubts.

Without thinking any further, compulsively, she said, "We can rent a boat and go out on the lake, Steven."

She watched him for a reaction, but he showed none except a tentative acceptance. "It'll be cold out there," he said.

"I don't care about that; it's not going to rain. We'll be alone, Steven, where Keller won't bother us."

"You do trust me, then," he said.

"I trust you." *Because you were inside me, innocent.*

He released a breath, extended his hand. She took it and let him hurry her down to where the boy was working at the side of the office.

KELLER

It had taken him only twelve minutes to change the murdered tire, put a live one in its place. But twelve minutes was a lifetime, a deathtime: you could kill twelve women in twelve minutes, twenty-four if you worked by twos, thirty-six if you lined them up and worked with a couple of knives. Now he was driving north on U.S. 9 in the empty wake of the Ripper's car. There was no traffic, no people. He might have been the only man alive in this area, except for the Ripper. The world had collapsed tight to the two of them: no one else, no other factor.

CROSS

I've got to show her the knife, Cross thought.

The idea, the conviction came to him just after he passed Stone Bridge Road, saw up ahead the entrance to the promontory road. Until then he had been on his way straight to the substation, to Lieutenant Rocca. Until then his stream of consciousness had been congealed to a low babble: Paula's murderer, Hook's knife, Hook the Ripper, my discovery, I solved it for Paula, full participant, catalyst and victim, change *The Ripper of Bloodstone* from a nonfiction novel to a personal memoir, call it instead *Triumph over Uncertainty: The Ripper Ordeal of Jack Cross.*

But now the focus of his mind turned fully to Florence. Florence up there alone in that big old crumbling house. Florence smiling when she learned Paula had been pregnant. Florence patronizing him, babying him, telling him in her caustic, martyred way that he was impotent and incompetent. Show her what he really was and what he had. Show her the truth and make her believe. Show her proof: the Ripper's knife.

Cross braked and turned onto the access road, drove up through the tunnel of trees and onto the surface of the promontory. The house loomed there, sinister and oppressive, seeming to reach for him as it did every time he came near it, ready to close down on him. God, how he hated that house. But soon he would never have to see it again, enter it again; soon it would be gone and Florence would be gone and Bloodstone and the Ripper would be gone. Like Paula. Out of his life forever. He would be free at last.

He stopped the car and got out, and just as he started onto the porch stairs, the door opened and Florence appeared there. He halted three steps up, staring at her. The fine, dense muscles of her face had loosened, giving the impression of collapse; her eyes were eviscerated. Sick old woman, he thought. No longer strong, no longer imposing. For the first time he felt himself as the dominant personality, superior to her in every way.

She looked at him for a long moment, saying nothing; then she turned back into the hallway. Her motions, her walk, were those of the elderly, and as he followed her, he thought that this was the way she would look thirty years from now, or even twenty, moving down a corridor in some nursing home.

When they were inside the parlor, he stood next to the Governor Winthrop secretary and watched her pivot in the middle of the room and face him again. "Lieutenant Rocca was here an hour ago," she said in a flat, dull voice. "He wanted to talk to me about you. He said they released the man they arrested last night, that that man isn't the Ripper."

"Well he was wrong," Cross said. "Hook's the Ripper, all right."

"Oh God, Jimmy, I can't stand it anymore. I can't stand the lies, the pretending, the horror."

"My name is Jack," he said. "Jack."

She brushed fingers like bent white twigs across her face. "When I heard you drive up, Jimmy, I was just starting to the phone. It took me awhile to work up the courage, but I just don't have any other choice, not now. I never really had a choice *ever*."

"I don't know what you're talking about," he said. Small ripples of confusion pushed at him, and the sense of dominance and superiority began to collapse. He touched fingertips to the cloth of his coat and pressed the knife against his side. "Listen, I've got something to tell you, something to show you—"

"There's nothing you can tell me or show me now. It's over, I can't protect you anymore."

"You're not making any sense, Mother."

"I didn't truly believe it, deep down in my heart, until today," she said. "I knew it was true, but there was always hope because I didn't really *know*. When you told me the state police had arrested the Ripper last night, I thought my prayers had been answered; I thought I had been wrong and I was almost ill with relief. But now there's no hope anymore, it's true, I accept it. I can't fight it any longer."

Understanding began to extrude into Cross' mind. The knife seemed to pulse luminously, to give off heat, inside his pocket. "Stop talking," he said desperately. "Just stop talking and let me show you—"

"I blanked out the terrible *evil* of it," she said as if she hadn't heard him. "I just . . . blanked it out, because all I could think of was you—my son. He's my own, I thought; whatever he may have become, he comes from me. But that was the sin of pride, Jimmy, because I was protecting myself as much as you. My own selfishness and false hope killed Paula. She would still be alive if I'd done the right thing. That's the hell I've made for myself."

"No," he said. "Shut up, Mother."

Her head rolled sideways on the stem of her neck. "There can't be any more lies, Jimmy. Don't you understand that? I can't lie anymore and neither can you. Not to each other and not to anybody."

The understanding grew, flamed. The feeling that came over him was the same he might have had watching an ax blade descend toward his head, his car hurtle out of control toward a high solid wall. Words burst out of his throat: "You weren't attacked at all the other night. You made the whole thing up!"

"You knew that from the first, Jimmy."

"Jesus," he said. "Oh Jesus, Jesus Christ!"

"How could you not know? God help me, I felt I had to keep them from finding out what I already knew in my heart, that I had to take suspicion away from you. I couldn't . . . I couldn't let them put you away in one of those places. The pain, the disgrace, I *couldn't* let it happen."

"You thought it was me," he said. "All along, you thought it was me. Jack the Ripper, that's what you thought. Your son: Jack the Ripper."

And he took out the knife.

Florence emitted a thin, terrified wail, and one hand came up as though to ward him off; the planes of her face turned the color of clabbered milk. "Oh my God!" she said. She backed up three steps, struck the edge of the coffee table with the back of one knee and then retreated at a different angle until she came up against one of the Peterborough cabinets.

He held the knife point downward. Blood pounded in his ears, diminishing to a whisper the sound of her and other, curious, sounds that came suddenly from the front entrance. Through the lenses of his glasses Florence seemed blurred and two-dimensional, shimmering like an apparition. Horror, shrieking mutely, capered through him and through the room.

"I'm your mother, you can't do anything to your own mother!"

His head jerked, drawn by the knife. He saw the dried blood staining the long, dull-bright blade, the gleaming point: the Ripper's knife. *She thinks Jack the Ripper is going to use it on her*. His fingers spasmed, and the knife fell clattering to the floor.

He backed away from it, and the horror danced out, and he was abruptly and painfully calm, calmer than he had ever been. "I found it," he said almost placidly. "I found it at the Hideaway Cabins, it doesn't belong to me, Jack's not the Ripper."

He swung around, started away—and a forearm struck him high across the chest, knocked him sprawling to the floor. His ears popped; Florence's screams burst against them. He shook his head, rolling over onto his buttocks, and looked up into the impending faces of Plummer and Daniel Smith.

SMITH

He holstered his drawn gun, picked up the knife, and turned it over carefully in his hand. Across the room Florence had stopped screaming, was now sobbing in a hysterical way. Plummer went to her and held her against him; he looked stricken, as he had from the moment they'd come onto the porch from the car and heard the loud voices carrying clearly from the parlor.

"Take her out of here," Smith said to him. "Get her calmed down."

Plummer looked past Florence's stiffened body at Cross still sitting on the floor. "Dan. . . ."

"Do what I say—now."

Plummer nodded desolately, looked at Cross again, and then led Florence through the rear archway.

Smith came back to Cross and grabbed the youth's arm and jerked him upright. Cross' breathing was rapid, uneven, but his aspect seemed calm, maybe too calm. "You came within two seconds of getting shot," Smith said, and held the knife in front of Cross' face.

The boy wouldn't look at it. He shook his head. "I know what she thought when I showed it to her, but it isn't mine. I found it at the Hideaway Cabins. You must have heard me say that." His voice was calm, too, controlled. "The gloves were there, the knife and the gloves. Bloody. Paula's blood."

"Where at the Hideaway Cabins?"

"Between Seven and Eight."

"All right—but exactly where?"

"In a little hole under a pile of papers and racing forms."

"Racing forms?"

Cross nodded. "Hook," he said. "Hook's the Ripper. He put those racing forms out there and he hid the knife and the gloves under them. I fell into the pile, there was this rat, and I broke it up like lumps of paste; but he must have moved it carefully each time, it didn't break up for him."

Hook, Smith thought. But even if Cross *had* found the knife and gloves where he claimed, it was not at all conclusive evidence against Hook. Anybody could have hidden them there; someone, the real assailant, could have done it to cast suspicion on Hook. Troopers had searched the area last night and they hadn't found anything, although the evidence could still have been there; they had screwed up in every way and one more screw-up was just as likely as not. It was even possible that the knife and the gloves had been hidden *after* the search, by someone other than Hook, late last night or sometime today.

"Maybe," he said. "What were you doing at the Hideaway Cabins?"

"I had to do something about the Ripper, because he killed Paula, because he made me a victim too. Ferrara said to visit the scenes of the crimes, but I couldn't do that. So I went to the Hideaway Cabins instead."

That did not make much sense to Smith, but at the moment it didn't particularly matter. He said, "If you found the knife as you say, why did you come here with it? Why didn't you go to the substation?"

"I was going to," Cross said. "I just wanted Florence to know I'd found it."

"Why?"

"She never believed I could do anything. I had to show it to her, prove to her what I could do. But then she started to accuse me, to confess. . . ."

"You didn't have any idea the attack on her was a phony?"

"No. No."

"Why would she believe you're the murderer?"

"She must be sick. Out of her mind."

Smith said, "Then she's got plenty of company." He pulled an antimacassar off the back of the sofa and wrapped the knife in it, put it into his coat pocket. "All right, Cross, sit down here and don't move. You understand?"

Cross moved his head disconnectedly and sat on the sofa, knees apart, body slumped forward. Smith went through the archway, located the spot from which Florence's sobs were coming: inside a partially open door, second on his right down the back hall. When he looked inside he saw her lying face down across an old four-poster bed, Plummer sitting beside her and stroking her hair awkwardly, helplessly with one hand.

"Plummer," he said.

Plummer looked up, then said something to Florence and stood and came into the hall. Smith leaned past him and drew the door closed.

"What did Jack say?" Plummer asked.

"Same thing we heard him say when we came in."

"Do you believe him, Dan?" Plummer's voice had a plaintive, imploring quality, that of a man trying desperately to hang onto his beliefs. The skin on his neck had a wattled appearance; his eyes were grayly opaque, like burned-out bulbs. He wasn't just old, Smith thought, he was shattered—more of a stranger than ever. "You don't really think Florence was right, do you? That he's the Ripper?"

"Maybe not," Smith said.

"What are you going to do?"

"Take him to the Hideaway Cabins, check out his story. I'll use your car; you stay here with Florence."

"Do you want me to call—"

"No. Don't call anyone. I'll handle things myself."

"Whatever you say." Plummer handed over his keys, then put a shaking hand on the doorknob. "Dan . . . she's a good woman. What she did was wrong, terribly wrong, and I hope to God she was wrong about Jack too. But you're a parent yourself, you can understand *why* she did it."

"No, I can't."

"Stop being a cop for one minute, can't you? Have pity on her."

"It's not up to me," Smith said, and pivoted and left Plummer there and went back into the parlor.

And stopped just inside the archway: Cross was gone.

He said, "Shit!" and ran out into the front hall, outside onto the porch, with his hand on his gun. A thick fart wedged itself in his rectal cavity, would move no farther. But Cross' car was still there, and a moment later he saw the boy standing off to the left of the house, next to a row of old stone bowls filled with ferns. He was looking out across the promontory at the lake.

Smith slowed and went over to him angrily. "What do you think you're doing? I told you to stay in the house."

"I couldn't stand it in there," Cross said. "I felt like I was suffocating in there. I had to get some air."

"All right, you've had your air. We—"

"There's a boat out there," Cross said suddenly. He raised an arm, pointing off to the north. "Man and woman in it. What would they be doing out in a boat on a day like this?"

"The hell with that," Smith said. He put a hand on the boy's arm.

Cross said, "Valerie Broome."

"What?"

"She was wearing a purple scarf at the town meeting yesterday. That woman out there has a purple scarf, the same color."

Smith looked out in the direction Cross was pointing. The boat, a small skiff, moved at an angle out from shore, north by northwest, too far away for him to be able to recognize the people in it, but he could see the bright patch of purple around the head of the smaller figure. The larger figure sat hunched at the tiller, back to the promontory—not a very big man, lean shoulders. . . .

"Hook," he said.

And Cross said, "The Ripper, she's out there with the

Ripper." He turned abruptly and ran away to where his car was parked. Smith came after him, faint flicks of pain coming from the ulcer now, the fart still wedged in his rectal cavity. Cross fumbled a key into the trunk lock, and when he got the lid open he reached inside and withdrew a pair of inexpensive binoculars from under a torn and greasy car blanket.

"All right," Smith said, and jerked the binoculars out of his hands, turned back to where he had an unobstructed view of the skiff. He lifted the glasses to his eyes, adjusted the roll knobs, and got the boat in focus. Valerie Broome's face was discernible now, and a moment later, as the man at the tiller turned to glance back toward shore, his face too, was recognizable in profile.

Steven Hook.

"It is Hook, isn't it?" Cross said.

Smith lowered the binoculars. "It might just be," he said. "Christ, it might just *be* Hook." Knife at the Hideaway Cabins, under a pile of racing forms; Cross had told him the truth. Florence admitting that the attack on her had been a sham, proving Smith right on that score, proving methodology right, rendering Hook's alibi worthless. Hook and his car at the cabins last night. Hook out on the lake now with Valerie Broome on a day no sane man in Bloodstone would go for a boat ride.

All of it together, then: Hook.

He spun at Cross, caught hold of him, pulled him urgently to Plummer's car, and pushed him inside. Then he went around and moved in at the wheel, dropping the binoculars on the seat cushion. No time to call in to the substation from the house, and since this was Plummer's car, no police band to use; and no point in calling in anyway, not after the foul-ups of last night, not when it was his case and his alone to win. He didn't need relievers out of the bullpen at this stage of the game.

"We're going after them, right?" Cross said. He still seemed very calm; there was no excitement in his voice. "Follow them to wherever they're going and stop Hook before he rips again."

Smith didn't answer. He started the engine and sent the car skimming around and onto the access road.

HOOK

Bitter cold on the lake: the wind sweeping against the fourteen-foot skiff, slapping at Hook's face and numbing his fingers around the hard-rubber grip of the tiller. The water, rumpled and flecked with white froth, was like a warped and clouded mirror, reflecting the leaden sky. Off to starboard, astern, was the small wooded island they had just passed, and beyond Valerie, sitting on the bow seat with her coat drawn tightly around her, he could see Fort Seneca and the high enclosing wall of the Colonial Village Amusement Park on the north shore.

He thought of a massive stage in an empty theater, with sets drab-painted but nonetheless majestic. Sets and scenery had always enhanced his performances in the theater. But here, he could not seem to remember his lines, he was not quite sure where to begin. The script was all there inside him, only it was fragmentary and disconnected, the words half assimilated. You could make strength out of weakness, truth out of artifice, sense out of the insensible—but not until you got into it, not until the dialogue commenced.

He looked at Valerie, at the wind-reddened surfaces of her face. She hadn't spoken since they had set out from Johnstone's Wharf: waiting for him to tell her what he had brought about their meeting to tell her, waiting for the curtain to rise. Enduring the cold and discomfort just for him.

"I've got so much to say," he said loudly, to make himself heard over the gusting wind and the whine of the outboard motor, "and I don't know where to begin."

"At the beginning," she said. "I know that's trite, but it's usually the best place."

"I don't know what the beginning is."

"Bloodstone? Everything seems to begin and end in Bloodstone."

"Not Bloodstone."

"Acting, then?"

"Maybe," he said. "I cared about that, I really cared about that. And I was good for just that reason, because I cared."

"Then shouldn't you have stuck with it?"

"It all went sour, it all dissolved into alcohol. But nothing else has ever touched me the same way since. I never cared about horseplaying. It was just a means of making money. Nothing up here touched me, I had no passion. I left my passion in New York."

"You might find it again if you went back."

He shook his head. It wasn't going right, not yet, but Valerie had gotten him into it, and he could feel the lines starting to come together. Somewhere at the rim of his consciousness, now, was an enormous insight. "Passion and feeling," he said, "I left those things in New York. I ran away from them. Acting was the last *thing* that made me feel, and until I met you, that bitch down there was the last *person* who made me feel."

"Your ex-wife?"

"Ginny," he said. "Virginia Warren Hook Bitch." The insight was coming in closer. "She ruined me; it was her and not the plays folding or the bad reviews or the alcohol. I might have been able to stay with it if she had stayed with me. But she didn't; she mocked me, she abandoned me when I needed her the most. She's the one who took feeling out of me for six years."

Valerie said something, but in a low voice this time, and he couldn't hear it.

"I could have lived with that," he said. "I did live with it and never even knew what it was. But then the parlay system began to fall apart, I started losing, and the machine I'd become started to break down. Then Bloodstone and the Ripper and—"

He stopped abruptly. The insight had started to break open in his mind.

"Steven?" Valerie said. "Steven, what is it?"

He stared at her, his hand shaking from the vibration of the engine and from the incursion of congealing knowledge.

And there it was. . . .

KELLER

Keller brought the cruiser bellowing onto the grounds of Johnstone's Wharf, slowed it to a stop behind the rented car in the parking area. He had seen the car from the highway, recognized it as Valerie Broome's, and his mind had begun to click and clack like a computer. It was still clicking and clacking, feeding out the same equations over and over: Hook needed to rip badly, and with the Bloodhound right behind him and the lid on tight, he didn't have time to go look for a random victim . . . he was screwing Valerie and it wouldn't have been hard, not hard at all, to talk her into meeting him before he made his run from the cottage . . . Valerie was going to be number six . . . the Ripper had her somewhere right this minute, here at the wharf, somewhere. . . .

Keller burst out of the cruiser, took a quick look inside the rented car, then spun away. Down near the office a kid in a baseball cap stood staring at him. He ran down there and said, "Where is she, the woman who was driving that car?"

The kid backed up a step. "She and this guy rented a boat, they went out on the lake—"

"What guy?"

"Well I'm not sure," the kid said. "She met him here, he parked his car behind the shed. I've seen him around, I think he might be Steven Hook, the one who—"

"How long ago'd they leave?"

"About ten minutes. I thought it was pretty unusual, them wanting to go out on a day like this. Did they do something, Constable? I mean, are you after them for something?"

He resisted an impulse to pull his gun on the kid. *Chicago, Chicago.* "They give you any idea where they were going?"

"No."

"Which direction?"

"North, out past the island."

The kid pointed into the lake. Several hundred yards offshore was a small pear-shaped island. It looked like a breast, a green-and-brown nippleless breast. There was nothing else to see out there, no sign of a boat on the slick silver water. Would the Ripper have taken her to the breast? Possibly. Or maybe he intended to do his ripping right there in the boat. You couldn't put anything past the Ripper.

He said, "All right, now you give *me* a boat."

"You are after them, aren't you?" the kid said. Then he seemed struck with a sudden thought, and his eyes got very wide. "Hey, that guy, that Hook . . . you don't think he's the *Ripper,* do you? Is that what—?"

You son of a bitch, Keller thought, and didn't know if he meant the kid or the Ripper or both of them. He touched his gun but did not draw it. That was good enough; that was as far as he was going to go. "A boat," he said. "A fucking boat, you understand?"

The kid's eyes followed the movement of Keller's hand.

"Well sure," he said hastily, "sure, we had two in the slips today, testing the engines. The other one's still there, a skiff with a Johnson Seahorse, fifteen horesepower. The one I gave them has an Evinrude ten, you should be able to. . . ."

Keller did not hear any more of it: he was already running for the slips.

CROSS

Sitting calmly beside Smith as the lieutenant swung the car north on U.S. 9, Cross examined matters and himself with a reporter's objective eye. Trial by fire, that's what all of this was, and he had come through the worst of it and was a better man for the experience. If he had actually been what Florence had taken him to be all these years, a weakling without character, he would have come apart long ago under all this stress and adversity. Instead, it was Florence herself who had come apart, faking that attack because she thought he was the Ripper. He really was stronger than her, as strong as anyone now. Which was why he could sit here very coolly while Smith went in pursuit of the Ripper, both full participant *and* detached observer now.

Triumph over Uncertainty: *The Ripper Ordeal of Jack Cross*. That certainly was a good new title for the book, all right.

He pressed against the cold glass of the door, peering out. They were coming to a high point in the road now where he could see the full northern sweep of the lake, and the boat came into sight again beyond an offshore island—heading straight toward the red-stone bastions of Fort Seneca. Or toward Colonial Village, he thought, and he said to Smith, "Do you think he's going to take her to the amusement park, where he killed the first one?"

Smith did not say anything.

"If he plans to kill her," Cross said, "I wonder how he'll do it now that he doesn't have his knife."

This time Smith made a grunting sound, but Cross couldn't tell what it meant, if anything.

He thought about Valerie and hoped that they would get to her in time to save her. Paula was dead, and he didn't want anyone else to be dead, particularly someone like Valerie, who was a decent person even though she had treated him pretty badly and turned him down when he asked her to have a cup of coffee with him. On his new plane of perception and self-control, he could forgive her that; he could even forgive Florence. He couldn't forgive the Ripper, though. That was the one person he could never forgive.

Stands of spruce and the buildings of cabin colonies and motels obstructed his view again for a quarter mile. Then the open grounds of Johnstone's Wharf appeared, and on the lake beyond he saw a red-hulled skiff cutting diagonally toward the island. A different boat, a second one with only a single person in it.

He reached around on the seat, caught up the binoculars, held them up to his glasses and adjusted the focus.

Smith said, "What are you doing?"

"There's another boat out there," Cross said. "Over by the island, one man in it."

Smith looked past him, and his breath made a hissing sound between his teeth. "Who is it?" he said.

The moving car made it difficult for Cross to get a steady fix on the second skiff, but he finally managed it just before trees flashed between again. "Keller," he said. "It's Keller."

"God*damn* it!" Smith said, and bore down on the accelerator until the car began to shimmy and the motor screamed.

HOOK

This was not a stage, Hook thought, and neither was New York City or Saratoga or Bloodstone or the Hideaway Cabins or any other place he had ever been. Life was not a play. There were no scripts, no set scenes, no ready answers available in the second or third acts.

You had to dig down deep within for the answers and then commit your own forgiveness; to do anything else—to take the easy way, to rely on the easy way, to *act*—was merely to sink deeper into your own destructiveness. And you could not use people, as he had tried to use Ginny, was trying to use Valerie, to work out your own pain. You had to do it on your own, because feeling was real and the responsibility for it was yours. That was what Ginny had maybe been trying to tell him long ago.

Hook sat rigidly at the tiller as the insight continued to widen. He had begun to understand a great many things now, in light of that insight: his own actions and reactions, the desire for alcohol, the inability to feel. He even knew what he had forgotten this afternoon. *Madness*. These past few days he had been teetering on the edge, had come perilously close to slipping over, but his subconscious mind had rebelled against it, pushed it out into his conscious mind. He was going sane again. For the first time in six long years he was going completely sane and thereby coming to a point where he could cope with his life. He could see hope, and in that hope there was the beginning of a vast release of tension and pain and horror. . . .

"Steven," Valerie said sharply.

He focused on her, started to tell her what was happening inside him. But he saw that she was looking past him, to something down the lake. "Steven," she said again, "there's another boat back there."

Hook snapped his head around. The other boat was two hundred yards away, moving faster than they were, pointed straight toward them. One man at the tiller—

Keller.

He said it aloud, "Keller," and fear cut at him. Keller *had* found him, was coming after him: deadly, implacable, as crazy as Hook himself might have been, with a gun on his hip that had already been fired at him twice today and twice last night. Hook reacted instinctively; he was going sane again, almost able to cope with matters now, but not quite sane enough to cope with Alex Keller.

He opened the Evinrude's throttle wide and began to run.

KELLER

Keller sent the red-hulled skiff slap-skipping through the ashen water, north on the leeside of the island and then around the outer tip. And as soon as he came into open water, he saw the Ripper's boat: not far ahead, drifting along, heading for the north shore.

Both of them were visible in the boat; the Ripper hadn't begun ripping yet. That was good, it was good, but he felt a vague letdown, a sharpening of his rage. He would do what he had to do, but afterward it would be better, easier with hard evidence, and hard evidence was coming in on the Ripper during or after the fact. Wasn't it? No, Christ, you had to *save* the victims, his job had always been to protect and save the victims. Make the streets safe and secure in Bloodstone, in Chicago, in America. Save the life of Valerie Broome, take the life of the Ripper, make them listen, make them understand.

He stared across the water, squinting against the wind-blown spray kicked up by the skiff's bouncing hull. He knew what the Ripper had in mind, now; he knew the Ripper better than the bastard knew himself. Planning to take her to Colonial Village. Planning to rip her there because that was where he had ripped the first one, Julia Larch. Recycling, that was it: starting, like Keller himself, to repeat the major moments of his history. Sooner or later the string ran out, and you found yourself doing what you had done at the beginnings, the change points, of your life. You thought you could move in ever-widening circles from your past, but that was a lie; the circles were a spiral instead, and eventually you backslid down it to the center, the off-center, of your existence.

Up there in the other boat the Ripper jerked around suddenly, looked back. He knew the Bloodhound was coming now. But that didn't matter. Nothing the Ripper knew or did from this point forward mattered in the slightest. He was a dead man, pure and simple. But not Valerie Broome. She wasn't going to die, she wasn't going to be ripped; no gaping wounds in her torso, no diamond-shaped marks, no pain, no death. Alive, alive-o.

The wind slashing across Keller's face had a brackish, metallic odor, like the bright smell of blood.

SMITH

Five miles north of the village, county road 9R intersected the highway, serpentining along the upper edges of Woodbine Lake to the east. Smith cut onto it, past a signpost that told him Fort Seneca and Colonial Village were two miles away, and then picked up speed again.

His stomach was hurting him sharply now, but he ignored the pain and the implications of the pain. He refused, too, to worry about Keller's presence. He concentrated only on the gray asphalt unfolding beneath the car, empty of traffic; on winking glimpses of the lake through the screening trees, almost subliminal flashes of the two boats heading shoreward.

And images of last night came to him, sudden and strong for half a dozen pulsebeats. He might have been back on Hobbler Way, pursuing his quarry through the empty landscape—*wasnt he? hadn't he been?*—and plunging toward a confrontation that would include Hook and Cross and Keller. But this time it would end differently, because the ulcer wasn't going to stop him, Keller wasn't going to stop him, nothing was going to stop him. Bottom of the ninth, runners at all corners of the diamond, two out, and the game about to be won, finally, in the regulation nine.

"Do you know anything about baseball, Cross?" he said without taking his eyes off the road. Trapped air burbled in his belly with an audible, boiling water sound, then built into a series of hard little farts that he began to squeeze out silently one by one, like marbles. "Do you know who had the longest team winning streak in major-league history?"

Cross turned his head and stared at him.

"The New York Giants, twenty-six games in 1916,"

Smith said. He blinked. "And they finished fourth that year."

VALERIE

She was afraid again—for Steven this time, not of him. Talking to her, he had seemed to find strength and calm and a kind of self-understanding, and she had felt close to him then, closer than on the night they had shared bed and orgasm. But now there was turmoil in him again, terror. His fear of Keller was even greater than she had thought, and it seemed to be tearing apart that new coalescence of self.

She gripped the skiff's curved gunwales. "Turn around, Steven!" she shouted over the accelerated roar of the engine. "Don't run away anymore, you'll only make things worse!"

He didn't answer, didn't even seem to hear her. His head moved in quick, jerky quadrants between Keller in the oncoming boat and beyond her to the north shore. She half turned on the bow seat, saw the massive walls of the fort and the wooden fence surrounding Colonial Village. The impression was of abandoned prison compounds: bleak, desolate, enfolding. She remembered the way the area had made her feel on Sunday and felt her own fright building.

"Please, Steven!"

But he sent the skiff planing between the little projecting peninsulas bounding the shore crescent. When they were twenty yards offshore, where thin little waves rolled in to lick at the grassy knoll equidistant between fort and amusement park, Hook cut back on the throttle. A moment later Valerie felt the keel jar against the slope, the boat rock dangerously as he stood up and swung himself over the side, into knee-deep water. The engine howled, then rattled and died.

Keller's boat, skipping high and low in the water, sending out spume in a gray-white fan, was less than a hundred yards away.

Hook caught the painter ring in the bow to keep the skiff from drifting, reached in his free hand, and tugged frantically at her. She scrambled out, and he released the ring then and pulled her onto the slope. "This is crazy," she said, "don't do it this way," but he shook his head, and his fingers—cold, stiff, like little shafts of metal—gripped her hand.

Stumble-footed, he took her upslope toward the jutting bastions of the fort.

KELLER

Keller throttles down as he comes into the cove, then sends his skiff plunging like a knife into the hard belly of the shore, next to the Ripper's boat. He jumps out, falls to one hand, thrusts himself erect and unbuttons the flap of his holster and takes out the gun. Above him he watches the Ripper and his sixth victim fleeing, and knows that the Ripper is running toward something as much as he is running away: running toward his final rip. He had to rip one last time, even with death on his heels; the need is too strong and growing within him. But he can't rip without Keller there, no way can he rip without the Bloodhound on the scene to complete the cycle, the three of them joined so that only then can the cutting and the blood begin.

Gun extended, he stumbles up the slope. And as he does, something new occurs to him. Of the three of them who will be together for this final rip, only two of them are really necessary. The third one does not have to be there. The woman, yes, no way to avoid her—but it can be either him or Hook, it does not matter, just so long as the Ripper is there. . . .

CROSS

The county road unfurled, curve after curve, and Smith took each of them at full speed, using the transmission to decelerate instead of the brakes. Hunched against the passenger door, Cross realized the danger of the car going out of control, lunging off the road and disintegrating against the unyielding surfaces of the trees, but he was not frightened. His new level of calm held him aloof and gave him an insight into Smith which he would have to include when he chronicled these events in the last pages of *Triumph over Uncertainty: The Ripper Ordeal of Jack Cross*. When you were emotionally wrought up, as Smith clearly was, you did and said certain things that were irrational, like driving recklessly and asking unreasonable questions about baseball. Cross knew all about that sort of thing, he had been there himself—the Superman business, for instance. But he was above it now.

Smith slid the car into another turn, and when they cleared it the entrance road to the fort came up on the right, flanked by tall signs that said FORT SENECA—NEW YORK STATE HISTORICAL LANDMARK AND MILITARY MUSEUM AND COLONIAL VILLAGE: A FUN-FILLED, EDUCATIONAL RE-CREATION OF OUR GREAT AMERICAN HERITAGE. They swung between the signs, down the road to where it blended into the half-acre parking lot, angled across the lot between fort and amusement park, toward the low concrete abutment that separated the paved area from the sloping lawn and the lake below.

Calmly, Cross waited for whatever was going to happen.

KELLER

He runs up the knoll, and sometimes he sees them and sometimes he does not as they flicker in and out of strange little dark spots in his line of vision. It will not be long now before he catches up with them. The first thing he will do is to put Hook out of the way, and one clear, deadly shot will do it. Then he will be able to turn his full attention to the girl; she will be lying on the grass, her body open, her face torn and twisted, and he will come down upon her in enormous power and force.

Keller tries to think of what he will say to her, but there do not seem to be any words. His vision darkens again, and all he can see is how she will look broken on the grass as he moves upon her.

HOOK

Hook heard Keller shouting behind them as they ran, but the words were made incoherent by either the wind or Keller's own voice. Terror was strong in him, yet tempered now by a rising sense of futility. This was no good;

Keller was too close, he could shoot him in the back with no trouble at all. Stop then, face him, fight him if—

Valerie's hand pulled suddenly from his, and she cried out. And that brought him up, more abruptly than any effort of will could have. Half turning, he saw that she had tripped and fallen to her knees, saw Keller running a few yards away, waving the gun. Run, run . . . but he couldn't leave Valerie there, he couldn't run away from her too. Keller was one thing; Valerie was another.

Something that might have been control slid into him. He moved to her and caught her arm and hoisted her to her feet. She was panting, saying his name. He shoved her behind him, faced Keller.

He was all through running away.

KELLER

He sees that they have stopped, that the girl is lying on the grass just as he had known she would be, Hook crouched over her. Then, as the Bloodhound closes—

The man there pulls her to her feet, to her feet, and wrenches her behind him, it should not be like that, and begins to shout. Keller sees the man between himself and the girl, this is not right, blocking him from the girl, not right, blocking him from his own necessity, and he stops too, but he should be moving in on her, the way the Ripper's knife moves in on the tender, open bodies of his victims, the way the Ripper's knife, and the diamonds, and the knife, the way the Ripper

The Ripper
He begins to know why this isn't right
It is not right because
He is not the Bloodhound at all and
He sees it fusing inside him
The truth
Oh my God, I
I am, I am, *I* am
The
I am the

THE RIPPER
Ah! Ah, crazylights!

HOOK

And Keller was screaming, "Oh my God, oh my God, I'm the Ripper, *I'm* the Ripper, *I'm the Ripper!*"

The look on Keller's face and in his eyes, the sound of his screeching voice, contained such horror and agony and madness that Hook accepted it instantly. Chills flowed along his back so deep and cold they were like fire. It was Keller, it had been Keller all along, the man who had hounded him, put fear into him, pulled a gun on him three times and fired that gun at him four times, wanted to kill him as he had killed five women, this broken shape of a man was the Ripper. . . .

The fury overtook him, and he stopped thinking altogether. Almost immediately the tableau broke apart in a clumsy, desperate implosion and explosion of forms, all of it happening very quickly in objective time but seeming to him to happen with terrible fluidity and deliberateness, as if they were moving in viscous liquid.

"Get out of the way!" Keller screamed. "You can't stand in the way of the Ripper!" He lunged forward, swinging the gun, coming not after him but after Valerie. Hook threw himself at the constable, came in under the weapon, and hit the bigger man with his shoulder, high on the chest. The gun went off close to his head, harmlessly, but the detonation deafened him, sealed him into a vacuum. Their bodies slammed into the wet earth, Hook on top, and the revolver kicked free then and sailed away across the grass in the direction of the amusement park.

They rolled against each other, broke momentum, and burst apart like enraged lovers. Keller's mouth was open, but if he was making sounds, Hook could not hear them in the awful ringing silence. There was froth on the thick lips, mad red glints in the protuberant eyes. He lifted to his knees and tried to thrust himself against Keller again, realized too late the mistake of that; Keller swung an arm that he saw coming and tried to dodge, failed to dodge, and took glancingly across the side of the head. Flashing pain, double vision. He shook himself doglike, got his hands up in front of his face.

And Keller hit him again, same place, greater force,

knocking him over backward this time and skidding him
headfirst downslope against a wall of blackness.

SMITH

When he brought the car past the outer edge of the
fort, the three of them burst into view midway up the
slope: Valerie and Hook and Keller, frozen in place, Keller with his gun drawn. Cross was saying something beside him, but Smith didn't listen; rage pulsed at his temples,
intensified the pain working in his stomach. He felt another fart building and made no effort to let it come out
silent this time; it erupted loud and sharp in the confines
of the car. Cross said, "What—" and Smith could feel
the startled cut of his eyes. He kept his own gaze on the
three of them down there.

Goddamn you, Keller! he thought. If you do any shooting—

And Hook and Keller began grappling, and Valerie
backed away toward the fort with her hands in fists against
her cheeks, and when the gun fired Smith bellowed, "No!"
and hit the brakes. The concrete abutment was only a
short distance away.

Beside him, Cross put out hands to brace himself against
the dash as the rear wheels locked, the tires shrieked.
Smith had a quick perception of the gun coming loose
from Keller's grasp and looping away, and then the car
fishtailed and slid into the abutment. Fender metal
crunched, and Smith banged his head against the door
glass. The car tilted slightly, settled again onto all four
tires; the engine died away.

Smith got the door open and stumbled out, ran around
to the front with his own weapon free in his hand. On the
slope Keller was stumbling away from Valerie and the
sprawled figure of Hook, toward where his gun had fallen
in the stubbled grass.

KELLER

He finds the revolver, dives for it, but loses his balance
and slides past it on his right side, fingers digging at the
muddy earth and wet grass as though at flesh and pubic

hair. He reaches back, gets his hand around the butt of the gun, and then drags himself onto his knees. At first he can't see, tears in his eyes, and he paws at the film and gets the man and the woman in focus again and steadies the barrel on his forearm. His vision is much better now; he is not seeing in flickers but in whole gulps of sight.

But he cannot pull the trigger. The Ripper never shot anybody; the Ripper only uses a knife and only on women. You couldn't rip with a gun, could you?

Where's my knife? he thinks. What did I do with my knife? I can't remember what I did with it and I need it, the ripping, and the diamonds, the diamonds . . . are not meaningless, had meaning all along, they . . . not diamonds, not diamonds . . . *squares*. A diamond is an off-center square and squares are . . . cells, jail cells, I . . . made them my prisoners, locked them away forever, because I'm not the Bloodhound I'm the Ripper of Bloodstone the bloody bloodspiller spilling the blood of Bloodstone and Chicago, Chi-ca-go. . . .

Someone shouts at him, and he staggers to his feet and whirls with the gun upraised. For the first time he sees the car on the parking area, the two men running toward him. Smith and Cross. Cross and Smith. Coming after him, chasing *him*. All along he has been chasing the Ripper, all along he has been chasing himself: snake eating its tail, dog eating its own turds, feeding on himself until there is just enough left for the rest of them to finish off.

But not yet. Not yet. "Not yet!" he screams at Smith and Cross, at Bloodstone and Chicago and the world. "The Ripper's not finished yet!"

SMITH

"Get down!" Smith shouted, and threw himself against Cross, who had followed him out of the car. The two of them sprawled forward onto the grass well beyond the abutment, skin scraping from Smith's left palm, right hand crooked up so that he wouldn't lose his weapon. The sound of Keller screaming, *what* Keller was screaming, rolled over him like floodwater, shocking and repellent.

"Keller," Cross said in a stunned voice beside him. "It's Keller, not Hook, my God. . . ."

Keller. Keller! Chaos, absurdity, still plucking at the edges. But methodology, order were still the more powerful; they had brought him here, brought him to the assailant no matter who or what he was, and they would bring him the whole truth as soon as he arrested Keller and dragged the answers out of him.

Smith held his gun steady. Aim for the legs if you have to shoot. But Keller did not fire at them; instead, he threw his own revolver down between his spread legs in a motion that was both savage and pathetic, wavered for a moment like a tree in a crosscurrent of wind, and then stumbled away along the slope—broke into a stuttering, awkward run in the direction of the entrance gates to Colonial Village.

"Shoot him," Cross said. "Why don't you shoot him?"

Smith shook his head violently, pulled himself up. Pain sliced razorlike under his breastbone, sending tendrils of weakness into his legs, and he thought *No, oh no, not this time,* and went full speed after Keller.

VALERIE

Steven had pulled himself onto his knees and was hunched there near the waterline, shaking his head, as Valerie ran toward him. She saw Keller moving opposite on the slope, Keller, the Ripper, God Keller; saw the two men—Lieutenant Smith and . . . Jack Cross?—who had come out of the suddenly arrived car now jammed against the abutment up on the parking area. She had been aware, until Keller threw down his gun and started running, that he might kill her, kill both her and Steven before the men up there could stop him; but her mind had reached an overload—too much had happened in too short a time—and getting to Steven was of immediate urgency.

Hook gained his feet just as she reached him, stared first at the three men running on the slope as if, confused, he thought they were an aberration. Valerie clutched at him, saying his name, but he seemed not to hear her; he slapped the heels of both palms against his ears, still shaking his head. She could feel the tension in his body that came with understanding of what was happening over there, and she knew that he was going to join the chase: knew as he did that the end of the Ripper meant the new beginning of Steven Hook.

She felt tears trying to form in her eyes. He was all right, he wasn't hurt; but much more than that was his complete and final absolution as the Ripper—she had *not* slept with a mass murderer. The relief that was spilling through her was as deep as pain, as sharp as love.

KELLER

He hits the juncture of the entrance gates without slowing, taking the impact on his left shoulder. The gates bow in, the locking chain creaks and rust like little flecks of dried blood sprays from it—but it holds. His vision has returned nearly to normal now, but inside there is an awful stillness, as if the very engines of his body have ceased.

Get away from them, he thinks, find a dark place, hiding place. He throws himself onto the cyclone fencing and climbs up in a frenzy, hands and shoes clawing at the pattern of diamonds. He catches the iron crossbar at the top, drags himself astraddle it, and then kicks his other leg over and drops down.

He falls to one knee, straightens, and looks back. They are still coming, coming. He raises his hands, the Ripper raises his hands to shut off the sight of them—and the hands are scarlet, curved, as if bearing gifts. He screams low in his throat, the Ripper screams the way Julia Larch and Arlene Wilson and Dona Lincoln and Linda Simmons and Paula Eaton have screamed. Then he turns and flees down the muddy main street of the village: crying and flying and dying inside. . . .

SMITH

Smith leaned panting against one of the gate halves and watched Keller running inside, past the brick-and-timber peasant houses that lined the near end of the street. He didn't think he was strong enough or agile enough to climb the gate the way Keller had, but he had to get in there. He shook the gates, fingers hooked through the diamond-pattern fencing; the chain lock showed no signs of yielding. Christ, a simple lock keeping him out, preventing him from—

Diamond patterns.

Lock.

Lock and key.

Latch key.

The latch keys Keller had been cleaning when he'd seen him last Sunday, the latch key Keller had had in his hand the night of the false Florence Cross attack. Square-headed latch key with rough surfaces, an inch in diameter. Shallow diamond-shaped marks on the victims' thighs, an inch in diameter.

And Keller was a cop; he could come up on women without making them suspicious. Women like Dona Lincoln, the visitor from Montreal. Approach them in his official capacity and then strike when their guard was down.

And Keller had planted the knife at the Hideaway Cabins last night or today, planted it under the stack of papers and racing forms to throw suspicion on the man he wanted everyone to believe was the assailant.

Keller. Of course it was Keller. Clues and facts pointing straight to him, just as earlier clues and facts had seemed to point straight to Hook. Smith should have seen it, *mea culpa,* no fault of the orderly universe cast in purpose by the hand of God.

Hook and Cross came running up, and Smith said immediately, "Stay out of this, both of you."

"It's too late for that," Hook said.

Cross said, "He's getting away in there."

Smith looked through the diamonds again, and Keller was nearing the artisan shops in the center of the village. "All right," he said, "one of you give me a boost up. But if you come in after me, stand clear when I catch up to him; I don't want you in my way."

Hook made a cradle of his hands, and Smith put one foot into them, caught hold of the fencing, and let Hook heave him upward. His fingers grasped the crossbar, and he pulled himself atop the gate, hung there for a second.

He could see Valerie Broome out on the slope midway between the fort and the amusement park, Cross and Hook peering up from below. He could see, too—turning his head—most of the village spread out before him, and it had an abandoned, ravaged aspect, as though it were a real village that had been unsuccessfully defended by the revolutionary troops of long ago, then raped and pillaged in the aftermath; it had the same desolate aura of Bloodstone. But the hell with Valerie and Cross and Hook, the hell with the village and Bloodstone itself. All that mattered was Keller, order, Keller, the truth—

All that mattered.

And as he dropped down inside, he realized that the assailant and the establishment of truth and order were all that had mattered almost from the beginning, that he had never really cared at all about the victims or the blood or the pain. . . .

KELLER

Where is he? What is this place?

The Ripper stops, suddenly and acutely aware of externals, and looks around him. Strange clapboard buildings with signs: Cooper, Wheelwright, Tallow Chandler, Blacksmith, Saddler. Merchant shops. Meetinghouse. A gristmill, a sawmill, a molasses rum distillery. Open sheds with simple wooden wagons and faded chaises. He stumbles sideways to one of the buildings and stares in through a streaked window; recoils. Males in buckskin yeoman's garb, in embroidered waistcoats and silk breeches and powdered and curled wigs; women in peasant dress, holding umbrellas. All piled together in a jumble of arms and legs and torsos. Mannikins? Or corpses awaiting the fire?

The Ripper turns, confused, sick. *What is this place?* And then he knows. The truth comes to him in a bright, singing rush of perception: it is a village in Colonial America. He has been taken back in time, back to the beginning, to a dead place at the beginning of America itself. Everyone dead, victims of a plague—and he understands why, the method is clear. *He* is death, Ripper-plague, and this is the place where all death comes to an end, at the beginning, to end at the beginning. Lost, all the generations strung out on the shiny ribbon of death, but the end, *his* end, is near, and all he has to do is find it and seize it.

He plunges away, around a stack of barrels at the side wall of the distillery. When he emerges at the rear he sees, first, a row of boarded-up booths and a maze of half-assembled machinery. These things don't belong here, why are they here? He feels truth slide and shimmer away from him, tilting, not vision but all perception involved now. But then he sees the lake, green and cold, glinting off to his left, the fronts of homes belonging to the landed aristocracy beyond it. Truth tilts back again and the anachronisms vanish and he lurches toward the water, arms outflung.

In front of him wooden constructions loom, glistening wetly, intruding on his consciousness. He recognizes them as pillories, stocks. Agencies of correction. Colonial punishments for the sins of scolds and prostitutes and dishonest tradesmen. Punishment for the Ripper? No. No common scold, the Ripper. Something else—

Ducking stool.

He sees it for the first time, it bursts massive and beckoning against the surfaces of his eyes and brain. This is it, he knows absolutely that this is the answer. Ducking stool for retribution and expiation, water for absolution, water to drown the unholy flames of the Ripper at once and forever.

A sob ripples in his throat and he races toward the lake, the ducking stool, his auto-da-fé.

HOOK

Over the fence himself now, running, Hook saw Keller disappear along the side of the rum distillery. Smith was twenty yards ahead, a hundred yards from Keller, and Cross—last over the gate—was somewhere behind.

He could not get out of his mind the image of Keller's face as it had looked when he'd begun screaming: the horror, shock, madness, pain. Keller hadn't *known* he was the Ripper until today, until maybe that very moment. Ferrara had been absolutely right. Anyone could have been the Ripper. *I* could have been the Ripper, he thought, it could be me running up there instead of Keller.

Hook lifted a hand, brushed cold sweat out of his eyes. He no longer hated or feared Keller; he could only pity him. And feel a consuming weariness, a kind of numb relief that it was almost over—for him and for all of them.

Ahead, Smith cut out of sight around the side of the distillery. Hook followed in his wake, splashed through a puddle of muddy gray water. He heard Smith begin shouting, "Keller! Stop, Keller!"

When Hook came out into the open he saw Keller running along the shore of the man-made lake seventy yards away, not heeding Smith's warnings. The constable threw himself instead against a wooden contraption mounted at the lake's edge, an outsized replica of a ducking stool, and caught hold of the long, upward-canted beam. Then he straddled it and began to crawl upward in little scooting movements, toward the armchair fastened to the upper end.

Hook saw Smith hesitate, poised on the balls of his feet. Smith held his left arm pressed hard under his breastbone, his right arm bent up at the elbow so that the muzzle of his gun pointed skyward. Hook ran up to him and stopped several feet to one side, staring at Keller crawling up the beam of the ducking stool like an animal up the trunk of a tree.

"Christ," he said, "what's he doing there?"

"Shut up," Smith said. "Stay out of the way."

There was something in Smith's voice that made Hook's neck feel cold. He pulled his eyes to the lieutenant: tight, hard mouth, bright stare, nostrils flared with the wheezing rasp of his breathing. He's no different from Keller, Hook thought. They're cut from the same relentless, inflexible, deadly mold.

"Keller!" Smith shouted again, and the word echoed once in the windblown stillness, fragmented and died.

Hook swallowed dryly, looked back to the ducking stool. Keller had reached the armchair, and he swung his legs now into a sitting position within it. His head and torso arched forward as though he were peering across the fence and across Woodbine Lake at the dark, impenetrable buildings of Bloodstone. Then he sat that way, immobile.

Cross pounded up and stopped on the other side of Smith. "Jesus," he said. And the three of them just stood there on a line, as they might have done, Hook thought, to give credence to the state.

KELLER

The iron retaining band is cold and wet and rough in the Ripper's hands, but he manages to get it fastened tightly around his chest. The wood of beam and chair creaks under his weight as he stares downward at the surface of the lake. It seems to congeal, to change color until it becomes thick and red like blood, like the blood of the women he has slain, those poor women! Then he blinks, and the blood drains away and the water winks gray at him, urgent and demanding.

Get to the water, expiation and absolution. But now that he is here, now that he is ready, he realizes that there is no one to help him, no one at the other end to duck him into those punitive depths. He has to do it himself. Of course he does. He has chased himself, the Ripper, and now that he has found him he has been given the means to punish and destroy him. He moans and struggles fretfully in the chair, begins to thrash his body up and down so that his buttocks slap with little flat cracking sounds against the seat.

The creaks grow louder, louder still; the chain which holds the beam fastened to the crosspiece at the bottom screeches with the pressure, like the cry of a woman dying.

CROSS

Cross watched Keller up on the ducking stool as though through crystal: clear, yet removed. And he kept thinking how really incredible it was that Keller had turned out to be the Ripper. The constable of Bloodstone was the man who had almost destroyed Bloodstone, had killed Paula, had made *him,* Jack Cross, a victim. There was fantastic irony in that. He would have to make sure to comment on it in his wrap-up chapter of the book—

"No!" Smith shouted suddenly. "You can't do that, you son of a bitch, I won't let you do that to me!" And he began running again.

Cross came forward too, Hook beside him. Keller kept on jerking atop the ducking stool: horrible, grotesque. Cross recalled that last night he had had pen and paper to put it all down as it developed, but that was obviously childish. Not professional, rational, adult conduct at all. What you had to do was to watch everything closely and then in tranquillity reflect and record. Be the emotionless seeing eye.

In front of him, Smith's gun kicked and fired a warning shot into the gray sky.

KELLER

The Ripper hears shouting, a hollow crash, but is transfixed by the sight of the water, the beckoning water. Hurry, hurry! He flings and lunges his body, up and down, back and forth. The beam wobbles, sways, tilts—

And the chain holding it to the crosspiece snaps free.

He is thrown forward against the iron band, feels the chill air rush past him as the ducking stool plummets downward, sees the glistening water reach for him. Yes! and he thunders against the brittle surface, it parts to let him through and then embraces him cold and red again, closes over him.

Leaning sideways in the chair, hands gripping the wooden arms, he opens his mouth and sucks the bloodwater into his lungs. Darkness swirls, the water swirls, the heart and loss of him swirl away. . . .

HOOK

They were fifty yards from the lake when Keller and the ducking stool went under. As Hook ran nearer, he saw bubbles rise popping in the frothy wake of the splash and then, just before Smith reached the edge, nothing but glassine smoothness. Smith dropped his gun on the shore and plunged into the water, half running, half swimming to the end of the submerged beam. When he reached it the water was at chest level; he ducked under frantically, groping for Keller's body in the armchair.

Hook went into the lake after Smith without thinking of what he was doing, automatic reflex. The chill of the water took his breath away. He struggled out to the beam, ducked under it to the other side. Smith was still working below the surface, trying to unfasten the iron retaining band that held Keller in the chair. Hook got his own hands on one of Keller's arms, tried to help, but it was another minute, maybe longer, before the band came free. Together, then, they pulled the limp body to the surface, held it there.

Keller's eyes were open and staring; his mouth, in rictus, seemed to be smiling. The cold wind, the icy water, put finger tremors on Hook's back. "Dead," he said. "Jesus," he said.

"No." Smith's lips were like a puckered, half-healed knife slash. "He isn't dead, I won't let him be dead." He ripped Keller's body out of Hook's grasp, in a way that was almost fiercely possessive, and began to drag it away to shore.

CROSS

From where he stood next to the base of the ducking stool, Cross watched Smith bring Keller from the lake and Hook wade out behind him. Then he moved there and leaned over Keller, stared into Keller's face. "Is he dead?" he said. "Is he dead?"

Without warning Smith hit him across the face—forehand slap, very hard. Cross reeled backward and went down on his buttocks, legs splayed out in front of him. He stared at Smith with hurt eyes. "Why did you do that? You didn't have to do that."

Smith didn't look at him, looked only at Keller. Cross pressed a palm against his stinging cheek and realized then that Smith had done it for the same reason that he had been driving recklessly and talking irrationally about baseball. Excusable; illogical but excusable. You had to make allowances for people, just as he would need allowances now, for the rest of his life, made for him. He wouldn't even mention it in the last pages of *Triumph over Uncertainty: The Ripper Ordeal of Jack Cross*.

He kept on sitting there in the mud, waiting for the pain to go away.

SMITH

Smith went to his knees beside Keller's supine body, then straddled him at the waist and folded his right hand across the back of his left and pressed down hard against the motionless stomach. Water dribbled out of the slack mouth, but the eyes remained open and staring and the chest was still.

Two paces away Hook said, "It's no use, he's dead." He had said it once before, just a moment ago.

"What the fuck do you know about it?" Smith shouted at him this time. He kept pressing against Keller's stomach. The eyes stared up at him, concealing knowledge, concealing the truth. "You son of a bitch, you're not dead. You hear me, Keller? I won't allow it. I want a complete confession out of you, I won't let you die until I get it."

Pain bubbled and slashed under his own breastbone, so sharp suddenly that it made him gasp. But he would not think about it. He stared into Keller's eyes, and his pumping motions were more violent. "You bastard, you can't do this to me!"

Keller did not move.

Smith leaned forward until his chest touched Keller's, until his face was an inch from Keller's. The pain cut at him again, and he felt himself begin to fart, heard the sound thin and squealing in the stillness. Then he took Keller's face tightly in his hands, growling noises low in his throat and low in his rectum, and began to breathe into the cold, wet mouth.

HOOK

He looked at Cross sitting there in the mud. He looked at Smith giving artificial respiration to the corpse of the Ripper, heard the stuttering, bizarre rumble of the lieutenant breaking wind again. He shivered, and this time it had nothing at all to do with the cold.

Hook put his back to all of them and walked stiff and straight through the empty park, to look for Valerie.

EPILOGUE

BLOODSTONE

And so it was over. The Ripper was dead, the Ripper was no longer a threat; Bloodstone, drained of fear, weary and disgusted, could now wait in peace for the advent of winter, for Christmas, the new year, spring, and finally the beginning of the Season, such as it was, which would keep the town alive.

Media people swarmed over Bloodstone, as could be expected, seeking interviews with principals in the case or with anyone at all who was willing to talk to them.

James Ferrara, over double Manhattans in the Homelite bar, said that it was unfortunate Constable Keller could not have been saved, for it would have been fascinating to delve into the complex, almost poetic nature of his psyche. But, Ferrara pointed out, his basic theory of the case was that the identity of the murderer would come as a complete surprise to the individual himself, to say nothing of the town, and this had been borne out by comments made by those persons involved in the events at Fort Seneca and Colonial Village. The identity of the assailant, ultimately, meant nothing; it was only the method and pattern of the crimes which were of social and psychiatric interest. One of the reporters asked him if he would elaborate on the method and pattern in those terms, and Ferrara said he would be glad to—and pointedly drained his glass. Properly cued, the reporter bought him another double Manhattan.

Lieutenant Joseph Rocca, interviewed at the Bloodstone substation, irritably refused to comment on reports that the attack on Florence Cross had never occurred, that for reasons of her own she had invented the entire episode. In answer to the question "Have you and Lieutenant Smith formulated any ideas or found any additional evidence to explain how Constable Keller was able to commit his crimes in total anonymity for so long a period of time?" Rocca said that they were preparing a statement for release shortly; he also said that Lieutenant Smith was with his family in Lake George, unavailable for comment, and that he was not at liberty to say what the nature of Smith's illness on Thursday night had been. Rocca stated flatly that he had no personal reaction to the fact that Keller had turned out to be the Ripper, and whatever feelings he might have as a resident of the Bloodstone area were private. When a reporter asked him what the *meaning* of the crimes was to him, he said that he didn't ever see any meaning in murder.

Henry Plummer, in his office at the Bloodstone *Sentinel,* also steadfastly refused to discuss Florence Cross. As to the outcome of the case, he admitted to being both shocked and relieved. He said that yes, he and the rest of the town council had known from the beginning that Keller was involved in that convention fiasco in Chicago in 1968 and had been aware of the exact reasons for Keller's dismissal from the Chicago force, but that the majority had felt he was just the kind of law officer Bloodstone needed at that time; and that yes, he had gone along with the majority without too much fuss, God help him, even though he deplored violence, because he had felt then that enforcement was minimal in a small town such as this, certainly never involving anything which would trigger Chicago-type reactions. One of the press people asked what sort of policeman Constable Keller had been during his time in Bloodstone, and Plummer frowned thoughtfully. "You know," he said, "I hadn't thought about that, but now you ask, he was always polite, dedicated, hardworking. A thorough man. Funny. I won't allow you to quote me on this, but he was a good cop for us. Damn it, he was really a very good cop."

Tony Manders, behind the plank at Bloodstone Tavern, said the outcome of the case just fucking made him sick. Your own constable, your own *policeman,* turns out to be the Ripper. Jesus! A reporter wanted to know if he felt that the adverse publicity Bloodstone had received would harm the community's reputation as a summer resort, and Manders said he didn't know, you could never tell how a fucking tourist would think. He didn't suppose it would do Bloodstone much good, but he said they would survive; they'd had to put up with a lot of shit in this little town of theirs over the years, and they had always survived. Then he paused, having just thought of something, and smiled thinly around at the reporters. "Keller came from Chicago, not from around here," he said. "By Christ, he wasn't one of *ours* at all."

HOOK

Lying on the bed in his cottage, Valerie beside him, Hook said, "You know something? We've been together ever since the finish of it yesterday, and we haven't said more than two hundred words between us."

"We're all talked out, Steven," she said. "We don't need any more talking."

"At the close of a drama you're supposed to have the obligatory scene, a kind of summing-up of perception and intention. Like I should tell you frankly and lucidly that I've come to realize what was wrong with my life, and how in the process I rediscovered manhood and self and the capacity for happiness. I'm supposed to pledge for a new beginning. Am I right? Isn't that the way it should go?"

"I don't know," she said. She leaned up on one elbow and stroked his forehead lightly. "You tell me."

"Well there can't be any obligatory scene because this isn't a play, life isn't a play. That was part of the insight that came to me in the boat yesterday. You can't sum things up in a nice neat package; you can't write a script or play a script or even improvise a script. Too many uncertainties."

"In other words, there are no happy endings in life."

"Not true," he said. "There are endings and a few of them are happy, but they don't happen right away if they happen at all." He paused. "I've got myself together again a little, I know that much, and I understand more about myself than ever before—but I don't know what's going to happen tomorrow or next week or next year. Maybe there'll be a happy ending and maybe there won't. All I know right now is that I've got to get out of Bloodstone as soon as possible and never come back again. If I tried to straighten out my life here, I'd never straighten it out at all."

"Corollary: if I tried to finish my article here," Valerie said, "I'd never finish it at all. I think I *can* do it now, but the farther away from Bloodstone the better. Maybe we'll leave together, Steven."

"Maybe we will," he said.

"To New York?"

"I think so. I belong in the city."

"Will you take up acting again?"

"No. I'm a failed actor; there's no room in the theater for failed actors. Hell, there's no room in the theater for *successful* actors, there's barely a theater anymore. No room for me, certainly."

"You'll need a place to stay until you decide what to do," Valerie said. "We could share my apartment for a while."

"We could get married for a while."

She took her hand away from his forehead and turned to look at the wall, then looked back at him. "Marriage isn't for us, Steven."

"I know, that wasn't an earnest proposal. Neither of us needs anyone to lean on. I thought I did, but I don't, not anymore. We'll see each other, maybe I'll stay with you at the beginning for a week or so, until I find a place, but we've got to live apart and we both know it. We're free spirits, you and I; we stand alone or we don't stand at all."

"Who said you can't do an obligatory scene?" Her fingers were moving on him again, on his chest now. "I think you're doing very well."

"Not so damned well," Hook said. He lit a cigarette and watched the glowing end for a time. "Poor Keller," he said, "poor crazy Keller."

"It's been a crazy time: poor everybody."

"That's right. That's it exactly. Poor crazy everybody. That's the real horror in what happened here, do you know that? The terrible little fact at the core of the whole thing."

"I'm not sure I understand what you mean."

"We were all crazy, in one way or another," he said.

"And we didn't know it. Just like Keller, we didn't know what was inside of us. Beasts, running scared—the running of beasts. Ferrara was right, more right than he ever realized."

"Right about what?"

"That anybody here could have been the Ripper," Hook said.

CROSS

TRIUMPH OVER UNCERTAINTY: THE RIPPER ORDEAL OF JACK CROSS--
add 228

maybe a novel. I think I could write a very good novel now that I have accepted the fact of who I am and have achieved utter and total and final control over my life and have triumphed over uncertainty. Never again will I take refuge in such fantasies as Superman, but of course writing a novel is not taking refuge in fantasy, it is merely setting down on paper your view of reality. In fact, I have packed up my collection of comic books and next week I will put an add in the Schenectady and Albany papers that it is for sale. I understand you can get a lot of money for comic book collections these days.

I even realize now why Valerie Broome treated me the way she did and would not have a cup of coffee with me when I asked her to. I was immature then, and she could see this. She grew up very fast and I grew up more slowly, but in the end we are both very much alike in that we are both writers of some stature and both deeply involved with Bloodstone and the terrible acts of the Ripper.

That about sums it up, I think. I am very tired now, for I have been writing these final chapters non-stop for the past fourteen hours. Tomorrow I will be ready to begin the final draft. As for tonight, I think what I had better do is go over to Paula's. If I don't she will only call again, as she has done several times while I have been writing these pages. Poor Paula! But I will take care of her too, and of the baby she is going to have, for they are my obligations and a mature man must always meet his obligations.

TRIUMPH OVER UNCERTAINTY: THE RIPPER ORDEAL OF JACK CROSS--
add 227

As for Florence, I have forgiven her completely. The state police have decided not to press charges against her-- I learned this through Plummer, who had a long talk with Lieutenant Rocca--but I think she has suffered enough, inside herself, for what she did. I can also see now that the failure of Florence is in many ways the failure of Jack Cross, or what was the failure of Jack Cross before I withstood the test of trial by fire and emerged whole and mature from the ashes.

It is certain now that I must stay here in Bloodstone, at least for a while, and attempt to help Florence. The strong must always help the weak. Plummer says she will marry him now, and maybe she will, but he still cannot ever do for her what I can. Obviously, she cares for me, her son, more than she could ever care for Plummer, else why would she have perpetrated a criminal hoax to protect me? I should have realized long ago how important I am to her, and should not have treated her so shoddily. But then, she should not have treated me so shoddily either. Things will change now. Our relationship will be much better, much more pleasant, the way a mother-son relationship should be. I think that even in time I can learn to like Plummer, although of course I can never think of him as Father.

Yes, I must stay in Bloodstone. When this book is finished I can send it out by mail just as easily from here as anywhere else, although maybe I'll go down to New York with it instead, just for a couple of days, and take it to a publisher personally, I haven't decided yet which one. Then I will begin another book,

SMITH

Smith went back into the hospital late Saturday, because of Marjorie's urging and because the pain had gotten very bad again. And because the case was over and there was nothing more he could do on it: Keller was dead, they had found nothing among his belongings to help toward an understanding of the whole truth about his actions and the case itself. The ending was unsatisfactory, and yet intrinsically he *had* to believe it bore out his faith in methodology and the ordered universe.

Metcalf examined him, ran him through X ray, and then told him there was no time for a full series of tests; grimly, he announced surgery for nine o'clock Sunday morning. Smith did not argue. He let them give him a private room and a sedative to help him sleep.

But the sedative wore off in the early hours of the morning, and he awoke, half awoke, to darkness and anxiety, fear of the cutting surgical knife. He lay restlessly in the bed. The blinds on the window to the left were raised, and he could look through at another wing of the hospital across the outer courtyard. Behind one of the windows there, the glow of a red bulb over an exit door put a faint sheen of crimson on the blackness—and he thought of the taillights on the car he had pursued from the scene of Paula Eaton's murder.

His mind drifted over the entire sequence, point to point. He had never really seen those taillights very clearly . . . had he actually seen them at all? Had he been pursuing a car or a phantom? No, it was a car all right, he remembered the engine sound, he *remembered* those lights. He had been chasing the assailant; there just wasn't any doubt of that.

And then he seemed to hear, whispering in his mind,

Rocca's voice on the telephone on Friday. Telling him things, filling him in on the entire network of Thursday night's events, telling him—

—that Keller had been at the Manders place on the false alarm when Smith's call on Paula Eaton went out over the radio.

Keller had been at the Manders place

Keller had been eight miles from Hobbler Way

Keller couldn't have been the man he had pursued from the scene of the Eaton murder

Keller couldn't have killed Paula Eaton

Keller could not have been the assailant.

He jerked into a sitting position, chills on his back, pain leaping like flames in his tomach. Not Keller. Driven by the intricacies of his own mind into madness and false belief of guilt. Not Keller. Anything could have made those diamond marks; not the latch key, maybe the knife itself, maybe that slender, square handle on the knife itself. Not Keller. I never saw him use a *tissue*, he wasn't the kind of man who would ever use a tissue—

Not Keller not Keller not Keller.

Chaos again, supreme chaos this time. The assailant still at large, laughing at them all, ready to kill again. Oh but Christ, Christ, only for the time being, it wasn't too late, he could still restore order, he could still capture the assailant; get out of here, get back on the job, tell Rocca and the others—and he flung himself out of bed, mouth open, breath exploding into the darkness, agony inside, and ran toward the door and got his hand on the knob and

And died of a massive peritoneal hemorrhage at five forty-five A.M., without regaining consciousness and despite the efforts of the hospital emergency staff.

THE RIPPER

Lost my knife at the Cabins forgot my *knife,* no more cutting and no more diamonds until I find a knife, but oh Ginny you cunt oh Ginny it hurts too much never knew how much it hurt until it got past the dullness with the hard ice of feeling, you Ginny winner sinner I'll marry you in fire and marry you in ice, carry you up and over the threshold and put the diamonds of our love off-center upon you, because the knife is the truth and the truth is the knife and the darkness is the binding, cutting and singing and ripping and wild sliding up and down the chilly blue of you Ginnycunt because still captive still captive still captive still captive—

Still captive the old wild king.

HEADLINE, NEW YORK DAILY NEWS, NOVEMBER 4

WRITER VALERIE BROOME MYSTERIOUSLY SLAIN IN WEST VILLAGE APARTMENT

BLACK LIZARD BOOKS

JIM THOMPSON
- *AFTER DARK, MY SWEET* $3.95
- *THE ALCOHOLICS* $3.95
- *THE CRIMINAL* $3.95
- *CROPPER'S CABIN* $3.95
- *THE GETAWAY* $3.95
- *THE GRIFTERS* $3.95
- *A HELL OF A WOMAN* $3.95
- *NOTHING MORE THAN MURDER* $3.95
- *POP. 1280* $3.95
- *RECOIL* $3.95
- *SAVAGE NIGHT* $3.95
- *A SWELL LOOKING BABE* $3.95
- *WILD TOWN* $3.95

HARRY WHITTINGTON
- *THE DEVIL WEARS WINGS* $3.95
- *FIRES THAT DESTROY* $4.95
- *FORGIVE ME, KILLER* $3.95
- *A MOMENT TO PREY* $4.95
- *A TICKET TO HELL* $3.95
- *WEB OF MURDER* $3.95

CHARLES WILLEFORD
- *THE BURNT ORANGE HERESY* $3.95
- *COCKFIGHTER* $3.95
- *PICK-UP* $3.95

ROBERT EDMOND ALTER
- *CARNY KILL* $3.95
- *SWAMP SISTER* $3.95

W.L. HEATH
- *ILL WIND* $3.95
- *VIOLENT SATURDAY* $3.95

PAUL CAIN
- *FAST ONE* $3.95
- *SEVEN SLAYERS* $3.95

FREDRIC BROWN
- *HIS NAME WAS DEATH* $3.95
- *THE FAR CRY* $3.95

DAVID GOODIS
- *BLACK FRIDAY* $3.95
- *CASSIDY'S GIRL* $3.95
- *NIGHTFALL* $3.95
- *SHOOT THE PIANO PLAYER* $3.95
- *STREET OF NO RETURN* $3.95

HELEN NIELSEN
- *DETOUR* $4.95
- *SING ME A MURDER* $4.95

DAN J. MARLOWE
- *THE NAME OF THE GAME IS DEATH* $4.95
- *NEVER LIVE TWICE* $4.95
- *STRONGARM* $4.95
- *VENGEANCE MAN* $4.95

MURRAY SINCLAIR
- *ONLY IN L.A.* $4.95
- *TOUGH LUCK L.A.* $4.95

JAMES M. CAIN
- *SINFUL WOMAN* $4.95
- *JEALOUS WOMAN* $4.95
- *THE ROOT OF HIS EVIL* $4.95

PETER RABE
- *KILL THE BOSS GOODBYE* $4.95
- *DIG MY GRAVE DEEP* $4.95
- *THE OUT IS DEATH* $4.95

HARDCOVER ORIGINALS:
LETHAL INJECTION by JIM NISBET $15.95
GOODBYE L.A. by MURRAY SINCLAIR $15.95

AND OTHERS...
- FRANCIS CARCO • *PERVERSITY* $3.95
- BARRY GIFFORD • *PORT TROPIQUE* $3.95
- NJAMI SIMON • *COFFIN & CO.* $3.95
- ERIC KIGHT (RICHARD HALLAS) • *YOU PLAY THE BLACK AND THE RED COMES UP* $3.95
- GERTRUDE STEIN • *BLOOD ON THE DINING ROOM FLOOR* $6.95
- KENT NELSON • *THE STRAIGHT MAN* $3.50
- JIM NISBET • *THE DAMNED DON'T DIE* $3.95
- STEVE FISHER • *I WAKE UP SCREAMING* $4.95
- LIONEL WHITE • *THE KILLING* $4.95
- JOHN LUTZ • *THE TRUTH OF THE MATTER* $4.95
- ROGER SIMON • *DEAD MEET* $4.95
- BILL PRONZINI • *MASQUES* $4.95
- BILL PRONZINI & BARRY MALZBERG • *THE RUNNING OF BEASTS* $4.95
- VICTORIA NICHOLS & SUSAN THOMPSON • *SILK STALKINGS* $12.95
- *THE BLACK LIZARD ANTHOLOGY OF CRIME FICTION*
  Edited by EDWARD GORMAN $8.95
- *THE SECOND BLACK LIZARD ANTHOLOGY OF CRIME FICTION*
  Edited by EDWARD GORMAN $13.95

Black Lizard Books are available at most bookstores or directly from the publisher. In addition to list price, please sent $1.00/postage for the first book and $.50 for each additional book to Black Lizard Books, 833 Bancroft Way, Berkeley, CA 94710. California residents please include sales tax.